Ece Temelkuran is one of the Turkey's best known novelists and political commentators. She has contributed to the *Guardian*, *Newstatesman*, *New Left Review*, *Le Monde Diplomatique*, *Frankfurter Rundschau*, *Der Spiegel*, *The New York Times* and *Berliner Zeitung*.

Her books of investigative journalism broach subjects that are highly controversial in Turkey, such as the Kurdish and Armenian issues and freedom of expression.

Her novel *Düğümlere Üfleyen Kadınlar* (*Women Who Blow on Knots*) won a PEN Translates award, sold over 120,000 copies in Turkey and has been published in translation in Germany, Croatia, Poland, Bosnia and France with editions also forthcoming in China, Italy and the USA.

Temelkuran was born into a political family in Izmir, known to be the most liberal city in the country. Educated as a lawyer in the capital city Ankara, she never practiced the profession except once to defend Kurdish children in a political class action as a symbolic act. Bored by Law School, she started to work for the newspaper *Cumhuriyet* during her second year at the university in 1993.

Her first novel, *Women Are All Confused*, was published in 1996, while she was working as a journalist. 20 years later the book is a touring stage play and performed in several cities in Turkey.

Then, as her journalism at the time was focusing on political prisoners and the Kurdish issue, she wrote *My Son My Daughter My State – Mothers of Political Prisoners* (1997). Afterwards, she moved to Istanbul to work for CNN International and carried on publishing her literary work including *The Book of Inside* (2000) and *The Book of Edge* (2010).

When she became a columnist for *Milliyet*, reality occupied her life, prevailing over literary truth. She started publishing her collection of articles and reportage, *The Words from the Edge*. She travelled to Venezuela whe   to write, *We are Making a Re*   me

a bestseller. She followed the piqueteros movement in Buenos Aires after the economic crisis and World Social Forums in Brazil and in India.

In 2006, while she was travelling to report from Malaysian, Russian, Iranian, Lebanese and European cities, her friend Hrant Dink encouraged her to travel to Armenia for reportage on the Armenian dispute, considered to be the toughest taboo in Turkey. After Armenia she travelled to France and to the US to meet the Armenian diaspora. The Armenian journalist Dink was assassinated in 2007. To fulfil her promise to him she wrote *The Deep Mountain – Across the Turkish-Armenian Divide*. The book is dedicated to Dink and she spent a year in Oxford as a visiting fellow of Saint Anthony's College to write it.

Temelkuran went to Beirut in 2008, a city she fell in love with while she was reporting from Lebanon after the 2006 Israel attack. She was planning to write a non-fiction book on Hezbollah but then, realising that it was time to turn back to literature, she started writing *Banana Sounds*, a love story combined with the unmentionable love of war, as romantic as it sounds.

She stayed in Beirut for almost a year to finish the novel, which has now been published in several languages. Due to political reasons, continuing with journalism became harder in the country. In 2012 she was fired from her job because of two articles she wrote about a massacre that left dozens of Kurdish children dead on the Turkish-Iraqi border, and the story was covered by the international media including *The Wall Street Journal*.

By then she had moved to Tunisia to write her novel, *Women Who Blow on Knots*. The novel has been published in several countries with the title *What good is a revolution if I cannot dance to it*. The original title is taken from the Koran and refers to witches practising witchcraft by blowing on knots.

Although she decided not to go back to journalism after the Gezi uprising in 2013, she edited the socialist newspaper *Birgün* for several months as a supportive act. She gave speeches about the

Gezi uprising in the House of Commons and at the Geneva Film Festival among several other venues. Since then her articles have appeared in several international media platforms including the *Guardian* and *Der Spiegel*. She was invited to Amsterdam as a writer in residence and gave the Freedom Lecture for the year 2013.

The lively political climate in the country stimulated her to write her political novel on Turkey, *Time of Mute Swans*, set in Ankara in the summer of 1980. It has been published in Germany and the US. Her political narrative non-fiction on Turkey – *Turkey: The Insane and Melancholy* (Euphorie und Wehmut / Zed Books) – has been reviewed widely in the German and British media.

She divides her time between Istanbul and Zagreb.

Praise for Ece Temelkuran:

'Temelkuran opens a battle against uniformed Muslim literary female characters.' – Özlem Ezer, Professor of Literature, Literary Critic

'This is an extraordinary novel, a stunning road story, a bitter fairytale and an awakening dream.' – Gülenay Börekçi – Literary Critic

'I applaud Temelkuran for creating this piece of world literature which is ultimate magic.' – Onur Bilge Kula – Professor of Literature

"Ece Temelkuran's second novel is like a firework. It is the book where Twitter and the Thousand and One Nights fairy tales meet." – Professor Hannes Kraus, KulturWest, 2014 (Germany)

"Women Who Blow On Knots is an extremely inspiring novel and it is the resistance of an independent intellectual" – Jean Baptiste Hamelin, Pages des Libraires, France

"A loving, feminist and fairytale-like 'partners in crime' novel which is a breathtaking thriller at the same time." – Le Progres Social, France

Author website: www.ecetemelkuran.com
Twitter: @ETemelkuran

CYNGOR LLYFRAU CYMRU
WELSH BOOKS COUNCIL

PARTHIAN

Women
Who Blow
on Knots

Translated by
Alexander Dawe

Ece Temelkuran

About the Translator:

Alexander Dawe studied French and Classical Guitar Performance at Oberlin College and Conservatory. He has translated several contemporary Turkish novels, including *Endgame* by Ahmet Altan. In collaboration with Maureen Freely he has translated *A Useless Man* by Sait Faik Abasıyanık, *The Time Regulation Institute* by Ahmet Hamdi Tanpınar and *The Madonna in a Fur Coat* by Sabahattin Ali. In 2010, he received a PEN/Heim Translation Fund grant to translate the short stories of Ahmet Hamdi Tanpınar. Currently he is translating a collection of short stories by Ercan Kesal. He lives and works in Turkey, on the Prince Islands Archipelago, in the sea of Marmara near Istanbul.

This book has been selected to receive financial assistance from English Pen's "Pen Translates" programme.

Parthian, Cardigan SA43 1ED
www.parthianbooks.com
Originally published in Turkey as Düğümlere Üfleyen Kadınlar (2013)
© Ece Temelkuran
Translation © Alexander Dawe 2017
All Rights Reserved
ISBN 978-1-910901-69-4
Cover design by Utku Lomlu
Typeset by Elaine Sharples
Printed by Pulsio Sarl
Published with the financial support of the Welsh Books Council
British Library Cataloguing in Publication Data
A cataloguing record for this book is available from the British Library.

"Say, I seek refuge in the Lord at daybreak. From the evil of that which He created. And from the evil of darkness when it settles. And from the evil in the blowers of knots. And from the evil of an envier when he envies."

Al-Falaq Verse 1-5
(The Holy Koran, Sahih International)

"But audiences no longer react well to heavy historical self-ironisation. They might at a pinch accept it from a man, but not from a woman.

Elizabeth Costello, J.M. Coetzee

"Tell all the truth but tell it slant."

Emily Dickinson

Women Who Blow On Knots

Tunisia

We are on the run. Barrelling south in a white car at a hundred and forty kilometres an hour. I'm in the back. On my left a woman with a yellow wig aslant on her head, as still as stone. On my right a bald woman wearing a white headscarf, her leg bouncing up and down. An old one-eyed man is at the wheel. An old grey-haired woman dressed in lilac silk is riding shotgun with her face to the wind, without a care in the world.

The bald woman says, "Where are we going?"

The old woman says, "South."

Angry, the bald woman digs in. "Just how far south?"

The old woman replies, "Way down south."

Not long ago I was about to make my way back to Istanbul. Now I am on the brink of the most terrifying and wonderful trip I have ever taken. I remember how it all began but to this day I still have a hard time believing it ever really happened.

1

I was trying to fall asleep when I heard slippers on the stone steps in the hotel. I heard footsteps. Even over all the noise from the wedding. The howling and fireworks. It had to be a woman's step. Light and young. Then another woman climbed the stairs. I heard her, too. I heard her little feet. I heard her nightdress, the sound of cloth. Thin cotton cloth. From her small steps I could even hear how tightly it clung to her body – and I knew the dress was white. But that night I wanted to be alone. Fired from my job at the paper I had no desire for life.

I was hungry and exhausted. After I'd complained to the receptionist for mixing up my registration, she'd got her own back and by the time I realized what was happening it was too late. It was the middle of the night but she'd said, "Of course" and only later would I understand that blank look in her eyes: she was a little devil.

After an awkward silence I'd asked her if the restaurants were open in the old city. "Of course," she'd said and I'd slipped into a dark labyrinth, shadows swirling out of every corner. Shadows you always see when you arrive in a city for the first time and wander off in the wrong direction. In the morning I knew I would wake up to realize that if I'd only walked the other way I would have ended up in the heart of town. But a traveller at night is no match for misfortune. Hunted down by all kinds of shadows, I made it back to my room at the Dar el-Medina, the window looking inwards. I skimmed hopelessly through Saudi channels brimming with discussions about the Koran. I struggled in vain to get online and I resigned myself to the fact that I would never kill the lone mosquito buzzing about the room ... so I tried falling asleep. That's when I heard the slippers.

Laughter: I started, as if a deer had just darted across my path. I heard a woman press her foot against her thigh, like a stork. I heard her slipper drop. I heard broken conversation. Then fingers over the jasmine blooming in the courtyard. I heard a flower being picked, branches bending. I suppose you only listen carefully to the sounds of the night when you're looking for adventure. Grabbing the bottle of whisky I'd bought last minute at the airport, I pinched three glasses between my fingers.

They stopped talking when they heard me coming. Two women leaning against the low white terrace walls of an old Tunisian villa now the Dar el-Medina Hotel, elbows on the low walls, hips pushed out. On our faces that stupid smile a tourist gets when she asks for her differences to be forgiven.

Their nightgowns really were white. And yes, the one with bigger hips had pressed her alluring foot against her thigh, just like a stork – she was more confident and more flirtatious than the other woman. "I can't sleep with all this noise," I said in English. Clearly we were all from the lower hemisphere but I didn't want to make things difficult by choosing one Arabic dialect over another. "The wedding, right? Come join us," said the one with the hips. "Come," echoed the other. They both spoke in Arabic. A word was enough to tip me off as to where they were from. The bubbly little one with the big hips was Tunisian – she hadn't used the feminine ending on her invitation. The other spoke with a stronger accent; she was a bold, shadowy, mysterious Egyptian, with the taut, tall body of a man. The Tunisian was the perfect little lady, sweet and more womanly. Then a firework cracked over our heads and we suddenly felt freed from the usual social niceties. I moved closer, putting the glasses on the low white wall. I looked at them to be sure ... yes, everyone was drinking.

"You can't really see the wedding from here," said the bold Egyptian.

"Look from here," said the Tunisian, pointing to one side.

Searching for the wedding, I said, "So this must be one of the wonders of Tunis. All the terraces are hidden from each other, no?"

"That's right," said the Tunisian with the hips. "The genius of the our country's architecture. Somehow we found a way to live side by side without actually seeing each other."

I turned away to look for the wedding and give the two women the chance to study my face. Bending over the wall, I finally spotted the celebration on a terrace below, in a cluster of rectangles and squares. The terrace was sliced into triangles by strings of colourful bulbs; old women were dancing and young girls were giggling with shame after every cry, covering their faces with hennaed hands. In her billowing gown the bride looked like she had parachuted into enemy lines with no hope but to surrender. The guests all danced around her like savages who'd stumbled on a tasty dinner.

"The bride looks miserable. I suppose it's the fear of the first night," I said, just making small talk.

The Tunisian burst out laughing. The same peal of laughter I'd heard from my room.

"That's what I was saying. She's in trouble tonight. Shock treatment!"

The Egyptian cracked an awkward smile.

"Maybe there is something to that old tradition among Tunisian Jews. You keep the bride absolutely still for twenty days, feeding her to fatten her up before consummation. Helps her withstand the brutal conditions of the first night." To downplay the sudden confidence with her new friend, she added, "We just met." A pause. Maybe she'd already forgotten the Tunisian's name.

"Where are you from?" said the Egyptian, adopting a serious tone. But the Tunisian steamrolled over the sudden formality: "It feels like we've known each other for years."

Ignoring her comment, the Egyptian turned to me. "You're a journalist, right?"

"You can tell in the dark?" I said.

Letting out an exaggerated laugh, the Tunisian said, "No, but I get a sense of your taste in underwear."

I was quiet. A subtle tension crackled in the air. I didn't appreciate the intimacy. But the Tunisian didn't seem particularly bothered. Turning to the Egyptian in the hope of encouraging a little decorum, I said, "I was. Now I'm out of a job. So I thought I'd come here to write a book about the Arab Spring."

Then I asked, "And I suppose you're an academic?"

All of sudden the Egyptian was a little girl laughing at something funny that had happened to her on the way home from school. Her tough-guy persona retreated a little.

"I'm Maryam," she said. "I came to Tunisia today. And yes, Cairo American University History Department, *at your service.*"

Although I was unimpressed by how freely the Tunisian was flashing her curves, I decided to give her a chance.

"I don't take you for an academic."

"I came here tonight. From New York." Pressing her glass of whisky to her lips, she smiled, drawing out the silence to set the stage for her opening act. And in neon lights, she said, "I'm Amira." And nothing more.

Another burst of fireworks exploded in the sky. We looked up. From up there the city must have looked like a giant dark crossword puzzle of terraces in the shapes of rectangles and squares. On one of the illuminated pieces was the first letter of the word for wedding and to finish the word you would have to switch on the lights of the surrounding terraces. We were three women standing on one of those dark squares, hidden from the naked eye. And only when the brightest firework burst open in the sky did we see each other's faces for a moment in that drunken square; from the sky to our faces and from our faces to our bellies, we could make out our shoulders, breasts, arms and wrists in the cascading light. If it weren't for her nightgown, Egyptian Maryam might have been mistaken for a boy. When she spoke you could feel the strength of her voice. Amira was shimmering in her nightgown like a fish. And when she shivered in a cool breeze it was like she was being kissed. Before I arrived it would have seemed like Maryam was the man and Amira the woman. Their opposing features highlighting their roles even more. We had stepped out onto this dark square of a giant puzzle to take refuge and watch the world from the dark.

When the fireworks ended, curiosity drove me to ask Amira, "Why are you staying here?"

Flashing me a wry smile she turned to the wedding, and

in a voice stripped of any emotion, with no sign of the previous laughter, she said, "There was a revolution and my dad died. I'm in no mood to go home."

Maryam expressed her condolences in Arabic and I was silent. Looking up, Amira nodded at Maryam, and, unwinding the silence, she said.

"It's weird being a tourist in your own city. When you leave home and stay in a hotel, you become someone else. Like walking into your own life through another door ... it's nice in that way..." Nodding her head, she muttered under her breath, "...nice that way, nice that way."

Amira was getting through her whisky fast when Maryam said, "It's like the movie suddenly stops and you step inside." *The Purple Rose of Tunisia*, I thought to myself. This is just that kind of night. I would have been scared at the thought of suddenly meeting a group of interesting men, a meeting which might have led to the bombing of Paris. But this felt more like the curtain at La Scala was rising and I was just getting to know some very interesting women. I was grateful. It was happening again...

Amira turned to Maryam as if to say, what are you doing here?

With little coloured lightbulbs flickering in her eyes, Maryam said, "Ostensibly I'm here for my research on Queen Dido, founder of Carthage. But I admit I'm also running away from my own movie, which is showing right now in Cairo."

Both of them stopped talking just when their stories were getting interesting – I wondered if this was because Arab women knew Scheherazade by heart.

With that we sat down at a wrought-iron table in the darkest corner of the square terrace, the moonlight falling in bands across our faces, the straps of our white dresses repeatedly falling off our damp shoulders, and we laughed together as we inspected our legs, stretched out drunkenly before us. We laughed about the hotel receptionist, laughed about the hotel rooms that looked more like prison cells, at the women dancing at the wedding... Amira imitated Tunisian men and her impersonations had us bent double. Then we had a go at Egyptian and Turkish men. If we could have decoded the banter, put it all down on paper, we might have ended up with a *Whimsical Encyclopedia of Middle Eastern Men*. Then we were quiet for a while. Amira still hadn't told us what she did for a living. I was curious.

"So?" said Amira to Maryam, "why did you leave Egypt?" For a moment it seemed Maryam was going to tell her story. Adjusting her dry academic tone to fit Amira's laidback style, she seemed to be drawing on a vocabulary she'd never used before.

"Sweetie, I messed up. I slept with someone. And so now you're graced with my presence."

Like a plump chicken, Amira clucked, "Go get 'em sister!"

As she spoke Maryam's body language switched from the male to female, but occasionally there was a blip and she got caught somewhere in between. One of her shoulders would jut out like a tough guy, but then suddenly she would throw her shoulders back like a woman. When Amira brought her breasts close to the table, Maryam leaned forward, and when Amira leaned back Maryam did so too. Inspired by the game, Maryam's voice grew husky.

"Till not so long ago your sister here was holding onto her innocence... I mean for that first night with that lucky man... But all bets are off now." She laughed.

The puffed-up street talk did her no favours, and neither did the attempt to sweep away her sadness. It was awkward to hear a proud, virile woman like Maryam resort to such loose talk. But Amira was compassionate and she quickly came to the rescue, scattering the sour taste in the air.

"Oh! So that means we have our own bride!"

With a finger Amira traced the curve of her smile up to her ear then raised her glass. The loud clink dispelled the lingering sadness that Maryam had failed to conceal beneath her words. She was clearly a woman who had a handle on the world but not on her heart. With visible good cheer, Amira jumped into a brighter mood. Maryam, however, still fumbled with the same forced slang.

"I'm thirty-six years old, buddy! Studied at Cambridge. Got my Masters and PHD at Princeton. I'm a Muslim. And I mean the praying kind. So what I'm saying, honey, is that I never had time for that sort of stuff. And then … of course … you know how conservative Egypt is. Nothing like Tunisia."

Amira laughed.

"Don't go there!" she said, still laughing. A bitter laugh. Which made the game of lightening the mood more difficult. Obviously there was something else Amira couldn't sweep away and it most likely had to do with Tunisia, and certainly with conservatism. Maryam suddenly pushed back from the table with a grim look on her face.

"Then there was Tahrir Square…"

Pulling a pack of cigarettes from her pocket, she went on. "When Tahrir happened … how can I put this? It was something else. Like magic … something like that…"

Amira leaned back. She didn't seem especially interested in hearing about magic and what actually happened at Tahrir Square. When people don't pay attention to a story that's being told for the first time I always get a terrible feeling, like someone might die.

"A feeling of solidarity?" I asked.

"Exactly. We were one. When people step out of themselves... It's like women, men, together, they become brothers and sisters in prayer. Like we were washing together, praying together. Taking refuge," Maryam said. An enchanted fairy-tale lantern was taking shape over her head.

"Of course no more fear, no more sin... And in such a setting, one night in Tahrir, I..."

"No way!" blurted Amira, anticipating the juicy details.

"That's right, mademoiselle," said Maryam, coolly nodding her head.

"You mean you did it in a tent?" I said, as if I had done the same and I wanted to give the impression that I fully understood how it happened. The truth was that Maryam didn't look like the kind of woman that would do anything so bold. You could take off all her clothes but you wouldn't find the woman inside. Still bent on teasing, Amira continued to make light of it all, deliberately shooting low.

"Well? Was he any good?"

Put off by the impertinence, Maryam didn't answer. She forced a smile, and kept up the tough-guy style. I had no choice but to try to smooth things over.

"A few years back I spent a year in Beirut. My mother was a little worried, and curious too. I went to see her in Turkey and we were talking in the kitchen. She wanted to know what I was doing in Beirut and what the Arabs were like. She wanted to know if they were all super religious, that sort of thing. Because when people in Turkey talk about Arabs they only think of the Gulf states or black Africa."

"Black Africa?" said Maryam.

"That's just the way it is, mademoiselle. Anyway, so then I tell my mum. I say, Mum, look, Beirut is more or less just like Turkey. Arabs aren't what you think. You don't just pray

11

in Arabic. You make love in Arabic, talk politics in Arabic, and everything else. I talked to her about politics, starting in the sixties with the history of the Arab left and all that, and then my dad comes in, munching on sunflower seeds, and he says, 'Of course, sweetie, you know there *are* modern Arabs!'"

They both laughed. "And you two are certainly modern Arabs," I said and they laughed even harder. Despite the posturing, loose talk and flirting – trying to work each other out – we were all trying to meet on common ground, that much was clear.

When our laughter died down, Amira suddenly tilted her head, like a poppy by the roadside.

"What's that!?"

We held our breath. Silence. The wedding was over, and then … faint music. Amira stood up, searching for the source, and as if catching the scent of the sound she tiptoed to other side of the terrace in her slippers. We shuffled after her. Amira leaned over and looked down at the neighbouring terrace to the left of the hotel entrance, and, draped over the wall, she said, "Yes, it's coming from down there."

On a sliver of the terrace below an old woman's hand reached out for a glass of wine. She wore a large emerald ring. Beside her glass was an old record player, playing *The Bridge of Love* by Oum Kalthoum. After every sip of wine she slowly, tremulously, placed her glass back down on the table, and, still holding the glass, she tapped out the rhythm of the song with her ring.

Under her breath Amira translated the words into English, as if she were savouring the remnants of marzipan on her tongue.

I have seen lovers... I have seen what will happen to them and that which they cannot see... / I have seen how they have fallen in love... I did not understand / could not understand / Then you suddenly came along... And then you...

We could only see the lower half of her arm, red nail polish on her fingers. Her emerald ring stopped clinking against her glass every time the man in the song 'suddenly came along'. And we watched from above, in the puzzle of the Old City. From one dark square to another dark square. Amira kept translating under her breath:

I have seen the lovers / they were naïve / I said, I can't be that way / And then you suddenly came along ... and then you...

Amira suddenly stopped translating and let out a deep sigh: "Ahhh... Oum Kalthoum... How many hearts has this woman broken? Asmahan, she's the one that gets me the most. What a woman! You just have to tip your cap to such beauty. But such grace can't command the kind of respect of a mannish woman like Oum Kalthoum."

Maryam was watching the wedding guests dramatically bid each other farewell, studying their hen-like gestures, so unlike her style, when she said, "Oum Kalthoum had no other choice. They left her no other choice but to become a man."

"I hate Oum Kalthoum!" said Amira but she was obviously referring to something else. Maryam laughed, trampling over Amira's heart that had just cracked open.

"There was this fervent Egyptian Imam," she said. "He used to say that Egypt had lost the Six Day War with Israel because of Oum Kalthoum. In a speech, he said, 'How could we expect our men to fight when her songs had softened their hearts.' As if that thick voice of hers could actually soften anyone's heart!"

I laughed and Amira's mood shifted. She was no longer a woman who had been through hard times, but a child thirsting for attention.

"I'm for Asmahan ... I like her. No reason to love someone just because she wins."

Maryam forced a smile.

"Sweetie, do you really think manly women can ever win?"

Our conversation and the song finished so abruptly that I thought we could hear the clouds drifting through the moonlight. And that might have been the end of our night – we were already out of whisky. But turning tough again, Maryam suddenly cried out in a young, rugged voice, "Madam! Madam! Good night! And bon appétit!"

The woman's hand quivered then clutched her glass. Her hand seemed to be thinking, surprised, sensing the surroundings. Then her face came into view, searching for Maryam's voice. The old woman looked up at us. Three women in white nightgowns, holding empty glasses. Slowly she rose to her feet, as if she had all the time in the world. Maybe she was smiling but we couldn't tell through all the wrinkles. She raised her glass. We did the same. With the intimacy of intoxication, we twirled our hands in salute to the old woman, La Scala-style. Then with her trembling hand she gestured, 'just a minute', and again, 'just a minute'. She put on a new record. We sensed what was coming: we had heard the sweet, dark, intimate, whimsical idea flutter through her mind. Then the song started. It was Warda.

Oh time... so much time without love!

We laughed, we laughed out loud to show that we had understood she was making light of the situation.

And that is how it all began. We were three women fated to take refuge in a story, looking out for each other as we moved forwards, three women soon to become four. We had no idea that the cure to all our problems was present in each other and that the balm we would blend together could protect humankind from evil. Indeed the strange events I am about to recount are entirely true. It's just that I have trouble believing it all really happened.

2

I am holding the torn wing of an angel in one hand and in the other a magic wand, a pink-white fuzzy ball on the top. Waving the wand wildly in the air, I am shouting at a woman in a black chador.

"Why in the world would you hit a kid like that? Why are you hitting her?"

With the wand I point out the barbed wire to Amira and Maryam and I say, "Wasn't there just a revolution in this country? The Arab Spring and all that? What's all the barbed wire for? I mean who's it supposed to protect?"

Amira and Maryam are trying not to laugh. Shopkeepers are milling outside their shops close to the government building, which is surrounded by barbed wire. They are laughing with soldiers standing guard on the other side of the fence. The one-winged little girl is tugging at my leg while her mother shouts at me in Tunisian, which I can't understand. The situation is desperate. With nothing to do but keep my cool, I say, "I'm talking to you, Amira! Wasn't there a revolution in this country?"

I have a good reason to be this wound up so early in the morning...

*

In a morning daze, Amira, Maryam and I are walking through the square at the entrance to the maze of the Old City, looking for a quiet coffeehouse. Barbed wire circles the Government Palace. This is the famous Kasbah Square, where the revolution started. Strolling about, we suddenly find ourselves in the middle of a situation.

"Hold on. Let me try it this way," I say, turning the child whose little angel wing has got caught in the barbed wire. The more she struggles to be free the more entangled she becomes. I look at her mother. She's useless. So worried about keeping her chador from slipping that she can't take care of her own daughter's wings. Clearly she thinks this matter of her little girl's wings is nothing more than an indulgence. When the girl sees that her wing is being torn, she starts to cry. And the silvery, feathery halo over her head slips down over her face; the feathers are now in her eyes, and she begins to sob. Then she starts whacking my back with her magic wand, a little wisp that couldn't hurt a fly. Then her mother is suddenly gripped by a desire to educate her child. She slaps her daughter harshly for hitting a stranger with a magic wand. The blow brings the halo down to her lips and the poor girls starts chewing on the ring, spittle dripping from the corners of her mouth. Now my scarf gets caught in the wire and starts to choke me. Now the mother's chador gets snared and suddenly we are two women and an angel caught in a web, flailing about and shouting. Springing out of their morning stupor, Maryam and Amira race over to help while I am yelling at the mother.

"Why do you need to go and hit your kid like that?"

We are three sea urchins trapped in a fisherman's net in front of the Government Palace, soldiers standing guard beyond the wire, shopkeepers on the other side delighting in the spectacle.

That's when I grab the kid's magic wand and wave it about in the air, crying out.

"Wasn't there a revolution in this country? The Arab Spring or whatever you call it?"

Maryam starts gently tugging at my arm while Amira says something in Tunisian to the mother who looks back at her defiantly to show she knows exactly what she is doing. Now the soldiers on the other side of the fence are cracking up with laughter. Maryam whips the magic wand out of my hand and gives it to the one-winged little girl. The woman behind me is still screaming. Amira spins round and screams back at her even more loudly. Now a furious trio, bringing a whole new meaning to the concept of rage, we dive into the maze of the Old City. A smiling shopkeeper is selling T-shirts, souvenirs from the revolutions. One of them reads: Game Over.

We are out of breath as we vent our exasperation and frustration at the needless beating of an anxious child and a crowd of men having such a good time looking on. Raising her arm high in the air, Amira says loudly, "What they should do is set up special units to deal with people who treat kids like that. Without any messing around they should say to offenders, 'Thanks for everything you have done till now but that will be all,' and take the kid away. If the revolution can't change this sort of behaviour then what's the point?"

A little more calmly Maryam mumbles something like,

"When everyone started laughing the woman felt ashamed and so…" But tying up the torn end of my scarf, I carry on in my rebellious mood. "I mean no way, I just don't get the need for the barbed wire. I don't get it. Isn't this Kasbah Square? Weren't you guys the ones who kicked everything off here? I mean who is the State still afraid of?"

"That's just the way it is," says Amira, despondently. That was enough analysis for one morning.

We walk single file into the labyrinthine maze of shops that is the Old City, keeping an eye on Amira's heels until we come to a coffee shop. Still rattled by the episode in the square, my voice is harsh when I order.

"Three coffees!"

Responding in a voice that sounded like he wouldn't care if the world came crumbling down, the proprietor says:

"Lavazza? Normal?"

"Normal," I say. Whatever that means. He clearly doesn't understand my quick reply and he snaps back, "Express? Amerikan?"

I look at his face to see if he's making fun of me. Then I snap.

"Express!" And I can't hold it back: "The Orient Express, *Habibi*!"

Laughing, Amira takes me by the arm and whispers in my ear, "This isn't Beirut, *hanimefendi*. You can't go around calling these guys *habibi* and that sort of thing!"

Maryam smiles and we feel the stress begin to slip away. Of course the 'express' refuses to come on time and the proprietor keeps wandering around us, nervous and threatening.

The coffee shop is like a cave. To get there you leave the lobby in the Dar el-Medina Hotel, go past the Zeytuna

19

Mosque and slip into the narrow passageway where they sell the souvenirs. Then take the passageway that leads downtown and it's the shop just a little ways ahead, the only coffee shop that allows women. To get inside you have to squeeze past all those other little shops selling spices, perfumes, soap and leather, making a narrow passageway even narrower. And when you finally burst through the fragrant clouds and wiggle through the cumbersome intimacy that goes with a bazaar, you suddenly realize you are inside.

"This coffee guy is really annoying, azizi," I say. Amira swiftly lets out a soft sigh, fans her face with her hand, sits up, puffs out her chest and flashes the man a coy smile. Maryam seems a little put off by the flirtatious display. Loudly she clears her sinuses, leans back in her chair, hikes up her trousers, spreads her legs wide and nervously bounces a leg up and down. Thanks to Amira's smile the Orient Express is already on the way. With the first sip of coffee my head must have cranked into gear. First I realized how right I was about my adventure the night before – if I had walked in the other direction I would have ended up in the centre of town. Then there were the fragments and shades of Amira and Maryam (and the dynamic between them) that I'd only just begun to make out in the light of the fireworks last night. They were much clearer in daylight. Amira had a body that seemed designed to support breasts. Her black eyes were almost too large for her face that always seemed to be smiling. Over her eyes were thin, striking eyebrows that looked like they were painted by a master artist in a single, deft stroke of his brush on the smooth, milk-chocolate canvas of her skin. That mysterious and enticing energy particular to small women turned her body into a kind of enticing treasure chest. She had bony feet but her hands were incredibly delicate. And she held herself in such a way that you felt she might suddenly spring into action, leaping to her feet in a flurry of motion. In her company you always felt a little on guard. She was a woman that gave you the feeling something big was about to happen.

Maryam was tall and her body was firm. Like well-mixed concrete, you could pull out all the supporting rods and she would still be standing. The features in her face were well balanced but she had a stony gaze like a sign that read 'Closed for Business'. But that body made you think long and hard: had she drifted away from the more usual feminine airs because she was born like that or had her body changed over time as she consciously grew more androgynous? When she looked at you she would narrow her eyes, and her chin and her nose would lift. But she possessed a rare warmth and intensity that poured out of her at unexpected moments, which wasn't common in women like her. This involuntary rush of compassion was directed more at Amira than me. Which is why she quickly tore open the oversized sugar sachet that came with Amira's coffee. Absently she popped the sugar into her coffee and started stirring. The tiniest details served to solidify their relationship. It blossomed before my eyes: Amira stirring Maryam's coffee with her spoon; Maryam trying to light Amira's cigarette and Amira saying 'you first'; Maryam checking to see if Amira's bag was safe and Amira saying, as if going through an old routine, 'just hang it there on the back of your chair'; Maryam taking four packs of cigarettes out of her bag and trying to squeeze them all on the table only for Amira to say, 'why don't I just keep this one pack in my bag?' And when the coffeehouse proprietor comes over with the pretext of emptying an ashtray, trying to get a closer look at Amira, tough guy Maryam holds it out for him before he can get too close.

In this way they both favour the roles they feel comfortable playing, like a couple sitting across from each other in a Ferris wheel compartment, trying to synchronize movements as they sway back and forth in the air before the wheel starts spinning, making little adjustments to get just the right balance. I could watch these two women for hours, marvelling at the way they worked off each other; they seemed far more interesting than anything in the bigger world, more interesting than the Arab Spring, or the political problems of any other country.

Observing my two new friends, I hear the word 'chai' in a strange accent, and then suddenly a glass of tea is under my nose. One of three older women at a neighbouring table want me to drink it. We are speaking English so she must think we're tourists. The big smiles on their faces make it clear they want to have a little fun with us. They want to see if I am willing to drink tea out of one of their glasses. Amira and Maryam stop and let the old ladies have a go at me just when the Ferris wheel starts turning. In the face of the male coffeehouse proprietor, I settle for an alliance with this troika of older ladies, plastering one of those silly tourist smiles on my face.

I pick up the glass of mint tea without a word of protest. Whose was it? Did it come from the one who was drooling because she hardly has any teeth? Shards of white nuts are floating on the surface of the tea. Nodding and arching their eyebrows, their lips opening like mothers trying to get a child to take her medicine, they encourage me to drink. I pretend I'm deathly ill and that if I just down the elixir I'll be miraculously cured. And it's gone in one gulp! Ouch! And there is a fresh wave of laughter. When they find out I'm from Istanbul we have a little chat about Turkish TV serials in a mixture of Arabic and English, peppered with 'ohs' and 'ahs'. And so we become an even stronger alliance in the face of the coffeehouse proprietor and I ask our group, shall we have more coffee? And they say, but of course. So I order three more expressos! It's clear Maryam and Amira are having a hard time coming to their senses in the morning. We are going to be sitting here for a little longer.

Two shadows appear in a doorway opening onto a sun-drenched street. A hunch-backed old man is holding the hand of a little boy with a bald, round head. In his other hand the man has an ice cream. The boy is reaching out for it, tugging on the old man, who raises the ice cream higher and higher as the boy lunges for it. They sit down directly across from us.

The boy jumps for the ice cream and nearly gets a hold of it. Greedily trying to finish, the old man says, 'Stop it, you're going to spill it,' as a little more disappears between his toothless gums. Finally he lets the boy have the cone, but the man is still devouring what's left with his eyes: the boy doesn't have any idea how precious a treat like that is for them as the old man's heart seems to drool with the ice cream. The boy is in heaven with every bite into the sweet coolness. There is a big smile stretching across his face, but then the old man snatches the ice cream out of his hand. The boy begins to cry while the old man licks the ice cream that has dribbled out of the cone and onto his hand. But before the boy really starts sobbing, the old man shoves the ice cream back in his hand. And the boy prepares for another trip back to heaven as if nothing has happened. But he's restless, one eye fixed on the heavenly delight and the other on the old man, watching his every movement: a potential threat. If he just goes fast enough this time he'll finish... But no luck. The old man's eyes are still locked on the cone; he'll find no peace as long as it remains in the boy's hand. The boy is eating all the ice cream the old man never had when he was a child. His nerves get the better of him and he cracks, swiping away the cone from the boy and gobbling up what's left. The boy starts to wail. Without an ounce of shame, the old man smacks his lips and hands the last bit of cone back to the child. A gooey lump in the bottom. In a fit the boy crushes the cone in the palm of his hand. He wants to shame the old man and make him angry. But instead he gets a beating, leaving ice-cream stains on a table. The boy is like an octopus fighting for his life when his granddad swoops down on him and they are gone.

Maryam, Amira and I turn our heads away to avoid making eye contact as we take deep drags on our cigarettes. "What is it with today, azizi?" I say. As if right on cue, Maryam, says, "Tunisia's National Oppress the Children Day."

Suddenly a jasmine peddler in a white robe shoves a handful of little bouquets under my nose. "*Maşmuum! Maşmuum!*" he says. Amira politely declines in Tunisian and shoos him away but with no luck. He has that serene Northern-African face of an itinerant peddler, pious, crinkled, compassionate, hopeless, loveable. He is pushing his jasmine, stuffed into large green shells, onto potential customers. Turning to me, Amira says, "Give me a dinar". I hand her one and she saves me. Taking after the peddler, I stick the *maşuum* behind my ear. Amira smiles.

"Woman don't wear *maşuum*. Those who do are considered 'loose' or 'easy'. Men wear them."

24

"Oh dear!" I say, putting the flowers on the table. Picking up the little bouquet, Mayram twirls it between her fingers. Very much the opposite of a 'loose' or 'easy' woman, she flicks it behind her ear and flashes a plucky smile.

The jasmine peddler takes off his traditional dark red fez, which he clearly only sports for the tourists, and, kicking off his sandals, he sits down on the doorstep, his fat feet and thick toenails dangling over the street. His coffee comes straightaway. Maryam and Amira can't see him from behind a pillar but I can see his profile. Without his fez his face no longer has that sweet folkloric look and he just looks glum. Two kids come and stand over him. Their hands are stuffed in their pockets. Probably brother and sister. The boy, who must be about ten, stands in front of his sister, who could be no more than twelve. Two hungry workers. Whatever it was they were doing yesterday they aren't doing it today but no doubt they have to hand over money when they get home. They say something to each other and with the grave expression of a grown man the boy approaches the jasmine peddler. Gazing into the distance, the peddler tries to brush them away, as if these two are poor featherweight fighters in the free market.

"How much do you sell those for?" asks the kid with a surprising level of seriousness, which suggests he's been around a while and knows the business as well as anyone. The old man doesn't even look at him. The boy looks at his sister. Her silence speaks of their desperation. Puffing up his chest, he puts on a sour face that he has probably picked up from his dad, because that's just how you look if you're a man, and he says, "How much do you sell those for, uncle?"

After wallowing in a long silence, the man says, "A dinar".

Like a codebreaker catching the right frequency on the front line, the kid shoots back the next question.

"How much you buy them for?"

The peddler doesn't need more competition; he sees a man in the child, but a man who does not yet pose a threat. He is still a boy holding the anger of a dozen men and the peddler only pities him. But the more the boy is rejected and pushed away the more he becomes a man.

"You get them from the flower sellers over at the station?"

All of a sudden the peddler half-heartedly kicks the boy right in his kidney. He falls to the ground. No one moves. I turn to Maryam and Amira and I say, "That man just kicked that kid!" Maryam leaps to her feet and Amira swivels on her stool, her legs still crossed. They still can't see anything from behind the pillar. The old man looks as peaceful as a cow swatting flies. The boy's face flushes bright red with rage. His sister gathers him up off the ground before the passers-by can step on him. Drawing on everything she's learned at home, she's now acting like his mother. As they run off a few men give the boy a tousle or two on his head – because he's such a cute little kid of course – and a couple of minutes later the two siblings have pulled themselves together, walking along like two normal kids. Shaking his head, the peddler rearranges his jasmine in his basket. His movements show that he was once beaten as a child so now he has every right to do the same. Shaking his head again, he forgives himself. The way a tyrant might forgive himself with overwhelming compassion.

"I can't take it anymore. This is just too much. Let's ask for the bill," I say. Of course Maryam handles it before Amira even looks up. The bill comes right away: express! Getting up at the same pace, I stick my jasmine back into the peddler's basket, just to make a point. He doesn't even blink. Maryam and Amira both flash him an evil glare in their own ways and hiss in solidarity: "How rude!" I see the boy a little further up the road, he sees us, and how we returned the jasmine to make a point to the peddler. He looks over his shoulder again before he races into the crowd and disappears.

Off we go jostling through the crowd, a dark cloud over our heads, feeling increasingly suffocated. We arrive at the exit to the Old City and stop under the Bab Baher Gate at the top of the bustling, sun-drenched, broad Habib Bourguiba Boulevard that runs down to the new city. There's a sea of people in front of the gate, a burning light, and a struggle. Frustrated, Maryam says, "I've got things to do. I suppose we'll see each other later on in the hotel." Nothing more. Amira says: "Me, too. See you later." I have nothing to do – which is why I am in this country – and so I keep quiet and as they both disappear into the crowd I slip back into the passageway to make my way back to the hotel.

I see the siblings walking ahead of me in slow motion ... the same boy and the girl bouncing like two tangerines in the skirt of a woman hurrying down a hill. It feels like my forehead has the mark of compassion. For Arab Muslims, the mark is left by a round, grey leather prayer tablet, which is made of mud from Kerbala, and comes after prostrating before God. Somehow hungry children and beggars can always recognize the mark. The little girl is holding one of those three-fingered Hand of Fatima prayer talismans. No doubt they have decided to try selling those after ruling out the jasmine. Feeling for them, I buy three talismans from the girl. When I get back to Istanbul, I'll give one to Ayşe. Casually I give the girl what turns out to be far too much money. The boy seems guilty about it and says, "Sister, why did you come to Tunis? Are you another journalist?"

"No," I say.

"Then why are you here?"

"Because they don't think much of kids in my country either."

His sister tugs on his arm and they disappear into the dim alleyways of the bazaar so quickly it seems like they were never there.

As I am stepping inside the hotel two street dogs start growling at my feet, the hair on their backs bristling. But they suddenly stop before pouncing. As if they both have a sudden and deep moment of clarity, they understand the futility of the fight and they back off. I watch them slink away, feeling the deep sense of relief that comes when you back out of a fight. Having left behind the growing conflict over political corruption in my home country, I feel like a child who has just got her first taste of her own snot; I am a slug holed up in a hotel room in a country I hardly know, a place that doesn't really interest me. I am a street dog that has pulled out of a fight, without any knowledge of what might have happened.

When I go into my room I find a jasmine-scented envelope with an invitation inside. I don't know this invitation is for three and that it will unlock all our secrets. Perhaps the scent of jasmine gives me the slightest premonition of the adventure that is to come. But when I tell you how it happens you'll see how it took us by surprise.

3

Night. We are in some kind of forest. Trees all around us. We see the feet of a woman. Running. A mature woman. My own two feet. The camera pans out and we see her running away from something or someone. Panicked breathing. There is the sound of other feet beside her but we only see hers. They are running together. Every now and then she turns to look over her shoulder. There's a howling behind her. A crowd is chasing them. She starts running again. She runs on and on. Then a close up of her feet again and suddenly they stop. The sound of heavy breathing. Desperation. The camera pans out just a little and we see her up against a wall! Slowly the camera rises and we see her completely surrounded. There's no way out. We see her slowly step back, then turn to face the crowd. The camera now directly overhead, we see the crowd from her point of view. Getting closer and closer and then they stop. The camera swings up even higher and we hear clicking. A volley of clicks. People in the crowd are cocking their guns. They take aim and wait. The camera slowly rises again. Looking from behind the woman, we see who is with her: a pelican and a baby bear! We see her confused, panting face, drenched in sweat. Reluctantly she raises her hands and says, "I'm sure your story is more interesting than mine. But now it's my turn to tell!"

A short pause. Opening her eyes like someone at least fifty years young, she asks, "What do you think? Gripping?"

Maryam, Amira and I are sitting on the other side of the dinner table, our mouths open in surprise. We could have stayed like that for hours. And we did. Well, we stayed like that for a while.

And then she let out a laugh that stampeded across the room. A long, hearty laugh. A caravan of laughter. She laughed at the sight of our open mouths and the more she laughed the more we stared in wonder. And that was how Amira, Maryam and I came to know the magnificent, one-and-only Madam Lilla.

We were shocked. When we had spotted the woman the night before drinking wine and listening to Oum Kalthoum, we were startled when she suddenly raised her glass to a toast in our honour, but this had now become more than we'd expected: she was, after all, the esteemed Madam Lilla. But we didn't know that yet. The jasmine-scented invitations had certainly piqued our curiosity but nothing could have prepared us for the one-woman wonderland this altogether magnificent personality presented to us. Besides, none of us were in any position to judge because earlier that evening things developed far too quickly.

*

"I'm not going anywhere," said Amira, holding her invitation. We were sitting on the hotel terrace, where we had met and drunk together the night before. Our eyes were swollen from the humidity, not tears! That's just what happens when you travel, she said. Amira's verve seemed to have died down and I didn't push her – eventually she'd come out and tell us whatever it was that was bothering her. I said, "What kind of invitation is this anyway? I don't get it."

My dear ladies, I would be delighted if you were
to honour my residence this evening

Menu
Mint turkey marinated in distilled jasmine
Rice with prunes and almonds cooked in tangerine juice
Blended powdered thyme salad with apple and sumac
Semolina halva with currants and mastic
Food served with homemade rose wine

"What I don't get is this: how do you do rice in tangerine juice?"

Amira smiled. "That was actually the only one I liked the sound of."

Suddenly smiling, her long face disappeared and so I asked:

"Or did you go home then?"

Her face fell again, almost into the palm of her open hand. She clearly had something very important to say but she couldn't come out and say it.

"Shall we order beer?" I asked. Amira's face now in her hands, she shook her head, her hair fluttering. "Yes," she said. By the time the beer arrived the sun was even lower. A touch of neon in the sky. With the sun low on the horizon the terrace seemed like an eye no longer squinting under the glare. Soon the young, spirited waiter, Kamal, who looked after almost everything in the hotel, wobbled up with our beers, a broad grin on his face. Sensing our sadness almost immediately, he quickly left the stage. As I poured beer into glasses, Amira came out with it as if leaping directly out of an interior monologue:

"What's a revolution if you can't dance!"

"Ah, Emma Goldman!"

"Huh?"

"That's Emma Goldman. The American anarchist. In the 1920s..."

"I don't know her. I'm just saying. I mean, I'm just saying."

I kept silent. Shaking her head and trying to calm down, Amira went on:

"You know it's about respect. Do you understand? They don't respect me. I thought that..."

"Did you think that things would change after the revolution?"

"Oh come on, what revolution? When my dad died ... I mean ... I thought the family oppression would end."

"Hmm..."

Now she was fuming, and at me. She assumed I didn't understand and she was so sure that it was making her really angry. She started to tear up. Just a little. Then it passed and she went on. "I couldn't tell you last night. I'm a dancer."

"No way. Really? That's great!"

"Yeah, really great. I'm also a journalist, of a sort ... more like an internet activist."

"Are you serious?"

In no mood to indulge my surprise she nevertheless forced herself to give an explanation.

"Before our dear dictator Ben Ali fell from power and when there was still all sorts of censorship in the country, Tunisians living abroad were hard at work. I was also pretty busy then. You know the Anonymous group? Well, working with them we were able to bring down government websites, that sort of thing, then..."

"Wait up! Just a minute! You did what? Sister, you can't just breeze over something like that. You did what?"

32

She flashed me a wicked look and I covered my mouth with my hands to show that I would keep quiet. She continued, "I don't want to talk about it anymore. Because after the revolution everyone was a revolutionary. Oh, it seems we had no idea just how heroic the entire nation had been! But we were just a handful of people. Now I look and see the public squares packed with all these 'revolutionaries'. I waited, tried to stay patient... But dad died before I could tell him. Now it's gnawing away at me. I'd told myself I should say it to his face – I didn't want to write to him about it. I mean, face to face! So I was going to say, 'your call girl, your dancing floozy of a daughter made this revolution, you beast!' But the bastard went and died!"

"So you beat Ben Ali but your dad had already kicked the ball out of bounds!"

She wasn't at all interested in the 'depth' of my observation.

"And yesterday, mum..."

She was overcome by more tears. Pulling herself together, she went on.

"They are deceiving people, you know? Total deceit. For years you think your dad is the bad guy and your mum is the miserable victim. But they actually have a secret pact. There you are struggling to protect your mum. And you suffer for her. In fact you become a mother to her in this weird way. Then ... then when your dad leaves the scene you see her real face, the face of someone who's always played the good cop. Check it out, she says to me, 'the way you're behaving doesn't do our family any favours.' You'd think we were the Trabelsi family!"

"Who's the Trabelsi family?"

She flashed me an infinitely humiliating look:

"What sort of journalist are you, buddy? Ben Ali's wife's

family. Before the revolution they owned more than half the country. Something like the mafia. You came here without reading up on this?"

"I came in a hurry. You see, the thing is, I was fired from my job..."

"Ah..." she said, looking at me out of the corner of her eye. Like it was the most natural thing to do. For some reason I was still feeling really good. Her trivializing the fact that I got fired gave me this feeling of relief. Amira went on:

"So she had to go and say, 'let's get you married and not suffer any more shame.' That was when I got the letter and left home."

"What letter?"

"Now that's the real story. I mean, that's why I'm crying."

"So you're saying everything you've just said isn't the real story."

"No. It actually has to do with Muhammed's letters."

We heard footsteps on the stairs leading up to the terrace.

A young man appeared in the twilight, hands in his pockets. Coming over to us, he said, "Hurry up and order me a beer!"

"Oh my God," I cried.

In a hushed voice Amira only managed to say, "What have you done?" Maryam was standing across us with a military buzz cut. Leaning over the wall, she smiled and called down to the lower courtyard.

"One more beer up here on the terrace, please!"

She came and sat down, leaning back in her chair like a bloke. With a Casanova smile beaming on her face, she jiggled her leg up and down.

"Just too hot. And they told me it was only going to get hotter. So I cut it off."

She ran her hand over her head from front to back.

"What do you think?" she asked. "Look good?"

"Oh yeah," I said both startled and amused, and then Amira started to cry.

"Whoa! What's with you?" Maryam said, taking her hand.

"How should I know?" Amira said, sniffing.

"Did you think I was someone else? Your lover or something?" said Mayram, laughing. Amira let out another sob. Puzzled, Maryam looked at me and then winked. I raised my eyebrows to say that I would tell her later. With Maryam now swaggering, Amira seemed nothing more than the stereotypical hypersensitive woman with nothing left to do but cry. Still holding Amira's hand, Maryam looked at the invitation on the table then turned to me.

"So you got one too. I say we go. Looks interesting. I'm especially curious about the rice in tangerine juice."

Amira laughed through the snot in her nose.

"Me too!"

Dressed and all done up, we knocked on Madam Lilla's blue door draped in jasmine, right next to the hotel. Waiting, I whispered to Maryam, "Why did you cut it?"

"I told you," she said. "It's hot."

"Interesting."

"That's right! Interesting," she answered.

Without any hair she no longer looked like a movie extra squirming because she was stuck with the wrong outfit. Now she was oddly at ease, even cheerful. The door swung open and an old man with one blind eye said, "Do come in ladies." He was dark and elegantly dressed in a suit. He wore patent leather shoes. The image of a perfect African gentleman. When he spoke, words came out one by one, like the counting of prayer beads: "Welcome and wonderful to have you with us, ladies. I am Eyüp, Madam Lilla's assistant. She is expecting you on the terrace."

As we climbed the stairs, we heard Oum Kalthoum's *He's Thinking of Me*. Moving as slowly as I could, I looked around the house. Everywhere there were mirrors, cracked and conspiratorial. It was impossible to see yourself completely in them. Maybe a natural choice for an old woman who wanted to remember her face as it once was. A jasmine vine grew straight up through the middle of the house, its branches winding around the stairwell and up to the terrace. A dark green velvet armchair was placed facing the door. An ugly cat with spindly legs moved away from us. There were colourful birds in a gigantic cage in the middle of the room and countless lanterns of coloured glass. There was a whip on the top of a cabinet. There were original paintings and piles of black and white photographs inside an open commode beside the armchair. Eyüp Bey seemed like a character out of a haunted house tour when he flashed me a razor-sharp look out of his good eye. He might have been imploring us to help him, or trying to tell us to get out now. It was difficult to know which with just that one eye. A cheerful woman's voice echoed through the room. "Welcome! Welcome!"

Stepping through the terrace door covered in jasmine, we came to meet the woman whose voice had bounced down the stairs like a marble. She was standing in the middle of the terrace, her arms flung open. She was a tiny woman who seemed taller than she really was. The kind of woman who seemed like she was in her late sixties but who had to be in her late seventies. You got the feeling her thin grey hair had been deftly pulled up into a bun years ago and had been like that ever since. She was a woman whose beautiful traits remained even after her beauty was gone. No doubt she could have starred in *The Lady of the Camellias* if they made a sequel to the film – she was that sort of lady. Her dark blue, gold-enamelled vintage belt draped down over her lilac-coloured dress with green patterns, nearly touching the floor. She stood with the patience of a lady of the salon who knew the weight of every moment. Her gestures seemed slow or rather she avoided the superfluous movements her younger counterparts might deploy to fill space. She was like a poem made plain with patience. Draped around her neck was a Hand of Fatima, a kind I had never seen before. Bracelets dangled from her wrist and her thin silvery hands were covered with rings adorned with diamonds and rubies. And there we were standing across from her like bums with shoulders slumped, one of us bald, one with swollen eyes and me a little drunk. Our modern day clothes fringed and frayed, we looked meek in the face of this black and white prima donna. We were steeped in the indifference of a decisive defeat. In the face of her womanhood, we looked like three young boys who had just finished a game of football.

"Please come in, ladies," she said. "Do make yourselves comfortable. Dinner will be ready soon! A glass of rosé wine?"

As the perfect cross between a gentleman and a lady, Maryam pulled a *maşmuum* bouquet from her pocket: jasmine about to bloom.

"Ah," said Madam Lilla, "you are so very kind!" She stopped and flashed a coy smile, a throwback to her thirties. "Do you know why they collect the jasmine early in the morning and make these *maşmuum* bouquets before the flowers have bloomed?"

With the flirtatious lilt of a baroness, every word she said flared up like a match.

"For then the jasmine will always remember their dreams. If you bring them home and place them on a silver tray they bloom slowly, remembering the night, whispering to you of their white dreams."

I hadn't brought my notebook. Sentences like that always slip away.

"Oh! But I am speaking English. I just assumed it was our common language," she said, embracing wholeheartedly the humility of her lead role. We sat down, keeping with our finest family dinner posture. Though we clearly looked like a second-league team, she must have taken us for women worthy of her social hours. Overlooking a pervasive anxiety and mistrust, she chose the momentary sadness of disappointment.

"I assume Kamal has already told you. They call me Madam Lilla around here. You can call me the same." Leaning over the table, we expected her to ask for our names.

"Last night ... when I raised a glass to you on the terrace ... as you might imagine such *grand* gestures don't happen in Tunis ... I wanted to meet you. And I hope that sending you an invitation was not strange. I thought that instead of wasting my time trying to tell that curious hotel waiter, Kemal, about my tangerine rice I would..."

We laughted loudly, with a dash of frustration.

"You have so much jasmine here. I wish I had brought you something else," said Maryam. Playing the role of offended child, Amira frowned and pouted and then said, "Forgive us for not really bringing anything."

"You have a wonderful home," I said, only to make small talk.

Choosing the line that best fit the unfolding play as she poured wine into antique crystal glasses, her frail hand trembling, Madam Lilla said, "The jasmine ... yes... I love the one by the front door especially. It took root there all on its own."

Amira had opened her mouth and was about to say something when Madam Lilla continued, "Ah! So here's the food. I can serve, Eyüp Bey. You have a rest."

Looking at Madam Lilla in the same way a fallen leaf might look up at a tree, Eyüp Bey quickly vanished. Then she served us rice as if that very morning she had travelled by phoenix over the hills of China to the mythical Mount Qaf to handpick each and every grain. Wafting out of the silver-lidded copper pots were bewildering smells. The faint scent of burnt almonds and, even fainter, the scent of tangerine swirled over the soft smell of rice. Then mint made a hairpin turn and lingered on the outskirts, as the sweet fragrance of prunes gathered in our noses and jasmine fluttered like a white paper airplane. To the naked nose it was a saturnalia of scents that was impossible to follow. And as for the taste...

"More than eating tangerines this is like wandering blindfolded through a tangerine grove," I said out loud. Madam Lilla let out a laugh as joyous as a queen.

"How well you put it! Are you a writer?"

"Not quite. But that's the plan," I said.

"And you?" I asked. But Amira leapt in.

"An actress! No?"

After much wiggling, pouting, frowning, jangling of her bracelets and twisting her neck there came an inviting pause – all to ratchet up the tension – and she said, "Ah, I don't want our first conversation to be like this."

How did she want it to be?

"What I mean is that seeing how we met under such curious circumstances, it's a little... How should I put this?

Let's not be like everyone else. And to be honest I have already given our first encounter some thought... So I say that each of us should describe a scene from a film. Imagine your life as a motion picture and you want it to start in the most riveting way. What would that scene be like?"

She ran her eyes over the three of us. And then she began to explain her opening scene.

Night. We are in some kind of forest..."

...

When we finally closed our mouths we looked at each other, hoping to find a flicker of enlightenment. "Did that really happen?" I asked. Madam Lilla let out another peal of laughter.

"Not quite! But that's the plan!"

We had surrendered ourselves to the astonishing storytelling of this phoenix hunter, jasmine grower, wily goddess – call her what you will – because for the time being we were convinced she wasn't normal.

With a voice like a pearl from the bottom of the sea, Maryam said, "Tahrir," and she went on:

"Tahrir Square. Yellow lights. The day Mubarak fell. Night is falling. The camera shows the interior of a car. A man is sitting next to me. A friend... We're in the car. We've been drinking, we're in a good mood. We want nothing else but to be in Tahrir. It's addictive. We're hurrying to get there. Our blood can't run freely through our veins until we do. Every moment away we're afraid we might suddenly slip into space. As long as there's Tahrir we can keep a hold on the world around us. That's why everyone's going. In fact the revolution is already over, but if we leave it means we have accepted the fact. I'm hiding something. Nobody knows about it. I won't tell. Only when I am in Tahrir do I feel some release

40

from the burden; you can understand that much from the look on my face. A close up. We reach the square. We're so happy. Elated. Singing. The camera pans out over all the people hugging. But I'm not hugging anyone. I'm on the brink of tears. Sadness and joy both at the same time. Cut to the top of a street leading into the square; we see a street dog. Oblivious to what's going on around him, he's startled and terribly afraid. Under a yellow light he looks like a stray. Everyone is so happy but no one has told him why. He's alone. I start running. From above the camera follows me darting through a crowd. My lungs expand. Fill with air. I run faster. I make it to the dog. I stop. He looks at me so calmly, as if Egypt isn't falling to pieces. He's filthy, thin as a rail, and covered in mange. But his tail is still wagging reluctantly. I start to cry. I sit down on the pavement. The dog is just standing there. I wrap my arms around him. It feels like this mangy dog is the only living thing that will still love me if I tell him my secret. He leans his head against mine. Then a man comes over. An old man in a grey robe, a very poor man. A dirty rag is wrapped around his head, an olive branch sticking out of it. Around his neck is a sign that reads: Justice. He walks as if he's walking on water. He puts one hand on my head and the other on the dog. I look. His eyes are shut. 'It's time for you to go,' he says, 'your secret is too much for this place.' The film ends with me buying a ticket to Lebanon the next day."

"Did that really happen?" I ask instinctively. Describing the scene Maryam seemed to shed layers of her outward appearance. But now she is sitting there like a tough guy again, all bottled up. Only a smile on her face.

Pushing grains of rice across her plate, Amira suddenly leaps into her scene as if she's lost her mind.

"They are beating me. The camera doesn't show their faces.

But I won't die. I'm so surprised I'm still alive I don't even feel the pain any more. They are mostly hitting me in the stomach. I guess they think I'm pregnant. You know I dance, I'm a dancer... Flashback: Images of dance, me being taken off the stage, pushed into a room. But I'm not pregnant or anything like that. We see faces. My dad, my two uncles. The camera turns to my mum. From behind a locked door, she shouts, 'Don't do it.' For some reason I'm counting. She shouts four times. I mean, 'not even five' is what I think at the time. My lips are fluttering and you see me counting between the blows. Why not five times for example? Why doesn't she try to break down the door, I'm thinking. Instead of feeling any pain I feel disappointment. I'm not crying, I'm not shouting. A close up of my hand. I'm pulling up my trousers. I'm wearing a G-string and I'm afraid they'll see. Your body feels bigger when you are being beaten. Not smaller but bigger. Till then I didn't know I had so many places for them to hit... Anyway... They leave me. Then a long, slow creaking of the door. It's been left open. Some time passes. I don't know how long. I am breathing like an animal. I stand up. A close up of my mother's face, crying, crumpled up at the foot of the door. Touching her head, I step outside. I leave the room. Cut scene. I am on a boat bound for Italy. They are trying to kill me and I'm running away. Cut scene. I am in France. Cut scene. I'm in England. Longing to be home. So homesick. I get news. 'There's a revolution,' he says, 'this couldn't be a better opportunity. I'm fleeing the country. Crossing the Mediterranean with refugees. I am leaving you letters here, in Tunisia, so that I can find them when you get back.' Then... Cut scene. I'm coming back to Tunis. I ask around. The man is missing. He was one of the many lost at sea ... that's it."

"Now that's for real," I whisper, leaning over to Maryam.

Now she has understood why Amira was crying on the terrace earlier that evening.

Madam Lilla lets out a deep sigh. "Ladies," she says. From then on that's how she would address us. "My dear ladies... In life you only get one chance to see your whole life in a scene, if you happen to be so lucky. And the rest of your life you spend either trying to recapture that scene or running away from it. You seem like women who have been through some profound scenes. You must understand what I'm talking about?"

With her lips pinched in a smile she turns to me. Clearly she is about to ask me for my story. Thinking quickly on my feet, I counter with a question. It comes with the trade.

"And you Madam Lilla. Which one are you? Are you running away or trying to reconnect?"

Instead of answering, she looks at Amira so intently she has no choice but to look back. For some reason she has her in the crosshairs.

"My dear Amira, it seems that we are going to get along just swimmingly. And of course with you two as well..."

She hasn't answered my question and now senses it might be dangerous to completely cut me out, so she offers an explanation: "But as her matter pertains to dance, things are different!"

Amira tries to look away but this only brings her back to the table.

She is so young. How many times would life call her back into the ring? First the centrifuge throws her out and then sucks her back in and, now flashing a smile, she says, why not? But Maryam isn't all that pleased – or so it seems – with this extra interest Madam Lilla is taking in Amira. She's jealous, and, like a man, she's tense and ashamed of the emotion. She feels she's slipping out of the game. Amira sends Madam Lilla a sparkling gaze while Maryam has her eyes fixed on Amira, who still isn't aware of the dynamic, but I can see everything from where I am sitting. And Madam Lilla is in her element.

"Given our situation, there are a few things I should explain," she says, handing us three separate envelopes. A new menu:

Pastry with violet thorns – cabbage cake with peanuts
Dessert
Pear cooked with chocolate and red pepper

Violet thorns?!

"Of course we won't be able to discuss everything tonight. But I do hope you will enjoy the thorns?"

More than an extraordinary and elegant character out of a novel, Madam Lilla was in her own way drawing us into a play in which it was clear not entirely good things would come to pass. The meal didn't last long. And she practically hurried us out of the house, successfully leaving the most elegant part of the night in our hearts.

Eyüp Bey showed us to the door. There was something about the look in his eye that I didn't like one bit – I couldn't quite place him. He was like an oarsman who had willingly signed up to row on Madam Lilla's vessel but then exhausted himself because he was the only one. Eyüp Bey was the backstage of the Scala Opera, its warehouse and the vast open maze beneath the stage: echoes, dust, silent ropes and pulleys. You always are a little suspicious of those people who downplay themselves to such a degree. Before he closes the door, he says, "So we will be seeing you the day after tomorrow." He has the patient elegance typical of the butler, who, with a self-confidence honed over time, knows everything but is never part of anything, until, eventually, he reveals that he is the killer after all.

Stepping through the front door of the hotel, Amira stops as if she has something important to say. "The jasmine. It's not like Madam Lilla says. It doesn't grow on its own." We stand and wait. As if this was the only odd moment out in an otherwise very odd evening; and, with the severity of a critic who has found a crucial error of continuity in a cinematic masterpiece, she says, "If you take a jasmine branch and plant it in the earth without breaking it, pulling the end out of the other side..."

Bending her arm at the elbow, she demonstrates the angle.

"Later when the branch gives root, you cut it off from the main branch. In other words jasmine doesn't grow on its own. Like a mother and child."

She whispers the last sentence under her breath.

It becomes clear Amira will need a little more time before she is herself again. Returning to our rooms, we feel utterly helpless, not knowing what will happen next, wondering what we would be eating the day after tomorrow. Like three armadillos flat on their backs we had no idea who was going to come round and kick us back over onto our feet.

4

Crash! Bang! Clang! Boom!

A Renault had crashed into a Mercedes, which had climbed up on a blue Peugeot 406 when the driver suddenly slammed on the brakes. Then a motorcycle swerved in from behind, clipped the Renault's bumper, wobbled and toppled over. All the drivers jumped out onto the street. Leading the group was a young hipster in a pair of loud sunglasses, then a well-heeled woman, a middle-aged man in a trim suit and skullcap, and finally a loose-robed Salafi[1] who had tumbled off his bike. The sudden three-car pile-up had happened right in front of us and in the blink of an eye had caused three busted fenders, the emotional breakdown of a motorcyclist, seven crying children, seventeen adults screaming at the top of their lungs and a street festival that would last the entire day. The police took their time in getting to the scene but soon the military took an interest. And as it all happened near the Ministry of Justice and courthouses on Bab Binet Street, lawyers, men and women in crumpled white ties who looked like children after an impromptu game of football, were already at the scene. And like anywhere else in the Middle East, coffeehouse proprietors, working in the best interest of their customers, had instantly set up an Inspection and Evaluation Board to keep tabs on the affair. With our eyebrows raised, we squeezed along the edge of the crowd, clutching paper cups full of coffee, pretending not to show the slightest interest in what was going on. The fact is

---

[1] a member of a strictly orthodox Sunni Muslim sect advocating a return to the early Islam of the Koran and Sunna.

*the three of us were the real cause of the accident. But, you see,
earlier that morning everything was completely under control.*

*

When I went down to the courtyard in the morning Amira
and Maryam were having breakfast. Amira seemed in a rush
while Maryam was taking her time, lingering over her food.
I didn't ask them what they had done the day before because
I didn't want to admit I had spent the entire day snoozing,
hoping a phone call wouldn't nudge me out of my daze. In
her necklace, lipstick and a slightly low-necked shirt, Amira
seemed ready for a big day.

"What are you up to today?" Maryam asked her.

As I stared into my cup of coffee, Amira explained, the
words bubbling off her tongue.

She was going to Nawaat. She had friends who worked
there for a news site that had contributed a lot to the
revolution. Maybe she'd find work as a journalist, and she'd
be much better off if she did or else … and in any case there
was something she needed to pick up from someone. Later
she planned to stop by the hamam. Not for a soak or a scrub,
but for work. Maybe she could dance for tourists, that sort
of thing. When she asked us what we had planned for the
day, Maryam and I sat there like the last scrawny, tongue-
tied old farts to be picked in the workers' market. "Then
come along with me," she said, and we were off. As we
passed the Government Palace in Kasbah Square, Amira
suggested we get coffee on the road to Nawaat and we went
into a coffeehouse. Amira had made a point of choosing the
one along the road that only served men and once we stepped
inside tension filled the room as men shifted in their chairs.
Deploying her breasts as a kind of shield in the face of an

47

abundance of male anxiety, Amira called out to the proprietor:

"Three express!"

So there we are: three women standing in the middle of the coffeehouse, our entrance causing a perfect horror-film style silence. Her hands stuffed in her pockets, Maryam is the picture of a strapping lad. Amira is more and more the quintessential woman. Like a statue of Venus, she coolly takes in the scene. I am searching for a safe place to rest my eyes: clocks on the wall that show all the different times around the world. What in the world are those clocks doing here in an old coffeehouse like this? Why would men who could fritter away all the time in the world in a coffeehouse need to know all the different times of the world? But they aren't ticking. I run my eyes over this vestige of French colonialism. London, Paris, New York... Men with the history of Western exploitation at their backs leered at us with Eastern indifference. The sons of a nation that once had its gaze fixed on the West were now glaring at women because they no longer have the slightest interest in the West. Then a middle-aged Salafi in a thick-clothed gown marches over to us. He stands there for a few seconds. Glaring. He's going to say something but which one of us will he choose? Amira is too much of a woman for him so he picks me.

"Lady, this is a men's only coffeehouse."

Before I could open my mouth Amira, who was of course expecting the attack, fires back:

"What do you mean 'men's only coffeehouse'? Who are you to tell us that? There's no such thing in Tunisia! You're talking nonsense! This is a secular country."

As the crowd rises to its feet, static tension shifts to kinetic energy and the proprietor quickly places the express coffees down on the counter. I collect the three paper cups while

Maryam gets in between Amira and the man, and, partly because she's the man on our team and a little bit because her head is covered, she appeals to the man's piety. Gesturing for calm, she speaks in those classic hushed tones. But with the vengeance of an entire army Amira yanks away the flag of surrender.

"We drove out a dictator! And now you are making trouble for us? Who are you to talk, brother? Who do you think you are?"

The man was ready to apologize but now Amira simply isn't going to shut up.

"Are we in Iran? What do you mean, a 'men's only coffeehouse'? And in Kasbah! People like me shed blood for you in this square. We made a revolution for you. Do you hear what I'm saying? And now you're here challenging me..."

Maryam finally manages to calm Amira and we make for the door. Bringing up the rear Maryam then gives something to the man as if in a gesture of apology. I am a little annoyed. Alright, Amira went overboard but now Maryam is suddenly collaborating with the man's world...

"What did you give the guy?" I ask. With a smile on her face, she says, "You'll see!"

As we are stepping outside, the man pushes past us, looking down at a chocolate candy in his hand. Mumbling, he tears open the chocolate, pops it in his mouth and then spits it out.

"Whores! There's alcohol in that chocolate!" he screams as the chocolate hits the windshield of the Peugeot 406, which suddenly brakes, and ... well you know the rest.

With coffees in hand we duck through the blue door of the Nawaat office in an old Tunisian building and double over laughing in the front hall.

"You're quite the swashbuckler, sister Maryam," I say. With a curtsy, she says, "At your service, my lady."

As we scramble up the narrow stairwell, laughing and joking, something happens, something none of us can articulate even as we go over all the details of the day. It's an evolution impossible to pinpoint: joyous, fast-weaving crystal spiders have bonded us in a web; something was crystalized while we were leaving the hotel side by side, walking single file, slipping into our settled roles in the open space of Kasbah Square, going into that coffeehouse, looking out for one another as we reached out for our coffees and pulled ourselves together, holding our ground in our own ways in the centre of that unseen, savage male arena in silence, looking out and then slinking away and stepping through that door and into the stairwell. A web cocooned us from the world, sheltered us from harm. In other words by the time we stepped into the Nawaat office to meet Amira's 'revolutionary friends' sitting on a landing in the middle of the room we were already old friends.

"We recognized the laugh," says a quiet, blondish, earnest man who looks more Irish than Arabic. Next to him a thin young covered woman and a man who seems to be drunk – a group of three. We are all introduced. I don't even catch the names. My plan is to be someone who doesn't draw attention and who doesn't pay attention. After all I'm unemployed and doing my best to lower my expectations of the world to a minimum. Amira and Maryam, however, jump straight into a passionate discussion. Suddenly they are talking about friends in Egypt, demonstrations in Bahrain, Syrian internet activists imprisoned for challenging Assad, sceptics of the election results in Tunisia, new publications in Beirut, and the collaboration of international hackers... It's like the world is playdough in their hands and they are shaping the Middle East. It is a serious business but they aren't wearing grave expressions. Cigarettes are lit and snuffed out. I only can make out names among the flurry of words: Raşa, Alaa, Razan, Wael, Ranwa, Ali, and then the other Alaa, Ranwa and Raşa, bloggers, hackers, the names of hacked government websites, WikiLeaks, revolution, revolution, Al Jazeera TV, the Al Akhbar daily... They all address each other by their Twitter handles, bringing up faraway friends, acquaintances, activists and heroes. They speak of a digital-membrane-world that covers the globe, made up of data shooting back and forth via satellites in space. Each datum fixed in a specified point is an electronic equation. Everyone in the world is one; every code a political act; every political act born of Arabic tapped out on a keyboard or a telephone screen, a blinking entity. Every name, every little point, every electronic presence is connected to another via the words "Al Thawra"– revolution. They are speaking of a new world in which they are the heroes. Meanwhile I'm swept away not so much by the content of the conversation as by the energy in their voices:

"How does it look from Turkey?" asks the stern Irish-looking fellow, his hand on his temple.

Sitting up straight after having slowly slumped deeper and deeper into my chair, I say, "Well you know. There's not much to be seen. When you talk about 'revolution' and all that you..."

My sarcastic smile hangs in the air: no one is backing me up. Pulling myself together, I say, "In Turkey they don't believe Arabs are going to change anything. Most people believe the CIA has a hand in all this." Reluctantly I go on.

"Now I don't know what to think when you talk like this, so full of hope. It's not like this in Turkey. Strange things have happened in our country... It's difficult to explain."

They are all ears and seeing that I can't dodge the issue I have to press on.

"Turkey isn't what it seems from the outside. Journalists, labour union leaders, students are in prison... There are stacks of lawsuits against them. Maybe we don't see the bigger world because we're consumed by all this."

I am uneasy now but the subject has taken on a serious tone. The Irish-looking Arab asks, "This is the issue of the Turkish model. After the Islamist Ennahda Party won the first election here... You know about that, right? The moderate Islamists... They are always talking about the Turkish model. What do you think about that?"

I look at him, unsure of what to say. Amira rescues me.

"Friends, I'm looking for a job."

The wisp of the woman in a headscarf flashes a rueful smile. The Irish-looking fellow says, "Oh, God! We just took someone on and now we're full." The young girl opens her hands as if to apologize. "But let's see," says the Irishman, "these days these foreign NGOs are cropping up like mushrooms. They're singing the praises of Tunisia as the only successful country in the wake of the Arab Spring."

His teasing smile is directed at Maryam who responds, "We got the message. But Egypt is no Tunisia. And you call this a revolution?"

"That Egyptian pride, this idea that you're the Mother of Civilization will do you in," says the Irishman.

Maryam raises the stakes. "Oh no, it's not pride. How could such pride make a revolution? Ben Ali left in just two weeks. 'Seems you don't want me anymore,' he says and clears out. Is Hosni Mübarak anything like that?"

Leaning even further back in his chair, he reaches out to touch a nerve.

"It's not a question of Mubarak. While you were handing the revolution over to the Egyptian military you should have thought about your collaboration with the soldiers."

Now the jokes were over.

"We sent Mübarak running! And we'll do the same with the soldiers!"

"You can't. They have US support. Have fun with that! Once the elections start, international TV channels will get right out of Tahrir. And you'll be left alone."

Maryam isn't going to give up her position that easily.

"They got the people to hate Tahrir. That was our challenge. The army nearly got people to turn on us. And Tahrir was already changing. There were stooges there we didn't know. Getting inside and provoking people."

Not backing down, the Irishman barrels on:

"You were naïve and you didn't make clear demands. That's why all this is happening!"

Raising her voice, Maryam affirms, "Our demands are clear. Freedom and dignity!"

Clearly the Irishman has picked up somewhere along the way the technique of lowering your voice to further infuriate women who are angry. Calmly, he replies, "And what is dignity? Who's going to deliver that? Who do think will give it to you? After everything that's happened do you think anyone would be willing to? You have lost yourselves in an Al Jazeera drama. 'The Arab youth is taking to the streets on its own without any ideology,' or so they say. The revolution has been coalescing for years. We started work ten years ago, but you broke away only to fit the Western recipe of who they think you are!"

Enraged, Maryam shouts, "You are being unfair. And you know it! When Ennahda settles nicely into power here and you become a new buddy to the USA in the Middle East, just like Turkey, and when you are put in your place by your Sunni government, you'll remember all too well what you've just said!"

Having achieved his goal of annoying Maryam, the Irishman flashes her a friendly smile and says, 'I'll make you a coffee.' And with that he believes he has ushered back in a calm and friendly atmosphere. As he heads for the kitchen he turns and calls playfully over his shoulder, "So you're finished with dancing, Amira?"

Her chest expands with an answer but then she fades. And there isn't a trace of the woman who has just been taking on the world. She has shrunk. In the face of the jest, she is torn between attack and defence and she stumbles into a ditch of hesitation, swallowing her words before they can come out. Clutching the bag in her lap, she gave up.

*

Now the man who seems to be half-drunk is telling the covered girl all about an anarchist fanzine they are preparing to publish and she is responding with a lady-like softness, teasing him because there are no women writers on the project.

"You anarchists and the hackers are a like an adolescent boys club."

Scrunching up his face, he isn't taking her seriously.

*

I look at Maryam's face. She seems uncomfortable. It has nothing to do with the political discussion but the way the man insulted Amira. Maryam is biding her time, waiting for

54

the chance to show the Irishman that he has crossed a line. For some time she keeps stirring her coffee. Meanwhile Amira is still searching for a topic. She looks guilty. Saying nothing.

Trying to maintain her composure, Maryam continues on her own.

"No, he knows. He was the one who mobilized the revolutionary activity. Didn't he organize the take down of government web sites and publish WikiLeaks documents? He's a friend of people in Egypt doing the same kind of work. But only to provoke me..."

This is an unexpected attempt to explain herself. Not an ounce of her manly pride left. Obviously the Irishman is an important figure and she can't draw her sword to challenge him. She addresses the group.

"This revolution is in our hearts. He also knows that. Nothing will be the same."

Coming back into the room with a tray filled with coffees, the Irishman is making a point of emphasizing that he is doing what is traditionally a woman's job – executed of course with a manly flourish. Then he calls out to Maryam.

"What were you saying, Mademoiselle?"

Her answer punches him right in the face.

"I was saying that only when you can speak to a woman who is both a dancer and a revolutionary will your revolution be complete."

The Irishman is stopped dead in his tracks. As if she's been holding her breath, Amira says, "hah," and leaves it there. She is back in her element. To conceal the sly grin on her face she looks down and rummages in her bag. Taking out a cigarette, she clicks a lighter. Maryam breathes in, preparing for another blow, or poised to twist the sword she has just plunged into the man's gut when there is a knock on the door. Maryam chose to draw her blade for Amira, not Egypt.

A group of poor, dark-skinned young men with wounded legs and arms shuffled into the room. They were accompanied by older women we assumed to be their mothers. With a diligence born of domestic courtesy, the young woman quickly rose to her feet. Compassionately she reached out and touched the women. The drunken anarchist sunk even deeper into his chair. Maryam greeted both the mothers and the young men, as if she knew them, as she had left behind similar young men in Tahrir Square when she fled to Tunisia. Disconcerted, the Irishman reluctantly introduced the new group:

"Friends, these are the people wounded in the revolution who haven't received medical treatment. For days they have been protesting outside the Ministry of Justice, all to no end. So now they will stay here and begin a hunger strike."

They stood in the middle of the room, like broken weapons of war, their faces held high but without ammunition and guns to fire. Their mothers looked shy and indecisive, like any other woman who might have left her kitchen to race after her child challenging the state. The boys moved between the bold gestures of street kids and broken pride. No one knew what to do. Finally the young woman broke the silence with the typical young-lady phrases women deploy when they are hosting – "Auntie, will you have a coffee or tea? Welcome. Are you tired? A glass of water?" Just to fill up space, break the silence. Signalling to her inebriated colleague, she said, "The chairs are inside, could you please bring them out?" The man reluctantly trudged off before swiftly returning with white plastic chairs which he placed on the landing. Amira wanted to speak with the boys but clearly they were revolutionaries who didn't have the time to learn how to speak with women; they spoke to them in the same way they spoke to girls in their neighborhoods; they didn't look Amira in the eye. And they couldn't choose which expression to adopt: the face of an angry, proud revolutionary or the oppressed but proud, mature face of a young man. The Irishman was just standing there, indifferent. Typical of men in this part of the world, he had left the business of relieving doubt and pulling a situation together to the women. So it fell to Maryam to put these men without guns at ease.

"Brother, how many days were you there outside the ministry?"

Sprinkling her sentences with brotherly words, Maryam was able to get them talking. Soon she had established a warm conversation with the guests, and the Irishman now looked more comfortable, a weight lifted from his shoulders. Short sentences, a broken accent with starts and stops, the young men spoke and their expressions changed. Their voices rose from among the back streets and coffeehouses, from the gratitude they felt for a revolution that had brought them to this office in the middle of an old building, their voices rose in the need for the revolution to be grateful to them. Their bandages were soaked in sweat and grime. Their mothers wore slippers. Casually sitting down on the armrest of a chair, the Irishman turned to me and said: "Write to people in Turkey about these folks." I felt restless. I was tired with the idea of writing about people destined to be a footnote in the history of a losing side. I held my tongue. And the birds began to sing. As if on cue, they were all singing together.

The chirping grew to such a pitch I no longer heard the word revolution stamped like a holy sign among the broken words the boys were saying nor the sighing of their mothers nor the sound of them wringing their cracked hands. Most likely tomorrow they would become a news story in a paper, ten centimetres on the fifth page. How many times had I seen such a thing in different countries, and those classic plastic white chairs, a symbol of unhappiness in the Middle East? The birds were now singing wildly. The conversation had stopped and Maryam suddenly stood up. And we all followed her lead – the three of us, a kind of battalion, responding to the new order. The Irishman took Amira by the arm, pulled her aside and whispered in her ear. Opening a drawer, he pulled out a stack of envelopes and handed it to her. Brushing tears out of her eyes, she hurried out of the room. "I have an errand to run," she said. She was reporting to Maryam, her protector, not me. Then as if ashamed, she added: "Let's meet at the hamam in two hours. You know it, right? Next to the hotel."

Walking back to the hotel with Maryam, I said: "I'm leaving in a couple of days. Are you staying?" Her hands in her pockets and her headscarf wrapped around her neck, she said: "I don't know. I need to have a look at Dido's tablets and visit a few libraries. Then I'll be leaving too... But I'll need to come back." She stopped and suddenly changed the subject.

"Why do you think an extremely powerful woman would commit suicide?"

I was still thinking about Amira.

"Amira's got a problem, and she's not telling us."

Maryam smiled.

"A woman in an Arab country who's a writer and a dancer and who has problems with her mother and unsettled accounts with her father. And there's a fugitive lover who suddenly comes home. There's a lot on her plate!"

"A lover coming home? " I said.

"She mentioned letters from a guy called Muhammed and we never talked more about it. She wants to open a dance school but she hasn't got the money."

"A dance school, eh? That sounds nice."

Maryam went on:

"She needs money and her mother has got it but she isn't willing to part with it. The only way is for her to save up money by working in this hamam of hers. But that's not easy... and if she can't do that... What was it that she said? Oh, yeah, 'nobody respects me'."

"Sister, you don't have it any easier. I mean in terms of respect and all that... In this 'men only' coffeehouse of a country."

Then I thought of how Madam Lilla had lorded over Eyüp Bey and I said,

"Madam Lilla really is a strange woman, isn't she?"

Twisting her words like they were a dirty rag, Maryam said, "Not that strange!"

We arrived at the hotel. In her room Maryam got down and prayed, the longest prayer I could imagine, and then she opened her computer and went online.

The long afternoon hours went by just like when you lie down on a cool bed and twist and turn until you get too warm under a single sheet, watching motes of dust lazily waft in the sunlight streaming through the curtains. But until we left to meet Amira in the hamam, where those strange and difficult events were set in motion, everything seemed like a dark conversation with myself.

5

As we undressed we were completely unprepared for what would happen next. Maryam and I had been under the impression that Amira only needed to speak with people in the office and then we would leave together. But treating us like we were European tourists, she insisted, saying, 'seeing as you're already here you can't leave without coming inside', and although we both told Amira how much we loathed hamams we ended up stripping down to our underwear and coughing and wheezing we clomped along the corridor in heavy wooden clogs, wobbling from side to side, clutching at the thin towels wrapped around our bodies until we finally found a safe haven on a ledge near one of the basins in the main room.

Disgusted by every particle – visible and invisible – in the world of a hamam, Maryam was squirming to reduce her body contact with surface area. I was in a bad mood after spending all afternoon fretting about the state of affairs back in Turkey and how I didn't have a job. Amira, however, was driving away whatever it was that had been troubling her. Humming under her breath, she danced flamboyantly in the middle of the chamber. I suppose Maryam and I were a little embarrassed by the public display. We found it hard even to look at her. But when she said, "ladies you have just heard a song by Amira, the rose of every stage," and delivered a dancer's curtsy, we couldn't help but smile.

At the basin across from us sat two women in their sixties who were chatting and pouring bowls of water over their heads. They couldn't have cared less about the way they looked. Waiting for the warm water to loosen up the grime still clinging to their skin, they looked like two old wooden ships, creaking as they carried on. To peel off the dead skin one of them would every now and then rub her arm or her leg or do the same to her friend. They must have been discussing a matter of grave consequence because all the water that fell from bowls and streamed down over their faces and down thin strands of hair, loosening their hamam towels, did nothing to dilute the conversation.

On the other side of the room were two middle-aged British tourists steadfast in their pursuit of the promised pleasure called *keyif*, as if out to fulfill a foreign mission assigned to them by their nation. Although red as beets, they were keen to conjure up an essence of *keyif*, which the Easterner finds by simply standing still and waiting. The women were holding out through the heat and the water so they would be justified when they would later expound upon the travails of their hamam experience as one segment in their holiday. Culturally estranged from the techniques of scrubbing and peeling, they suffered the most, along with Maryam.

In the corner basin were three young Tunisian women who were doing everything they could to attract attention. Dressed in bikinis, they must have been in their thirties, and the way they held the copper bowls as if they were strange objects, dipped their fingers in the water as if they had never seen such a wondrous thing before and loudly carried on and fooled around in their own little world, all suggested one thing: they had come to the hamam to enjoy themselves.

"It's like the class distinctions are still there even when they are naked," I said to Maryam as I nodded toward the women. "I mean the smoothness of their skin, the immaculate waxing, everything perfectly balanced ...

61

everything they do looks good…" Her lips glued shut, Maryam was afraid bacteria – or who knows what else – might hop inside her mouth. She only nodded in agreement. I continued to study the girls:

"Is that kind of fussiness only a thing with middle-class women? I mean, just when everything seems to be in place there's always something missing. Do you see what I mean?" Maryam was rooted to the spot, still dreading the germs.

Meanwhile Amira was tapping out time on a bowl. But it was as if my observations had an effect on her and now she was frustrated with the Tunisian girls. It was only a matter of time before she would launch an attack.

"How pretentious can you be, for crying out loud? It's like they're from Switzerland. Why all the drama?" Amira said. The girls let out a peal of orientalist laughter as they insulted the hamams of their country, slipping into French at least twice in every sentence. Amira stood up in preparation. I stayed put but Maryam finally separated herself from the marble. She was just taking her position next to Amira – indeed she stepped out in front of her to intervene – when one of the girls cried out, "Ah! It's Amira!"

In wooden clogs the woman teetered over to middle of the room, pinching and pulling her bikini top. She stopped to give the impression that Amira was the one walking over to her. One of the sly little games upper class women will play. I narrowed my gaze. And then – bam – she kisses Amira on the cheek! "Cherie, I was just thinking about you the other day! Girrrls! Amira's back."

In a few seconds Amira became the housemaid at a private high school tea party, dressed up in her finest holiday clothes. Her face was blurred in the steam but she was so clearly a woman: the way she held herself and the way she moved, even the muscles in her back. How horrible to be such a woman in this world...

Maryam was unsure whether or not to leave Amira on her own. The girls brought her to the centre of the room. For them Amira was a class act but she wasn't one of them – she was an interesting specimen. Indeed they must have lived vicariously through her; she was someone they watched, a kind of TV serial. "So you were in the US!" "Oh! That's so interesting!" "We read your blog!" "You did so much work for the revolution." "Of course you suffered the most because you had to run away and everything, I mean, how terrible." "We were all in Kasbah that day." "We wished you were there. The day the revolution started." "So what are you going to do now?" "Of course, she's going into politics, sweetie." "Now I'm working at the Ettakatol Party. Why don't you come?" "Oh sweetie, that's real light weight for someone like Amira!"

Now Maryam stood up, ready to challenge the girls. There was an eerie silence. Amira was saying something important... in whispers and then whistling. There was the sudden contortion of their faces, twisting into all different shapes. We had no idea what Amira had just said but like a victorious commander she tightened her towel over her breasts and came over to us with her head held high and sat down at the basin. Pouring cold water over her head and her breasts, she let out a series of sighs. And with the nervous energy of show horses, the girls retreated to their basin. If they hadn't gathered up their things and left the room the tension might have jumped from basin to basin.

"Whatever you just did there you did it right, sister," I said.

"Sometimes I get the job done," said Amira. "Sometimes I'm able to remind people just who they are. If only I could do it all the time..."

Once the girls were gone we were free of all their 'oh's' and 'ah's' and we could settle down. Scrubbing dead skin off her leg, Amira was now speaking from the heart.

"Those girls, I mean the whole lot of them, they're tourists in their own country. They hit the streets once Ben Ali was gone. You'd think they were the ones who'd started the revolution. Now they are all racing after 'democracy positions'. Proud to be Tunisian. And supposedly they're planning to work for the current political parties. Now they say the most important thing is doing something positive for their country. But not one of them can write in Arabic, they don't even really know their own language. They are all interested in politics now because they are afraid of Sharia law."

"Aren't they Tunisians? Why can't they write in Arabic?'

'Of course, they're Tunisian. That's how it is here. Not everyone can write in Arabic. It's all French. *Très intéressant, chérie,*"

I felt Maryam's indignation cut my cheek like a knife. "Tell us what you said to them?" she asked Amira.

"I told them I'd slept with all their husbands."

We stared at her as she continued dumping water over her head.

"I didn't do anything of the sort of course, but it just came out…"

Maryam was angry and I imagined her tangled thoughts racing: you are handling a problem with exaggerated womanhood and then you get so disappointed because you are perceived only as a woman and not getting any respect so then why do you talk about sleeping with men? But she didn't want to draw it all out. Turning to me, she said, "So when exactly are you leaving?"

"I don't know. I should be gone in three or four days."

"Good, let's head out to Dido's together before you go. I need to go to Carthage. You know the tablets I was talking about..."

"Sure, let's do it. In any case maybe..."

"Maybe what?"

"Maybe I'll come back. Maybe I'll write a book. I mean it would be good if I did. Something about women. I mean..."

"Ah," said Amira on a new wave of enthusiasm, "so will we be in it?"

Relaxing a little, Maryam said, "If that's the case then you better change my name."

I teased them.

"Oh, so you're already so sure you deserve to be heroines in a book? I don't know, I'll have to keep a close eye on you."

They laughed and for a moment I lost myself in the scene. They were two women, two men, two cowboys, husband and wife, mother and child... Everything contrary to initial appearances. The refugee made the asylum real. The one who seems most in need of protection is more powerful than the protector. They weren't entirely Thelma and Louise but they might make for a good film if someone actually watched it.

"For example I could call it *The Country of Fugitives*. Let's say... Rokolan! Rokolan Fugitive Country! And of course Madam Lilla would be the protagonist. Something totally outrageous."

And this is how things unfolded as we laughed and doused ourselves in bowls of water and scrubbed off slews of dead skin:

Amira: "Madam Lilla's mother should be a real weirdo. Full of life; a powerful woman."

Maryam: "They should live on an island. An island with no men."

65

Amira: "That's not possible... Maybe an island where all the men have women's names."

Maryam: "Because they don't want to send the men to war."

Me: "What war are you talking about?"

Amira: "There's a war on the mainland. They've fled the city. All the cowards are gathered on the island. So everyone is out of touch. Wait, now that's good. *The Cowardly Fugitive Island of Rokolan*!"

Maryam: "That's where Madam Lilla gets her love of film. Her grandad ownded a cinema."

Amira: "Everyone on the island is crazy about film. They're fugitives, right? So they are always trying to get their minds off things."

Maryam: "That's why... Look, now this is it: the names of everything on the island come from names of old films. For example... *The Butcher Tarzan*."

Our laughter filled the hamam like full purple grapes and big fleshy chunks of watermelon.

Amira: "Wait! Wait! I got it! *The Haberdasher's Little Shop of Fears*."

Maryam: "*Kill Bill's Beauty Salon*."

Me: "*The Male Barber of Siberia*."

Before my very eyes they conjured up the image of an island garlanded with laughter. There was nothing more I needed to do. Like two discoverers drawing up a topographical map, they charted the novel. They came up with such bizarre ideas that it got to the point where Madam Lilla was endowed with super powers.

Maryam: "Ah, yes that's it! You're right! She should be a superhero! With tights and all the gear!"

Amira: "Super Madam!"

For a good while we shook with laughter, rising and falling.

66

And when Amira hopped up onto the centre stone with a second towel wrapped around her neck like a cape to perform the superhero dance, her hips quivering in all directions, we really cracked up.

"I'm getting the feeling that you people have turned feisty since the Jasmine Revolution. Superheroes or whatever you want to call them!" I said, laughing. Suddenly serious, Amira said, "Now don't you dare go and use that term again, like you're some kind of tourist. The name is *Thawrat el-Karama*. The Dignity Revolution. The Jasmine bit was made up by an American."

"Now look, when you say this is a matter of dignity... Have you seen *My Fair Lady*? Not the Audrey Hepburn version, the older one?"

"I swear I'm the spitting image of Gilda!" claimed Amira.

"For the love of God, would you just stop for a second, I'm talking about something else. Have you seen it? Bernard Shaw wrote the scenario. In the Hepburn version they cut a section. There's this English professor in it. He picks up a flower peddler and teaches her how to speak properly and the girl's father goes to the professor's house and asks for money. Five pounds! And so the professor shames the man and says, what kind of father are you, trying to sell me your daughter and all that. But the vagabond father gives this crazy speech. On dignity. He says something like this: "I'm a man with no money. Which means I am opposed to all middle-class values! Always!"

Maryam looked at me "And? So what are you trying to say?"

"I mean this dignity deal and all that sounds a little like a middle-class thing in your countries. I mean when people are starving..."

"Don't be ridiculous!"

The conversation got stuck. Lost in another mood, Amira said, "Ah, I'm going crazy. What was Gilda's real name? In fact didn't she have that line: 'The boys sleep with Gilda at night ... and wake up with – whatever her name was – and they leave in the morning.' Ah, what was the woman's name?"

Maryam seemed lost as she tried to recall the name.

"Wait, wait," said Amira, "those ladies over there are from the generation that watched all those summer drive-in movies that were so popular in the colonial period. They would know something like this." Amira was clowning around again as she called out to the women: "Hey, you over there! What was the woman's name?" And she got up on the central stone, struck a pose, and started to sing.

"Put the blame on the mame! Put the blame on the mame!"

Her hamam towel slid off her waist and she was indeed the perfect Arab Gilda!

The women were as delighted as village children who sell flowers in the mountains and joyously greet a car only to have the driver take their pictures. Clapping, they sang along with Amira, tossing in whatever bits they knew; toothless and laughing they were beautiful. Then finally one of them shouted, "Rita Hayworth! May she rest in peace!"

"Aha!" said Amira and turning to us she added, "She's the one I'm rooting for!"

Amira's cheeks were flushed bright red. I saw the way Maryam was looking at her. She looked as if she might murder anyone who didn't hold Amira in high esteem, but most of all, she looked like she wanted to strangle all the men who slept with Gilda by night and left Rita in the morning...

6

"Dido? I'm rooting for Kahina!" said Amira, laughing as she walked away. "See you tonight at Madam Lilla's." Amira's clear stance on everything was sealed with a smile, like that first joke we had all shared together. Amira had to do some shopping for her new job at the hamam – or at least that's what she said – so she left me and Maryam to enjoy a morning cup of coffee at the Café Univers on Burgiba Boulevard in the city centre, an imitation Champs-Elysée panelled with enormous men.

"So who's al-Kahina?" I asked Maryam.

"One of Dido's girls," she replied. With the gruff precision of a serious academic, she went on: "I don't mean she was her daughter. I've just always thought of it that way. But first tell me what you know about Dido."

"Oh sister, no more than the average tourist."

"That's all you need. Dido was the young queen of the Phoenician Kingdom in Sur in Southern Lebanon. But her husband's brothers killed her husband. In fact they were going to kill her too, and they set a trap for her. But turns out she has a dream warning her. And she flees on a boat with a bull hide packed with gold. Truth is I think she took more than that but anyway... She sails to northern Tunisia. To Carthage. But they say to her, 'you can't have it, madam'."

"Can't have what?"

"The land. I mean they wouldn't sell Dido anything in Carthage. They mocked her, made an enemy of her and all that. Dido says, 'I don't want very much. Only what can be covered with the hide of an ox.' That night she cuts the ox hide into thin strips and the next day she covers the entire hill in Carthage with strips all linked together at the ends. Shocked, the locals sell her the land."

"Huh? That's ridiculous. How can that be? I've never heard of a community submitting to the smarts of a desperate woman and not putting up a fight. Have you?"

"Sister, the story is part myth. No documents. Half of it's just a fairy tale. Though later the question of covering the largest amount of land with the strips of an ox hide came to be known as the Dido Problem in ancient Greek mathematics. Are you listening?"

"Yes."

"The land she got became Carthage. They build a port, and trade and sea transport booms and the city flourishes. But in no time there is this bastard who leaves his kingdom in Macedonia, crosses the Mediterranean, and arrives at the shores of Carthage and in a week he has the mighty Queen of Carthage's head spinning..."

"Of course. They wouldn't just let her be! And?"

Pausing, she smiled:

"I can't tell you the rest. You need to do the research. That's enough of Dido for now. Let's move on to Kahina."

"Don't go and make stuff up for my sake! Don't you dare!"

Maryam was really getting into her swing as she lit a cigarette. Then she told the story like she was a sweet old man.

"Madam al-Kahina... That was the name they gave her. But the Muslims didn't like her one bit and spread the rumour that she was a wizard soothsayer!"

"Allah, of course the Muslims!"

We laughed a little as she playfully parodied an overly sensitive pious woman adjusting her headscarf. Then she went on:

"Well madam, al-Kahina, came onto the scene sometime after Christ. Do you know about the Islamic Empire's transition to the Umayyad? Ali, Omer, Kerbela and all that?"

"Sister, you mean how the control of Islam passed from the poor to the rich, from oppressed to oppressor. We know that chapter in history."

"And the switch to male dominance! Don't forget that. The Umayyad worked to spread Islam through Africa. They made up all sorts of rumours about al-Kahina: she was Jewish, a sorceress, a Christian and so on. But if you ask me, she was a loner. And a significant part of modern Libya belonged to her."

"Why don't I know these things? These are first-rate stories."

"Then listen and learn. So these Umayyad do a full press. They are defeated in the first battle. You see al-Kahina was quite a powerful warrior. But then, and I'll make this short, they finally get her cornered. And..."

"Now you better tell me the end to this one."

I said those words with the sheer severity of a child and I almost laughed at the way they sounded. She went on:

"al-Kahina retreats to the south. She relies on the tactic

71

of destroying all available resources. Nothing is planted, watered or harvested. Al-Kahina knew it was the end. In the desert she dies along with her enemies. In the books it's written, 'the drought we're still suffering today stretches back to that time.' Get a load of the misogyny. The whole thing happened in a desert and it was a woman's fault. And over a thousand years ago."

Maryam was now really riled up. I asked, "So you're also for al-Kahina?"

"Don't be ridiculous!" she blurted. Being with Maryam could make you feel alone in company of another. There was only one thing she was determined not to talk about and, provided that we didn't go there, she was strong as a rock.

Fifteen minutes later we were in a taxi and Maryam was shouting in Tunisian Arabic:

"Uncle, do you see any other left? That's it! I told you we were going to Carthage!"

Maryam was having a lighthearted squabble with the taxi driver. He wore coke bottle glasses and his face was pushed close up against the windshield. The radio was blasting techno and the windows were wide open. He was wearing a coat. Zooming along at a hundred kilometres an hour with a driver who was out of his mind, we made a glorious entrance into Carthage. He drove sharply away, leaving us at the bottom of the museum complex. We started up the hill to the palace perched on top of a windy hill. On the hillside overlooking the sea sat the awkward concrete museum buildings. From the other side you looked out over an expanse of hills. There was no trace of the glories of history in either the museum or in the dry weathered ruins of the old city. The place didn't attract many visitors; apart from the museum there was nothing more than a cluster of tents with old souvenirs lined up in front of them. The museum officials sported a large amount of that complete, ongoing holiday languor that was everywhere in the country. "Sister, this country seems lost in a daze. Is this revolution fatigue or what?" Before I could offer any more analysis I was interrupted by the official at the ticket office:

"Welcome, Madam Maryam!"

"How's that?" I turned to Maryam.

"They know me by now. After all it is my fifteenth visit," she says. "Think of it like a pilgrimage." Collecting the tickets she puts them in her pocket and takes me by the arm. Murmuring to herself her step grows heavy and her face slips into a reverence, and she partly closes her eyes like a woman in fervent prayer.

"A woman never abandons her goddess. Don't forget that. They only weave them new clothes to help them hide!"

I thought of the Hand of Fatima around Madam Lilla's neck. "Wasn't that charm around Madam Lilla's neck pretty weird?"

"That wasn't exactly a Hand of Fatima talisman, or was it?"

"You're right! Because it had a ring or a necklace or something like that, no?"

"Fatima, Dido, al-Kahina, Sibel, Meryem... Use whatever name you like. Female gods in different clothes. As you might imagine, in a man's world you have to be quick on your feet to stay alive. Onward. Let's go see the tablets."

We stepped inside the museum building. Maryam knew exactly where she was going, occasionally reaching out and touching images of Dido in the mosaics on the walls and the floor. She was inside a kind of solitary prayer. With one finger raised, Dido seemed to be explaining something. We stopped in front of a tablet. Standing there still for so long, I grew restless and asked, "What's Dido saying?"

"'We built this road and if you damage it we'll do such and such to you. It's a threat. I mean you have no idea what will go down as history...

"Take these slabs for example. Say there's nothing left of the palace but then someone chisels out a poem and it's great but there's nothing left of that, and then you see it's just a cheap bowl that survives?"

"Huh?"

Maryam wasn't listening.

"I think it's silly. We're living for no reason. Just take this big deal about Dido... Maybe she was nothing but a damn loser. How can you know? I mean maybe Amira's right. Maybe there was an Asmahan in her time and your Dido was Oum Kalthoum, like a man, a woman as hard as concrete. Seeing that she ended up a victorious queen..."

"Where do you get the victorious part?"

"Well, that's you what you said...?"

"It's not like that. Give me a couple minutes to check something. You have a look around."

Maryam was starting to treat me like I was an idiotic contractor wandering about a construction site for no apparent reason. So I had a look around. There was nothing worth seeing. And what was there was labelled in French and I couldn't understand a word. I went outside and walked until I could see the sea. Beautiful. A little way ahead was the Carthage pier. I wondered if the sun was stronger when the cicadas were humming? It seemed that way. If only I could take an afternoon nap. Jump in the sea, splash about, stretch out on the sand and wake up to find myself inside a cloud that smelled like flowers. And if only all the problems in Turkey could just go away. How sweet. What in the world was I doing in this godforsaken country anyway? I should just leave...

74

"Come on, we're going to Sidi Bou Said. We can have a coffee there."

My hands stuffed in my pockets, I followed Maryam. She was like a mother keen to get the shopping done and I was the kid dragging her feet. "Just what is it you're looking for in these tablets?" I ask. "Something!" she says over her shoulder. "Great," I say. Going through the same left-versus-right disputes with the taxi driver we finally made it to Sidi Bou Said.

"So this is postcard Tunisia," I say.

Blue and white houses on a hilltop overlooking the sea. Blue window-eyes staring over the sea. You could almost make out hands shielding those eyes from the sun.

Wandering through narrow, cobblestoned streets, passing empty gift shops and despondent shopkeepers, we arrived at an outdoor coffeehouse on one of the terraces overlooking the sea. The only other people there were an old man and his wife. We choose a shady spot sectioned off by a low wall. I don't feel like talking to Maryam so I watch the couple. They've ordered a crepe – it's on the way. They're like a scratched section of a record, moving in fits and starts. Their faces are scrunched up as if they are trying to pluck something out of the distant past as they look out over the sea. In a way they don't look like a couple; now the man forgets his wife and now she loses track of him. On the other hand they seem so much an inseparable part of each other: linked by a cable, they seem to communicate without words. Clearly the woman has dressed him – he looks sharp as a tack. As for the man he surely doesn't do anything for his wife, apart from acting like a child to make her feel younger and more adept. They exchange a few words about the crepe. Words that have been said a thousand times, words understood in a mumble. They sit there like two ancient countries wondering why they ever settled on a ceasefire way back when. Compared to the old couple the waiter seems to be sprinting when he comes over to them with their orange juices, his arrival almost an act of terror. But then their faces light up. When he leaves, their eyes go dry and they slip into a dark mood. Now a bee is going for their juice. First the man listlessly tries to wave it away, grumbling all the while. Seizing the opportunity before the bee even launches its first attack, the woman says, "I told you that if we ordered orange juice..." Belligerent, the man says, "You're the one who got it annoyed. Now it's all in a fuss." Maliciously, the woman snaps, "Oh, don't you just know everything!" The man seems ready to pick up the table and smash it over his wife's head. "You never let me eat in peace." Fifty years of sacrifice firmly under the woman's belt, she says stridently and with full confidence, "Did I say we should come here? I told you it was too hot!" The bitter taste of a rotten lifetime on his tongue, he says, "In any case this crepe smells like egg. We should've eaten at home..." They're just about to have another go at each other when the woman slams her hand down on the bee. And with a menace in her voice showing the extent of her rage, she says: "Just eat already. Eat!" Once upon a time these two, cheek to cheek, posed for a black and white picture.

"Let's get out of here before another bee comes," says the man. "Yes, yes," says the woman. "Hurry up and finish your crepe."

As I watch in astonishment, Maryam says, "She's dead."

"No, she didn't die. The woman got it but then it got up and flew away."

Facing the sea, Maryam says, "She died. She killed herself when that bastard from the Trojan War sailed away."

76

"So Dido committed suicide?"

"She did, but why? It couldn't have been only love. Yesterday I asked you why a powerful woman would kill herself?"

"She killed herself because the man left?"

"There has to be something else. It couldn't just be love... For some reason it just doesn't sound credible to me."

"Maybe it's just better that way. Instead of rotting with some guy the woman killed herself. Look at Madam Lilla. She's a good model of an entirely different kind. Going crazy all alone. They are these different models. It seems like you've blown Dido up in your mind. She fell in love, was rejected and in the end she killed herself out of grief."

"It still doesn't sound believable."

She was gone again, gazing at the sea, her forefinger between her lips, staring into the distance. I suppose it was from out there that the man had arrived by ship, the one who ravished Dido with love and drove her to suicide. As Maryam slipped deeper into sadness, I said, "Why did you cut your hair?" Her eyes still fastened on the waters, her finger on her lips. Suddenly she came out with something completely unrelated.

"I'm not like Amira, living with everything out in the open... I can't understand her."

She expected me to say something but I kept silent. She went on. "Is she really that much of a child or is she just acting like that so I look out for her?"

She looked at me. I didn't answer. My only thought was that this wasn't good. In the crystal web that cocooned us a knot was coming loose and who knew when it would unravel. The events at dinner *chez* Madam Lilla would bring an unexpected answer.

7

Holding back a mocking smile as she pretended to laugh along with Amira and Madam Lilla, Maryam was poised for a ruthless attack. She seemed to be saying, 'Is that so? Well then show me your hand,' as she shook her head, her elbows propped on the table. I saw the red flashes in her eyes before she even opened her mouth. But there was no stopping her. She was intent on her victim: Madam Lilla.

"You're very kind, Madam, and so gracious. Yes, you are and you are aware of this as much as we are. Very much so. I wonder what they said about you when you were young? Seductive? Devastating? Surely you got whatever you wanted? You became a master at managing others. That much we understand. Clearly you're a master at getting what you want whatever the human cost. Who knows how many skeletons you have stuffed away in your closet? Have you counted? Or you don't even remember? And now you've decided to drag Amira along with you, just like that, for the thrill of it. Is that right? How long has it been, Madam Lilla? It must be some time since you tested your powers on others. Did you decide to suck the blood of young women when you saw us? Or have there been recent victims? Oh, but of course! You're too above it all to even keep count. Does Eyüp Bey oversee the accounts? Bury the bodies for you? Just what is it you're doing in Tunisia? Where were you before? What sort of game are you trying to play here? Do you really think you can still play the mysterious games people let you play when you were young and beautiful? Just who are you, Madam Lilla?"

As she raised her right hand to her chest, Madam Lilla seemed ready to take an oath before the gods. Then she shook her head as if to say, 'OK, be quiet now, I've had enough.' Her leg bouncing under the table, Maryam was a restless racehorse in the starting block and there was no jockey. But as the silence around the table grew she leaned back, determined to hold her ground. And this is how Madam Lilla made her appeal:

"Ladies… There comes a time when nothing can bring you back your old life. The more you try the more you obsess about it. One little mistake… One tiny little slip and your entire life is gone. And everyone laughs and laughs. You know they're talking about you and laughing, behind your back. You feel humiliated and defeated… They once looked at your face with admiration but now it evokes disgust. They turn away from you. As if they've been caught in the act of loving you. And they shun people who still dare to mention your name. A few adoring knights will remain, a faithful few… But a handful of people are nothing in the face of the cynics, and it is shameful to even honour the respect they bestow upon you. It's as if … as if a bunch of madmen have gathered around a false prophet. You don't even want to see the people who love you. These friends, who remind you of the unjustness you've faced, cause more pain than loneliness. You just want to be forgotten… Someone from the past sees you and stutters out your name and you would rather hide. So that you don't have to hear her say, 'once upon a time you were so important for us.' A few friends feel compelled to say, 'bad luck. If only you hadn't gone and done what you did. I wish it had worked out differently for you.' Then they talk about little details from the past you cannot change. And you want to cry out at the injustice. People like me are slapped by fate, fallen from grace… Like the sails of a ship bound to the chances of the wind. Ladies … sometimes the wind doesn't blow. For years the waters are still. Disappointment is the utmost damage a person can inflict on herself. On the one hand there is the mockery of others and on the other an endless torment of your own making…. And there is no balm for the suffering. The droughts come and go when we are young. But in middle age…"

Smiling at Maryam, Madam Lilla gently leaned over to her and said as if inviting her to suffer the same fate:

"My dear Maryam, imagine a single woman close to fifty. All the men in the Arab world are ready to cut their wrists for a chance to see this woman and all other women are so worn out from jealousy they surrender to this woman's magic, a woman who sings and dances and shuttles the secrets of the world's rulers from ear to ear, a woman who is suddenly taken by her Achilles heel and then there is no more of her beloved stage… My dear Maryam, you are left with no choice but to run away and build your own little stage where you can beg from a handful of spectators… Say I was a vampire, and I ruined hundreds of lives. Say that of all the heartless people in the world I was the most drunk. But you see, my dear soul, I was on my own!"

Snatching her glass off the table, she downed her wine in a single gulp. We were under a spell. When she began her speech she was ten times ruder than Maryam and a thousand times rougher than us all. As the words fell from her mouth the awning of an enormous tent seemed to stretch out over the table and her body seemed to embrace the three of us like a great cape. But gradually her voice softened like the sea drawing over the sand. It was clear that she hadn't prepared her speech in advance. But if she really did… I didn't even want to think it was possible. A wisp of hair slipped out of the aristocratic bun on the top of her head. It *hit your heart like a catastrophe, as scandalous as the Mona Lisa skewed against the wall. An untended silver tendril dangling over her face like the stroke of a sword, she went on:*

"And then there was a man who laid waste to the stage, who came and left, never to return. Now if I cannot find him when I am at death's door... In that event, my dear friends, my entire life will have turned out to be false. Oh, that will mean I was entirely deceived, that I've lived all my life the wrong way round..."

"Enough!" said Amira, placing her hands down on the table. She avoided our collective gaze. She had not yet decided if she was 'rooting' for Maryam or Madam Lilla. Silence fell over the room. We were still as silent birds waiting for a rain cloud to pass. The silence was intro music to an old Egyptian song, Madam Lilla sizing up her audience before she took the stage. She knew precisely when emotions would leap from joy to expectation, from tension to anger and then submission. Drawing on her wisdom, she asked at the very moment we had given in:

"So then what do you say, ladies? Are you in?"

Like a military commander fresh out of ammunition, Maryam answered as if there was nothing left to lose but pride:

"We will let you know, Madam Lilla."

It was the end to an evening in stark contrast to its beginning. But in a way it made perfect sense.

*

What happened back in the hotel before leaving for Madam Lilla's had foreshadowed events to come. Amira was busy showing us the treasures she had picked up on her shopping spree. Dressed in her strange dance outfit and clacking

81

beads in our faces, I could read what was coming in Maryam's face. She asked, "Can you really live on dancing alone?" and Amira was even more delighted in her dancing toys, pushing aside the more esteemed personality to whom the question had been posed. Clearly she felt the need to pack up that other Amira, the person who wrote and cared about politics, wrap her in a sack and stuff her in a closet. Since our trip to visit her Dido, Maryam had not relinquished her sword. I was frustrated with the way she kept going after Amira but... it would take a lot of courage to come out and say, "A woman angry with the desperation of another woman is no doubt angry with her own life. So what's your deal?" Or thinking quickly on my feet I could spin something clever like: "If you willfully reveal another woman's secret then surely you're hiding from another woman who lives in you." But in that moment I had neither my wits about me nor the courage and I simply watched the network of crackling electric cables that ran between Maryam and Amira. Maryam was a darkening shadow and this made it increasingly hard to handle Amira's rising exuberance. And of course when those charged lines hit Madam Lilla's stage, there was no stopping them.

Is the evening set in motion when Amira gives Madam Lilla a present – her purple belly-dancing skirt adorned with antique silver coins – or is it when Maryam and I retreat into our shadows? I'm not sure. But I do know the dinner will now feature two solo performers – an adolescent and a grown-up who will graciously share the stage. Amira seems to be constantly throwing a thought over her shoulder like a chiffon scarf blown back by the wind. Who knows what she is thinking. When we're out of sight I can clearly see she's deep in thought but she keeps it bottled up. But now and then she speaks. Madam Lilla leaves the brightest spot on the stage for Amira, as if setting up a trap. It's as if she is going to fire up the audience for her then jump into a role no one would have expected. There's a dangerous cunning about Lilla but Amira is in no state to see it. Drunk in her own dance in the spotlight, she's dazzling the world around her. Turning, twirling... Madam Lilla poses questions and Amira gives long and elaborate answers as she plays along. Laughing, she talks about all the different jobs she's had to stay afloat in Europe and America:

"Oh and once ... I played the role of defendant for law students."

Madam Lilla mimed surprise.

"Of course they have that kind of thing in the US. They call in actors to play either the witness or the defendant so that law students can get used to the process. Of course as an Arab I had to play a terrorist. And once I was a woman who was abetting terrorists. And once you start with terrorism it never ends. Later I played a terrorist for the US army. They needed Arab actors when they were conducting drills. It was hilarious. You act all afraid and then not. You're in tears then extremely dangerous. Like a school play, nothing very difficult!"

Maryam and I forced out smiles but Madam Lilla was throwing coal on the fire.

"Oh! Well then tell me about the most interesting one, Amira!"

"In Spain. This woman set up the weirdest company, called Destroyers Inc. Later she was arrested for it. So here's the story: Let's say a man ruins your life. You go to Destroyers Inc and they guarantee to send a group of actors to ruin the man's life in the same way he ruined yours. Like a private law firm. A revenge firm. Of course there were some really interesting stories. And in the end it was always a matter of cleaning up the mess."

Madam Lilla maintained her teasingly seductive air. There was a feather in Amira's wing that would help her fly and Lilla was twirling it, and the more she twirled, the more Amira looked like a dove doing somersaults.

"I am amazed, Amira. These are truly invaluable experiences. Please tell us more," said Madam Lilla and then Maryam was waving her sword again.

"Seeing as you've had so much work experience yourself, staying up on your feet and all that, you must have very thick skin? Either it's thicker than you're letting on or you really haven't lived ... wouldn't you say?"

Amira's smile was suddenly frozen on her face, her eyes flickering like a young girl stabbed in the back. Picking her up from the fall, Madam Lilla said, "And dance? Did you ever dance in those places?"

Amira shrugged away the role of fallen child, steadied her voice and with a few words she was back up on stage again.

"Some ... I mean not how I would have wanted to. But in a couple of hotels, at weddings. Actually I was part of the play in a dance theatre once, I came out in the 'oriental' role. But I wasn't really dancing, just doing an imitation of the style..."

"So you either cater to Western deceit or become it, right?" snapped Maryam.

It didn't look like Amira was going to let this one slide. With a blank expression on her face, she looked like a child suddenly plucked out of a dream. But Madam Lilla was determined to finish the play on her own schedule. The audience might have been hurling rotten vegetables but this show was going to unfold exactly when she wanted it to.

"Alright then, Amira, so now that you are here in Tunisia... What is it you are thinking of doing?"

Falling short this time, Amira stopped and looked at Maryam. I felt the need to jump in.

"Amira wants to open a dance school here in Tunisia."

Amira and Maryam's electric cables crackled and Madam Lilla said with delight, "Ah!" and she sat up in her chair. "Oh, how wonderful. When?"

Her eyes still fixed on Maryam, Amira only managed to say, "Not yet". No doubt under the impression we could all simply ignore Maryam's fury, Madam Lilla went on.

"Why not right away? I think you should get right down to it. No need to delay!"

With Amira still faltering, I said, "There's no money right now."

"Money?" said Lilla, laughing. We were startled, Maryam included, by the sudden outburst and we watched her closely as she continued:

"Now why are you worrying about such a thing, Amira! If the matter is money then leave it to me! And if that's the only problem then when are we opening?"

Even Maryam's jaw dropped. We were taken aback by the sudden offer to front Amira's school but Madam Lilla went on as if there was nothing to be surprised about. "As for the matter of dance, Amira..." And she stood up. She stopped. As she raised her hands up into the air, the baggy sleeves of her chiffon dress fell in a quick and decisive flourish. Her face turned towards the red light on the terrace. She closed her eyes. The light was cast over her face. Slightly turning, a beam fell over her cheek. Like that she began to slowly twirl her wrists, broadening her shoulders. And in a single, sudden, startlingly fluid movement a wave shot through her neck and her shoulders and down her body. Then she stopped and turning to us she shot a glance at Amira.

"Look at the light. Only at the light."

Slowly she began to dance. Snakes seemed to slither out of every part of her body, twisting and curling. No music was playing but she heard something. The rustling of her chiffon dress hummed music only we could hear and only this once. Madam Lilla's body was broadcasting a crystal clear message from a distant planet called youth. And as we marvelled at the quick, coy movements of the hips and breasts of such a woman, she danced and spoke in twilight tones.

"You need to get lost, Amira. Close your eyes and make them feel like you're in another world…"

With another turn that seemed to bring her chiffon dress to life, "They should think that you're reeling wildly from pleasure in that place and that they cannot get there."

Madam Lilla grimaced, crinkling her brow, and shutting her eyes.

"They should have the feeling that you'll drown if you're left alone to writhe in that sea of pleasure. You must make love with yourself until you give them the feeling that they are the only one who can save you."

Madam Lilla wraps her arms around her waist and bows her head like a dead bird. Then, as if alive and resisting capture, she flings open her arms and lets them fall at her sides.

"Then dropping the tempo you need to make them feel, this time so sweetly, how beautiful it would be if they were also in that world."

She smiles and begins to twirl, faster and faster and faster, dashes of red light shimmering on her chiffon dress flying in the night.

"Then one last time, in a final frisson, you call them to your world of pleasure, summoning them to your body and you collapse."

Suddenly Lilla sits down among the clouds swiftly stirring out of her chiffon.

"And then you must open your eyes to the light you feel on your face, that light you feel over your eyelids. You must to look at them in such a way... Amira you must look at them in such a way that"

That's how she was looking at us then. "You must look at them as if they ruined your life."

I was overwhelmed by her gaze; as if she has died and I hadn't reached out my hand.

"Great dancers truly suffer, Amira. The motion is in their eyes. Especially when they are shut. Sin must be present on that stage. And the heart of the audience should sink with the desire to be a part of it. To get them to fall at your feet, Amira, you must make them feel guilty as they never have felt guilt before. They should feel guilty because they watched you and were in awe of you and later they couldn't drag you out of that world... You must never forgive them, Amira. Do you understand what I'm saying, my dear?" And with that Madam Lilla was back in her old body, sitting down solemnly at the table as if she had not danced at all.

Amira looked like a young girl seeing a bride for the first time. Rising to her feet like a sleepwalker, she took Madam Lilla's hand, kissed it and gently placed it on the table. Madam Lilla brought two fingers to her lips and nodded reverently as she blew Amira a kiss. Then humbly tilting her head, she let out a foppish sigh. She seemed exhausted, truly worn out, as she raised her glass.

"Well then, let's drink to Amira's dance school?"

The mild manner Maryam was now putting on seemed phony and my attempts at any intervention were feeble as Madam Lilla and Amira were swept away by a powerful enthusiasm. They clinked glasses and all the coloured bulbs in Tunisia seemed to light up in Amira's eyes and she said, "Then let's call it Madam Lilla's Dance School, if you agree of course!" We expected Madam Lilla to acknowledge the gesture:

"My dear Amira, I have but one request. Which of course goes for you ladies, too."

Silence. Again Madam Lilla was eying the stage. Puckering her lips, she took a sip of wine, placed her hands on the table, tapped out a dramatic rhythm with her ring and then gracefully presented her request as if it was nothing more than a tasty little dessert.

"I want us all to go on a trip."

Her red fingernail began playing with a crumb on the table, pushing it back and forth. Without knowing where this trip would take us and what was supposed to happen if we agreed, without knowing anything at all, Amira looked at us with imploring eyes, again she was like a child. Madam Lilla pressed gently down on the crumb without crushing it and said, "To Syria."

"What? To Syria?" I cried.

Maryam leaned back in her chair to show that the play had ended. It was all too clear she was lying low before a powerful counterattack. As if she had just proposed something entirely feasible, Madam Lilla had raised the stakes with deadly confidence. Quickly and delicately licking the end of her finger, she dabbed the crumb on the table.

"Of course as I no longer fly we will have to travel over land."

Shaking her head, Maryam looked into the distance, she looked about to explode. Smiling, Madam Lilla turned to Amira.

"Amira, if you agree to come with me on this little adventure you will have the most beautiful dance school in all of Tunisia, no, in all of the Arab world! Are you with me?"

Helpless, Amira looked at me, and then Maryam, and then back at me, trying to extract an answer from us. I started to smile.

"Amira … Madam Lilla … I mean, you are very kind, truly. Oh my God! I mean this sounds so outrageous it actually seems impossible."

"But my dear aren't you a writer? To my mind this is going to be an invaluable adventure. Surely you would agree with me on that."

I felt the need to say, 'alright so we've laughed about all this and had some fun but it's over now,' but then I thought I shouldn't be the one to knock down Madam Lilla's carefully constructed castle made of sand in a single kick. So I searched for a relatively civil way to change the subject, drawing on the right words, knowing I'd be more convincing if I could stop myself from laughing.

"I mean of course it would b… my God! But this has nothing to do with me. In the end you and Amira will go…"

"Oh no," said Madam Lilla. "It won't do if you two don't come along. Maryam Hanım should come too. If you ask me, a journey like this will be the perfect cure to the grief that drove her to chop off all her hair. Yes, yes, it'll be good for all of you. Ladies, I am promising you a road trip the like of which you have never seen before!"

And she threw open her arms and Amira looked so excited she seemed on the brink of bursting into a round of applause. Convinced of the power of her charms, Madam Lilla was ready to receive the praise… But before little red riding hood Amira fell prey to the wolf in grandma's clothes, Maryam angrily said, *"You're very kind, Madam, and so gracious too …"*

89

And you know the rest. When she danced she took our hearts in the palm of her hand but they cracked after everything she said in the face of Maryam's assault and then she threw them to the ground like they were cracked goblets. Maryam had said, "We'll let you know our decision," and we awkwardly hurried out onto the street. For the rest of the night Maryam wore that dreadful, teasing expression of a child soldier clutching a Kalashnikov as she tried to make light of the situation and make us feel the same way. But there was hesitation in her voice.

"What kind of woman is that? Out of nowhere she wants to take us to Syria! I suppose she thinks Amira is as crazy as she is."

Amira was as still as a stone. Flashing Maryam a venomous look, she said, "So now you're going to play the oppressor, Maryam Hanım? You're going to test your powers out on an old woman? Is that it?! We're the kids here and you're the only grown up, eh? Hah! Well then let me tell you this, Maryam Efendi, you still haven't seen crazy! Just because you saw me dancing and laughing like that ... you think that I ... because I have thin skin..."

And Amira lost it and broke down crying. I tried taking her by the arm but she pulled away: she was tougher than all of us, including Madam Lilla. Maryam didn't know where to look. She looked like a mother who got needier with age but who once played the role of tyrant.

"Look at me, Maryam! I'm talking to you! I don't know what's running through that bald head of yours but don't you dare think you're any smarter than me. There's something eating away at you and we know it and you won't tell us. At least I am struggling with my problem. Oh yes, I'm right in the middle of it!"

Flinging open her arms, Amira was but a woman in a dark

street in Tunisia, but in that moment she must have been visible from space, standing there like the wall of China.

"Are you going to try your powers on old women or on a woman like me? I'm right here! And you? Where are you? What's your story?"

Amira wasn't acting. This was real.

"Come off it, we understand this one here," she said, pointing at me. "Out of a job and all that, a messed-up situation. She takes whatever you give her. Clearly she's guilty for something she can't pay off. But you, Maryam Efendi... What are you afraid of? Life? Well then let me tell you something, Maryam Efendi! Life's all around us!"

Amira picked up her bag and walked off. The bullet had gone straight to Maryam's heart. I couldn't salvage the situation. Had she just abandoned Maryam? Like a baby animal who had found shelter in a larger hollow. It seemed Maryam was still hungry.

Maryam and I were like torn paper lanterns and the lights had gone out. When I got to my room, I said, "I'll be leaving tomorrow then. There's a plane in the afternoon." She didn't say a word. "See you tomorrow," I said, and still no reply. She only nodded. Then she made a gesture to say, OK. Madam Lilla's castle made of sand might have fallen but there was no longer any trace of ours. Our story ended there. At least for me, it was the end of this adventure.

8

Afternoon. We're barrelling down the highway that runs through town at over a hundred and forty kilometres an hour. A yellow wig aslant on her head, Amira is crying. Maryam is whistling through her teeth. I'm wedged in the middle of the back seat, silent as a lamb. Madam Lilla is riding shotgun, cool and comfortable, like she's posing in a documentary about herself. Eyüp Bey is at the wheel. One eye looking at us in the rearview mirror. We are moving ... moving...

*

The night before last Amira was holding a can of beer and shouting at a taxi driver: "So you're not going to take us then?"

Twilight. It was my last night and Amira and Maryam had come together like a bride and her future sister-in-law on a holiday visit with no choice but to kiss and make up. I was stressed about the thought of going back to Turkey. They were scooping up journalists, bundling them into prison. I was in no mood for all the drama between my two new friends. Despite an awkward silence the ceasefire worked in my favour. Most likely I would never see them again. Both had been missing all day. Though at one point I peeked through Maryam's window and watched her pray, like the last time she went on for a while. I hadn't seen Amira since morning. When she got back to the hotel she was a bundle of nerves, shouting and cursing at everything around her:

the flies, the jasmine, the weather, the bellboy Kamal. I didn't bother asking her what was wrong. I couldn't care less. All day I'd been gathering ammunition for my trip home. I was constantly online, trying to figure out what was going on.

When we finally all met in the lower courtyard we had somehow shaken off the bad vibe and for whatever reason Maryam kept saying, 'I really need a drink tonight.' In a flash of inspiration we decided to try the market because drinks were too expensive in the hotel. Alcohol was always sold in a secret section. In the whole city there were only two places that sold booze. When the three of us walked into that market we understood how time can come to a halt. Every human and commercial transaction was suspended. Everyone held their breath as they stared. We filled up bags of local Celtia beer. As both conservative and drinking customers, Maryam and Amira displayed their own brands of passive aggressive behavior. Finally we were out on the street with four beers wrapped in four layers of plastic bags, waiting for a taxi. A car pulled up. As Amira moved to get in she kneed the bag of beers, knocking one to the ground. The driver was stunned and like a dutiful American post officer who had detected a potential SARS threat, he cried out: "Alcohol! Alcohol! No, No! You can't get in!"

Amira already has one leg in the car and she keeps it there. She looks at the man. The swordsmen in her head have already drawn their blades. I can hear the rattling. She shouts: *"So you won't let us in a public taxi?"*

Almost out of his mind, the man shouts:

"Alcohol! Alcohol!"

Amira continues in a voice so low I get really worried.

"So you are not letting us in? Is that right?" And then she

cracks open a beer and dumps the brew over the back seat.

The man hits the gas and Amira rolls back onto the street. We are too shocked to say anything when Amira starts laughing. Sitting there on the road she has clearly survived the tumble and now she's laughing so hard she can hardly speak:

"Oh did you see... How I..."

Shaking the empty beer can in the air, she says, "Now he'll give his car a good spiritual cleansing!"

Maryam burst out laughing.

"If nothing else he now has his own ride straight to hell!" Out there in the middle of the street we laughed like we were the only people left in the world. It was like no other feeling. In the end we found a sufficiently sinful driver to take us back to the hotel and when Kamal brought us our third beer a message from Madam Lilla lay on the tray beside them...

"The woman doesn't give up," said Maryam, "is she crazy or what?"

The woman in question had sent fried potatoes carved into roses and large peanuts roasted with red pepper. Nothing else. I made small talk to steer us away from the topic.

"So I'm going back to Turkey. If they don't throw me in prison you should come for a visit. I'll take you to some place like Bodrum."

Nothing. Not a word in response. This silent dialogue between Maryam and Amira was more strained than Turkish politics.

"Eh?" says Maryam, pushing Amira for an answer to Madam Lilla's crazy offer. Pushing peanuts back and forth on the tray, Amira shrugs. "So what?" says Maryam. "Are you going or what?" Leaving the peanuts, Amira moves on to the potato. She's drawing out her game with the food. In the end I just can't bear it any more.

"Just say something, woman! Are you going or not?"

Smiling, she covers her face and shakes her head. Finally she decides to speak.

"I want to trust her…"

Maryam: "What? Trust Madam Lilla?"

Amira: "What I mean to say is, how could I go without you two? Out there in the desert with an old woman, what's that all about?"

Maryam: "Oh and it all makes sense if we go with you?"

Amira: "No, I just mean that if we all go things will be different."

Maryam: "This one here is leaving tomorrow afternoon, and me, too… With all due respect I realize you might have already thought all this through but… Haven't you once thought about why this woman wants to go on a trip with all of us? Who are we to her? Think about it. We don't even know her. Which means…"

Amira and I look at Maryam as if we are watching the invention of logistics.

Maryam: "Which means she knows all too well that the people who know her wouldn't go on a trip with her."

Amira: "What's the big deal? In the end I'll open a dance school. It'll change my life completely."

Maryam: "So you're convinced she'll give you the money. Brava!"

Leaping in, I say, "I swear on that point I actually believe her." Shaking her head, Maryam shoots me daggers for interrupting her psychiatric therapy session at such a critical moment and encouraging Amira. I only say *"yani,"* that pliant Arabic word of many meanings, which in this case begs empathy.

Maryam: "Look Amira, my dear friend, last night I was in a bad mood and I was a little harsh but in the end... God damn it I can't believe we're even talking about this!"

Amira: "I swear I've done some crazy things before so one more isn't going to make much of a difference. And..."

Again she stopped. Adjusted her breasts, "Is there anyone expecting you back home? No one's expecting me. The guy who was supposed to be waiting for me just upped and disappeared."

"Aw come on, will you just tell us about him already?" I said. "We never really talked about Muhammed."

Amira laughed brightly, her eyes glimmering. "If we take the trip I'll tell you."

Maryam snaps back with an ironic, "oh now that's just brilliant," and it's suddenly clear that we are honing in on the tension of last night. "For the love of God let's not open up this discussion again. You can talk about it after I've left. Just send me an email or a tweet or whatever and let me know the outcome," I said and the topic was closed.

Silence. I have no memory of what we talked about after that. I just wanted to get drunk and the same went for Maryam, and Amira was oddly all over the place. We said goodbye that night and we went to bed.

I didn't see either of them in the morning. I felt like if I went to the airport ahead of time and had to wait three hours before departure the pilot and crew would feel embarrassed for me and we would all take off early. To me no place is more comfortable than an airport. It is the spot where travellers can write up a Z report for their holiday. I sat down and started to dash off ideas about Amira and Maryam and I loosely imagined the male characters I could cook up if I really was going to write a novel. For a good two-and-a-half hours, I let my mind wander as I thought about all those notes I had scribbled down in different airports and how wonderful it would be for my grandchildren – if I ever had them – to find them. When I finally heard my flight being announced, I saw those words on the bottom right of a cartoon strip – "the adventure ends here" – and then my phone rang.

"I'm just about to board my plane. What? Oh shit... How many? Who? Him too? I can't believe it! (Silence.) Eh? So what should I do now? You mean I shouldn't come? Huh? What are you saying? Oh man, but you never know why the hell they throw people in jail... Oh my God! My plane's about to take off. I'm boarding. I'm coming, yes, I'm coming, I'm getting on that plane."

When you are about to fly home and one of your friends calls to say that they are rounding up journalists and arresting them and says, "just stay where you are for a while, things are getting out of hand," the boarding process suddenly picks up speed. There I am standing alone in the middle of the airport. All kinds of terrible things could happen to me if I go home, and nothing could happen at all. Should I go back? Board that plane? I check my heart, my instincts are quiet – they don't know either. I call my lawyer. He says, "What are you worried about? There's nothing for you to be afraid of!"

He speaks to me in a strange theatrical tone of voice. Clearly his phone is tapped and he wants his advice to go on the record. If this goes down in a police report he knows the prosecutor on my case will ask me why I was afraid to come home. But then he adds with a slightly less dramatic flourish, "*Yani* of course if you're nervous why would you come *yani*?"

Two *yani*'s in the sentence... That wasn't a good sign.

"So you're saying I shouldn't come, *yani*?" He's silent, obviously angry with me. He's thinking, 'girl, don't drag this out, you got the message.' An airport official looks me in the eye as I hand him my passport then pull it back. I call someone else who says, "I can't tell you to come and I can't tell you to stay. You know how we never know who they are going to round up and why?" And when I heard that…

If you ever decide not to board a plane after you have checked in you have no choice but to become really friendly with airport security guards. Otherwise they won't actually return your luggage until your plane has arrived at its intended destination.

After downing five murky mint teas, I dragged my suitcase back to the hotel. "I knew that you were going to miss this place," says Kamal. This has to be the classic joke reserved for all the customers who fail to leave. All I could say was, 'and where else am I supposed to go Kamal…' Fear is a miserable prison house. Like a ghost I slink back into my room. Locking the door I pop a sleeping pill and plop down on the bed. I sleep until night and then right through till the morning. Finally I get up and head down to the courtyard without a thought in my head. I take my luggage with me. I suppose I'm planning to go somewhere. Or so it seems when I have a look at myself in the mirror. I hear Maryam's voice above me – is she shouting or throwing up? Strange noises echo through the courtyard. Maryam can really drink; her stomach must be a wreck. Kamal sits me down in the courtyard and makes me a coffee. I sip my coffee through tears. "I'm going to give Maryam Hanım the news," says Kamal. He disappears. Vacantly I look around, unable to recognize anything, the names not coming to mind. My thoughts slip underwater and there is a deep hum in the base of my ear. I vaguely sense time is passing. So alone in the courtyard I could hardly sense the sinking feeling when the front door loudly swings open. Amira comes running in. Startled like a baby zebra who has woken up to find she's in a zoo. Breathlessly she says, "We need to go!"

She takes me by the arms. Without thinking about asking me why I'm sitting there. Trying to catch her breath, she's whispering and shouting at the same time:

"I ... I think I killed someone!"

With a swollen face, Maryam appears at the door:

"What? Who?"

Openly taking refuge in Maryam for the first time, Amira pleads, "Let's go. Please, let's get out of here right away! Now!"

I'm holding a cup of coffee and my suitcase is at my feet. Our faces turn red like beets; the three of us are transfixed. The entire city could probably hear Amira's breath echoing through the courtyard. Planting her hands on her hips, she looks at me, desperately waiting for an answer. I... And it just happens. There are times when such strange things happen that it feels like I'm watching a film and not really living. Watching with a numb fascination, waiting to see what I'm going to say. Waiting to see if I'll get up and go. Minutes pass, or so I think, I can't say. With a voice as deep as a dungeon, Maryam says to Kamal, "Kamal, go and tell Madam Lilla we're ready. But tell her we need to leave straightaway! Get our bills ready as well! Now!"

Kamal's even more prepared than I am. It is like I am the only one who has come to the scene without reading through my lines. Still holding my coffee, I'm watching. Now Maryam takes me by the arm.

"Look at me! Are you in some kind of shock? If so then snap out of it! Hey, is anyone there?"

Her face buried in Maryam's shoulder, Amira says, "I didn't mean for it to happen," then she mumbles something else I can't understand. She starts rattling something off in Arabic. For some reason it reminds me of an old couple that started speaking Kurdish with each other after a break of forty years when the big earthquake hit Istanbul in 1999. I drift off into that world. I imagine their children shocked to hear them and their own shock. I wonder if they forgot how to speak Kurdish simply because they hadn't spoken it for so long. What was the first thing they said to each other? I wonder if I'd forget my Turkish if I was always on the run. All I want to do is get out of this moment, be anywhere else; I'd even welcome an earthquake for the chance to run away. I am about to open my mouth, about to say something like, 'I couldn't bring myself to go back home. I was scared.' Why I can't put down this cup of coffee, I have no idea. Maryam pulls out a cigarette and stuffs it between my lips.

"Look at me! We're leaving. I ... I mean Amira needs to go. So we're going too. Do you hear me? Look at me! Hey! Seeing as you're still here you're coming with us."

If I could only open my mouth I'd ask, "But why are you going?"

In bits and spurts Amira is giving Maryam the story and occasionally I can make out the word 'hamam' and 'bride' then 'but me' and then a string of curses, and then something – and did she really say this – 'Michael Jackson'. I can't piece together all the fragments. I feel ashamed and frustrated with myself but there is nothing that I can do. Slowly Maryam takes the coffee out of my hand and puts it down on the table. "You wait here," she says. She's just about to let go of my hand when – and this isn't really me because I am watching myself moving in a film – I reach out

100

and take her arm. "Maryam," I say in a cracked voice, "I think I'm homeless." As tears roll down my cheeks, she caresses my face and says, "So am I. Don't worry." In my mind's eye Maryam's stomach – which was hardly a stomach at all – seemed so big we could have all hidden inside.

When had we become so close? Who are these two women? And what was Madam Lilla to us? Shouldn't a camera now pan out to show a speaker who steps in from stage right and says, "Ladies and gentlemen, this has all been nothing but a pack of lies?"

Kamal comes racing back while everyone struggles to keep the show moving along. From the entrance, he cries out, "Madam Lilla is ready. She told me you should meet her outside the hotel in half an hour."

Amira scrambles up to her room on the first floor with Maryam at her heels. I pick up my coffee. It feels like nothing is really happening to me. The characters in the film have left and I'm alone in the courtyard. None of this has happened. I look at the jasmine then up at the sky. A heavy silence. Light should have sound. Otherwise we wouldn't hear mosquitoes so clearly in the dark. Light must have mass. Otherwise making love in the dark wouldn't seem so vast. If we put a stop to the excessive compassion we feel for swallows and ants. Though both are truly aggravating predatory creatures... All these thoughts are banging about in my head when suddenly 'Boom!' A seagull falls into the middle of the courtyard. Blood splashes all over my face. I scream, "Maryaaaaam! Amiraaaaaa!"

When seagull blood splashes over your face you'd better trust the people who first spring to mind.

Strange. I am not the one screaming, it is the *I* in the film. I am actually thinking of something else. I have always wondered where all the dead gulls go. I am split in two. And it seems one part of me has no qualms about heading out on some strange trip. For *I* am nothing more than a watching eye.

Amira comes downstairs wearing a yellow wig. How ridiculous, I think to myself. If only I can move my face I might even laugh. As Eyüp Bey keeps the car moving at a hundred and forty kilometres per hour, I keep loudly telling myself this isn't a movie. *I* am not moving at all.

9

"But I actually didn't do anything. That girl, I mean the bride, was asking for it. I didn't do anything."

Madness swirling in her eyes and her yellow wig now tilted from the bumpy ride, Amira is about to tell us what happened. Maryam is trying to calm her down. Madam Lilla is wearing a lilac-coloured headscarf and Eyüp Bey sits at the wheel dressed in his finest duds. Madam Lilla looks as cool as a wealthy leading lady in a love film set in 1950s Morocco. When elderly women hit the road in these parts they don't wear tracksuits like they do back home; they have the right respect for a journey and whatever might crop up along the way. Apparently I am also in the car. Maryam finally manages to calm Amira, who gets herself together enough to start telling the story.

"You remember the girls we saw in the hamam... I don't know why but they asked me to come back. One of them was getting married. Maybe they wanted to flaunt it in my face, maybe they wanted to get revenge... Anyway, they were going to have a party for the bride in the hamam. They were all there and I was cool with it. Just a lot of giggling and laughing. Everything was normal. It was just a job for me and that means money. So I couldn't care less what they were really thinking. They were talking about all sorts of things. The bride was supposedly going into politics – you'd think she was Joan of Arc – it was that over the top. 'For our country, for Tunisia', and all that kind of crap. They say they are proud to be Tunisian, that it was already high time for a revolution. That they saw it coming. But then they go on

103

about the Islamists and all that... Honestly I was trying not to listen. In the end it was time for me to dance. My head was somewhere else. I mean that's just how I was feeling. But then when they started acting like they were the other day, as if they'd grown up somewhere else and suddenly found themselves in Tunisia ... but even then I didn't let it get to me, I kept calm. They were in their bikinis and all that and for a while we danced along to music. The bride was this little pipsqueak. Wouldn't you know she says, 'in honour of Michael Jackson'. And then they were all up on their feet, singing something from Michael Jackson. And then the girl says to me, 'seems like you don't really know these tunes.' And they all laughed. So I said, 'come on then, let me teach you sweeties the moonwalk.' No, wait up, no, just a minute, I didn't say 'sweeties'. I couldn't have said that."

"Just tell us the story. What happened next?"

"Then I go out into the middle. To the centre stone. And I start moonwalking. Giggling, they all give it a go. But they can't do it and then they start really laughing. Then I suppose the bride has got to show me how it's done and she says, 'You might have slept with everyone, Miss Dance, but you can't do a real moonwalk,' and she throws herself in the middle. And when she steps up on the stone..."

Amira stops and Maryam goes berserk. "And! Say something Amira!"

"Boom, she falls down and dies."

"Huh?"

"She just died. Broke her neck and bang she was dead."

"What?"

At the top of her lungs, Amira stamped out each syllable. "I am saying that the bride is dead!"

Silence in the car. Lowering her voice, she adds, "I didn't do anything. Really."

Maryam covers her face and tugs on her cheeks like she can't breathe. She closes her lips like she might throw up. Eyüp Bey seems deaf; there isn't the slightest twitch on his face to show he's registered anything. Madam Lilla looks unfazed. And me, well I'm not even there.

Maryam says, "Let's think about this." And she's lost in thought. "Alright," she says, "did you touch the girl at all?"

"I didn't push her."

"I'm not asking you if you pushed her," snaps Maryam. "But did you touch her?" Amira is silent. Maryam claps her hands: "Okay. We're up shit creek!"

"But they can't prove anything," says Amira, panicking.

"If they can't prove anything then why are we running away, Amira Hanım?"

Her voice a notch louder, Amira says: "I'm the one running away. Why are you coming with me, Maryam Hanım?"

Silence. I don't know when they had officially formed their coalition but the two of them turned and looked at me as if I was a penguin who had just taken flight. I kept quiet, thinking about when I might be able to get out of the car. If I could only open my mouth and speak. Whatever the expression on my face is, it isn't encouraging either of them to ask me why I gave up on leaving the country. A pregnant silence. We're about to leave Tunis when Maryam crosses her arms and takes it upon herself to ask, "Just where are we going, Madam Lilla?"

As if woken from her beauty sleep at just the right time, she cheerfully replies:

"*We're heading south!*"

"*How far south?*"

"*Way down south.*"

Maryam looks at both of us. Amira is gazing out the

window like she has every intention of going way down south. Maryam looks at me and I can hear her whispering to herself, "Once there were two crazies and now there are three. Oh God, give us patience. Oh Lord."

As if Amira had not killed a bride and Maryam was not a bald bundle of nerves and I was not mute and we had never actually met each other, Madam Lilla said in a tone of voice that defied reality, "Don't worry about it. We won't cross the border at night. We'll stop somewhere and sleep for a few hours and cross in the morning."

With her forefinger between her lips, her elbow against the window, Amira seemed to have surrendered to fate as if her sole saviour was a woman living in a fantasy world and she asked, "What border?"

"You mean Libya, Madam Lilla?" asked Maryam, in a brittle and sarcastic tone.

"Oh yes! Libya. Once we get there everything else is easy."

"Madam Lilla, are you out of your mind?" said Maryam. She had leaned close to her, put her hand on her shoulder and posed the question in a cool and collected tone of voice with the intention of getting a real answer. Mirroring the same cool tone, Madam Lilla pinned Maryam to the spot.

"Not crazy enough to kill a bride in a hamam, young mademoiselle!" Bound to Amira's fate, Maryam kept quiet even though she had no doubt that all the signs indicated this adventure was going to leave us somewhere near the end of the world.

"War?" said Amira to Madam Lilla.

As if she wasn't driving south along bumpy Tunisian roads but racing straight back to her youth, Madam Lilla came out with a line right out of a film. "Well that's why there's absolutely nothing to worry about!"

Wildly cursing Maryam spoke of all the atrocities of a

sexual nature that would befall three women travelling through a desert. But Madam Lilla wasn't hearing any of it. Maryam stopped to apologize to Eyüp Bey for the bad language. He looked cracked and broken. I thought it was a good thing that we were driving on the right side of the road, made perfect sense as our driver was blind in his left eye. We were blasting along but the blank expression on Eyüp's face made you think the car was moving on its own. I don't know how far we had gone when I saw the sign for Sfax, which meant we were halfway to the border. I was struggling to rally my voice to say, "There's an airport in this town, right? You can drop me off there." Mustering the will to push a pebble up a mountain, I finally got a sentence out. "I'm getting out. At the airport."

Screech! Eyüp Bey had stopped at five minutes to death o'clock. As I struggled to figure out how my scant announcement had created such a stir, Eyüp Bey was already out on the street, flinging open the boot and slamming it shut before he came back and started driving as if nothing had happened. Gently he said, "I was checking to see if we had the covers." And with that we were back on our way. As I was trying to figure out if he'd heard me a minute ago or if I hadn't said anything at all, Maryam said: "I'm coming with you." Bouncing in her seat, Amira said, "If you were just going to leave then why did you even come? And why didn't you leave before?"

"I was going to go," I said, "but they were throwing journalists in prison..." And suddenly Madam Lilla says, "Let's stop here." And we did. We got out of the car. It was all desert beyond Sfax. I saw an eagle circling in the sky. It wasn't the wind we heard but the whoosh of its wings. Her chiffon scarf draped over her shoulders, Lilla took a deep breath.

"Oh, how I have missed the desert. There's an old saying:

'Drink from the desert waters and you'll find yourself back in the desert.' You don't know it now, but you'll be back, too."

We stood there in the middle of the desert under the burning sun, the shimmering sand rising to meet the sky. The eagle was directly above us now, swirling in smaller circles. Except for Eyüp Bey, we all looked up and watched it for a while. Madam Lilla turned and looked at us as if we were her daughters, as if we were about to go our separate ways... Then in a worldly voice that clashed with the beauty of the desert, she said, "From here on we might not have a mobile signal. So call anyone you need to call."

We paused. Amira flashed an evil smile. Maryam fixed her piercing eyes on Madam Lilla as if to say, 'you shouldn't have done it, Mum.' Neither was even moving anymore. Only standing in the middle of the desert. Madam Lilla kept quiet, playing with the expected silence to ratchet up the tension. I was the only one who moved through the dream space as I pulled out my phone. Once I had it in my hand it beeped to announce a new message like an accursed sign. I read it and sat down. The eagle flapped its wings. Taking my phone, Maryam read the message.

"What does it say," she asked.

"Don't come."

"Why?" asked Amira.

"I told you, they're throwing journalists in jail." I am still barely getting words out but I am slowly coming to my senses.

"And what does that have to do with you?" asks Maryam.

"Nothing," I say, "but they could pick me up if they wanted to, they are taking anyone in the opposition."

"If there's nothing directly to do with you then why are you scared," asks Maryam. Amira adds, "yeah, why?" For a moment I just look at them. The two of them are pushing this too far. It seems that if we all jump back in the car it will be for my sake, like we are all running away for me, and that way everything would seem more justified, more reasonable, more meaningful. I feel like I am deep under water. And from the bottom I can hear them, and a little higher I can understand them, and even higher I can imagine us setting off together but then higher we are not going at all and just near the surface I am speaking.

"Should I be scared or not? That's just why I am scared," I say. Maryam scuffs a couple times at the sand. Sitting down beside me, Amira puts her arm around my shoulder and with her other hand over her mouth she gazes into the distance. Maryam is standing silently over us. She bumps me with her knee and then Amira. We are the last three sea bass on the counter of a fishmonger whose throat is dry. No one wants us. In the sky the eagle is circling south.

I really wanted to know how Madam Lilla knew precisely when a risky move was least likely to be rejected. She knew just when to strike. Tapping each of us lightly on the shoulder, she said, "Come on. We've got a long journey ahead." Turning to Eyüp Bey she said, "Let's go. We'll stop at Shusha."

She caresses Amira's hair and Amira rests her head on her chest. She pats her affectionately a couple times on the back but keeps a distance to prevent her from falling apart altogether. She's playing the mother role perfectly. Maryam doesn't see any of this as she goes and sits down in the back of the car. Her arms crossed, she has given up. The eagle turns south and disappears.

The sun slowly sinks below the horizon. Our faces are crimson in the car. The desert is purple. If you stay out long enough you disappear, or so the desert says, in strips and strands it says nothing. Making you so light you are hardly even there. Nothing left to be explained. Purging you of words, it is that beautiful. You could die here with a peaceful heart. Which is why you can live there with a peaceful heart. We're going...

"Did you know they filmed *Star Wars* here?" says Amira. Just when I think no one's in a mood to respond, Maryam says, "Oh! OK! Why don't you just come out and say it's the perfect place for a moon walk!"

Maryam and I burst out laughing. Laughter cascades through us against our will. Madam Lilla joins us. And still staring out the window with her finger between her lips, Amira starts laughing, too. Even Eyüp Bey might be laughing.

We stop an hour later. Night is falling. Only after a careful look around can we make out a desert camp of yellow tents off to the right. I look at the gate and read the sign: The United Nations. A refugee camp. My head is finally up and running again. Libya, the war, refugees pouring over the border into Tunisia...

"How are we going to get in here, Madam Lilla? This is a refugee camp," says Maryam. No longer a frail woman afflicted with rheumatoid arthritis, Madam Lilla looks like a war commander who has just hopped off her horse to draw up a battle plan.

"It was checked out. – Who checked it out? – Security in the camp is really light so we'll be safe. – Oh my God! – They don't even keep tabs on who comes and goes. – Oh!

That's really rich. – The other week three people were killed and no one blinked. – Oh! – Which is why we'll just park the car inside and sleep in a tent. Eyüp Bey will pitch it for us. In the morning we'll get up early and hit the road."

"And what if the hungry Libyan refugees slit our throats in the middle of the night, Madam Lilla?" said Maryam.

Like a general evaluating the concerns of a ranking officer, she answered gravely.

"There aren't any Libyans in this camp. Just people from all over Africa. Ethiopians, Nigerians, Somalis…"

"Great," said Amira, "they'll eat us whole."

"Ugh!" I said, springing to my senses, the racist comment serving as shock therapy. But Amira and Maryam ignored me because they were Africans. "You wait here," said Madam Lilla. And without giving us the chance to rebel, she brazenly walked off in a cloud of dust. Eyüp Bey went after her. She went into the closest tent. Leaning against the car, we waited. One by one the stars flickered into the night sky. It was getting cooler. Maryam was running the tip of her boot through the sand. I took a handful of the stuff. Lost in thought. It was as fine as silk. Unlike dust this wasn't hiding a thing. Every grain was nothing but the whisper of people dying millions of years ago. Flecks of nothing, as light as air. Of course such a land would have such a god…"

"Just look at us… It's all your fault," said Maryam.

"It's too late," said Amira. "No reason to grumble about it now. It's night and we're in the middle of the desert. Don't make this any more difficult."

That's as far as it went. Half an hour later Madam Lilla, Eyüp Bey and two large black men come over to the car. Without even looking at us the men fling open the boot, pull out a yellow tent and start pitching it near the camp gate. The sound of rock against the metal spikes echo over Africa as thin dark shadows of all different sizes come out of the other tents. Men and women and children come out and line up outside the tents. No one says a word to us, in fact no one says anything at all. When they had finished pitching our tent the dark shadows slipped back into their tents as if nothing had happened. Everything was done. Like a dream you want to keep dreaming and then it slips through your fingers. Eyüp Bey sat down at the front of the tent with the two men. We lay down and started to roll into sleep. Just as I was drifting off, I said, and I don't know why this came to mind: "Is *erguvan* an Arabic word?" As if she had been expecting the random question, Amira quickly answered, "No. And nearly no one in this county knows the Arabic name for *erguvan*."

She let out a strange sound, like someone trying to laugh through her tears. Then we were silent again. The sound of our breathing blended into a soothing magical lullaby or maybe we were entranced by the concern that everything was just a dream. In my dream that night we were surrounded by centipedes, scorpions and snakes. Circling around but never touching us. I think all three of us slept soundly until dawn. In the morning we woke to Madam Lilla caressing our hair. Then like a commander up at the crack of dawn, she said, "We're off!"

When we finally really woke up we found ourselves in a village coffeehouse sipping coffees and nibbling on croissants with sour expressions on our faces. 'Colonialism is such a strange thing,' I thought to myself as I looked down at my croissant. Why in the world were we eating croissants in the middle of the desert? Surely these people had their own bread before the French showed up. How could they forsake such a thing? And when? If you could do that wouldn't you forget your own gods, just a little? If you consider a bread crumb a godly thing... Then my wandering mind slipped into focus.

"What did you give those men to get them to look out for us last night?" I asked Madam Lilla.

"A few telephone numbers, a few names," she said. Faking a light cough, Maryam leaned into my ear and said, "I'm telling you the woman's an agent. If she's not crazy she's a spy! For sure."

I pushed her. "What phone numbers?"

"Friends' numbers. Old friends who work at the United Nations. When Somalis are next in line, Nigerian refugees can't get permission to cross into a third country. People in the West rate their success stories against the tragedies of people like us. Now the Somalis are all the rage so nobody is interested in the Nigerians. I gave them numbers of people who can make things easier for them if they just pass on my regards."

"And they believed it?" I said.

"And you don't, mademoiselle?" she said. It was the first time since we had left that she sounded so defiant.

"How do you know these people, Madam Lilla?" asked Maryam, pushing her for more answers. Madam Lilla answered briefly, "A woman on her own must have people whom she can trust," and she changed the topic.

"We're late now. We need to get over the border."

Putting her arm in Amira's, she walked over to the car.

No one bothered to ask, 'late for what?' Eyüp Bey looked despondent, tears welling up in his eye. And the moment we all got in the car we learned why.

"Eyüp Bey won't be coming with us. He'll drop us off at the border and we'll walk across. He's turning around."

Although Madam Lilla had said to this to us it seemed

like she had repeated herself to help Eyüp Bey accept the grim reality. Without looking at him, she went on, "Eyüp Bey, once you are back home please do exactly what I have told you to do. In particular those matters to do with Egypt. They can be sure that we'll arrive on time. And they need to be there if everything is to go as planned."

Eyüp Bey didn't so much as nod. The two of them looked like a picture from an ancient schoolbook on Social Graces. I thought of the old bickering couple in the café in Sidi Busaid. If they were photographed they might be the negative to this image of Madam Lilla and Eyüp Bey. They were as fresh as a topic that had been sealed shut for years.

"Now pull over and we'll get dressed."

"Excuse me but just what are we going to wear?" Maryam said brusquely.

Madam Lilla answered sternly: "I felt it would be prudent for us to wear chadors during our crossing into Libya."

As Maryam looked at me for support, I asked, "And why do we need to wear chadors?"

"Ladies," Madam Lilla began, leaning back in her seat. She was about to say something even more severe when I suppose she realized that we had not crossed the border and that she still needed to keep us with her.

"Just until we meet up with friends. For a couple hours or so. I don't suppose you want the militia to detain you at the border where they can give you a good look over."

"It goes against my principles," said Maryam. "It's just two hours, Maryam," said Amira. "Please." I was only concerned with how I was going to walk in a chador without tripping and tumbling to the ground. Now that would be a disaster. We drove on until we saw a crowd in the distance and then finally the sign at the border. Hundreds of luxury

114

cars were lined up waiting to cross into Tunisia. No one was crossing in the other direction. We seemed to be the only ones enthusiastic about entering a Libya where people were rising up against Gaddafi. We stopped. We went to the back of the car as Eyüp Bey took out the chadors. In a single swoosh more skillful than a matador, Madam Lilla slipped into her chador that was the colour of an eggplant. Ours were all the same: the colour of the desert. They could have left us there in the desert and no one would have noticed. This was more like camouflage than a chador. Though chadors are already a sort of camouflage... What a great word, I thought to myself, camouflage. It's got its own charm. It's been like this since yesterday. My mind was in the moment but it kept slipping away to escape the reality of what I was experiencing. I wondered if everything from this part of the world would be left behind after crossing the border? I was losing my mind and maybe it would be better if I never got it back.

"Let's walk," said Madam Lilla. We walked ahead. I looked over my shoulder to see her stuff an envelope in Eyüp Bey's hand. Amira asked her what it was. With a deep sigh, she replied, "My will. But don't worry, you're in it. And so is the dance school." Amira missed a step then kept walking. I looked back again to see Eyüp Bey leaning against the car, waiting, as if speaking with God. As Madam Lilla passed us she seemed to be endowed with the spirit of the last relative to the Romanov family. An eggplant-coloured woman in the desert, the three of us stumbling after her, our heads bowed, looking only at the ground beneath our feet. I heard Maryam praying, full of nervous energy. When we reached the checkpoint everything came to a halt, on both sides of the border, everyone stopped. Naturally they stopped to

115

look at four women who had just emerged from the desert. We were about to present our passports when...

"Call your commanding officer," said Lilla. There was no doubt she had an incredible power over people. But the cinematic effect of four women walking right out of the desert was what really made the difference this time. We looked as helpless as we looked mysterious and, dressed in chadors, we were legitimate and entirely submissive, and, for whatever reason, this had an effect on the men the likes of which I had never seen or felt before. The militia greeted us as women in need of help. The chador isn't all that bad then, I thought. Creates an effect you could never get from jeans. At least in a desert.

The commander arrives. Madam Lilla begins spinning a story that leaves us flabbergasted and our jaws drop (it's a good thing we're all completely covered).

"My husband has gone to the bosom of God, commander! My son and my sons-in-law crossed the border to Libya and did not come back. Poor as we are we have no passports. We need only to cross into Libya..."

Peppering her story with compliments and winks, Madam Lilla proceeds to tell the commander all kinds of elaborate, made-up, indeed entirely far-fetched stories. And so dressed as downcast women, it takes us a grand total of seven minutes to make the crossing. We walk towards the run-down border gate where Libyan militia stands guard. We cross into Libya. Madam Lilla stops in the middle of the road. The militia are staring at us and so are the Tunisian soldiers. Everyone in the convoy desperate to get the hell out of Libya is watching this strange film. In that moment Madam Lilla is suddenly above all the lies she has been spinning and entirely sure of how we will interact with the militia, and, taking Maryam by the arm, she speaks calmly.

116

"Young lady, you will take yourself seriously. Neither you nor your principles nor the secrets you keep from all of us are important. And if you think so the day will come when you will take your own life…" Looking at us all closely, she softens her voice: "Trust me. You're setting out on the journey of a lifetime. Enjoy it while you can."

Ten minutes later Madam Lilla is chatting away with the Libyan militia in perfect Libyan Arabic, Amira is sipping tea and Maryam and I are looking at the modest war installation the militia have constructed at the border. Bomb fuses, broken Kalashnikovs, anti-aircraft ramps, nostalgic photographs pinned to a sign that reads *Bienvenue Free Libya*… The militia has been stuck here for months, and they are bored out of their minds. They pretend to question us but they really couldn't care less about what we have to say. One is a former teacher, another an engineer and the rest are clearly down-and-out types with no work. The teacher and the engineer are just young kids. Initially they try putting on grave soldier faces but they can't contain their joy: they have the chance to talk to someone new. They have no idea about the civil war raging in their country. The Internet is down, which is really depressing. The computers are hardly working and they can't play video games. So we end up shooting the breeze in the middle of the desert. Madam Lilla cooks up problems to fit the character she's now playing. And we throw into the mix whatever God gives us. Me and Amira play Lilla's daughters and Maryam is the family bride. We are suffering, oh yes we are. Our brothers are all fighting in the civil war. Oh and we have no idea where they are. Gaddafi has brought such evil upon us… Madam Lilla's husband is Libyan and we escaped years ago, which is why we only speak English. But when the revolution broke out… Oh because you see there is nothing like a homeland. Long live free Libya! Madam Lilla invents all the names. And when she voices them there is suddenly such love for the person, longing, she fears for them, asks after them.

"Have you ever heard of them?"

She asks with such sadness that we grieve with the militia. I see that Amira is deep in her role, seated with her head in her hands. If Lilla takes this any further she might cry.

It is the first time our stories, hidden beneath these covers, are beginning to crystallize. We are on a journey with an old woman who is tracking down a man in some distant land, a man she once loved, and she is close to dying. But now she is alive and we are simply following. She is chasing someone and we are running away from something. It's good our faces are covered: there isn't a trace of this woman's lust for life in any of our expressions.

Later we see a strange, busted-up jeep covered in "Free Libya" slogans in both Arabic and English, kicking up a crazy cloud of dust. "Here at last," says Lilla. A woman hops out of the jeep and suddenly everything that has happened until then seems as interesting as a phone bill with a detailed call list. From a distance the strange driver calls out to Madam Lilla, "Welcome, Thirina!"

Libya

Three Tuareg are standing as still as statues. The helicopter above is blowing sand all over the place, whipping hair across our faces. Madam Lilla shouts:

"Fire! Fire!"

How did we end up here? What in the world were we doing in such a situation? Once you cross a border you have no idea how many more you keep crossing. But the desert you get lost in is the one that finds you...

10

"Forgive me, Thirina, I'm late. The English wouldn't stop talking," she said, throwing an eagle-eye over her shoulder to see Maryam to my right, Amira to my left, and me in the middle, sticking to our three-person grouping in the back seat. She asked, "Who are they?"

"My girls," said Lilla, wiggling out of her chador. Then, laughing, "I gave birth to them this morning and they bloomed right away!"

We were racing along in a black jeep at over two-hundred kilometres an hour when Madam Lilla introduced us to the fierce warrior in the driver's seat, whose headscarf looked like desert camouflage, she was like some kind of desert cowboy.

"Ladies, allow me to introduce to you to Saida, the most brave-hearted of the Amazigh women. A true warrior. A woman who radiates all the beauty of her forty years. And mother to a daughter, who must be ten now, no?"

Saida proudly nodded, her eyes fixed on the road. She was a tall, sturdy woman but her delicately defined dark face concealed all her emotions – she was that kind of woman. The palm of her dark mother-of-pearl hand only barely touched the steering wheel when she turned and although she was tall we could only see her forehead in the rearview mirror because she drove like a man, leaning back with one hand on the wheel. She probably hardly ever even looked back when she was driving. Sitting up a little she caught our eyes for a moment and greeted us with a nod. Then we heard something rumble in back of the truck. She slammed on the brakes and adjusting her headscarf like it was a cap she hopped out and walked to the back. Crawling in under the green tarp, she rummaged about pushing and shoving, her hips up in the air before she marched back to the driver's seat. "Always the same old Kalashnikovs, Thirina. Some things never change."

Madam Lilla smiled at her like a cold-blooded killer.

"Ah, that's my girl, Saida!"

They smiled at each other like old war buddies, alluding to a mysterious partnership. As if the word Kalashnikov was a sweet breeze from the past, Lilla twirled her hand in the air. All this would have sounded very different the night before but now the word Kalashnikov seemed a natural part of her lexicon. Turning to us, she said:

"Ladies, you can take off those chadors. We are in our country now."

Our country?

She looked at us and her face seemed a reflection of the exalted word. "Amazigh country!"

Taking advantage of the chadors rustling over our heads, I whispered in Maryam's ear:

"What's Amazigh, girl?"

"Berbers."

"Oh!"

Predicting what might come next, she scolded me.

"But don't you dare use that word! Oh no!"

I thought about it for a moment:

"Berber ... barbar ... ah barbarian ... got it."

In Maryam's expression I could see that hint of sadness in the face of fast-approaching apocalyptic scenarios. Amira, however, was far away. Far from the scene of her crime.

Madam Lilla was enjoying the breeze, like a mare on a jaunt over a mountain plateau. Wisps of grey hair that had slipped out of her bun fluttered in the wind racing through a crack in the window, and now she looked like an artist and now a guide for alternative tourism.

"Saida is like a daughter to me. How many years has it been, Saida? Thirty? Maybe more? The Amazigh uprising... Oh the good old days! But I am so happy that they will never return.... Oh, the days we had here. Saida's uncle ... let's call him an old friend ... he died years ago. He was one of the bravest leaders in the Amazigh uprising. A man of truth. A man who understood life and women."

Indeed Saida wasn't really a woman: she was more an Eastern man who hadn't forgotten how to feel shame; and so whenever we started talking about her or her uncle and certainly when the subject turned romantic she would start fiddling with the rearview mirror and then with the side mirrors – in short she would spend all this time peering into mirrors. And we were the only car on the road. Madam Lilla was having fun teasing her.

"Back then Saida was a young girl. I talked with her uncle all the time, arranging for her study in London. And it was a good thing she went. What do you say, Saida? You sort of owe me for all those nights in London, no? Ah! What a sweet girl. What happened in Soho stays in Soho! So tell us what's going on here then."

Saida seemed sweetly taken by surprise, it was as if she wanted to present Madam Lilla – or Thirina – to us in the same way Madam Lilla introduced her: through their shared past and spirited adventures. Glancing at us in the rearview mirror she said. "Thirina, or as you know her, Madam Lilla, has done incredible things for the Amazighen. If the world is talking about us today much of that is thanks to Madam Lilla."

Pausing like a soldier about to lower her voice before a commanding officer, she turned to Madam Lilla and said, "The English are helping a lot. The Americans, too. This time it's all OK, Thirina. Once we get rid of Gaddafi... We are getting close to that day of honour and independence we have been waiting for for so long."

Gazing out the window Lilla spoke to the clouds with a confidence that came with a sacrifice she had made and that we knew nothing about.

"Sadly, Saida, this is true. You will pay for the alliances you have made and be all the more compromised for them."

Saida began nervously adjusting the mirrors again: clearly she either agreed with Lilla or didn't want to question her out of respect. Lilla went on.

"I'm following the situation. There will be a civil war. Families weren't ready for everything to move this quickly. The English will come back for revenge and the Americans will come for the oil. Your uncle's fears will come to pass... Tribal wars... Which is why we turned down foreign aid... But now..."

Then sensing she might have come down too hard, Madam Lilla changed tack.

"But still my only hope lies in the Amazigh. You are the only educated community. The Amazigh women in particular. If they remember where they come from then the true meaning of those cave signs will be revealed."

I looked at Maryam. Signs in a cave? No answer. I looked over at Amira. She was still out of reach. Lost in a dream world, she hadn't said a word since we crossed the border. Lilla let out a mournful sigh.

"Your uncle wouldn't have wished for it to be this way. He died because he didn't want things to turn out like this."

Frustrated, Saida said, "You weren't here, Thirina. We had no other option but to cooperate."

Without hesitating Madam Lilla reached out to her. "I know Saida. How could I not... There is no pure rebellion if there is no self-sabotage in the equation."

I looked at Maryam and Amira. This much was clear: we were a capable crew ready for the storm which was all good. Because in a storm there is no time to question what came before (remember the tall tale we told the Libyan militia) or what comes next (exactly where Saida was taking us). But when the wind died down we would lose our footing. As we sped along that road I looked closely at Maryam and Amira, and Madam Lilla. We looked like people who wouldn't know how to stomach still waters. Even Amira, who'd been silent since we set out on this lightning adventure, seemed as peaceful as a child in a cradle. Maryam's frustration was no more than what you might get from a fly buzzing about in your car. And of course it goes without saying that Madam Lilla was a prima donna ready to burst into song after a long musical introduction. So it just seemed better to plough through the waves than ask the tough questions...
.

We hear the rattling of the guns in the boot again, but Saida doesn't stop. She pops in a CD, hoping the music will drown out the sound. Asmahan's *Joyous Viennese Nights*. She must trust us as 'Thirina's girls', because she says, "if only those Kalashnikovs were as buttoned up as the English," and she laughs.

Quietly listening to a Viennese waltz sung in Arabic, we travelled down that stretch of land stained with desert. We were with an Amazigh woman buying Kalashnikovs from the Brits; Madam Lilla, codename Thirina, whom we'd just learned had played a key role in several former Amazigh uprisings; and the three of us who looked like three flamingos forced into the city by a sudden catastrophe, and, as if that wasn't enough, were crushed on the asphalt between two bodies of water. We might have resorted to the standard gestures to express concern but a mysterious inner peace had come with our willful abduction.

Deserts should be nobler than this. This was nothing but a stretch of land full of stones the size of your hand. There wasn't a trace of the dignity of the desert or the fruit of the earth. God must have got bored before he could decide which one he wanted. The landscape was a sharp, strong, dirty yellow. It was the place where the ambitiously lazy and disengaged decided to stay when the rest of humankind was lining up for the great first migration wave out of Africa. I mean you wouldn't even miss Libya if she wasn't on the map. Those aware that an abundance of human life was sacrificed for the most inhospitable swaths of land might ask why would people even squabble over such a place.

"Oh my dear Saida," said Madam Lilla, cutting the silence as she geared up for a speech. "The people here took up arms for oil and for revenge. But you ... oh, they have no idea..."

Turning to us, she went on, "Ladies, the mother goddesses and the women who ruled these lands hundreds of years ago have all gone underground. Dido, al-Kahina, Tanit, Tin Hinan and so many more powerful women. They have changed their names and covered themselves..."

126

Elbowing Maryam, I said, "She's talking about your lot."

As Madam Lilla went on in her documentary tone Maryam seemed to hang on her every word, "And the Amazigh women kept the words of those ancient mothers close to their breasts so that these accursed lands would have meaning again. So they would have a tongue to speak. So there would be life, do you see?"

Startled, Maryam nodded her head with the enthusiasm of a hardworking student who was faithful to her teacher. Lilla went on, "The Amazighen, indeed feel free to call them Berbers, which is what they should be called in my opinion, for is there anything nobler in this world than being a barbarian? If only they had protected their lands and their independence..."

Madam Lilla stopped mid-sentence and Maryam was left openmouthed. Some of what Madam Lilla was saying must have come from the heart because now and then her voice cracked.

"Do you remember what your uncle used to say, Saida?"

Madam Lilla looked at Saida. She was looking back over those years as if staring at some something that had broken down along the way and she trembled with disappointment. Then, as if addressing that lost world, she continued, "'Thirina, when we win the legend does too.' Yes, that's what he used to say. The legend will win!"

"What does 'Thirina' even mean?" said Amira finally breaking her silence.

Madam Lilla tossed the question to Saida, trying to get her to play along in a new game. Saida looked as stressed as on the first day at school.

"What does it mean, Saida?"

Saida fiddled with a mirror and then spoke, her voice like crumpled paper.

"Love."

Madam Lilla was silent, leaving us a space where our dreams could grow. A shard of glass sunk into Amira's heart as she gazed out of the window and Maryam only whispered, "of course". I imagined Madam Lilla pushing fifty and racing along the horizon on horseback, a bundle of grace and laughter. The uncle in question is in his forties. The ornaments on his wild black horse ring across the desert as he charges after her. In his dark-skinned face his tame eyes glimmer with a hungry passion. On and on they gallop...

"Why did you leave, Thirina?"

Suddenly reproachful Saida had posed the question. But clearly there was more: this was a long unwritten angry letter... She stopped looking at the road and turned to face Madam Lilla. But the old woman was not to be deterred by such tactics.

"Keep your eyes on the road, Saida," she said sharply and then as if Saida had never asked the question she said, "Eyüp Bey must have told you on the phone. We won't be staying long. So we need to draw up our itinerary tonight. I trust you can help us choose the best routes given family situations and the state of the war. And I am assuming you can take us as far as the Egyptian border."

How many times had Saida's heart been broken in the same place and no doubt by the same person? Now she is a little girl asking her mother about her greatest disappointment only to find that her mother remembers absolutely nothing of the day. And yet when Madam Lilla speaks of goddesses and fairy tales and poetry the expression on Saida's face reveals the boredom of having listened to these shimmering lies so many times.

"Could we stop somewhere?" asks Maryam in her

harshest growl. She receives an equally harsh look from Saida in the rearview mirror. Figuring I should back her up, I say, "Just when do we get to wherever it is we're going?"

Not bothering to look back Saida says, "We're close," and nothing more; a scornful freedom fighter forced to suffer the whims of three abducted tourists.

Deaf to any dissent, Madam Lilla carries on in the same tone, "But I really must get to Yefren by the day after tomorrow." She's playing a game, pretending that we aren't even there. Clearly disturbed, Maryam's face goes white and I take her hand.

Finally we see posters on the remaining walls along the side of the road, which gives us the feeling we are getting close to something. Again Madam Lilla is like a tour guide talking from another time.

"Ah! Saida, what bliss! Who would have guessed that one day we would see such signs along this road? Ladies, these signs here have the colours of the Amazigh flag: red, white and blue. Gaddafi banned Amazigh flags and their languages and so to see them here now... Oh God! That sign there is an Amazigh symbol. A free person standing between earth and sky, bringing the two together. Zin. As for that one of a woman who looks like young girl in a skirt, she's Tanit, the mother goddess. Oh, Saida! Just admit that the legend is winning ..."

Madam Lilla was in her own world, which made everyone in the car uncomfortable, except Amira who was still somewhere else. At last we saw a market village in the distance. Typical late period Middle Eastern architecture: iron sprouts reaching out of unshapely concrete chunks splattered with whitewash.

"So you no longer live in the old city then. But these new

houses are all cockeyed," said Madam Lilla. Looking around I couldn't find a trace of anything that looked like an Old City. Only a sea of dirty yellow stones. Suddenly children swarmed around the jeep as if they had popped up out from the earth in the twinkling of an eye. They were all doing the same thing. Holding up three fingers on one hand and a victory sign on the other.

"What's the three mean?" I asked.

"It's an Amazigh sign," said Saida. And she continued – of course addressing Madam Lilla – with a slight touch of pride in her voice.

"We started our own education programmes at school. Teaching the Amazigh alphabet, Amazigh history... In fact we're building a museum at the school, a little museum to tell what happened during the war. Do you remember Maren and his sister? When you left..." her voice dipped then rose "...they were still kids. They have both left their jobs and come back from London. After we took control of the state-owned radio tower, they began working on a broadcast in Amazigh. So it looks like once people come back from America and Europe things will get moving. In the near future they will start studies on our oral history. And we are shooting a film showing local historical remains, a documentary that should be ready in a few months."

"Now you're talking, Saida! Brava!" said Madam Lilla. It seemed like empty praise, I thought to myself, as Lilla put her hand on Saida's hand that clutched the stick. She squeezed tightly and let go. However Lilla must have had the power to repair all the hearts she had ever broken in a single touch. Saida flashed her a shy smile. That was the first time I realized Madam Lilla was a truly dangerous woman.

At the entrance to the village were men in T-shirts and sunglasses who looked more like gun-toting surfers from California than soldiers on active duty, their feet dangling off jeeps. Somewhere a war was in full swing, which we understood from the writing on the jeeps and all the bullet holes. Yet it didn't seem real.

"The men go to fight in the morning and come back in the evenings... Sometimes they don't come back," says Saida, "but the clashes have been pushed farther north. Nothing's really happening around here any more. So we have finally retaken our land. Tooth and nail. Just a month ago there were snipers up on those hills. Thank God we succeeded in driving them away. Now the fighting is only in the north. Which is why you need to head south, which will draw out your trip a little."

Madam Lilla echoed her earlier sentiments, "Just as I thought. Now that's my girl!"

Her face now a shade of green, Maryam looked like she might throw up if she only opened her mouth. Taking deep breaths, she threw herself out of the car. Amira was silent as she walked beside Madam Lilla. Most likely she was thinking about the bride and the incident at the hamam. With an air of indifference Madam Lilla gave Saida her handbag and we stopped at an undistinguished house. This was Saida's home and I was shocked to see all the lace, plastic flowers and cut-glass sugar bowls in a glass display case. A young girl raced over to us and suddenly stopped as if there was a wall of glass between us. Her skirt was still billowing.

"Say hello to mother Thirina, my little girl," said Saida. Madam Lilla stood there like a queen waiting for her hand to be kissed. The girl seemed unruffled. "My daughter is quite famous now, Thirina," Saida said and the little girl covered her mouth and smiled.

"She called Gaddafi a donkey live on Al Jazeera TV. Tell them what you said to Gaddafi, sweetie?"

Hopping from foot to foot and first turning the words over in her mouth, she cried out, "'Don't you get it, donkey Gaddafi! We don't want you!' That's what I said." And she raced out of the room. Madam Lilla and Saida broke out laughing. We joined in to liven the mood, Maryam seemed a bit better. Amira was having a look around and, as if she was Madam Lilla's daughter, she said. "Thank you for having us." And with that humble 'thank you' we went into our room. Four beds each with a different bed cover and patterns on the pillow covers were lined up in a row. It made the room feel like a flower garden in full bloom. "I need to get going," Saida says. "The women are working at the school. I should check up on them. And you should rest. If you're hungry there's food in the kitchen. There's no bread so we're always making pizza but what can you do. I'll leave some on the table. I should be back late. I also need to check the radio tower."

Madam Lilla turned up her nose at our made-up room like it was full of dirt that might get on her skirt. "Please wait, Saida," she says, "we'll come with you." We? Maryam was in no state to go anywhere and she was already making for her bed. So clearly she wasn't coming. The trip must have taken a lot out of her. But Amira looked like she didn't want to be alone, hanging on Madam Lilla's every word. "I want to see what my girls are doing," says Madam Lilla.

So the three of us follow Saida and her daughter down a narrow street with the usual trail of children as is standard in this part of the world. Saida's little girl takes after her mother, proud as a little anchovy trying to be a shark. The houses are empty and so are the streets and we hear only the sound of our footsteps. I look down at my shoes now covered in dust. 'They look much better this way,' I think to myself. With all the dust in my shoes, I feel like I have run away from home but also like I have deliberately set out on a trip that is a chain of bizarre events. I once wrote, "Truth is in the dust." Now looking down at my shoes I think, 'if that's not the case then we're done for.' It felt like everything that happened in the airport and everything that was happening in Turkey had happened years ago. Crossing the border we had crossed into another time and place and now I didn't have to think about what I'd left behind. All three of us could feel the weight of what we had left behind lifting, and the peace of mind in the here and now. We avoid looking each other in the eye because we are afraid one of us might say, 'have we gone crazy? Come on, let's get out of here.' Best to live for the moment. My heart contracts and I turn to Amira who is walking silently beside me. "Are you alright?" I ask. As if picking up a conversation she's been having with herself since we set off together she suddenly turns to me and says in a trembling voice, "No, it wasn't an accident. I killed someone. I suppose it was revenge. I mean I suppose I got my revenge. And it wasn't just for me... I think it was for him, too."

Catching the sudden nervous energy in her voice, Saida and her daughter and Madam Lilla look over at us. Only when we start walking again do I ask, "Who's that? Whose revenge?"

She looks at me. Like she is weighing my heart as well as the secret she is about to share. Shaking her lowered head, she says, "Muhammed. My Muhammed." Before I can say, "Sister, just who is this Muhammed!" I bump into Saida.

We are standing at an open door of a one-storey building.

133

We can hear singing inside. Children are coming and going. Girls are skipping with ropes on the street. This is a flurry of life in stark contrast to the war out in the desert. This little rundown school looks like a picture drawn by a happy child with a pure heart. If this village embodies the desert then this wobbly-looking school must be its oasis. The sounds of women and children seem to waver in a mirage. Water must be only one part of an oasis. A desert is made up of lost and withered men, and women are the watery heart that is the oasis.

Madam Lilla is holding Saida's hand. Leaning close, she speaks softly but I overhear.

"Both your uncle and you ... you know Saida ... I loved you both. But people like me need to move on. You know that... Please help me. If there is any part of me in the woman you are today then help me, Saida."

Placing her hand on Madam Lilla's back like a quiet child forgiving her mother, Saida looks away. She nods. And, as if Madam Lilla never asked for help, she raises her head in a way that implies that the brief conversation is over and off the record and she announces in the voice of a school inspector.

"Yeees... So let's see what the Amazigh women are up to? The daughters of al-Kahina!'

As we step through the front door a young girl runs over to us in a fit of joy. Shaking a camera in the air, she cries, "Saida! Did you see it, Saida? We made a recording, did you see it? We got all of it!"

11

"The series of events to unfold on this adventure, ladies, will leave you in a daze. Which is a good thing. For then your mind is muddy but your heart is clear. Free from what you must do you become the women you must be. Look around. You will see that life is in our breath."

Amira and I are squeezed into a large ring of women seated on the ground, watching Madam Lilla hold forth. Boxes of sweets and little notes are moving both ways around the ring. In the heart of war we are all crouched down like this but Madam Lilla is still playing the lead role in her film. Having survived the latest whirlwind we are still not entirely sure how we ended up here.

*

We stood at the front of the school with the image of a mother goddess on the door. But when the girl with a camera came running over to Saida, letting out whoops of joy, the mood suddenly changed. Women stepped up and took us by the hand and led us to the other women inside. Quickly moving from room to room, they breathlessly explained so many different things. Bewildered, we suddenly found ourselves seated among a group of women working. Just a couple minutes ago I was keen to hear about Amira's Muhammed. She was about to tell me. And now we were sitting cross-legged with a group of women, both young and old. We sat in silence, as if we had been sitting

135

there since the beginning of time, and might stay there until the end. A young girl was softly singing. When she finished someone picked up where she left off. Their heads were bowed while other women continued working. Madam Lilla was merrily carrying on, not at all taken aback by this ring of women and the work that they were doing.

In one corner of the room a circle of seated women were mixing soft sweets and pastries on trays. Everything looked unusually small: they were these tiny little colourful sweets. The women kneaded them with the tips of their fingers and carved out designs with their fingernails. Other women in the ring lined the little sweets on a large tray. The trays were then passed to another part of the ring. There women divided the sweets into little packets. Beside them were seven young women writing on little pieces of paper. Sweets now in the little packets come from one part of the circle and the little notes come from another and meet where we are seated and are then placed together in little boxes wrapped in nylon. At first I tried reading the notes in Arabic but I slow down the pace of production because my Arabic is not good. Now and then Amira – if she felt inspired – would translate one for me. They were little poems penned on separate pieces of paper. Poems of love and freedom. Some of them were miniature letters, words of bravery and compassion not addressed to any particular person. These little boxes of sweets and words were then sent to the men fighting on the front line. The young girl who met at us at the door with such enthusiasm manages this elaborate production line. Saida has left us to her care. As leader of poetry and sweets, she eagerly collects the poems and brings them to the ring. She counts the trays, the poems and the boxes. She is responsible for sending a woman's heart to every man at the front, a poem for every gun. She breathes out her work like a peal of laughter. Now and then she sets her camera on the ground, the same camera she showed Saida and us when we came into the school. When the activity slows down she goes back to watching her recordings. One recording shows her and seven women in the ring. Reading their poems to the camera. When repairs to the radio tower are finished the plan is to broadcast these poems. Like fairies in the middle of the desert. Tiny little things. Poetry blended with sweets sent to the front where human flesh meets steel. But the boxes hold more than just candy and a poem. In our ring sit two very old women. When the packets arrive they take each one in their hands and read a prayer through fluttering lips and then blow on each packet before placing them in cardboard boxes. Is it simply that everything here seems smaller than it really is in the light of a war that is always waged extra large? Maps, guns, planes and ships, they are all spoken of in terms of size.

"You will come to understand that life is in your breath. Nowhere else and in nothing else. You will make your life. You will breathe out … life… As far as your breath will go," continues Madam Lilla. She speaks with a gravity that wavers between poetry and prayer. We are a little embarrassed by these theatrical flights that seem out of touch with reality. We try not to hear as we help the women packing. Swept away by her own lusty voice, Madam Lilla continues.

"In truth, ladies, women live in a world within the world. Into that world they blow their love and magic. Men are forever ravaging this world, destroying. Women lay the foundations for it with every new breath. And women breathe life into men. The sum of a man is the breath of a woman, nothing more."

Amira leaned close to my ear and said, "I don't think that's how it is. Muhammed wasn't like that." But she left it there. Madam Lilla then elaborated on her thesis: "But there are a few. Every once and a while there comes a man who understands that his sole responsibility is expressing his admiration at a world made by the breath of women." Amira nodded her head in agreement and sighed in even deeper agreement. Now that we had drifted away from the subjects of poems and candies and war I could ask: "I suppose that at some point you're going to tell me who this Muhammed is?"

Amira looked at me and paused. Madam Lilla went on, now in a more vitriolic tone.

"Yet sadly those rare men also have something to race after. A war, a god, a story. Certainly something drags them away. And we are not the ones to wait for them!"

Looking long and hard into my eyes, Amira nodded at what Madam Lilla was saying. "Certainly," Amira echoed. Madam Lilla then rose and silently sat down among the women blending sugar. I said to Amira, "You're going to tell me." When she nodded, I stood up.

I went into another room where they were teaching children Amazigh. There were reading cards on the wall and Amazigh letters on the blackboard. These people were working to free themselves of a language they had been forced to learn and to return to their mother tongue, and in the middle of a war. It must have been something like reading history backwards. I suppose they were trying to remember the forgotten words of their ancestors; and the more quickly these children remembered them the more quickly they would learn the language. They were moving closer to their native tongue but Amira and Maryam and I were moving further away from ours. Yet we understood each other better than anyone could understand us in our own languages. This was a different language that had come to life the day we met. We couldn't speak in any one mother tongue so we'd made a little English-speaking nest for the three of us. Far from the comfort of our native languages, we were wintering in a foreign language of limited vocabulary and purged of references, ornaments, intricacies and needless words. What remained was only that which could not be said through silence. And it was fun. The three of us had been exiled into a personalized, ragbag English. Amira would add words from Tunisian Arabic, Mayram from Egyptian Arabic and I would toss in Turkish. Words from the Muslim world like *inşallah*, *maşallah*, *valla* and *bilahi* jingled like beads in our English. These words opened new passages in English. In the icy London weather of English they were warm Middle Eastern arcades. And over a few days we'd developed our own unique language. A brand new English with Arabic almond paste, seasoned with Turkish rose jam. Sadly it was a language we could never teach. It was a language that came to life through us and that would melt into the sky when we went parted.

I go into the classroom that is now a war museum. In the middle of the room sits the base of an anti-aircraft gun. Broken Kalashnikovs lean up against it. On the walls are scenes of war drawn by adults with less talent than children. Not pictures but individual symbols. Though they are crudely drawn, I am sure they move the hearts of those who have actually been through such trauma. Anger must have driven them to collectively remember as a way to seek revenge. Maybe the wars that began in this part of the world would end this stage of human history. Maybe these primitive drawings would start a new era that might even include us.

Blood, cracked skulls, bodies strewn on the earth, bodies wrapped in funeral shrouds... Every sketched composition on the wall told the story of a moment before the war and during the war. Why would they show such things to children? To explain them? Is there nothing but blood that unites generations? Do people come together only to honour their fallen? The fate of humankind. Even the history of us three now carried a corpse, a bond of blood. No matter how you looked at it there was a bride whom Amira felt she had killed, and maybe she had. When I disappeared and decided to go on this trip, I felt half-dead. And who knows how many male bodies Madam Lilla had left behind? As for Maryam ... honestly, why did she agree to come? A spark went off in my mind. When you pulled together all those loose ends... Shaving her head, her constant nausea, the sudden decision to leave with us... Maryam was sick. She was really sick. Oh my God! Why didn't I get it? Does Amira know?

"Come over here!" Amira is calling me over from the door, a smile on her face. I go back into room where they are making sweets. A young man is standing at the door, keeping a cool air about him. He is wearing a T-shirt that says *Free Libya* and has a five-o'clock shadow that gives him this carefree attitude and that man-of-adventure look. He leans his Kalashnikov against the door. He cocks his eyebrows and flashes a Casanova smile. The young poets are all excited, fixing their headscarves and jumping to their feet. There's a gauzy flicker in the air. The old women try to ignore this storm of infatuation that stirs up everything in the room but soon the skirts of the young girls are billowing and the young man's hands are now eagerly gesturing as he tells stories of the front line. The old women don't look because they know they will only make things worse. All the girls are now blushing. With a sly smile on his face and coolly leaning back, the young man speaks.

"Everything's fine. God willing we'll go back tonight. Everyone's good. There were a couple of clashes but none of our men were hurt. And how are things here? I hope all is OK. Are the boxes ready?"

When he puts his hands on his hips you see that spoiled behaviour particular to Middle Eastern men that can be enticing to watch but only causes pain if you actually love the man. Oh, how he is so very pleased with himself. He sees himself as a gift to the world. Ah! He deserves it all. So you see if you are loved enough you turn out like this. It was like every part of his body was alluring in its own way and with every movement he was reminded of the fact. Who would be the lucky girl? It seemed like he was lazily mulling it over. Or would he simply deign to grace someone with his presence? He's rubbing his belly and the girls are swooning. Telling arrogant jokes, he scratches his beard. And the girls are swooning. He hooks one finger in his back pocket like a tough guy. And the girls are swooning. Nothing but smiles all around. He is generating an overwhelming lust, as if he isn't aware of it. He knows he will be loved all his life and never abandoned. There will always someone waiting for him, no one will ever try his limits. He'll always be forgiven. And if he is ever asked for an ounce of love he'll get terribly bored and restless and say so and leave. Then he'll be rewarded by other loving women who think he deserves better. None of these dear girls will ever know what it's like to be so easy. They will tell each other how bitter and sweet it is to love a man like that. "How cruel," they say. He's indulgent, self-centered, and the ultimate scoundrel but in the end he's called a "man-child" and forgiven and loved again. He will take everything they have, give nothing back, then maybe – if you're patient enough – he might smile at you again. Oops... and everything is laid out at his feet again. And this is precisely why he smiles like that because he is so sure that the same thing is going to happen all over again. It is the smile of a Middle Eastern man whose heart has never known malaria. It is the smile of a man who will test his strength on softhearted women who believe that they always have to try harder to be loved.

The girls began carrying boxes of sweets to the door. No direct eye contact was made but the young war hero who was still rooted to the spot received a volley of furtive glances that spoiled him like they would any other Arab man. Then came a brief and flirtatious scene. Girls with fingers graced with poetry and sweets giggled into their headscarves and the boy looked ashamed, as if he had been kissed, his lips aslant, stealing glances from under his eyebrows. The poet leader's body suddenly grew taut as she handed a box to the young man. The scene went on. Away from the eyes of the old women, their fingertips touch behind the box. In that lay the meaning of war. In an instant. In that touch a wave went through them. Into that moment rushed an entire world. When it ended the box swayed in his arms. The carefully arranged sweets graced with a poem and breath suddenly shook in his arms. Jostling everything inside. In his arms compassion was thrown into disarray. The war front rattles anything it touches in the world of women. But the poet leader was not bothered. The intoxication of that momentary touch was worth it all. She could no longer see the box, blind to the fact that a crude touch, a thrill bereft of grace, had disturbed the consonance in the world of poetry and sweets that she had made. She must have felt it was worth it. Or she was still very young. In any event she could still breathe into the same world and with the same compassion, in the same rush of air, a powerful breath that would bring it to life again. In any event those poems could be written again and shaken hearts would come to rest and then blended into sweets that would be arranged anew in boxes. Madam Lilla was right, women were that way: they were the sum of their breath. And with the breath of women this world...

"It is enough if men show respect and admiration for the world of women. And that is the breath of men over women. Women will find the strength to rebuild a world in constant decay when they see this respect and admiration. This powerful magic will frighten men. Which is why they go on about the 'sorcery of women'. When men understand that women can thrive without them at their side, that they can live on that magic... That's when they begin calling us sorcerers. You will learn it. You will learn how not to fear this magic, learn how life is made of it."

Madam Lilla whispered all this in my ear. It left me feeling frustrated. I was sick of this way of talking and how she imparted these life lessons, never leaving us alone. Especially after just witnessing a man going on about everything he can do while doing absolutely nothing. And I was still thinking about Maryam. Without realizing it I found myself teasing Madam Lilla in Turkish when I said aloud: "Oh my God, just watch you go!" With her hands clasped on her stomach, she looked like a headmistress. Throwing her head back with an eyebrow raised she responded in Turkish: "No need to worry."

I was stopped cold. The boy must have left because a sudden joyous clamour broke out in the room. The girls were now laughing and the older women were praying out loud in full breath after the young man who had just left the room, sending their magic with him to the front line. The girls surrounded the leader poet and made fun of her. One of them kicked off a song. It was sheer joy. Sure of herself, Madam Lilla swaggered over to the old ladies. Frozen, I kept my eyes on her. After making me wait for a good while she looked up and flashed me a playful smile. I hadn't really done anything wrong but somehow her forgiving me like that felt good. I understood Saida and I thought again about how Madam Lilla was indeed a dangerous force of nature who could take a human heart in the palm of her hand and do whatever she wanted with it. I thought of how we'd set out on the journey of a lifetime and how everything we had left behind deserved to die. Of how I didn't want to waste time explaining even to myself how everything had happened, how it was just a matter of getting swept away and how this journey was worth it. How life was happening precisely now in this moment and that I didn't want to contact anyone. I only wanted to get lost because I knew it would be good. Everything that was happening was extraordinary and if I could slip out of the role of someone dashing off explanations to newspapers I could explain things as I saw them myself. I could push away the things I had to do and then I could be the person I needed to be so that everyone could "breathe over this world" by doing what they are meant to do. I could live only with truth and beyond explanation, knowing that this journey could take us to our true selves.

"Write all this down, will you?" said Amira.

"We need to leave it behind," I said. "We need to leave

everything where it is. That's what you said, right? Life is happening here and now."

"Huh?"

"I can live now that I have died."

"What are you on about?"

"I'm not going to write anything... I think Maryam's really sick. She might have cancer or something like that."

"What?"

"That's what I think. And do you know that Madam Lilla speaks Turkish?"

"What does that have to do with anything?"

"Nothing. Anyway ... I think Maryam's sick. Did she say anything to you?"

"No ... where did you come up with that idea anyway? Wait a second. Yes ... yes, you might be right."

"She's trying to kill herself. That's why she agreed to take the trip."

Amira stopped to think, trying to remember something.

"She won't say anything about it. Let's ask but if she doesn't say anything... She's writing something, in a notebook. I saw her put it under her bed in the hotel room. She must have it with her."

We looked at each other. Of course we were going to rifle through Maryam's personal belongings.

When night fell Saida came back and we walked back to her house together. Again the desert looked like a purple lake. Madam Lilla took me by the arm, encircling the two of us in silence. The pebbles crunching under our feet seemed that much louder. Only her breathing broke the silence that underscored the importance of what she had to say. She looked out at the hills in the distance and at the drifting clouds ringed in dark blue and purple that were incredibly beautiful.

"I learned the languages I know from men but everything I have just told you I learned from women. It is no coincidence we now find ourselves here together. You need to know that. You are someone who will always challenge fate. People who write stories about people need to know this: you are writing fate. And with that comes loneliness. A great loneliness."

With the deepest compassion I had ever felt, she looked at me to see if I had grasped the bitterness of her words. I felt like crying and my throat contracted. Satisfied that I was speechless, she went on.

"To set out on a journey with a woman like me – and I'm not talking about you alone – you must have been kicked out of your own world. It seems you don't have a place there anymore. Neither do I for that matter. Ah, my dear … the world, your country, people and family that you have feared for so long and worked so hard to make a part of your life, well, it will take years until you accept the fact that they fear you. It takes even more time indeed until you understand that you cannot change them. So there is no other hope for you but to trust your breath. We must breath to create the world and the men who live in it. But for now the three of you must now be out of breath. You must be tired."

She stopped. And recited the *Bismillah* prayer in praise of God. Then she recited a prayer in Arabic. Smiling: "*Neffasati fil' u'gad*!" Do you know the Koran?"

If I could have spoken I knew that I would cry so I simply shook my head.

"It's from the *Fellak* verse… The verse begins with a decree, *Neffasati fil' u'gad*, 'Keep away from the inauspicious women who blow on knots.' Keep away from the inauspicious enchantresses…. For God knows just what we are capable of. Both for good and evil. But we have forgotten. But now that we have crossed the border ... I will help you remember. And you will help me. You will stay with me until I find the man who destroyed the world I brought to life with my breath."

With a trembling hand she squeezed my arm. A man who destroyed the world of a woman who'd destroyed so many men with the flick of her skirt? Surely she was lying. There couldn't be such a man. And even if there was, how would we find him? She was concocting a vast, multilayered story around us with no possible way for us to get to the heart of it. By then the two of us had become a single purple shadow among the houses. It wasn't Madam Lilla, prophetess of weariness and loneliness, that got to me but the depth of compassion in her words that stuck in my throat like a grenade of tears, and that stayed with me until I saw Maryam. Once we were back in our bedroom Amira and I went to work straightaway – it was time to investigate. Whatever this secret was it was going to come to light. But in fact the fate of our trio would turn out to be far funnier than either of us expected.

12

We are in front of a mirror. Our cheeks are tired from laughing but we can't stop. "The Women Who Blow on Knots Dance School! Yes, now that's got to be the name!" said Amira, bursting with laughter. "Yes! We'll have the opening right here in the Libyan desert! Ladies and gentlemen, come and dance with us like we're all out of our minds! BOOM-chick BOOM-chick!" In front of the mirror Maryam lustily tries to belly dance with a belly she doesn't even have, her tongue stuck out of the corner of her mouth. I strike ironic femme fatale dance poses. Like a prima donna, Amira thrusts herself in front of us, bows and blows kisses at the mirror. We salute our audience of three women dressed in white night gowns. We're back in our white night gowns. Afraid we might be making too much noise, we struggle to hold back the laughter. But every now and then one of us explodes and we double over and come back up with grave faces only to start dancing again until we collapse on each other's shoulders. Pulling up her shoulder strap, Amira says to the mirror, "Oh come on, sweetie, forget about it already! What was it saintly Albert Camus said!?"

I look at these two in the mirror. I watch the rosy hue take over their olive-skinned bodies. Maryam has forgotten all about her lack of hair … beads of sweat have clustered on Amira's skin like mother of pearl… If Madam Lilla was right and women really are the sum of their breath then surely something happens to women during mouth-to-mouth resuscitation. And just when they are about to die. There was simply no other way we could have ended up like this at this

148

*moment. We hadn't come to this room in Saida's home so full
of joy....*

*

Striding into Maryam's bedroom, Amira put her hand on
her hip and cried out: "Maryam!"

Before I even could tell Amira to calm down for a minute,
the question had already been dropped like a bomb.

"Look, do you have cancer? If you do then you're going
to tell me! I won't stand for this any more."

The expression on Maryam's face was far too composed
for someone who'd just been caught concealing the fact that
she had cancer. Lying on her bed, she was writing in a
notebook. She hesitated and Amira became even more
impatient.

"On top of that we know you keep writing in that
notebook. Which means if you aren't going to tell us now
we are going to have a look anyway. That's right! We're
listening."

With her arms crossed like that she looked more
frightening than the grim reaper himself. I sort of thought
we were going a bit too far with someone who might
actually have cancer but then again I was convinced that
keeping a secret like that from us for all this time was
worse. In the end we had all set out on this trip together.
So yes, we were listening!

Maryam's belly began to lightly shake before laughter
rolled off her lips.

"And just what are you going to do about it?' she said
laughing. "Will you beat me up if I do?"

"Yes," said Amira, clear as a bell. She went on like a
plump little mother.

"So what's this all about then? You weren't going to tell us? You were just going to roll over and die in the middle of the desert? Leave us to bury you? Was that your plan? Wonderful! Brava! You complete moron! You were going to leave me alone on this adventure?"

Amira was angry at the idea of a loved one dying but it was an anger born of compassion. While Maryam was still laughing at the idea of a friend who cared so much that she wanted to beat her up because she had cancer. When Amira's face twisted into the face of tearful little girl left alone with her foul temper, Maryam finally stopped. Smiling, she rose and took Amira's arm and shook it... "So you're going to read my notebook, eh?"

Still angry and unwilling to back down, Amira said, "Stop it. Are you dying?"

Maryam gave her a bear hug. "Don't be ridiculous. I don't have anything like cancer. For the love of God where did you come up with that idea? If I did, would the treatment be a good thrashing? At least I've learned something."

"So what then?" said Amira. "What aren't you telling us?"

"Yes," I said. And trying to wiggle out of my embarrassing diagnosis by bombarding Maryam with questions, I went on. "Why did you decide to come with us in the first place?"

That mysterious dark-skinned woman, who never seemed exposed no matter how many layers were peeled away, was gone altogether: she now had a lightness of being we had never seen before.

"I thought you'd never ask!"

Pausing for a moment, she went on, "But Madam Lilla should never know. I don't trust that woman one bit. Where is she now?"

Madam Lilla was busy with Saida. And with something we should have been busy with too: namely our itinerary. But here we were fretting over a disease Maryam didn't even have. The only thing we knew was that we would be travelling further into southern Libya. Thanks to Saida we learned that much; Madam Lilla was hardly sharing very much with us. When Maryam heard that our trip would take us deep into the deserts of Libya, she said: "OK, enough. We'll talk to Madam Lilla tomorrow and put an end to this nonsense. What is all this, *yani*? Alright, so we got swept away but really, just where are we headed? What's really going on?"

"You know the guy who ruined her life, we're going to find him," said Amira, with the grave expression of a child.

"Hah, hah, hah... Madam Lilla's life? She's lying," Maryam replied

"I agree," I said wholeheartedly.

Maryam continued, "There isn't a man alive who could wreck that woman's world! Now if we are setting out on a road trip, and clearly that's what we are doing, she needs to tell us the truth. Enough is enough."

"Forget about tomorrow," said Amira, "you need to talk to us, lady. What is your story?"

"Hmm," said Maryam, sitting down on her bed. For a split second she flashed Amira a different kind of look. It was as if she were thinking about the way Amira had asked her all these questions with a mixture of intense curiosity, compassion and fragility all masked as obstinacy. I suppose this alone was why she decided to talk.

"I ... I mean, I suppose you already know ... it's not easy to talk about it. I can't describe it like you. But this notebook you're so interested in..."

"We are not interested in your notebook, mademoiselle.

But we were under the impression you had cancer and..."

"Alright, alright, I get it," said Maryam. "I can read it to you if you want. Because..." She stopped and made an abracadabra type gesture in the air directed at Amira and she said, "Because my big secret is here in this notebook!"

I got the feeling she had already decided to share this secret with us before we had even come into the room.

"On one condition. Every night I'll read you one part from this notebook. And this friend of ours will..."

She pointed at me.

"She is going tell us her problem. Why is she running away from her country? Is she a spy? A terrorist? A fugitive? We don't know."

She was both pulling my leg and deadly serious. "Azizi, I swear there's no such secret," I said.

"Allah, Allah!" cried Maryam. Both of them had picked up this ironic doubling of 'Allah' from me. They really liked it.

"I swear that's the way it is. I'm just tired and the country's a mess. Nothing more than that. I've lost my faith in writing. And I probably won't write again. That's it."

When I saw the strained expressions on their faces I understood just how much mine had fallen. So Maryam didn't push. She reached out for a cigarette and lit up to blow away any bad vibe and with a smile she asked:.

"Well then out with it, what are you going to do (again those abracadabra gestures) in return for my big secret?"

Amira was suddenly bright as a child again.

"I've got it," she said, laughing at the idea that had sprung to mind. Then she said, "She'll dance!"

"OK. Make her dance!"

If I didn't accept this invitation to a good time I knew the moment would pass. I forced a smile.

"Ok," I said. "In any case I've always wanted to be a belly dancer. This might give my life some meaning."

"Really?" said Amira, seriously asking and seriously surprised. If only I could have taken a photograph of that startled expression: those wide-open eyes that were proof she would be fooled by life a thousand times more. If only we could document that look of surprise that remained, despite everything she had experienced, we might succeed in setting up a Museum of Unappreciated Moments. There is no way this woman could have killed anyone. Whenever I saw Amira like this my heart would melt at the sheer beauty. And Maryam would become proud as a warrior ready to protect her helpless child. That was how they completed one another. Like apples and cinnamon, Amira always called out for Maryam. And I am the dough that brings the two together.

"Just a minute!" says Maryam, cutting her off. "This friend of ours…"

"What? What?" says Amira. How could a person be so full of enthusiasm for a life she doesn't even have?

"Now as for you, my dear, these letters…"

"How do you know about those?" I said.

"Eh… You aren't the only one without any shame around here. Maybe I thought Amira had cancer and… I actually did my own little bit of investigative research. Seems the mademoiselle here is hiding letters from us."

"You read them?" said Amira, flustered.

Maryam shook her head. "You are going to tell us about those letters and the person who wrote them. What was his name?"

I quickly whispered: "Muhammed".

And that's how we came to our agreement. Like solemn children with pure hearts making a castle out of cookies…

"You first," said Amira to Maryam. "Read us something from that notebook."

"Strip!" Maryam said and she laughed. We put on our white nightgowns. Maryam took out her notebook. We lay down on our beds. "I already told her (meaning me) the story but you (she meant Amira)," she said, "you must know Dido." Amira nodded and said, "Our friend the queen who came from Phoenicia to Tunisia and founded Carthage. I know her."

Enjoying Amira's increasingly childlike air, Maryam drew out the introduction.

"But you know the whole story, right? She founds Carthage and that godforsaken man Aeneas comes from Troy and she falls in love with him and then..."

"I know, I know, and she kills herself out of love..."

"No, the story doesn't end that way," said Maryam and she went on.

"The ending you know is the one written by men or let's say the ending they take to be true. The real ending is totally different. And my secret lies in Dido's unknown story. *Yani* (and she slipped into an imitation of Lilla, adopting the air of a prophetess, her hands open wide). You need to read Dido's full story to learn my secret. There are seven tablets here. And the secret lies in the last one."

Unable to hold myself back, I said, "Azizi, now look, no matter how you look at it, I'm still a journalist. So for the love of God tell us the end of the story first and then go back and give us the details."

Slipping out from under the Madam Lilla mask, Maryam looked serious and she smiled.

"You, my friend, the moment you crossed that border you stopped being a journalist. Now you're just an ordinary human being."

154

Restless, Amira said, "Oh, now you're just rambling! Just read whatever it is you're going to read."

And with that Maryam began to read Dido's first tablet.

*

Dido's First Tablet

That ship will come and I am waiting. Waiting among the marble columns of my victories with a heart that does not know the shadow of a doubt.

I know that even gods need seven days and seven nights. So then that ship will spend six more days and nights on the horizon of the sea where the sun is born. Gathering courage. Courage for a new life. Everything that has happened will be forgotten to open space for everything to come.

That ship will bring to me a bold warrior, a weary conqueror and a hungry lover.

I will cry out to him: O brave warrior! My name is Dido. The sun and the stars have brought you to this country of mine. O proud sailor! Welcome to these compassionate lands, to the most beautiful country in all the Mediterranean: Carthage! My home is your home!"

When I return to my palace dressed in light purple silks from Phoenicia, my ladies with warm, gentle hands will present jasmine sweets, rose-scented candies and of course full-bodied wines to our guests. They will lay cool cotton beds on the purple-white terrace. Draw the silk nettings around them. Sprinkle orange essences over the dream-laden pillows. Goats and camels will be sacrificed in your honour. The nimble hands of my ladies will peel the meat from the bone. They will feed you the most succulent pieces by hand, piece by piece. Our generosity will astound the stranger. He will grow curious. His solemn airs will melt under the spell of wine. The weary conqueror will ask: "Who is your master? Tell me! Is she some kind of sorceress? Or an angel? Who is your mistress? Who shames us with this unrivalled elegance?"

The denizens will say to him: "Her name is Dido. She came from afar. From the shores of Lebanon to us. When she arrived she was a young and miserable widow. We said that she would fall prey to us in the end. We expected her to marry one of our own; we wanted her to give herself to the village. In the end we said that she would be one of us. We expected her to be as mortal and as cowardly as we were. Finally she would fall into our trap, bow her head and her face would resemble ours. "Dido will submit," we said. Dido will no doubt be defeated!"

O stranger! Dido did more than just found a city for them. She went beyond possessing all the vineyards and wells and ships. It was not enough for her to show them treasures they never knew existed. My anger burned even after they kneeled before me, stranger. Dido made them say, "We are merciless traitors and oppressors." She made them say, "In the end Dido was victorious."

And later these words were written in stone so that gods and mortals could read about it. So that people could see how the widow Dido took her revenge on the denizens who withheld their mercy. She did not stop at building a city but went on to make the naysayers face their shame. O honorable warrior, ask them about Dido. For they will explain it all to you:

"Dido forgave us. Because she is the most good-hearted of all mortals."

Mortals will never attain goodness if they cannot face their shame. They will not find peace until a ruler forgives them. They taught me oppression, and I became the oppressor. I was *disgusted by their clever tricks and I deceived them all. O eagle-heart, they did not receive me as their equal and so I became their ruler.*

I do not despise them. Nor am I revolted by them. I do not love them. Carthage is now a sea without waves, a poem without blood, a rusty sword. There is no enemy I fear and no danger to rouse me. It is a long windless day. I need more air to breathe than there is air in all of Africa. This continent I have conquered is the hide of a defeated lion draped over my shoulders.

O mysterious stranger! I do not cower in the face of your terror. For my warriors could finish you in an instant. They will massacre every one of your men. Now there is but one shadow in my heart: that the ship will bring me nothing. But surely there is something greater than this victory bequeathed to me by the Gods. Something greater than Carthage. My life must bring me something greater than the sum of what I have done. That must be you, stranger. Tell me, great warrior! Let it all begin! Let my heart sail in strong winds again.

O sad and lonely stranger, I am preparing Dido and Carthage for you. Make your heart ready for me! Open your sails for me! Bring me the wind, oh beautiful one. So that a fresh breath fills me.

*

We were supposed to leave an extended hushed silence. Or at least so it would have been like that in a film. But I spoke before Maryam could even get the last word out.

157

"Madam Lilla ... I mean it's strange. She told me that ... she said that, 'Women are the sum of their breath.' Then she read me something from the *Felak* verse in the Koran. *Nefassati Fi'l-u' gad*. I wonder if Dido was out of breath. I mean in the end she says to the man... 'Bring me the wind,' in other words, breath."

Furrowing her brow and twirling her fingers, Amira asked: "Did you write that or was that really written by Dido?"

"I did," said Maryam, "or let's say Dido made me write it."

Amira insisted. "So there's no such thing as these tablets, right? This is just your own story?"

With her hands behind her head, Maryam looked up at the ceiling.

"Let's just say it's the story of any woman who can carry her own weight ... but yes ... It's my story. Let's say Dido's secret is my secret."

We were silent.

"Your turn," Maryam said, turning to Amira, who was rubbing her face. Then she paused, smiling hopelessly.

"Do you have a cigarette?"

Maryam gave her one.

Settling down a little, Amira continued.

"These are the letters Muhammed left behind for me when he left. I won't say anything else. You'll understand once you hear it all."

And with that Amira began reading...

*

Muhammed's First Letter

Bismillahirrahmanihrahim
With the everlasting compassion of love and mercy...

Hey! Don't go and say it's strange for me to recite the basmala. *Accept it. You're a Muslim but you think you don't believe. But Islam is such that some among us become a part of it without even knowing of their fortune. Or else do you really think I would go so far as to fall in love with a heathen! But thinking about it, you probably have already fallen away from me...*

For someone like you blessed with immense goodness in your heart at birth, you will have a place in the Muslim theatre box all your life. And in this mortal play we all have our heads raised, looking up at you. And you, sometimes, if we are so fortunate, will cast a glance down through your little golden viewing glasses to see our public rows. In our ignorance we are paralyzed with shame. Me most of all... Fine then, let me speak of the terrible crime I committed against you. But there are a few things that I need to tell you first.

Counting only the sensual acts we shared together, there are so many marvels we have made and set aside. Though I donated a great portion of it to the poor house the place is still filled to the brim with those good deeds.

So then you have a permanent place in heaven and you should never forget that. You were sent to be among us ignorant savages for a while to give us one more chance to believe. And as for you... Alright, I know, the world is not the greatest place. But you know God and how he bends his mind to those beloved mortals. God is deeply concerned with you. Hey! Come on. Cheer up.

You know the greatest sin is disbelief. Like me you weren't raised with the Koran. Fine then, so the only pious person you know is a fool like me, but surely you know this: <u>That you have to believe. If not your breath that makes this world will run out.</u> It is important to know this: piety means surrendering to shame in the face of the Prophet's good deeds. Piety is putting your soul in order in return for the Prophet's faith in humanity and his commitment to remain gracious in a crude and stale world. My breath is full because God believes in me. And your lungs must be that much larger than all of ours because he believes in you more than he believes in all of us. The only thing you have to do is show the courage to surrender to your everlasting breath. I hope my prayers will take care of the rest.

You know I'm praying for you. If everything goes according to plan you will find a pocketful of prayers when you get to the other side.

There are so many reasons you shouldn't pay attention to those hopeless and feeble attacks that fools who dare to call themselves human beings and even Muslims launch against you, and that includes your mother and father. This might hurt the angels always toiling for you. The one thing you must do is dance. When you dance you give poor people like us a three-dimensional picture of just what heaven might be like. In fact every once in a while I think that a loose-talking angel, who couldn't resist such beautiful dancing, told you everything. And I suppose you don't tell us anything about the world beyond because you don't want to inspire all those people who are trying to get there to kill themselves. Your patience and your mercy is dazzling to the eye.

Don't lend an ear to those fools who think they know

anything about you. A real Muslim does not hold back his love. The rest of the religion is merely the tangled contemplations of experts. Fine then, but you already know all that. Considering you can love more than any of us… And that you couldn't even willingly hurt a soul, you must be the most joyous student in the class. You graduated on day one. And top of the class. What do you say to that?

Hmmm… I suppose there are a few things I should explain about my departure. I'll try to make this brief. Things happened here that they decided to call revolutionary and they are still going on. You know how badly I wanted to leave and for so long. So it seems to me it wouldn't be such a bad idea for me to take advantage of this turbulent time. I feel like it would be crazy to cross the Mediterranean right now, but in fact it would be just the right thing to do. Fine then, just don't worry about me. Ever since that dictator Ben Ali threw me in jail with those idiots, the so-called Islamic revolutionaries who tried to drive me out of my mind, nothing has been as exciting. I don't want you to worry and think I'm under threat. It's just that after five years in jail I came out to see that the bridges had been painted blue. Seems Ben Ali's favorite colour purple is on the way out and people are doing everything they can to paint over all the purple. I suppose our conservative team got involved in the blue trend and now there's a raging market for it in Tunisia. But I never cared for that kind of blue. So I decided I had to leave. Fine then, I suppose that wasn't convincing enough. OK, yes, there is also the reality that one day my brothers with whom we set out in the name of God together will be transformed into petty statesmen in a day. For so many years they must have been secretly exercising because all of sudden they came out looking like the men who imprisoned us. Seeing them I questioned my belief in human beings, not God, but that's still a little dangerous, don't you think? If you don't find this sufficiently convincing either then imagine me reading the Koran from the beginning to end and over again and losing my mind.

I get the feeling you'll come back from wherever you are. With so many merciful angels fluttering around your head, I doubt you could ever ignore the suffering in this world for very long. So I am leaving you these humble letters for you to read when you get back.

You said one day: "You give me such a look that I want to go and get up and come back right away. Like a little girl twirling her skirt, not knowing what disappointment means." Now twirl around for me once. Then step in front of the mirror and tell yourself how wonderful you are. Be all ears...

As the English put it:
Ever yours,
Muhammed

*

This time I didn't dispel the magic in the air because the moment Amira finished, Maryam said, "So just where is this guy?"

I suppose she was stuck on the idea that such a graceful man could actually exist but then later disappear.

Amira laughed bitterly to herself. "Not here," she said. Then she added mischievously. "When you tell us your secret I will tell you where he is, *mademoiselle!*"

"Just what did this guy do to you then?" I asked. Amira

only grunted. She wasn't going to say. Not yet. She only said, "You'll see when I read the other letters."

I persisted. "So this is the Muhammed you got revenge on? Why did you need to get revenge?"

Amira's answer hardly shed any light on the matter.

"Because this country doesn't take men like him seriously. Not Muslims, not the secular elite. They didn't let him live here."

Stories of this kind of injustice dealt to gracious souls were rife in all three of our countries, and more or less all the same, so there was no need for us to say anymore. I broke the silence.

"You said something about twirling skirts... It's like he loves you like a father, with such admiration. Today Madam Lilla said, 'if only men could just admire...' It feels like he has that kind of admiration for you."

Drumming her fingers, Amira replied, "No, no... He loved me like a lover should. But also like my granddad. You understand?"

Who wouldn't?

"That's harrowing, don't you think? I mean everything that Madam Lilla said about breathing in Dido's tablets and Muhammed's letters..." But before I could finish Maryam cut me off.

"Forget about Madam Lilla!" But the colour hadn't drained from Maryam's face because of Madam Lilla. It seemed more like Maryam was upset to see that sour expression on Amira's face after finishing the letter. Brusquely Maryam fired up a cigarette and raised her hand.

"Let's see your dance then, azizi!"

Amira bounced out of bed flashing one of those looks that was perfect for the Museum of Unappreciated Moments and cried, "*Yalla!*"

She took her place in front of the full-length mirror, and like a Casanova, Maryam stood there beside us ready to take it all in. I got up, too. There was no escape.

That was when Amira struck a pose the way a belly dancer lays eyes on women. "Well then let's start with the *Khavagi* from Egypt. The word means 'foreigner' and compared to other Egyptian dances, it's the lustiest one of all. With the same playful flirtatiousness, she invited Maryam to the dance floor, a space no larger than three queen-sized beds. Maryam joined the madness and we were off. Dancing to a mirror in the home of the female leader of the Amazigh militia in Libya. Humming quickly under her breath, Amira made the music. And with quick thrusts of our hips and bellies, we danced. Eyeing one another. Making fun of our own bodies. With no men around we could do a free parody of womanhood, with all kinds of moves. At one point I stopped. "Madam Lilla said…" I began and they both dropped their arms, tired of hearing about her. "Just a minute," I said, "this is important." As we carried on with our dance, I continued, "On our way here she told me… 'Breathing is key to the making of the world and in the making of men.' She said the three of us came on this trip because we were shunned from our worlds. That woman…"

"That woman, azizi, is out of her mind. We ended up going on this trip with her by sheer chance. In other words there's nothing else to it," said Maryam, laughing. With her tongue hanging out of the side of her mouth and vigorously thrusting her hips like a woman from Finland trying the dance for the first time. "No, azizi, it doesn't stop there. I think there's something far stranger about that woman. She left behind those fancy airs when we crossed the border and now she's serious. I think she's far more interesting than those airs she put on when we first met," I said. Maryam pouted to show she couldn't care less. Twisting her hands like they were snakes and marvelling at them in the mirror, Amira said, "Me too. She seems like a solid woman this Madam Lilla." Maryam still seem unfazed. I went on.

"Tonight, I mean a little before we got here ... I don't know ... I felt like she really got me, got me at a deep level. What she said really moved me. Maybe I'm just tired."

The dancing went on and so did I, "This fatigue comes from pushing a pebble up a hill, forget the rock, you get what I mean? You get to the top and it just tumbles down. Get it up and it tumbles down."

"How could I not know that?" said Amira. "I want to believe in people. Always. If I ever lose hope... Over time I would get like that ... you know those kinds of women..."

With grave expressions on our faces, we watch ourselves wiggling in the glass.

"Bitter women," said Maryam smiling through her dark thoughts and throwing her hips out like she was fighting on both sides. Through an increasingly dreamy dance, Amira asked, "I wonder if that's what I will become? Or what we'll become in the end?" She paused and one of those spirited looks flickered in her eyes as she craned her neck.

"Maybe that's why Dido killed herself. So that she wouldn't turn into one of those bitter women."

"No," said Maryam as she sidled up to Amira.

"The more I read the more you'll understand."

And we danced. "I swear," I said. "I don't have the energy to push this pebble up the hill one more time. I just want to sit at the base, smoke a cigarette and think deep thoughts. Friends, just why am I still pushing the damn thing up the hill! I just want to have a long think about this."

As Maryam struggled in vain to liven up her dance, she laughed.

"Here's the rub, ladies. Do we have the strength to carry destinies that resemble no others?"

I added, "Or to use Madam Lilla's words: will our breath be strong enough?"

Maryam answered without missing a beat.

"Or what if we weren't to push that pebble back up to the top of the hill?"

In that moment it all seemed so hilarious that we started to laugh. That's when Amira's shoulder strap fell and placing one hand on her hip and waving the other hand in the air she said:

"Oh Lord, sweetie, Just forget it. What was it that saintly Albert Camus said?"

"What did he say, madam?" I said, leaning back and swirling around Amira.

"He said, 'We need to design a contented Sisyphus.'"

"Really?" I said. "Was there something like that in his essay on Sisyphus?"

That was when Maryam said the words in French as she struggled to make her entire body quiver. They both looked fabulous.

"This breathing business is serious stuff," I said. Bent on making light of it, Maryam laughed. "Then quit smoking!"

"Oh, azizi, what if life is really nothing but the sum of our breath. What if there's no other trick at play. If the magic doesn't just come on its own... If men are the sum of our breath..."

"OK then, but so what?" said Amira, with the gravest of expressions on her face. "Well who the hell cares, we'll just have to become one those spiritual healers that blow prayers in your face!"

Maryam burst out laughing. Me too. Then Amira joined

in. Together we laughed and laughed. We couldn't stop ourselves. And laughter purges you of pain far more than flowing tears. We laughed and laughed. Now and then it seemed like someone might say something but couldn't. That's when Amira said: "And for the Dance School .... ha ha ha... we'll name it... wait for it. The Women Who Blow on Knots Dance School!"

The laughter only got worse the more we tried to hold it back. That's when we heard the scream at the door. And like most Middle Easterners who fervently believe that a punishment comes on the heels of every happy moment, we weren't surprised and the guilt hit us straightaway.

13

The poet leader hit the ground and the women who had been holding her stood there with empty arms. She grasped a handful of dirt. In the palm of her hand dry yellow stones that would never become desert sand. You wouldn't call this crying; her checks were riven with tears. Her face was a dripping cave... She held the earth in her hand, tight, she opened her hand and stared... Then she ate. She ate the earth. The women tried to take the stones out of her mouth, but her lips were already sealed. Stones crunching between her teeth. "Libyaaaaa!" she cried, stones spurting out instead of spittle. The poet leader was mashing, biting, grinding Libya in her mouth. She let out a sigh, blowing desert sand into the sky. And so she joined the other women. Her lips grew thin and then locked. Now she was only breathing in and out. Beyond her there was only a dirty blanket. A night that began with a scream and ended with a scream. Daylight was breaking but it wasn't quite morning yet.

*

Our dance performed in white nightgowns in honour of the opening of the Women Who Blow on Knots Dance School was cut short by a scream. The sound was a black bird whose wings were torn apart in flight. We got dressed and went outside. Women were screaming at a fleet of approaching jeeps; a cloud of dust marked their approach. As they pulled up in front of Saida's house the headlights of the vehicles seemed to freeze the women who emerged from the house. Men pulled out a body wrapped in a blanket from one of the vehicles. They were in a hurry. They wanted to hand over the body as fast as possible, as they had no idea what to do with it. The women knew what to do. The men left the body on the ground. The corpse had been brought home and their work was done. The women moved as if under a silent accord. Some of them were crying, musically. Some of them were shouting. They must have been sisters of the deceased. Six young girls, the poet leader in the middle, slowly walked over to the men. The poet leader stopped when she saw the body in the light.

Four women help an old woman into the illuminated ring – the Mother. She wants to break free of the women holding her back and race over to him. They hold her tightly. Her legs give out but the women hold her upper body as she comes to the head of her son. She begins to ululate. No need for anyone to say anything. And no one does. She wraps her arms around her son. The dust rising in the headlights grows thicker and thicker.

The men are quiet. Lighting cigarettes one after the other. Smoke mingles with the dust. In the headlights and in the shadows they become frail, meaningless, dry scarecrows. Smoking scarecrows. A young man, who must be the brother of the deceased, just stands there. The father arrives. Kneels beside his fallen son: He wails, "God is great!"

Raising his head, he cries again, "God is great!"

His wail is like a bloody vow. An avenging scream before God. From a distance it seems that way. But when the headlights strike the man's face... You see that the old man is screaming to hold back profanity.

"God is great!"

To say, 'Come to mercy, oh merciless one,' he screams, "God is great!"

To crush his rebellion he must suffer. There is no other way.

"God is great!"

The seated mother is swaying from side to side. She is the line on a horizon no caravan will ever cross. A desert without so much as a mirage. Everyone can see through their eyes; the mother fades and fades but she will break.

Head bowed, the poets support the head of their leader who is like stone, her expression blank. She whispers, "Let's go back. To the house."

The poet leader has not fully grasped the situation. Maybe she thinks this is a dream. She's still young enough to think that anything bad that happens at night might be a dream. Together they are devastated. They walk to Saida's house reading prayers in Amazigh, biting back their voices to stifle the screams. The leader isn't crying, not a sound. She is only falling to pieces. Gathering up the pieces, the poets take their leader to Saida's house. Bloody rags on the floor.

Standing in front of Saida's house, the three of us are no longer seen: arms crossed, shrunken and with shoulders hunched. Madam Lilla arrives and stands over the deceased. As the men around her wither and slink away, she stands even taller. Saida is next to Madam Lilla, whose hand now and then falls on the father's shoulder. Everyone is still.

Saida first takes the mother by the shoulders and when she falls she locks her arms around her waist. She holds her. Not one of the men is helping. Madam Lilla is standing beside them. Holding the face of the mother, Saida trembles every time the old woman trembles. She says something to the woman we can't make out. Neither can the woman. She runs her fingers over the woman's cheeks, again and again... Saida then takes her in her arms and sits her down. The woman lets out a scream once, twice, three times and then like a flag falling to the ground she crumples on the ground. Her husband isn't holding her. Saida wraps herself around the woman. Smothering the pain with her own body. Standing there as if she isn't even there, Madam Lilla gazes into the distance.

As the young men are at a loss for what to do they can only adjust the blanket covering the corpse: a musty, patterned blanket. Wrap anyone inside and the name is gone. This boy wrapped in the raggedy, old, patterned blanket would soon join the caravan travelling to the sky, like all the other boys wrapped in blankets just like that one. Maryam's voice goes cold as she whispers in my ear, "Our kids always end up in blankets like that. God damn it, do they always use the same blanket?"

In countries where people carry a picture of death about in their inner pockets, like some kind of lover, why are they so unprepared when it comes to an actual funeral? Those foul and filthy embroidered blankets... All the blankets I've have seen with boys inside... Young men whom I can't even bring myself to write about now...

"I've had enough," I said. Maryam shushes me with an elbow. Amira has her hand on my back. We retreat inside.

They have taken off their headscarves. Hair is plastered to their brows. Faces strewn with hair they leave untouched. Swaying with thin black wounds, they are withering and growing old in Saida's home. The poet leader is sitting in the middle and there isn't a sound or even a poem ringing in the room. Suddenly she sits up. Unbuttoning her shirt, she digs through the layers of clothing covering her chest. Finally she reaches flesh, the point where her two breasts meet. Looking down she buries her chin deep between her collarbones. She looks at that point where her breasts meet. She runs her fingers over her flesh then she scratches with her nails, a little more... She is looking for her heart in the same way you would search for a welt. If she could only find her heart and pull it out she would crush that painful source and be done with it. The girls hold her hands. Stretching out her body from all four sides. Like a dead bat stretched out on a wall she opens up, she's a tortured baby panther, she's a mare that has to be put down, a gazelle on the spit, a stretched-out cobra left to die... One by one all her animals die: all the inner animals that recite her poems. One of the girls starts a song. It is the song they sing when they roll the sweets. But now they are rolling the girl. In the palms of their hands they are lightening her pain, giving shape to an emptying body, a body becoming dough, boneless, quivering with tears. From now on this girl will have new life, a new body. Shaped by the force of grief, she will continue to live in a different form on this earth. Like a sweet that has lost shape on its journey to the front line...

We join the women who are caressing the girl, and blowing and whistling. Amira is crying. Maryam wraps her head tightly and then prays. I remain there as an eye that cannot turn vision into words. Amira puts her head on Maryam's shoulder and trembles. After some time the tears turn into yawning as if she is a child who has been placed in trustworthy arms and read the Nazar prayer. Amira can't stop yawning. I help her up and take her to bed. Her eyes swollen, she seems to be fainting as she drifts off to sleep and says, "the groom. I never thought about him." Closing the door behind me, I hope she will not remember the nightmare she is about to have.

I go to the kitchen. Always the perfect escape. Maryam

comes in behind me. Raising the last words of her prayer she says 'Amen,' and, rubbing her hands over her face, she says *Bismillahirrahmanirahim* then she slips off her headscarf and opens the cupboard. She takes out a frying pan. Finds some flour, a little salt and oil. "Knead," she says. I dip my hands in the warm flour. The oil licks my fingers. The salt crunches as I squeeze and the oil spurts. It must be because I'm thinking of all the other embroidered blankets I have seen that the dough is sticking to my fingers. Maryam is studying the funk I have fallen into. Rubbing her bald head, she pushes me aside. She scrapes the dough off my fingers and throws it back in the bowl. Then only a little more flour. It seems we are getting close to the perfect blend. The rise and fall of dough sticking to every part of the bottom of the aluminum pan. As Maryam pushes and shoves the dough, a steady rhythm comes from the pan. She speaks to the rhythm.

"I don't know if the sum of a life is your breath... But if life isn't as serious as I think it is well then..."

She takes her hands out of the dough, fingers draped with strips of dough. As she speaks she looks at them, clasping her sticky fingers together then pulling them apart. She holds her hands up at the morning sunlight streaming through the window and as she opens her fingers she looks at the thinning dough between her fingers. Her head looks even balder next to all that dough. "Did you know that I took it seriously? When they told me to cover myself I covered my heart. When they told me to believe, I believed right down to my bones." A bitter smile takes shape on her lips. "When they said, 'we're having a revolution,' I slept day and night in Tahrir, got lost, disappeared, became one..."

She paused for a moment, blew over the dough in the palm of her hand, threw it back in the pan, looked out the window and bowed her bald head over the bowl again...

173

"Friendship, politics, love, marriage, living... I mean I took it all so seriously." Turning around, she checked to see if I was listening.

"I understand," I said.

She pressed the palms of her hands down on the dough again, returning to that strong, steady rhythm.

"But later... It's as if... People have two parallel lives. They actually don't take anything seriously but they all seem to take everything more seriously than I do. Same goes for the revolution, for love, covering ourselves, God, death... It's like... Do you know what I feel like?"

"Like you have been cheated?"

"But not the kind from above..."

"What then?"

"'Getting shunned by the world,' Madam Lilla said. Not from Egypt or from society, or anything like that ... but really, getting thrown out of the world..."

She paused again, looked out the window and spoke as if she were speaking to God:

"Azizi, seeing that things are not all that serious, seeing that everything just happens on the sidelines... I mean then why choose me to deceive...?" She turned to me again with dough hanging from her fingers. "You get it?"

"How could I not, azizi. How could I not..."

"There's a scene which I think explains it all perfectly... Could you roll up these sleeves?"

I touched her thin, feathery, dark-skinned arms with the tips of my fingers. If I roll up her sleeves they'll just fall down. So I fold them one by one. Folding them just twice isn't high enough so I undo them and I make three folds. For both arms. I stick my fingers under to see if it's too tight. No. So I roll up them up just little higher and leave it there. Maryam continues:

174

"Thanks... So when I think of that scene I want to cry. I want to cry for my whole life. The superintendent is washing the apartment stairwell. And he told us – we're kids, I'm around eight – he says, 'Come over and help.' And I'm wearing – you see we were going to visit someone – I'm wearing a white dress. But I get all carried away with the broom and I'm furiously sweeping the floors. Water is splashing up at me and I don't even notice. I'm cleaning like crazy. I guess the other kids were with the super, like me. I don't even look around. Then I guess everything is finished and I'm standing there out of breath. I'm a mess and drenched in sweat. Then I look up and I see the kids playing and the super puffing on a cigarette... The rest was always like that. Always like that. You get it? I mean if..."

She started to cry. One dough-covered hand went to her nose and the other held the counter.

"I mean if ... if that guy was anything like me ... if he'd been swept away like me, taking it more seriously than the others..."

She turned to me, her eyes bloodshot, the back of her hand over her mouth, her voice quivering.

"You get it?"

I hugged her. Maryam was like dough, like a child: they both have the same beautiful smell. We breathe in through our noses a couple times. Look out the window.

After the body is taken out of the blanket they give it to his mother. Tonight she will sleep under it. God is great!

"This dough is no good," says Maryam. "I suppose we shouldn't be the ones making it."

She wipes her snot on her sleeve.

All the women inside scream and the dough trembles. The poet leader throws herself outside. She falls to the ground. She looks at the earth, on her hands and her knees. As if she is seeing it for the first time. And then she took that handful and began to eat. Screaming, yellow dust flies out with her breath.

"*Libyaaaa!*"

Opening and closing her mouth, she crunches sand between her teeth.

"Libyaaaa! You wanted blood then? You wanted blood, eh?"

And with that her face begins to look like the faces of the other women. Her lips grow thin and lock. This oasis of women in the middle of the desert tightened around her. She was now a line on the horizon, and no caravan would pass. Dawn was breaking, but it still wasn't morning.

Maryam and I stood at the door. We were like two freshly nibbled, freshly cooked loaves of bread. Two pieces of raw dough. If someone didn't come along and throw us in the oven we would fall then swell and then rot. Clearly we were people who found suffering on the road and not in the bread that women made in times of mourning. Surely that was why we agreed to Madam Lilla's strange, sudden, meaningless offer.

14

"Ladies! You must learn how to kill!"

On the threshold Madam Lilla turned to us in the semi-darkness and declaimed these words that echoed in the cave. The announcement might have chilled us to the bone if things hadn't played out the way they had. Now we knew her words were driven by a deep concern. And the truth is we desperately needed the kind of compassion that slapped you right in the face.

*

Madam Lilla literally dragged Amira out of bed. "We need to go," she said, "Now!"

I could see that in her sudden panic she was really struggling with herself and not us for being slow on the uptake. "We're late," she kept saying. "We need to hurry up!" Her concern was laced with a striking desperation.

"She's gone crazy," said Maryam.

"But she was so strong during the funeral," I said.

"She's not OK. She clearly wants to get out of here fast," said Amira.

"Madam Lilla?" Maryam asked incredulously.

Shaking her head and rubbing the sleep out of her eyes, Amira said, "She can't take it anymore. Was it all the women crying? The boy's death? If we don't go with her she really might lose her mind!"

Saida was standing at the doorway. Lilla stormed out of the room without even acknowledging her. For the first time Saida looked at us as if we weren't spoiled tourists, as if she understood our predicament. Leaning against the wall, she watched us put on our shoes. Maryam looked up at her as Saida gravely said, "Thirina never mourns. You'll see. She can't take the helplessness. Go with her and..."

She seemed about to add, "look after her" but she couldn't and she went into an inner room where she slipped out of her headscarf. She stopped, took a breath and then stepped into the room where all the girls were crying.

While the women continued to fill Saida's home with clouds of tears, Madam Lilla, our queen of salt, hurried out of the house opening her umbrella. The sun was high in the sky but this woman was determined. The plan was to go first to the old city, just three-hundred metres away, and from there to the holy cave. At a time when everyone was leaving Saida's home to bury the young soldier we were on our way underground. Or rather we were stumbling after Madam Lilla who marched ahead under a black satin umbrella marked *Hotel Ritz-Paris*. Madam Lilla was continuously rattling out sharp, rapid notes.

"You can't come all the way here and not visit Tanit. We must go in and give our respects to the Goddess Tanit. You can't start a day like that. We aren't just going to sit down and cry. Or suffocate in that house. We need to get out and walk. You can sleep later. Get some rest later. You might be tired but that doesn't matter. Now we have to walk. Yes, we have to walk. Yes, it'll be good for you to see Tanit. Very good for you. Yes. Yes."

Softly Maryam said to me, "We're being rude to the other women. We should have stayed home." Stones crunching under our boots, Madam Lilla turned to us and gave us a dark look from under her umbrella. She took three steps forward then stopped and peered into our faces.

"Ladies... You cannot stay home. Courtesy should be your last concern. We are pilgrims. So you can't go home. If you go home you'll suffocate and die. You aren't like them. You have to keep walking."

She started walking again, mumbling to herself: "The only thing you need now is Tanit."

She was striding forward as if everyone in Saida's home had rallied together and was coming after us. She was practically running. She was afraid of that suffering paste that stretched from hand to hand, infectious, thick, expanding. She was afraid that if it reached her she would be stuck. If that crying circle got her inside she was afraid she would fade away in the ring. To keep from falling or fading she was searching for something to hold onto. The best thing for her would be to go and see Tanit.

Even Maryam had toned down her usual sarcasm. As for Amira... She was the one among us that seemed most in need of a god. Someone she could pray to and ask forgiveness. I was looking at their faces as all of this raced through my mind but the expression on mine must have been blank because Maryam felt the need to share some of her encyclopedic knowledge:

"Tanit ... a goddess, yes ... Like Cybele or Artemis in your part of the word. For the Tuareg she's Tin Hinan... You see a mother goddess. Tanit is just another stage name."

"We got that part already!" I said. And then I think I understood why Madam Lilla was racing to the mother goddess, fearful that she might arrive too late and miss her, racing to see a mother goddess who had been waiting there for thousands of years.

We stood in front of a hole in the rock that was so small even someone as slight as Madam Lilla had to bend over to get through. She snapped her umbrella shut. Looking up at the sky, she said, "Thank God for giving us these days," and with that she leaned over and shuffled into the cave. She was gone, fast enough to slip away into another world. We scrambled in after her. We stopped and waited for our eyes to adjust to the gloom, until we could make out each other's faces. Then Madam Lilla said, "This way," flashing her light down the middle passage of three. Then running the light over our feet, she said, "Come on, there's nothing to be afraid of." The deeper we went into the cave the cooler and more humid the air. Surfaces became softer and smoother. Amira was still sleepy and teetering along, moaning and griping as she stumbled over her feet. Maryam was letting out little grunts of discontent. I am breathing – my breath was so loud. Madam Lilla's long skirt is rustling. We are rolling forward like a ball of sound. Now and then I can see black drawings on the walls, signs. Madam Lilla begins whispering something, like a prayer. I think it might be Arabic but I can't be sure. Touching Maryam, I flash her a quizzical look. She doesn't know.

As Madam Lilla finishes whispering we arrive at an opening in the wall just big enough for a small group of people to pass through. "Here," said Lilla, "Tanit!" We marvelled at the signs on the walls: triangles, a circle placed on the top corner of one, and between the circle and the triangle a horizontal shape pointing upwards at both ends. So this was the sign of Tanit. It looked like a young girl in a dress. There were signs on every part of this opening in the cave all with various depictions of Tanit. It was as if everyone – maybe only women – had dropped everything they were doing one day and came into this cave to do all this in a single burst of activity. Maybe a thousand years ago women who were thinking about the same things we think about but in an entirely different language sat down here and made a god, like they were kneading dough. Rubbing, murmuring prayers and breathing over them. A sweet humidity filled the cave, a refreshing coolness, a deep relaxing warmth, a prenatal sleep in the waters of the womb. The women had woven for themselves a womb of stone. It felt like we were entirely safe here, apart from the rest of the world. The women before us were the sum of their breath, full of good wishes.

Madam Lilla finished a prayer with her eyes shut. She was either giving thanks to a higher power or making some kind of solemn promise. This wasn't our place, this temple didn't belong to us and like awkward tourists we were silent with our hands respectfully crossed over our stomachs. Madam Lilla opened her eyes, looked again at the image of Tanit, then turned to us and said in a surprisingly polite tone of voice, "Please have a seat."

She stepped over to the image of Tanit and stood there. She placed the flashlight between us. The heavenly beam of the light must have made Maryam nervous. "Madam Lilla for the love of God where are we going with all this?"

"I am taking you to the real you, ladies," said Madam Lilla and Maryam hissed at her like she was hawking a ball of phlegm. "Oh, great God!"

Madam Lilla was unfazed and raising her hand she closed each finger one by one, leaving her forefinger extended, as if to say, "Just a minute." And she began her speech.

"You ... people like us ... we don't agree to a trip like

this out of the blue... We don't take a trip like this to please anyone. You didn't come here for my sake. And not because Amira might have killed someone. You each know why you're here. People like us cannot thrive in the savagery of a home. Certainly there is no need for blood: but in a story that unfolds in just one place someone is bound to be killed. And being on the road brings people together. Defeat, setback and ruin – it's all there – but there's no animosity. That is why we set out on these journeys. But now I know you well enough, you see your own choices as a stroke of ill fate. And now you walk along this road as victims and not as heroes because you cannot come to grips with the fact that you have chosen this path. Ladies, you must learn to drink your own tears and change pain into anger."

Maryam shuddered. She shuddered and I felt a cold sweat oozing out of my pores. I didn't know why. But something happened to Maryam when Madam Lilla said we had to learn to drink our own tears. Only later would we understand why. Madam Lilla went on.

"To stop is to settle, to build a castle. You reject the idea of living like all the others but you aren't willing to show the courage in your hearts. Just who are you then? You aren't the kind of women to build a castle, that much I know for sure."

This time Amira started and quivered and she let out a deep sigh. Maryam and I could hear the moist echo of her breath. She was moved by something.

Madam Lilla continued, "You have clearly fallen into this world. Like all your counterparts throughout the course of history, you are one of a kind and alone. You take life seriously but you do not know how."

I looked at Maryam. This was precisely what she was telling me earlier when she was kneading the dough.

"You must learn this from the Goddess Tanit and all the other wise women and from my humble self. Not because I feel compassion for you, and certainly not pity. It is only that it would be a sin for me to watch others like myself go to ruin, a sin in the eyes of Tanit. That's why I seized you. I took you in my hands, ladies. The first night I saw you, I saw who you really *are*. But how is it that you are now three women in solidarity and so miserable at the same time? Yes, we must change with the help of Tanit. We have to heal you. We must mend. You need to trust me. You are souls that only have a home in each other, you are souls bound to the road. When we come back nothing will be the same. Now that you have crossed the border consider yourselves dead and ready to live. Now you can lose yourselves without any doubts."

Now I was the one who shuddered and Amira turned to look at me. She must have remembered what I had said to her in the school building where the women were mixing sugar: "Now that I have died I can live." As if she knew Madam Lilla was speaking about getting lost. And considering that both Amira and Maryam had just shuddered in the same way, Madam Lilla must have said something that hit them in the heart too.

Blind to our startled reactions, Madam Lilla went on, "Now I am going to take you away from here. We will head south where we'll cross the border into Egypt and make our way to Alexandria. And if all goes according to plan we'll get on a boat and sail to Lebanon. There we will decide what to do next. But I promise you this: it will all be magnificent. You'll find new strength along the way. I have faith in you. And you must have faith in life. Now … is there anything you need to ask?"

What could we ask her? She asked when we had nothing

to say. She asked when we were not really there. As if up against a powerful mother, we were speechless and we had clearly surrendered – though we all had different reasons.

"So then make an oath to Tanit. Right here and now. Say, 'we have died and when we step outside we will be born again.' Ladies, have faith in this and you will have victory."

"Let's go," said Madam Lilla. "Take my hand, I don't want you to get lost." We took each other by the hand and as we made our way out of the cave along a surprisingly shorter route than the one we had come in by, Amira stuttered like a child, "So then ... you'll teach us ... what we don't know... What was it?"

That's when Madam Lilla turned back to the cave and spoke. "Ladies! You will learn how to kill! You will learn how to kill the one that has killed you!"

This wise woman who so wanted to protect us from the world was one of us and her compassionate smack in the face felt good.

She stepped outside. She opened her umbrella. The expression on her face was the one she wore on the night we first met. A little later, as if nothing of any consequence had happened in the cave, she lightheartedly said, "Now you go and get some rest." Smiling, she marched ahead. We were still standing in the cave. Taking my arm, Maryam flashed her torch on one of the walls.

"Have you seen this?"

Specks of metal glimmered in the two tunnels on either side of the one we had gone through. Adjusting her eyes to the gloom, Maryam slowly stepped into the one on the right. Then we saw the chests filled with guns. Another packed with grenades. English writing on them. Others were marked with Qatar flags. Maryam said:

"So I suppose Madam Lilla doesn't see all this? She calls it a temple but it's actually a weapons depot."

"Yes," I said, "she definitely lives in another world."

Maryam was now really angry:

"We've lost our marbles, azizi. The woman is like Don Quixote, lost in a dream."

Amira was the only one who wasn't prepared to betray her reason for shuddering a little while ago.

"But she's our Don Quixote!"

And she walked out of the cave. Like a rosary with only three beads left, we walked home single file. No one said a word. I asked just one question to them both: "Why did you shudder like that when she gave that speech?"

Neither of them answered. The question fell to the earth like a piece of raw meat, rotted there. We went inside the house and we fell asleep.

When we woke up a few hours later the sun was setting. The desert was the colour of cotton candy. Without saying a word we got dressed and went outside for some fresh air. Maryam mumbled to Amira, "bring your letters with you". She said nothing more as we left the house. It was like nothing had happened that morning, the funeral and everything with Madam Lilla. I suppose it was only after walking for some time that we slowly came to understand that what had happened was more than a troubled afternoon dream. We walked up the hill overlooking the village where we could watch the full setting sun in all its glory. Maryam sat down on the sand and we sat down beside her. She lit a cigarette and we followed her lead. Pulling a notebook from her back pocket, she said, "This woman … this woman will either lead us to disaster or, like she said, we'll take the trip of our lives… You asked me why I shuddered. Well here's why…"

And with that she began to read as Dido:

Dido's Second Tablet

Stranger, tonight I had them light all the candles. So that from a distance the palace windows might look like flames. The painful truth is that the sea of your dreams is not vast enough to imagine my existence as queen. What a pity that I am now ready for you. Ah, it is all so clear! Your ignorance will be my negligence.

Stranger, the wine is now coursing through my veins. Heavy red dreams are pressing down on my bosom. In order to tell you my tale, I am tearing it to pieces, wringing it in the palms of my hands, weaving it with silver words.

It was years and years ago, stranger, when the Gods told me that I would be killed, for the most dreadful assassin from the kingdom of Phoenicia was after me. I was young and in my eyes he was horrific. Horrific because we were brother and sister. And horrific because they ordered the murder of my husband king. They took the beloved spirit of my palace with a blunt knife. When such a catastrophe looms it brings a mysterious calm to its victims. I was sleeping as if unaware of what was to come. But the gods woke me with portentous nightmares. Victims believe their innocence might bring them mercy at the hand of an oppressive fate. Before the night was through I hastily filled the hide of a bull with all my gold and all my worldly knowledge. I was only able bring with me but a handful of mementos. And unfurling our sails we struck out upon the Mediterranean, leaving behind the cardamom-

scented pleasures of that place, its cerulean glass and light pink silk pillows, leaving all to fade into a purple cloud. Those who weren't agile enough to save themselves from the cruellest fate had no choice but to stay behind.

With a handful of faithful soldiers we set sail on the Mediterranean Sea. And Penelope... My dear young Penelope. She was born to love me and would die for me. Of course she was there by my side. To this day she still does not know. Her fear is the source of my courage. She cowers and for that I have the heart of a lion. Her fear is the antidote to my fear.

I boarded our ship and the winds swirled around us. Winds are the hands made by the gods for people like me. Unmerciful hands. The gods say what they will say to us with flaming whips. If our hearts overflow it is a proof of their wild passions. Ah! Gods love the mortals who write their own stories the way they love their own peers.

You know so much, traveller! You will board your ship because there is nowhere else for you to go.

I was but a fresh flower, a stranger, all alone, and when I landed on these shores, the savage Berbers were wrapped in crude cloth. On their faces they wore those fearful desert marks. They knew not how to love glass or sand or children. They lived hidden from each other, from the gods, from the wind and the sea.... They hardly spoke. They were crude. When I reached those shores I saw that the gods had left me no place of refuge in this new land.

Rain was pouring down from the skies when I arrived. Through autumn I washed my memories of Phoenicia with my tears. But I gathered those tears in an inkwell. And one night, stranger, in the darkest hour, I woke up with a dream. I knew if I could not dispel it with my breath – if I did not breathe strongly – that this malady called sadness would remain and I would never uncoil that dark giant knot in my chest. The gods told me so much. The gods said, drink your gathered tears. They told me to make anger of my fear. Your anger should become revenge, they said, your revenge should become human life. Drink your tears and let copper water flow over your flesh that seeks mercy. The sky broke open in a thunderous clap and at last the rain came pouring down. I drank my tears and slipped into a dreamless sleep. The morning was gilded like Phoenician glass. I woke with nothing in my breast. Taking Penelope with me, we climbed to the highest hilltop. I breathed in, and, breathing out my eyes were opened and saw what the savages had not seen. I saw the place where the sea hugged the land and I foresaw my victory. The sea is just like me in the way she embraces the shore. If only I could take that shore and make of her a shelter for ships like mine.

The savages laughed at me. They mocked me for taking the land where buffaloes wallowed in the mud. They called me Madam Buffalo. Only to mock me they asked for more gold and then for even more. I fell from grace in the eyes of my warriors. The savages made up distasteful stories about me, and they sang disgraceful songs in the town square. I am Dido, stranger! I founded my city like any other exile unfurling the sails of courage because she is done with fear. With the patience that comes with the desire for revenge I bore the ridicule of the underworld gods and the savages that roamed the earth. And I named this land. I named it Byrsa. A place of refuge. The gods told me: that the exiles pursuing me would come here. Every man and woman crossing the Mediterranean in fear, every ruler fallen from grace, every brave warrior suffering injustice, every princess whose heart has withered after shedding too many tears, they will all find their way to Carthage.

Hey lion heart who came to me without knowing that he had unfurled his sails for me! I have founded this country for people like me. I know that you have also fled. That you are looking for something. For the waves will only bring people like us to these shores.

Hey stranger, I now taste on my tongue the tears that I have drunk. Wine is calling me back to an innocence. My mind is foggy, I am angry for showing weakness, I am afraid at night. Are you curious to know my story? The marble pillars of my city are not strong enough to bear my city at night. Will you hear that which I will not say? In the dark my eyes cannot make out the glorious silk. Ah! Graceful man! Will you be able to deceive Dido who is weary of her powers?

"People grow weary of their powers," I said as Maryam's voice trailed off into the sky. "In any event," said Maryam, "that's how an invitation to a major tragedy comes about; but it seems only women do it like that..."

Pinching her thumb and her index finger, Amira flicked her cigarette butt into the distance. She rubbed her face a couple of times and she looked down at the letter crumpled up in her lap. And she started to read...

Muhammed's Second Letter

Greetings, sweetie,

Hey! You're looking as wonderful as always! But I should remind you again to take care of yourself. If anything ever happened to you the beauty God assembled on this earth would be knocked out of balance.

Fine then, seeing that you have come back home I'll just tell you a few things the angels told me to tell you and then I'll finish without going on for too long. I shouldn't take up too much of your time when your fans, who must have gone wild when they heard you were coming back to town, are chasing after you.

So you see, sweetie, for some of us, the rules of Islam are but a string of prohibitions to reel in our slipshod ways and idleness, but for unique beings like yourself, it is an institution that harnesses the desires in your heart and encourages you to do good. For example, if you as our princess don't have any idea about the proper distribution of religious alms, you might just go ahead and recklessly hand out everything you have, forgetting yourself altogether. You might lose your mind turning every which way to make all the children and the cats happy with what you have to offer. For people like you, who only come around every hundred years, God puts a limit on your goodness and beauty. If we let go you would never stop praying, don't you think, sweetheart?

Hey! Your new haircut really looks good. Looks like you just came back from handing out sweets to kids in heaven. It's only natural you look a little worn out.

Fine then, have a look around. Look at the market stretching into the Old City. Most of the people you see there know how to look after themselves. Though there isn't even one notable statue inside and not one unrivalled mosaic, those people are experts in building castle walls. Now you've been so busy with matters of excellence since the day you were born that you haven't had the time to look into such things. If you could only look up and look around instead of handing out your beauty to the world, you might have the time to consider a defence strategy – you could call a meeting of defence engineers. But you have other things to do and we are all aware of their importance. So you need to set aside this role of victim you often slip into when you say, 'People won't leave me alone, the whole world is out to get me.' It doesn't suit you and you should trust in your angels. If I could just manage to adjust these things and if my prayers made it to the right address then everything from here on will work out in your favour. In the end you should only think about being you. That is to say there is no need to mix cement when you're making a sculpture out of ice.

We all know how you sometimes spend too much time mulling over past misfortunes. That's no good. Set that stuff aside. Here's what I think you need to focus on: through dance you bestow the world with meaning. Now look back at the main square. Every day those madmen are pounding copper, selling beads, trading leather. Is any one of them even interested in where copper comes from? What it smells like and why? What were the wishes of the people who touched this copper before me? What kind of meaning can I bestow on the person who will buy this copper from me? Every damn day he is preoccupied with copper but he has no idea what copper really is. I won't even start with the guys who sell beads. If they had spent a little time trying to figure out why ladies like beads they might become great lovers. As for leather peddlers, I don't think they spend more than a moment thinking about the animal's soul. They are in pursuit of gain and you are in pursuit of giving. And this shouldn't change one bit. Please don't let your past misfortunes say you did something wrong.

You often tell me that they are trying to drive you crazy. You are too graceful to play the woman who gets angry and suddenly cries, "these people are trying to make me crazy," on a brief visit to an insane asylum. If they aren't capable of uttering a single wise word to you it isn't because they are out to get you. It's simply as much as they can do. Fine then, you had no choice but to leave this place because a large group of people mistreated you for so long. You did your time and then you came back. Now you need to trust people. The rest will come after. That's what I told you, we are coming after you with angels. I know I should have been there to protect you with my sword but now I'll have to make do with these lightning bolts I am sending to you to help you in these trying times.

Fine then, you know the Yasin verse from the Koran has always been my favourite. But I suppose I should tell you about the Rahman verse. The gulf between accepting and belief is like the gulf between you and those people. It is important you get this just right so that when you peer into that gulf between you and others you don't go tumbling down. But enough of that. The meaningful message that comes out of the Rahman verse is this: in theory you have faith but you don't really understand a thing.

Turn to the market and take a good look. They are accepting. You are faithful because you understand. Already in your heart there is a mountain plateau that has been touched by the hand of God. The moment you shed tears while listening to the songs of Asmahan you know that God is speaking to you. If we let you go then you will lose yourself in that conversation with God and forget about everything else, right? You are pious because you know that this Godly fingerprint in your heart offers enough healing for all of us. You don't decide to believe, it isn't in your hands, you're faithful because you know without learning how to know. Go to them with mercy, and not with anger, sweetie. They can defeat you with their anger but you have the golden belt of mercy. So take them to the mat where you can beat them! I think you get the picture.

If for just once you can dance long enough I have the feeling you would make the most fortunate leap year in centuries. Kiss your wrists for me. Oh God! Have I gone too far?

> *Your servant,*
> *Muhammed*

"Mercy huh," said Maryam, nearly laughing as she lit another cigarette and stuffed her lighter back in her pocket. "So Muhammed is saying just the opposite of Madam Lilla." Then goggling her eyes and waving her hands about in the air in a parody of a prophetess, she went on, "Madam Lilla said, 'You will learn to kill.'" But your Muhammed is still going on about 'showing mercy.' Which one's true? Muhammed's God or Madam Lilla's goddesses?"

Amira only shrugged her shoulders. I spoke in her place:

"But really, what did Madam Lilla want to say? I guess she was talking about really killing someone."

"I swear you can never tell," said Maryam. "If our Madam has made up her mind on the matter she might very well go through with it. That's to say she would show no mercy!"

"I didn't show any mercy either. Not to Muhammed or to myself," said Amira. She was shrinking down to her core, to her smallest matryoshka doll. I put my hand in my pocket. My fingers touched something made of metal. I pulled out the three Hand of Fatima talismans I was planning to take back to Istanbul, thinking I would give them to friends. Amira didn't seem fazed to see them. "See, these were meant for us," I said. "Look, they were missing and now they are found."

Amira was like a child expecting to be pressured into making up with another child – she was half indifferent, half interested.

"Hey Amira," I said. "Do you know what they do in my country when they find something that was lost?"

"What?" she said, uninterested.

"They do seven belly dance thrusts at the sun. Of course while you're looking for the thing you need to say a tongue twister."

Not because she was very curious but to bring Amira around by getting the story going, Maryam asked, "And how does it go?"

"It goes like this: 'Father Ethem, Father Ethem with the linen shirt, Father Ethem if I find what I am looking for I'll do seven thrusts at the sun.' Then when you find what you're looking for … yes…"

I took Amira by the arm and lifted her up. "We all have to do seven thrusts at the sun."

Amira smiled as if rain drops were sliding down the back of her neck. She was fooled again. And with that we all stood up. In the face of the setting sun the three of us belly danced, sending powerfully wild thrusts at the sun seven times, with the hamsa talismans around our necks. After the third thrust we started to laugh and like all the others whoever went through the ritual we laughed and we laughed.

We got home to find three girls eating pizza and watching *Sex and the City*, their eyes red from crying. It was the episode when the Arab women help Carrie Bradshaw and her friends. The Libyan women stared at the Arab women created by Hollywood. It was a strange sight. When we went into our room Madam Lilla was already asleep. "Just a minute," Maryam said. "You never told us why you shuddered in the cave."

"We can live now that we have died," I whispered into her ear with cheerful relief.

I suppose that was how we chose to live.

15

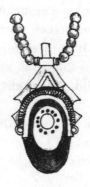

Saida's chador whirled in the air as if she were the matador and the bull. Before we had even stepped out of the car she had whipped out her rifle with astonishing speed, pumped the chamber, clicked open the safety catch, raised the barrel and levelled her eyes on the men sitting in the coffeehouse. It was one of those moments when the whole world stopped, everything suspended. The men were frozen, grins plastered on their faces. Saida took the three heaviest steps in the world towards the coffeehouse. She stopped, narrowed her eyes, and ran them over everyone in the crowd. "Now," she said. "Tell me who's going to park my car."

The back of her jeep stuck out in the middle of the road and the front was up on the sidewalk – it was far from parallel to the street. But Saida was out to avenge all the women in the world who had been mocked for not being able to park a car. The proprietor came out from the back of the coffeehouse with a coffee tray dangling from one hand and walked right into the frozen scene of men with frozen grins. Although he was short, plump and bald and had as much charisma as Zagor's Chico, he slipped into the role of negotiator.

"Oh please Madam Saida! Please!"

The coffee tray swaying under his hand the proprietor then turned round to face the men and said, "But now you gents… " Then spinning back to Saida, "Sister, my dear. For the love of God!" Then hopping back to the men, "as if you don't know Saida's jeep…" and with another bounce back to Saida, "the ignoramuses haven't grasped the situation, but please go easy on them, Saida Hanım!" When Chico finished his little game of hopscotch, Saida showed mercy and relented. Slowly she lowered her gun, her desert eagle eyes still fixed on him. Right away Chico shooed away a group of young men sitting in a corner of the terrace and made a fuss of setting chairs around a table, preparing a place for us. Saida was making a mental note of the faces of the men who had laughed the most when she had attempted the parallel park. Some of them now flashed faltering, apologetic smiles. But like a matador again she twirled her chador to say that she was not going to apologize. The men had accepted defeat and now they wavered between getting the hell out of the coffeehouse or staying and pretending like nothing had happened. The proprietor was still pushing and pulling chairs.

We got out of the jeep. We had no other option but to march over to our table like we were part of Saida's militia. With eyebrows cocked, Madam Lilla looked about as if nothing out of the ordinary had just happened, as if casually taking in the good weather. When she sat down she quickly leaned over to Saida and through pursed lips she said with sarcasm tingling in her words, "Perhaps you need a holiday, my dear Saida!"

Oblivious to Madam Lilla, Saida was still staring at the

men. Her face was still as stone, two lines etched in forehead. If you could read those lines the meaning would be all too clear... They told the story of what had happened two nights before...

*

After the funeral march for the young man arrived at the village, the sweets production line came to a halt. Throughout the day the women worked as if lifeless. They had spent the whole day longing for night to fall. No one spoke. Not even us. Death had spoken. Everyone and everything in the village had slipped into lukewarm silence. Only when night had fallen and the sweet-makers had finally settled down did we understand when it was time for Saida to break her silence.

I couldn't sleep. There was a light at the window. Drawing the curtain, I looked out. There were three floodlights in front of the house. Around them men sat in three rings. Now and then they huffed and puffed, snorted and coughed. Cigarette smoke swirled in the light. Smoke like an accursed prayer. Weaving in and out of the rings, Saida was like a goddess directing the smoke with her skirt. They spoke in whispers. Even the sound of clinking metal seemed muted. In place of the ring of women at the school who made sweets and dough, Saida had formed a metal ring of bearded men. They were unloading the Kalashnikovs Saida had got from the English, wrapping them in pieces of blanket and stacking them.

In one ring men were writing in little notebooks. Other men were inspecting the guns and calling out numbers. They must have been taking down the serial numbers. Saida was probably preparing for blackmail in the event they didn't get what they wanted from the white men when the war was over. In a way she was compiling a written record of the sins on both sides. The words Madam Lilla uttered when we first arrived – you will pay for this collaboration – slithered among the men like an accursed snake...

In another group the guns were being placed in wooden boxes, then loaded into the boot of another truck. Saida was working with such animated precision it gave you the impression the bullets of these guns would never actually take a human life. This was more like a feast of metal. In the white light her skirt spun tiny motes of dust through the air. Dust rises wherever she goes. As she walks she kneads the desert sand, not flour, sugar and salt. That night Saida wasn't making bread, she was preparing for death. As she turned the wheels with her skirt, war was a kind of poetic act.

Saida's daughter wakes and comes to the door. Her mother doesn't notice because she is lost in the operation of inspecting the guns. Here and there the rifles slice the darkness like smoke-grey light sabres and once out of the light they slip into the ire of the night as shades of black metal. Saida watches every movement of the guns, like she's watching fire. Her daughter takes a step or two to catch her mother's attention. It doesn't take her long to understand it won't be easy to capture – she is busy capturing guns. With a finger hanging on her lips she tries to decide if she should go to her mother or go back to bed. Filled with the courage of a frightened child she chooses her mother's anger over the monsters hunting her down in her bedroom. She races towards the floodlights. For the first time I see Saida's face in the light. When she sees her little girl the overwhelming emotion of commanding this ring of death, whirling the wheels of death with her skirt, overseeing this production line of men, falls from her face piece by piece. Her motherhood unravels in the taut lines on her brow. The little one runs over to her mother and stands in front of her. From the shuffling of her feet I can she's on the brink of crying. Reaching out her hand Saida pulls her in, pressing her daughter's face to her belly. Shrinking in fear, the little girl wedges in between her mother's legs, disappears into her dress. Now you can only make out her eyes. A little girl peering at the wheel of death from her mother's belly. Her head quivers only when her mother gives an order.

"Check the serial numbers twice."

She masks that line of frailty that formed in her brow with the arrival of her child by making her voice sound even more like a saw. In that moment Saida looks so much like Madam Lilla.

I am watching Saida. Imagining her as a student in London. Worn out, she's climbing up the steps in Oxford Circus. She's walking by the BBC building, no one noticing her. Holding plastic bags she suddenly wants to sit down in the middle of the road. I can see her giving up on everything. Coming home and scrunching up all those plastic bags into another plastic bag. And then lining a trash bin with one of those bags... I imagine her thinking about how concepts like 'civilization', and 'security' and 'peace of mind' are all filled with those plastic bags.

And then World History suddenly presents Saida with such turbulence, her seat belt is fastened and tray table shut and her seat in the upright position, and her flight is rerouted. And plastic bag civilization is left behind.

She prefers being killed by a single bullet to drowning in plastic bags. Maybe there is a Foucault's Pendulum inside every human heart, which is made of burning steel. When you are standing at a certain place in the world and standing at a certain angle, it begins to swing, knocking into your ribs, breaking open your chest. At midnight in the middle of the dusty desert with her child between her legs and within this ring of guns, Saida knows that the pendulum in her chest is swinging slowly, tapping her ribs but not burning the flesh.

I looked to see that Maryam had woken up. She came over and peered around the curtain with me. "What's happening now?" she grumbled through her sleep. "They're counting our Kalashnikovs," I said, pointing to Saida.

"Do you see her daughter? Under her skirt."

Maryam looked at her. Not at the guns. For some time she gazed at Saida's little girl. They had finished packing and I felt tired. Maryam stayed at the window, staring at the little girl. From my bed I watched her. She had a lump in her throat. She swallowed and there was another. As I drifted off to sleep she was still at the window.

When we left two days later, Saida's little girl was crying. Even though we never really got the chance to talk to her, and hardly ever saw her. In the end she was a little girl trying to be a part of her mother's war; so maybe she was tired. Saida tried to calm her. First she deployed the standard rounds of compassion, sounds, gestures, caresses listed in the code of motherhood around the world. But when her little girl wouldn't stop whimpering she went for an exaggerated display of anger. Though her daughter hadn't said a word about Madam Lilla, Saida suddenly shouted.

"She's not with us anymore. She doesn't live here. Thirina is only a guest. And she'll always be a guest!"

The girl didn't stop. Saida grabbed her and shook her

"Don't cry. There is nothing to cry about."

Saida was shaking her own fragile childhood. To toughen her up she couldn't decide if she should show more compassion or more anger. Her daughter rattling in her hands, she finally came to her senses and smothered the little girl with exaggerated affection.

*

Now staring down these men in the coffee shop, you could see the whole story from the other night and the morning after take shape in her deepening brow. But the men didn't know the backstory in those two lines. Most likely they kept quiet because that crinkled brow reminded them of the way their mothers looked at them, and the Kalashnikov Saida was holding probably had something to do with it as well.

Then a jeep pulled up in front of the coffeehouse. Madam Lilla must have known who it was and she seemed to be suddenly sprucing herself up, slipping into a Welcome Summer Party mode. First a young man dressed in jeans, a white shirt and sunglasses jumped out of the jeep. He looked like he could have been entering a café in Milan shooting a commercial for Lavazza. Amira scratched about like a turtledove. Maryam spread her legs and nervously tapped the ash off the end of her cigarette with her middle finger. Saida gathered up her chador and went inside. She seemed to be running away from a confrontation. The man opened the side door of the jeep. First came the foot, in a white sock and sheathed in a shiny white, studded moccasin, something out of the 80s, but still in perfect condition. We had to wait some time for the second shoe to arrive. Then a cane struck the ground beside them. Black, shiny and ornamented, then a hand, olive-skinned, blue-veined. The hand seemed to say, 'now just a little push', and with that an old man emerged from the car. Coming out he was an old man but as he straightened his back he looked

202

like a lord and when he refused the young man's arm he was suddenly a knight. Could a man really walk with such ceremonial solemnity? "Here we go. Now the film's rolling," said Maryam. She was looking at Madam Lilla, who seemed to be idly passing the time. It was as if she wasn't in the middle of the desert but in Paris about to bump into an old acquaintance; she wasn't paying any particular attention to her surroundings; her role play was just right – she was captivating. Covering only half her head, her scarf managed to expertly catch the wind and undo itself. Somehow her hair was still perfectly in place, loosely tied up in a sweet little bun. Then slowly she turned to look at the approaching man and she fixed her eyes on him, Madam Lilla the female desert eagle. Her neck seemed to grow longer and now standing before her the man was pinned to the spot. His two hands gripping his cane. In the sun he looked like the figurine of a god carved out of a mahogany. They looked at one another. When the old man slowly raised his chin the young man sprang to action, leaping over to the glove compartment in the jeep where he pulled out a box. Like a character moving quickly in a film shot in slow motion, he came back over to us and looked. What eyes. They shimmered like two black marbles.

First he put a large, brightly ornamented, blue wooden box down on the table and then three little green boxes. Pursing her lips, Madam Lilla kept her head high. She made a gesture with her chin that was similar to the one the old man had made. But nothing happened. We stood there. Lightly she turned to us, her lips so tightly locked they had almost disappeared and she raised an eyebrow, nothing more. I got the message and I opened the box directly in front of her. Inside was a large silver necklace. Madam Lilla looked down at it with indifference. Her head still bowed her eyes swivelled to the man and a smile played on the corner of her mouth. Then with another subtle gesture she asked us to open the other boxes. Amira opened them to find three smaller silver necklaces with the same sign. Madam Lilla only shut her eyes in approval. Then the old man walked over to us, as if walking to his past. That's when I realized what was strange about him: his face was blue. Bluish. From a certain angle it was like looking at blue pines. He came and stood over us with no intention of sitting down. Madam Lilla didn't offer him a seat. Leaning his head back, his bluish face shimmered in the sunlight.

"Tin," was all he said and then again.

"Tin... Tin.... Tin Abutut!"

Madam Lilla only ever so gently and imperceptibly nodded. Silence again. The man narrowed his eyes as if he had spotted something in the distance. Madam Lilla brought her hand to her ear. I hadn't ever noticed before, none of us had noticed – she wore silver earrings that bore the same sign as the necklace. She touched an earring then folded her hands on her lap. The man bowed his head and, I think, he was smiling as he looked down at his cane. Then he brought his trembling hand to his inner jacket pocket and pulled out a white handkerchief that was stained blue. He wiped his eyes and put the handkerchief back in his pocket. This time Madam Lilla lowered her head. I don't think she smiled, she only seemed to have accepted something.

"They are waiting for you," said the man, and that was all. He turned and left but then stopped and slowly turned around to face us.

"Do they know how to ride camels?"

Madam Lilla lowered her chin once and kept silent. The old man raised his hand and waved as he left. Piece by piece, he climbed back into the jeep.

"Yes," said Maryam, "unfortunately we have already learned how to ride camels!"

*

"Yallah! Yallah! Yallah!"

"What do you mean *yallah*!? What do you mean *yallah*? Wait a minute! I screamed, looking more and more miserable as my camel suddenly reared up on its hind legs. "Allah, Allah, Allah," I kept repeating until the fear that I might really frighten the beast overcame my desire to cry out.

Sitting on top of a camel is like being up in a skyscraper that can breathe and think; only add to the experience all the bones and layers of skin you feel crackling and rippling underneath you. It's the kind of shock that makes you think – if you are up there on a camel – 'this is the end for me', and if you are just watching you might think, 'how nice if we could just watch this all the time'. Sounding like a father chucking his boy into the sea to sink or swim, Madam Lilla cries out, "You can do so much more than you think! You must learn to overcome your fears. The boundaries..."

I was about to unleash a curse that would travel all the way to Timbuktu. But the crazy camel (of course the camel was perfectly sane, quite mild-mannered even) – ponderously turned round to look me with that gloomy glare, which said something like, "but why all the ruckus, my dear friend? Does such behaviour befit you? Befit either of us for that matter?" I felt ashamed. And in a remarkably short period of time my camel friend and I became quite the team. Better said he treated me with maturity and I came to my senses. In that moment I understood why women gave those quick short breaths when they went into labour.

205

They huffed and puffed like that so that the gusts of air they had swallowed in fear wouldn't burst their lungs. Now I was breathing exactly the same way: in quick, rapid puffs. And it seemed the camel was cursing under his breath; now he was suspiciously silent.

Maryam and Amira had been discussing the Arab Spring from the moment they had opened their eyes that morning. While I was on the top of my camel struggling for dear life, they were still talking.

Maryam: "I don't know how all this sits with Saida... Taking guns from the English then calling it a people's revolution."

Amira: "But it's different for the Amazigh, they've been seeking official recognition for years. For them it's a bona fide uprising."

Maryam: "But you know Libyans..." (laughing sarcastically) "I mean..."

Amira: (laughing) "*Yani...*"

Perched on top of my camel I couldn't help but catch the racist undertones in the discussion. As they ripped into the Libyans, Maryam and Amira were getting on like a house on fire.

Below me Madam Lilla was still talking.

"You already know how to do it. It's just that you've forgotten. Think about it that way. Now remember, just let your body go and move with the camel."

Providing there was a return route from Timbuktu! A two-way street! I said under my breath. Coming out of me were those quick, rapid puffs! That's how we started our aerial dance. With every step the camel took a wave went up my spine and I was suddenly breakdancing, my head shaking like I was making buttermilk. In no time this stupid grin somehow took shape on my face, and Madam Lilla kept bellowing from below, "Don't let yourself go so much, you'll feel drunk."

Maryam and Amira were still at it.

Maryam: "I mean Madam Lilla is right on that issue. Libya is going to pay for this collaboration when all is said and done."

Amira: "First of all I really don't think things here are going to work themselves out any time soon. These Libyan Arabs will never let the Amazigh get what they want, give them recognition and all that, I mean I really don't think so. But in terms of this collaboration the Egyptians... (laughing) Yani... "

Maryam: "What? What's that you say, mademoiselle?"

Amira: "Oh sister, you have got to drop this Egypt-is-the mother-of-the-world posturing of yours. You also collaborated with the army, and let's see how the people in Tahrir get their noses out of that mess."

Maryam: "Egypt, not Tunisia."

Amira: "Oh come off it... Just accept it, sister. We were the only ones who pulled this off."

Maryam: "What does that have to do with anything? You can't pull off a real revolution in such a short time. The spirit in Egypt is changing. You need time for these kinds of things."

Amira: "What do you mean by that? That Tunisia isn't changing? Haven't you seen the people there? They're starting to talk."

Maryam: "Your grassroots organization pre-revolution was nothing next to what we had in Egypt. In Egypt we have civil society groups in poor regions. I have little hope in the opposition in Tunisia. People in Egypt will open up a space for politics once all the fuss in Tahrir is over. Tunisia isn't like that. You only have all this online activity."

Amira: "So only you have such a space. We don't understand shit about what's going on? And when you talk about grassroots organization you're talking about the Muslim Brotherhood. In both elections and in civil group organizations they'll destroy you. Yani!"

Maryam: "Even if no one else knows this, you know that all this nonsense in Tunisia about being 'western' is nothing but window dressing."

Amira: "You got that right but when they draw up a new constitution they won't let a single item in there that has to do with Sharia law."

Maryam: "Sweet dreams, mademoiselle."

Amira: "As if they would actually set up a Tahrir government in Cairo. You never know what will come out of it. Our people won't give the revolution away to people promoting Sharia law."

Maryam: "We'll see about that."

Amira: "Oh yes, we will."

I'd had enough I suppose. I could hear Maryam and Amira speaking to each other hurriedly in hushed tones over the sweet, deep breathing of the camel. Now there was nothing else in the world but me and the creature. It was as if I could no longer see the old man who was leading us. When you truly let your body go everything did fall into place. For instance I could have drifted off on camelback if I just let go. Slipping into a trance, I would cross into the Sahara, the rocking motion was that sweet. Just let me go! Of course the exhilaration didn't last long because when the camel lightly shook his head from side to side, there they were again: my quick, rapid puffs! Madam Lilla was laughing at me from below:

"Brava! Brava! Good, very good indeed. Now he will bring

the camel to its knees. Lean back, not on the tips of your feet, but with your weight on your heels."

I followed her instructions and with a shudder that seemed like an earthquake the camel-skyscraper collapsed with me trying to keep my balance on the top. And then in a flash the building was up again. This time I leaned back and finally the camel sat down on its back legs. Madam Lilla called out: "Tense up your ankles when you jump, but first slide down."

Following her instructions, I managed to climb off. The adrenaline felt like a fresh spring rain; I was drunk on happiness. Before they had even called for her, Maryam hopped over to the camel. When she had woken up that morning she was in a right state looking as if she had stomach-ache. But clearly she was now fine as she stubbornly climbed up onto the camel. As if born in the desert her intention was to get the camel running straight away. Madam Lilla intervened. Looking at me and Amira, she said, "What's wrong with this woman? She looked sick this morning." To which both of us replied, "Oh no, it's always like that, it passes pretty quickly." Raising an eyebrow, she continued to issue Maryam commands. But Maryam was already a camel rider of forty years, joking with the man holding the reins.

Then it was Amira's turn. She reluctantly walked over to the animal and Madam Lilla said, "It's like dancing. You'll do it perfectly. So hop on up and sit there like a lady."

With the man's help Amira sprang up onto the camel in such a way you might think she was a desert princess.

"Getting on and off are the important parts," says Madam Lilla when Amira finished her tour. And with that we set off on a second round. Several times Madam Lilla cried out for us to lean back on our heels. She also had some fascinating things to say about camels.

"The animal you are now sitting on is a hundred times stronger than you are. But he doesn't know that. Only you know that. So you keep that to yourself." Then laughing, she adds, "Just like men."

It was impossible to keep control of the camel and marvel at Madam Lilla at the same time; the first time she really exploded with laughter.

She went on. "The camel should never forget who is in control. Don't assume that control isn't in your hands even for a moment. Then he'll understand. They might not understand anything else but they'll understand this; again just like men. Ha ha ha!"

When we were all up on our camels, Madam Lilla was really having a grand old time.

"Don't look at the camel, keep your eyes fixed ahead. Otherwise you'll get sick to your stomach," she calls out to Maryam.

"Just like men," laughs Amira.

Suddenly serious, Madam Lilla says, "Only if you're stupid enough to pick the worst of the lot. If you actually get tricked into marrying." Her words rang out in the air, creating an odd alienating effect, and she laughed to see her joke had fallen on deaf ears.

I think I was secretly in love with Madam Lilla. Her otherworldly flights aside and ignoring the whole mother goddess spiel and her playing the role of the prophetess, she really was a fun woman. It was like she never took herself quite as seriously as other people took her. And now that we were members of the inner circle, it was like we had tickets to a private show: Madam Lilla Makes Fun of Herself. Amira let out a reluctant laugh and asked, "Have you ever been married, Madam Lilla?"

She was in a great mood and seemed ready to take any question thrown at her.

"Marriage, my sweet lady, is a kind of relationship where you see the patterns of porcelain sets more than you see the face of a man. As for me, thank God, I always had more exciting things in my life than porcelain sets. Ha ha ha!

"Oh my dear Amira, no man would have you for a lifetime. No man would even marry someone like you. And the man who does ... well no doubt he'd need huge amounts of self-confidence."

Frustrated, Amira said, "And so we're always going to be alone?"

Madam Lilla fixed Amira's hair.

"No, sweetie, it's just that from time to time you will be alone. For even the most boorish men will know how to defend themselves against people like you. If they know nothing else they'll know this. I have always believed this is knowledge that comes down to them from their hunting past. And seeing as you aren't birds of prey... Otherwise you wouldn't be up here on the backs of camels."

Amira pouted her lips and looked into the distance as Madam Lilla laughed. She seemed a little offended so Madam Lilla tried to bring her back into the silly game.

"My dear friend, you've been given something that people rarely receive: the gift of dance. When the chance for such a wondrous life awaits you why go for the porcelain set?"

Amira and Madam Lilla laughed together. "And as for you," she said, turning to me with a finger raised.

"You, young lady, it seems to me that you're not looking after your inner garden. I get the impression that..."

She was interrupted by a scream. The man leading the camel in front of us was shouting wildly at Maryam, and

211

calling out to Madam Lilla, angrily kicking up dust. Letting go of the camel, he came over to us. Madam Lilla was waving her hand as if to say, 'what's the matter?' as the man continued to shout at the top of his lungs. It was Libyan dialect which I couldn't really understand.

Amira exclaimed, "Maryam has thrown herself off her camel?"

Maryam returned on foot, "Oh for Allah, why would I do such a thing. I didn't do anything of the sort."

Madam Lilla narrowed her eyes suspiciously: "There's something strange about this woman," she said. It was the third time she'd said the same thing.

*

That morning I was wandering about the house in a daze. Wondering if there were any tomatoes, peppers, cucumbers, olives and things for breakfast, maybe a little white cheese, too, mundane dreams banging about in my head, when I hear Saida suddenly shouting in the living room: "Mother f...!" I peer inside the room where those three girls were watching *Sex and the City* the night before to see Saida standing in front of the television, watching CNN, with the same three girls.

She probably hadn't slept in the night, overseeing the packing of all those guns, but now she looked totally refreshed. Struggling to focus on the screen I made out a map of Libya. Every now and then the heads of three middle-aged men appeared. Then a broadcaster was standing in front of a map of Libya, asking questions. Finally I grasped what was going on. This was truly worthy of some foul language. The representatives of three multinational oil companies and an English man were

212

discussing the matter of Libyan oil. Cool and collected, they were going over what, in their minds, needed to be done... Going on about how they would manage this particular oil-rich region versus that region. A conversation with a running theme of 'oh-we'll-all-get-along-just-fine' but even more astounding than that was Saida's second volley of profanity, far fouler than the first, while the broadcaster went on in his grave tone of voice: "Now of course we do not know how many people will be able to go back to work for these petrol companies as they are actively engaged in the current civil war. We are thus confronted with a problem."

Still wondering if sleeplessness was deceiving me, Saida let fly a real sting of a curse. Now I was sure all this was really happening. "Did you hear that? Did you hear what they are saying?" she said, turning to me. I cursed, half in Turkish, and Saida let rip a few more at the TV screen.

Then she turned to the girls, "We're making pizzas till noon. Then we meet at the school and carry on with the packing."

They would make food packets for the front as if betrayal wasn't galloping full speed right at them with flags flying... and that's how they would defeat these multinational companies. They were going to make pizzas – you still couldn't buy bread. The TV broadcasting would continue. They would continue to stack guns and sweets.

Madam Lilla appeared at the door – we had no idea she was already up and dressed. "Good morning! Today we're going to get you up on camels. Wake up the others."

Say what?

"You might need the skill at some stage during the journey. I thought it might be a good thing for you to know. I'll be waiting for you outside in an hour."

What?

"There's no need to make a fuss, you'll pick it up in half an hour."

Allah, Allah!

"You'll be a bit tired afterwards but then you can have a rest. I'll be waiting outside."

Without giving me the chance to get a word in the conversation was finished. Then Maryam appeared at the door. Madam Lilla called out to her.

"Good morning, mademoiselle. Get ready, you're going to learn the art of camel riding."

"OK," she said, excited. It was said with an enthusiasm I couldn't quite pinpoint. Madam Lilla looked at me questioningly and said quietly, "There's something strange about this woman."

I felt the same. I told Maryam about the TV program on Libya and then Amira, emphasizing how disgusting it all was. It was strange how the two of them weren't equally disturbed. "This is Libya after all," said Maryam and Amira added, "Certainly not Tunisia, and not Egypt either."

Allah, Allah...

*

Our lesson with camels made everything seem strange. Was it the sun or the camel or Madam Lilla's enigmatic words that made our heads spin? We were so terribly tired by evening that before going to bed I couldn't even muster the strength to ask Madam Lilla, who was pacing about the room, what had she meant about my inner garden? All I remember is hearing her warning as I drifted off to sleep:

"You will have a dream tonight. After riding a camel for the first time you always have a desert dream. Pay attention

214

to it. It will tell you something about the lies you tell yourself."

We fell asleep right after sunset and slept straight through till morning. But we weren't really awake until we heard Saida's daughter crying and Saida's show with the gun at the coffeehouse and only when those boxes brought by the old blue-faced man were opened. We had to wait for the blue man to go until we could get back to this matter of the dream. Yet we should have known by then that Madam Lilla's stories would be more than our questions.

16

"It was the night before I saw the three of you tipsy on the hotel terrace in your white nightgowns. Ah! Maybe I shouldn't tell you this but I am going to anyway. (Laughter.) Even if you wanted to there's no turning back now. In any event I believed in you because I saw you that night, like I'd seen some kind of sign. If you ask me even then I already knew we'd be setting out on this journey together. That night you saw me, it was sort of linked to the big dinner the night before. As they say in English, I was feeling blue. For the first time in years I was drinking alone. That's why I played Walla Zaman for you. All those years and no love. Oh, sister Warda. What a woman she was! In any case... The night before I'd hosted a large dinner party. I sat everyone down at the table... (laughter) All the men of my love life. All of them! Around the same table. They came from all over the world, some from very far away (laughter that took your breath away). Oh how they had aged. But not me, oh no (clasping her hands and placing them in her lap, she inspected her manicured nails). I'm a lucky woman. You see I can call and have dinner with all those people who would normally end up as a photograph in an album. That night was like going through everything in my album before burning it. I made all of them their favorite food, which truly surprised them to say the least. Only one person didn't come. He was the old man you saw this morning, (then, turning to me) the one you call the man with the blue face. Perhaps you don't know why he's blue. I'll tell you. He merely sent me a short note, explaining how he loved me too much to come to such a dinner and so on. And he sent me these earrings. (*The same ones she had shown to the blue man that morning in the coffeehouse.*) With the same symbol on the necklaces he gave to you. (*Again looking at me.*) The blue-faced man didn't come to the dinner because he loved me while I was entangled in a passionate affair with Saida's uncle. But he wanted me. So they arranged for an elaborate duel in the middle of the desert. On camel back. He doesn't use that cane just because he's old: it's because he wounded his leg that day and it never fully healed. He used to call me Tin Abutut. And you see, he still does. (*Smiling she quickly turned to the mirror and looked.*) In the Tuareg language those words mean, 'the woman with a vast shore'. At the same time it was also the ancient name for Timbuktu. He loved me and he suffered dearly for it … so much. (*She held back a growing smile to show she wasn't all that cruel.*) After all those years and everything that has happened, he still does whatever he wants. He is a gentlemen and well-respected among the nomadic tribes. We cannot pass through the desert without his permission. I didn't want to say all this in front of Saida because she still believes I left because of the duel. That is the story of the earrings and the old blue man. Truth is I was surprised to see him come and curious that he was willing to help us. I thought he despised me. This means he still loves me. (*Again she stared down at her hands in admiration for some time.*) As for why we came to Yafran…"

Yes, this was the story we had been waiting for since morning. Waiting since we'd left the coffeehouse in Saida's jeep and set out for Yafran. When we were finally settled in that strange hotel room, Madam Lilla, dressed in her purple nightgown, told us everything. We had waited for this since Maryam had cried out in the car "Alright then but why do we need to go to Yafran!"

217

*

Maryam might very well have been in a sleep-addled daze or unnerved by Saida's armed parking operation and the dramatic encounter with the blue man, but her attention was still fixed on all the mundane details of our impending journey. As we left the coffeehouse and made for Yafran, she asked Saida for a map of Libya. When she finally managed to unroll the map and pinpoint Yafran, she protested.

"Fine, but why Yafran? It's not even on the way! It's north of here. Aren't we travelling south? And on top of that there are still skirmishes flaring up in the north. I'm getting the feeling you're trying to get us killed, Madam Lilla!"

Madam Lilla was clearly irritated by this interrogation to do with such trivial details as north and south, war and death. Amira and I had left the matter in the hands of God but it wasn't going to be easy to convince Maryam. Madam Lilla pretended not to hear as Maryam shouted in her ear, "Fine then, but why Yafran?"

Raising an eyebrow, Madam Lilla turned slightly but with no intention of answering Maryam's question, and, as if speaking to a void, "I thought it would be a good idea to go to Yafran. There is a house there that I think you might like to see."

Then as if she hadn't heard her previous question and as if she'd just noticed Maryam was leaning over her:

"Especially you, Maryam Hanım. I think it might be a very good idea for you to visit Dido's home."

Her eyes wide open in surprise, Maryam responded like a robot, right on cue

"Which Dido?"

"Aren't you a professor on the subject? I'm talking about *the* Dido," said Madam Lilla.

Ruffled by a scrap of unknown information to do with her area of interest, Maryam was suddenly the classic academic caught off guard, and, fumbling about like a child, she said:

"Huh? Um ... hmm ... Dido doesn't have a house there. I mean, there's nothing like that in Yafran. There shouldn't be."

Madam Lilla responded, "Hmm," flashed half a smile and then added, "My dear Maryam, the house you are going to sleep in tonight is none other than the house of Dido. You can be sure of that."

Maryam slowly let go of the seat in front of her and as she leaned back a strange expression came over her face. Amira and I were holding back our laughter – you could see it in the twisted expressions on our faces. My forehead was scrunched up into a number eight and I couldn't help but say: "Weren't you researching Dido, my dear Maryam?" Making a face, she looked at me. Forcing back her laughter, Amira answered for her.

"She's also known as Elissa!"

Maryam was still mumbling:

"There couldn't be such a place there. Absolutely no way."

"I spoke to Eyüp Bey this morning," said Madam Lilla. "And I made a point of bringing up this matter regarding the hamam." She was clearly addressing Amira. "We need to wait a little longer. But it seems Eyüp Bey will be able to settle everything."

"Settle what?" asked Amira.

"It's still too early to say. But I can give you a definite answer in a week or two. For now we can only wait." And with that she left Amira hanging on a thread, her curiosity aroused. She looked over at us.

219

"So we'll be on the road for a week or two or more, is that it?" said Maryam, slightly on edge. In a sweetly teasing tone of voice, Madam Lilla struck back.

"Is that so bad? Some of us are learning something new every day!"

Amira and I laughed and Saida joined in. Of course Maryam looked at me and Amira and said, 'Ha ha ha!' She was not prepared to relinquish her bad mood.

Madam Lilla had been putting on airs all morning. She was already in a different mood when we left Jadu and even when she spoke of reaching the open sea, she had found the poet leader among the girls who were seeing us off. In a flat tone of voice this is what she said.

"What you have in your heart will always be with you. It has nothing to do with anyone else and won't have in the future. Love had nothing to do with him and won't have anything to do with him. Someone else will come to take his place, and love will always stay with you. Make space for what is to come."

Like a robot, just like a robot. Sometimes you wanted to kill the woman. And just when you thought you might actually do it she would come up with some new trick and... It wasn't love or warmth you felt for this woman but fascination. And because you were so eager to hear the rest of her story you couldn't risk giving up on her – she was that kind of woman. Not someone out of a dreamy art film about Scheherazade. Our Madam Lilla was a documentary in herself: entirely real.

The poet leader didn't say a word. She only looked as if she might curse us. Madam Lilla wasn't bothered by the look in the slightest. Taking Amira by the arm, she said, "It's time to get going," and then she whispered, "When the pain passes those are the only words she'll remember."

Once again Madam Lilla was the captain and commander. When she was in her stride she looked at least twenty years younger. It was something to see. And that's how we set out together. As we travelled further and further I couldn't stop thinking about the poet leader's stony face. As if someone very similar to me was born in the desert. They had grown and blossomed but now a branch was broken off by the war.

"What will happen to the poet?" I asked Saida without giving it much thought. Just like that. She looked to the left and to the right, fiddled with the rearview mirror and finally pushed a CD into the player, thinking she could just pretend she hadn't heard me. I felt really down. What was the deal with these guerilla leaders and their butch style? I'd asked a simple question. And as I was brooding over the dumb tourist treatment I was receiving, the song kicked in:

And I go back to black...

I curse out of joy. Amy Winehouse's voice can cover all of the earth. We are barrelling along. Amy is singing in the middle of the desert. Saida is gravely thumping out the rhythm on the wheel, humming along to the chorus. The three of us are sitting in the back in a mild state of shock, befuddled expressions on our faces. Madam Lilla is nodding her head, lost in thought. Is she thinking about the poet leader or is she trying to make sense of Amy Winehouse, who is the outcome of this age of ours? All of a sudden she says, "The poet leader will learn that her gift will not end with someone's death. And that love belongs to her. This poor girl, for example (referring to Amy Winehouse)... she can't handle what she's been given. You can tell from her voice. Just like Billie Holiday. And then... What was that poor girl's name... Janis Joplin..."

How can this woman be so sure?

"It's always the same story. They can't pull themselves together. They can't protect themselves; they can't possess what is given to them; they are like colourful birds that can't fly. And someone is bound to shoot them. Tell me who shot this girl because she carries such pain in her voice?"

Our mouths open in surprise; none of us have an answer. Then Saida said, "Her husband. Or I should say the man she married. A good-for-nothing shit."

Nodding her head as she tapped out the rhythm of the song on the window, Madam Lilla seemed to be saying, of course. She went on speaking with *Back to Black* in the background.

"Now I'm talking about you two in particular (she meant me and Amira). You need to believe in your ability to use the talent you've been given. Because such talent ... sadly this is the world we live in ... my dear Amira, you're listening to me, right? With the talent you have they are going to try to destroy you instead of protecting and caring for you. They will try to convince you that you are worthless. To beat them you must believe that something or someone loves you deeply. That is why you need to believe in a god or a goddess. You can't just love yourself out of the blue. You can love yourself only if you believe that a god loves you, that someone loves you. You must believe this or else you'll lose your mind. Look, this poor girl lost hers. She'll take her own life. Or did she already?"

Saida nodded and let a sarcastic grumble out of the corner of her mouth. It was like a bullet had lodged in her flesh and ached. "Alright Thirina," she said, "go ahead and tell them, when no one is willing to love them and they are all alone with their gifts, like you promised..."

She couldn't finish. Though she sounded tough, she left the sentence in mid-air, her voice trembling.

"Is this what you're trying to say, dear Saida? 'That you will always be with them like you promised?' I think that might be it..."

Saida's eyes flashed angrily in the rearview mirror. Madam Lilla's voice was completely flat, the same voice she used while speaking to the poet leader:

"No, I will not. I will do everything to help these people as much as I can. Not with compassion but with a road map. I am nobody's mother. If I wanted to be a mother..."

Saida was tough but Madam Lilla was a rock. If her voice so much as trembled you'd think there'd been an earthquake and not a tremor. She had taken up her position. Saida only shook her head as if to say, let's drop it. Clearly this was an old scar and she didn't want to pick at it now. And so we listened to Amy Winehouse songs over and over again. The third time through Maryam lit a cigarette during 'I Cheated Myself', without asking Madam Lilla, even though Maryam knew she was uncomfortable with smoke in the car, although she occasionally had a cigarette too. I followed her example. Then Amira. Then Saida jumped in and lit up even though she never smoked, thinking what the hell let's burn.

"So this blue-faced man..." Maryam suddenly said, drawing out the words. Saida shivered even before the question was finished. Madam Lilla seemed ever so slightly on edge. Then before Maryam could finish, she said, "later" making it clear the conversation was closed. Taut as a bow, Saida turned to Madam Lilla.

"Anyway," said Madam Lilla. "We're now in the lands of al-Kahina. But I suppose you already know that."

She looked at me again because I was the most ignorant

of the group. But thanks to Maryam I already had this particular piece of information, which she'd explained to me when we talked about Dido in Tunisia. She was the woman ruler who retreated to the desert and ordered her people to leave the fields barren at the expense of decimating her own army, and who refused to be taken as a slave and eventually risked mass suicide with her army when the Umayyads were taking control of northern Africa.

Madam Lilla turned to Saida.

"I know this is going to make you angry but don't be, Saida. I will make this clear. You are losing. You are losing because you are winning. You are losing because your victory has come to you too easily. If your uncle were here … I wish things had worked as he said they would. If only the dream would come true with your victory. But now it's only drawing the Americans and the English in, who have wriggled out from under their sins as if they have done nothing wrong. Everyone is more excited than they should be. Especially the youth… They don't understand. In the end they will be…"

For the first time Saida spoke with real sincerity in her voice.

"Madam Lilla, you aren't here anymore. Times have changed. This is a different country. Forget about the magic, and your belief in fairy tales. You're getting old. You don't know anything anymore. The life you're talking about never even existed, nothing is the way you imagine it to be. That goes for people and for life… You're … smothering everything in a magic blanket. And when you pull it back you don't like what you see, no? Well welcome to the world, Madam Lilla, where everything is more flat, ugly and ordinary than you ever thought. None of us are worthy of you. None of us can match your flights of fancy. None of us are good enough. You'll die before you can accept the world for what it is. And the thing is you're doing such a good job of deceiving yourself that you always find new adoring fans that love to watch." She motioned at us before continuing. "But they'll see the truth as well. They will grow tired of your lies. When this hippy craze is over they'll see that you always leave!"

We were like ice. It was like a wrecking ball had just smashed into one of the supporting pillars of La Scala. A second passed in icy silence and then unexpectedly Maryam shouted, "Pull yourself together, Saida Hanım. Watch what you're saying!" And she didn't stop there. "Or I will do it for you!"

For the next hour we only stared out of the windows.

"At last," said Madam Lilla as we pull into a little village. Yafran. We stop in front of a green garden that stands out against a background of dirty yellow. An old plump woman with a smile on her face is standing in front of the garden gate with her hands clasped. As if there is a motor in her hips powered by joy, she begins shuffling over to us the moment she sees us, letting out sharp exhalations, shifting her weight from one hip to the other as she makes for the jeep. This is the sheer joy that is particular to people who live far from others and fill a garden with flowers. Next to her there is a middle-aged woman and a younger woman with a little girl tugging on her dress. They all had similar faces. Madam Lilla got quickly out of the car. And the old woman spoke to Madam Lilla as if she were reciting a prayer of joy.

"Welcome, Thirina. Welcome to the house of Dido."

In the face of the woman's joy Madam Lilla's lofty air seemed even more imperious. But this old woman could bring a smile to anyone's face. She really was funny. Meanwhile we climbed out of the jeep one by one, a chain of rising tension. Maryam seemed keen to get into the garden as soon as possible with no desire to say goodbye to Saida.

But Saida had something to say before she left us. For the past three days her tough guerilla style kept her at arm's length but now she must have felt that Madam Lilla had turned us all into her sidekicks. Or maybe she wanted to explain the rift between her and Madam Lilla. She couldn't say this to Maryam because of her outburst on the road. And maybe because she felt Amira was too beholden to Madam Lilla she didn't speak to her either. In the end she opted for me.

"I'll only say this…"

Biting her lower lip, she looked like the kind of mother who behaved like her own daughter when she wasn't around. And like her own daughter her feet were fidgeting nervously.

"I know she can't hurt you like she hurt me. I was a child then. My only crime was falling in love. And giving up on myself altogether… Her name is Thirina. A name that means love. But she punished me for my love. She would only ever give up on another man in the name of love, and she never gave up on herself. I know her boundaries and that's why she hurt me."

Tears welled up in her eyes and, turning away, she began to shuffle her feet again. She wanted to say things that would make her seem even more cruel; things about 'mother Thirina' but she managed to pull herself together and her guilt overtook her anger.

"You need to remind her that she has responsibilities. Because she dragged you into this brilliant world of hers… she can't just kick you out … leave you high and dry."

She drove her heel into the ground as if she were trying to drive back the tears. As a woman who knew how to kill in a desert, she was now ashamed to be shedding tears for an old memory in that same desert.

Meanwhile Madam Lilla was standing over the boot of the car. Naturally she was waiting for someone to come to help her with her bags. Saida was the first to react. She went over to her and muttered, "They'll come to get you in two days. If they don't, let me know." Madam Lilla only waited before Saida added, "I will always be there for you."

Madam Lilla didn't answer and Saida wasn't expecting to be forgiven. Clearly their stormy relationship was always like this. And then, jumping back into the jeep, Saida was gone in a cloud of dust.

The young girl came over and whisked the bags out of the boot. Looking up at us, she said, "good morning," even though the sun was just setting. Then she let out a sisterly giggle. In a flash she gathered up our bags and disappeared into the garden. Behind me was the youngest girl, who must have been about six or seven years old. I couldn't see her face. For a moment slipping away from her bubbly good cheer, the old woman took each of us by the hand. For a moment, only a moment, a grave expression appeared on her face as if she was checking for a pulse. Like she was carefully taking our temperatures from the heat in our hands. When she finished with each of us she returned to her former lively self, laughing as if she knew a funny story about each of us. The middle-aged woman was more balanced in expressing her joy and putting her arm around the older woman she invited us to come inside, the two of them saying together:

"Welcome. Welcome. Welcome to the house of Dido."

Maryam looked at the house. She was intent on working

out whether Dido had really ever lived here. She wanted to know. Her intense curiosity made her seem like a humourless judge in comparison to the lighthearted women of the household. The middle-aged woman then took Maryam and Amira by the arm and said, "This is Dido's home, come in. The door is always open for Thirina's girls."

Madam Lilla put her arm in mine and we stepped into the garden. Which was bursting with blooming redbuds which should have been impossible in that climate and season.

The middle-aged woman stopped on the threshold, her eyes suddenly brimming with tears.

"It's been years, Thirina. Welcome home."

Looking around like a proud interior minister overseeing newly constructed bridges and dams, Madam Lilla took in the place. "We will get some rest, Hatice, are the rooms ready?" she said, and nothing more. For our arrival the woman had thought of everything: everything was sparkling clean and white. There was such peace and quiet. We went into an underground house that was nestled inside a cave. There were no windows but it was elegant beyond belief. Dark red satin, gold studded pillows, dusky rooms. It felt cool, maybe because the walls were covered in wicker. And the soft wicker under your feet gave you the overwhelming desire to kneel down and touch it. The centre hall opened onto three rooms. The bathroom was along another corridor. The kitchen was underground. Candles flickered in every corner. There couldn't be a better place to tell a story or share a secret. It was underground and windowless but you didn't feel smothered or suffocated, only this surreal sense of release and comfort. It was as if every bit of lace, every detail, had been designed in a long played game of house. If you were to create a house of compassion in a fairytale this would be it. The desert outside was another world altogether.

Madam Lilla went into a bedroom with a single bed and we went into one with three. It seemed like Madam Lilla was back in a house she'd only left a few minutes ago. The three of us were watching silently, trying to understand this game of house that had started before we arrived, trying to figure out the roles of the objects and their stories, and waiting for this dream space to settle in our minds so that we could get on with the game.

Slowly we went into the little bathroom, one by one, where we sat in the basin under the cascading water. Silently we swaddled ourselves in white towels. Then we slipped into our nightgowns. After the deadly, panic-struck world of Jadu, world of guns, we slipped into the silence of Yafran that healed everything that crossed our minds, joyfully licking each of our wounds. The room was spotless. And cool. Not a trace of the desert. Madam Lilla appeared before we went to sleep. In her purple silk-satin, dotted nightgown she looked like a wise sprite wrapped in tissue paper. As she walked the purple silk seemed to hover weightlessly in the air. She sat down on the corner of Maryam's bed. "Let's leave this matter of how this house in the middle of the desert once belonged to Dido until morning. But as for the blue-faced man … whom I couldn't tell you about in front of Saida…" Then she told us what we had been dying to know since the morning.

"It was the night before I saw the three of you ladies dressed in white nightgowns on the terrace of that hotel. Ah! Perhaps I shouldn't tell you this, but I will…"

Oh the joy and pleasure she got from recounting the story. But we could sense that there was something she wasn't telling us. She stopped before getting to why the man's face was blue and the symbolism behind the earrings and the necklaces. Turning to Maryam, she said, "As for why we have come to Yafran. This is a special place. And my... There is something I need to collect here. Something special. Certain private affairs must be handled with special implements. Because..."

Suddenly she stopped again, "I'm tired. We'll talk tomorrow."

No one took offence. Amira said, "You didn't ask about our dreams. The ones we were going to see after riding a camel for the first time." Madam Lilla let out a sly laugh.

"You seem like the kind of women who can decipher a dream. There's no need to tell me about them."

We didn't push the matter further and she was gone.

As Maryam drifted off to sleep she said, "I shouldn't say this but...

"I know you like Madam Lilla and her secrets and all that but this matter of the blue-faced man. The man is a Tuareg. The Tuaregs are known as the blue people. They are the largest nomadic group in Africa. The men cover their faces with a thick blue cloth. Over time the cloth leaves a lasting blue stain. So they are called the blue men. The necklaces... Each one is a symbol of a tribe. In other words the symbol on that necklace refers to his tribe. So I guess Madam Lilla doesn't really have all these wild secrets after all."

"The women in those tribes don't cover themselves then?" whispered Amira sleepily.

Pleased to use her knowledge to rattle Madam Lilla's throne, Maryam said:

"Do you want the truth? Or the fuss to do with the fairytale?"

We all laughed. Maryam went on.

"They say that in the Old Wars women fought on the front

lines because the men were too scared. Since then the men have always covered their faces in shame. But the truth of the matter is…"

"Azizi, we couldn't care less about that," I said. "And neither do we really trust you anymore, Maryam Efendi. Look, you totally missed something as big as Dido's house!"

And we all laughed. The room filled with joy and took hold of us and we drifted off to sleep. It was a room made ready for us by the women of Dido's home.

None of us ever spoke about the dreams we'd had the night before, the dreams that, according to Madam Lilla, had to do with the lies we told ourselves. For Madam Lilla it was always tomorrow. She had stories that stopped in the middle because the following day was still coming. Madam Lilla carried the weight of secrets that couldn't keep up with time. She had blank pages in her stories that were mentioned but never explained. A new day came so quickly that we could hardly remember the troubles of the day before. Saida had called this, "covering with a veil of magic," and for Maryam it was just a lie. As for Amira, she had called Madam Lilla our Don Quixote. But one way or another this woman kept time moving. And what she was going to take from Yafran was truly special. We waited until dawn for it. Scheherazade had nothing on us! A miserable slave talking to stave off death. With our stories we kept the world spinning for one more day. Oh and what a story we would hear on the following day! And as for our dreams … the time would come for those too.

17

Holding the long handle of a broom, Maryam dashed out of the garden tent where we were having breakfast.

"I don't want to get better. There is nothing wrong with me! Just leave me alone. I only want the truth."

The sun was already high in the sky.

"Hasn't anyone ever healed you?" asked Madam Lilla, cold as ice. With a crushing tone of voice dressed in the finest shades of compassion, she said, "Hasn't anyone ever helped you get better, my child?"

Suddenly pulling herself together after her 'therapy' session (she had been crying off and on ever since), Amira answered Madam Lilla's question, "No, Madam Lilla. And I'm sure that you already know that. In any event didn't you tell us that already! Nobody can do anything for people like us because we…"

Once again it fell to me to finish her sentence. But my mouth was sealed and I didn't know what to say.

"People like us have to self-heal. No one would believe that we really needed help."

Amira turned to Maryam. And she recited from Dido's tablet.

"The Gods love us as they love their equals."

The three women of Dido's home stood in the corner of the pavilion, watching this sudden eruption of emotion. We must have looked really funny. In the face of our three-person, small-scale revolt, Madam Lilla was hardly shaken – she only flashed us a knowing smile from the divan where she was stretched out and said, "That's what I thought, too."

The three women of the house of Dido stood silently together. All our fussing and fighting in the middle of the desert seemed all the more meaningless in the face of their purity. They looked at Madam Lilla to find out what they should do but she only smiled. At last she slowly sat up, left the tent and approached Maryam.

"So you want the truth, huh? Then you will have it! Samira! You can now bring me what I entrusted to you."

Samira shuffled towards us with a little velvet pouch. We might have been frightened to discover what was in it if we hadn't been through so much over the last few days. Indeed if we hadn't been through so much that morning we might have been surprised.

*

We didn't realize how early it was when we got up that morning. As she made her bed, Maryam seemed to pick up a thread from the night before.

"But of course it would have been impossible for me to know. I mean who would have guessed that Dido had a house in the middle of the desert in Libya? In any case this is more a tourism matter than academic. I mean three strange women, including a mother and child, get swept away with the wild idea of opening up such a place to the public. What does that have to do with academic research? It's entirely normal for me not to know anything about this."

"Of course," I said, teasing her. "Azizi, it's nothing but a piece of information for tourists!"

Amira woke up in a totally different mood, laughing and messing around. She had the sweet madness a loner has when she is joking with herself, "I wonder if I should set

233

up my dance school in the middle of the desert? Wouldn't that be something? I could dance without anyone ever seeing me."

Suddenly it seemed like she'd heard a voice in her head, and her eyes were on a fixed point in the distance, like she was trying to catch the slippery tail end of a dream. Both Maryam and I were quiet because we knew what a subtle game that was. Then grabbing the tale and the gist of the dream, she said, "I'm travelling from somewhere. Holding suitcases. Maybe from New York. There's a big house. Made up of boxes of little houses. It's our house. I go inside. Then... wait... This part's confusing. I think I see my mother. Yes, yes, I see her and she says, 'We're going to have something to eat. Everyone's here.' I go to my room. No, no, I can't find it. Mother isn't surprised that I've come, and I'm upset. Then I go into a corridor but the house is like a maze and I can't find my room. Then I do. It's full of light. I'm confused. I wonder if this really is my room. Then I start to change but I stop, naked, looking out of the window at all my relatives. They see me like that. They wave. But in a garden far away. I think to myself, no they can't see me. I'm not sure. Then I leave to go to the garden but this time the house is even more of a maze. I can't find the front door. I get frustrated and scared. Finally I find the door and I step outside. Mother is there waiting for me with all our relatives. 'Oh I was so worried about you,' she says. Angry with her, I say, 'If you were that worried you would have called.' Turning to our relatives, she says, laughing, 'Ah she's so angry with me!' I'm about to cry. Actually I think I did cry. Then I woke up."

We listened carefully to everything she said, as if it had really happened. My own dream had just left the station of my mind and the moment I began thinking about it the train

234

was already roaring ahead, "Did I cry, too? I think I did. But why in the world would I?" They didn't break the silence. They were waiting for me to race after it, jump on and walk up to the engine room from where I could explain the entire dream. Finally it came.

"There was this young girl I really adored. She said, 'I am going out to get the news.' She's going to a really dangerous place, and I'm upset about it. There's a press meeting going on in a room, all men. Laughing. No one is paying attention to the girl. I go inside and shout, 'don't you see what's happening? The girl's leaving!' When no one even turns to look at me I feel like crying. I go out right away. I say to the girl, 'Look, no one said anything like that to me. But I am with you all the way.' Stuff like that. Then the girl takes a carpet and throws it over her back. The carpet is her home. I feel even more upset. I feel ashamed for having just lost my cool in front of those men. I go out straightaway. It's night and I look up at the clouds. There's something Godly there. God has written something in the clouds but if I read it I know I'll lose my mind. I go back inside. I am going back to the meeting room and I'm going to be strong. But my legs are shrinking. So I start pulling up my skirt so they won't notice. When I go in I see all these little boys licking the men's penises. Everyone is laughing. I feel like I'm going to lose my mind. Then I wake up."

"One of those dreams that makes you pity yourself when you remember it," said Maryam, chuckling a little. For a moment I also felt sick at the meaning behind the dream.

"And you?" I said. "Did you have a dream?" Letting out a sigh, she threw herself down on the bed she'd just made. Running her hands through the hair newly sprouting on the back of her head and looking up at the ceiling, she recounted her dream.

"That damned Madam Lilla must have got to me because I certainly had one of her famous camel dreams. We were in Mecca."

Playfully Amira recited a prayer of good fortune, imitating an old auntie. Maryam smiled and continued.

"But it turns out Mecca was Tahrir. Or we were in Tahrir but it was really Mecca. Some kind of dream trick. We are spinning, then running, then we stop and start spinning again. Sometimes I was really angry when we stopped because there was a well in the middle of the square. Someone's fallen in. If we don't spin she'll never get out and while we keep spinning it's like we are turning something. It's someone very small. I'm totally serious and they're all laughing. And that's when it happens.... Now no talking to Madam Lilla about this dream. No way. She already takes herself too seriously."

Impatiently we vowed we'd never bring it up and Maryam went on again.

"That's when I feel a hand on my back. Madam Lilla has slapped me on the back. With that I begin to spin the whole crowd. And spinning like that we come closer to the well. I hear a scream from below. And that's it," she said, jumping to her feet.

"And? Did you save her?" asked Amira, excited. Maryam snapped, "Don't be crazy! It was just a silly dream!"

Amira looked at me. I gestured to say, just leave it. Holding out the corner of a sheet that looked like a white flag of surrender, Maryam said to Amira, "Here, take this."

As a sisterly peace offering they wrapped the dreams of our losses in a shroud made of white sheets.

"So if Madam Lilla's right," I said, "these dreams should say something about the lies we tell ourselves. As we all know. A camel dream!"

Maryam wouldn't let me say any more.

"Oh leave it. We're not even up yet."

The door creaked open and a little girl came in and said with sweet arrogance, "Hello. My name is Melika. I'm six years old. I think you all need to get a move on. Because it's going to get really hot and you'll lose your appetite. I can't tell you how fed up I am up with all these people getting up so late."

The little girl finished with a supercilious hoisting of her eyebrows as she stood still in the doorway.

"Allah Allah!" I said, laughing. Amira laughed, too.

"OK then," I said. "Melika Hanım. And what if we don't come?"

Standing at the door like an angry housewife, Melika said, "Then you will have to go fishing. And that might be a little difficult because my swordfish is nowhere to be found. She was the swordfish who knew these parts best."

Open-mouthed, Amira and Maryam were on the brink of laughing out loud. Keeping a straight face, I went back to folding sheets and said, "Well it's a good thing I brought my banana fish with me. So it won't be a problem for us. You just need to point us to the sea."

Suddenly full of excitement she looked like an alien reuniting with someone from her home planet. She carried on with her mischievous little game.

"I'll show you where the sea is but right now I need to take care of Amin. Have you met?"

"No, but we would very much like to. That's just what we were hoping to do this morning."

Thrilled she had found someone to take part in her game, Melika slipped out of the know-it-all routine and dashed out of the room. Before we could even laugh she was back. With a box in her hand, she said, "This is Amin!"

She opened up the cardboard box full of leaves and brushing the leaves aside she whispered:

"Amiiin! Amiiiin!"

Then she squeaked, "Ah, here you are, you little devil." There was a spot at the end of her finger. A ladybird. "Hello Amin," we said, as gravely as we could. "Sometimes he gets out and tries to hide from me. But today he didn't because we have a TV programme," said Melika. As if she were a man, Maryam said to Melika, "So what kind of programme?" She stroked the little girl's hair. Flinging open her two little arms, she loudly announced, "Summer Nights with Melika!"

Until then she probably hadn't thought of a name for the programme or exactly what she would say. But as we sat down Melika made the flash decision to play an imaginary piano:

"Ta da! Melika and the Summer nights! Yeeees, ladies and gentlemen (she thought for a moment) Yeeeees! Now the horse is on the way (she paused, unable to come up with what to say next and twirled her finger at Amira) you tell me, what is a horse?"

Taking the game very seriously, Amira blurted out, "An animal with four legs!"

"You're wrong! It's a brown animal that runs straight ahead!"

Then she pounded away at the piano again.

"Ta da! Now ladies and gentlemen, a zebra is on the way Pointing at me, she said, "so what's a zebra!?"

"A horse in pajamas!"

"Hmmm," she said and left it there. It was becoming clear that she wasn't used to people taking her games seriously and that she was a lonely child. She turned back to the piano and made it clear she wouldn't stop tinkling with the keys until we changed the topic. Maryam said: "You have such beautiful hair, Melika."

Melika dropped the TV programme and said, "Yes, I got my hair in Tripoli."

"How much did you pay for it?" I said.

On the next beat, she said, "1,500."

Swiftly she turned her focus to Maryam's head.

"I think you'd look good with red hair. I think we should get you some red hair."

That was probably the best possible comment anyone could make about Maryam's hair and we couldn't help but laugh. Melika, however, was a little put out. "Didn't I tell you that breakfast was ready!" she shouted and suddenly she was gone.

In the whole wide world there couldn't have been a more beautiful morning sprite. She had rubbed the rust off our dreams. Or at least that's how it felt to me then. When she was going over to the pavilion in the garden, Maryam said, "How do they break the spirits of these little girls later on? How do they make them fall into line? It's like murder. Maybe we were like this once too. If only we could have grown up without being crippled. I wish there was a computer program. One that could show how we might have turned out if our spirits weren't crushed along the way. To show us how we might have been," she said, wistfully. I didn't realize Amira was listening.

"If only we hadn't suffered," she said. "Imagine the kind of women we'd be if we hadn't suffered a single major setback. How wonderful we might have been?"

"We wouldn't have seen those dreams," I added. "I mean, if nothing else."

We heaved a communal sigh. I imagined Melika as a grown woman but in her current state. What a truly wonderful woman she would be.

"Melika wouldn't give an inch to all those fools and tyrants," I said, "if she could grow up without losing that spirit."

"She would need to be loved the way we are," said Amira.

"She could go on adventures alone and never feel lonely," said Maryam. The tangled nerves in our heads had turned Melika's cheerful mood into a source of sadness. Surely it was ridiculously melodramatic to feel so low so early in the morning, but we weren't laughing. Suddenly the bubbling voice of an old woman, who had materialized behind us like a playful ghost, interrupted our communal lament.

"Oh my lord! Good morning to you all. Good morning!"

This woman had the joy of a pressure cooker.

"No need to fret my pretties. You can still get back to that pure state. I'm here to help. Not a problem!"

Then she waddled out, her entire body giggling. It was sweet to think of our sorrow as something like a headache you could beat with an aspirin and a glass of water. Laughing at the old woman we were caught by Melika's mother standing there with Melika between her legs.

"So you have met Melika," she said, stroking her daughter's hair.

"We even joined her TV programme," I said. Widening her eyes, her mother said, "Ooooooh... I suppose that's something new. We still haven't been on that one."

Melika was too young to know the value of the joy she brought to our lives and ashamed by our laughter she scurried off. "Where is she going?" said Amira. Not even looking over her shoulder, her mother said, "She'll be back." And she laughed. "Come, have breakfast. The pavilion is still cool." For a second Maryam looked at the woman, stunned.

I was just wondering how the Judas trees could survive

in this heat when Amira said, "Judas trees." Echoing her, Maryam said, "Judas trees, how strange." They looked at each other. As if surprised they could think the same thing at the same time and understand it without words.

Madam Lilla had long since stretched out in the pavilion when she called out, "Samira, tell your granny to get ready. We may need a cure."

The bright-faced young mother smiled and, after running her eyes over the table she had set for breakfast, she left.

Maryam then asked the question that must have dented her pride.

"So where are we? Dido's house? Who in their right mind would think of opening up a hostel in the middle of the desert and call it Dido's home?"

We started tearing off pieces of bread, catching whiffs of fresh butter and some kind of wonderful unsalted cheese. After so many days without a proper breakfast, our anticipation was high. Madam Lilla waited for us to calm down before she answered.

"It's mine!" she exclaimed.

She spent time relishing her good mood, swishing the end of her skirt over her feet and striking poses.

"You already know Dido's story. She falls in love with some fool and kills herself. I decided there should be a place in the middle of nowhere for women, a kind of oasis that men could never find. Over the last few years I think many people have heard about it. Tourists and the like are coming. I made the place for women on the run and I donated it to Fatima. She looks after everything. Of course now she's a grandmother. But she's only five years older than me."

She said all this with such grace we might have thought she felt for the woman and wasn't simply pleased with her own situation by comparison ... if we didn't know Madam

Lilla better. Letting out a phony sigh, she said, "The only thing she has to do is keep those Judas trees alive."

The expression on her face fell.

"So, Madam Lilla, I think you have something to share with us," said Maryam.

"Yes indeed!" said Madam Lilla.

"So, getting to the essential story. Dido shouldn't have killed herself but the one who stole her heart. Show no mercy to people like that. Rip out the roots of those barren hearts so that they will do no harm to anyone again. So that they can never hurt people like us again..."

She paused and looked at me.

"You saw the whip at my home. You looked at it carefully. I saw you. Well that whip..."

I had forgotten all about the whip. Now addressing everyone, she went on:

"It belongs to a heartless man. The only thing he left me was a whip. As a sign of his taking me prisoner."

Turning to Maryam, she said, "You, mademoiselle, you know all too well what I'm talking about. You know Dido, and how she fell, gave herself to the dogs. You know how such a seductive, independent woman (she turned to Amira) could turn out to be such a coward, leaving her fate to be written up as a tale of defeat, fear and shame. You know too. That's how I fell. (Now turning to me.) The only way we can have a say is to write our own stories. But you also know that perhaps it's sweeter to watch the miserable wretch suffer than to write the greatest love story. To stay up on your feet ... that's the most important thing. To never give up."

Madam Lilla had taken the joy out of breakfast. I could feel the lumps of food stuck in my throat. The moment breakfast was over Samira came out with little sweets. She

242

held the tray out to Madam Lilla, who instead of taking the tray and placing it on the table grabbed a sweet. Slowly she munched. Samira stood there with her back bent. Madam Lilla took another sweet. She was making the girl wait. Samira started to smile. Without looking at her, Madam Lilla took another sweet from the tray. In such a gentle voice Samira said, "Thirina, mother and gran have always said so much about you. But you're something else altogether. You're truly wonderful."

There was such a ring in her voice ... balanced on the fine line between compliment and mockery. Madam Lilla wasn't pleased with the sass and she immediately dropped the game of sweet torture she was playing with Samira for her own pleasure. Samira had sweetly schooled her elder and we hadn't missed it. Madam Lilla turned to us and said, "Samira's grandmother is a healer. She saves women from the weight of secrets and the shadow of fear. In my opinion what you need is..."

As Madam Lilla went on, Nana Fatima came chuckling into the pavilion, holding a long broom handle. She paid no attention to Madam Lilla holding court, perhaps thanks to her unstoppable cheer, or maybe she was just too old to care about much at all. It seemed she didn't even realize she was cutting Madam Lilla off.

"Would the pretties like their healing now? In that case," she giggled, "we will walk forward and not backwards." We were shaken by a strange need to laugh. There was such a cloud over the woman that the moment you saw her you began to think less of the world. Squinting her eyes she practically had to sniff out Amira. She took her arm. Though her hands were trembling once her plump fingers got a hold of her, Amira couldn't move. With a century's worth of knowledge of the human body, she could take any part of

Amira and slowly lower her onto the divan. Mumbling a prayer, her hand found Amira's forehead and she breathed over her face as she continued to recite the prayer. "Ah! Ah!" she moaned, as if on Amira's behalf, as if sucking out all her pain through the palm of her hand. Then placing the end of the broom on Amira's belly button, she said:

"Now there is no longer any need for you to fear. Your belly contracts from fear. I will bring it back. But your belly will be strong again, my pretty. You will believe again."

She clutched the broom handle with both hands as she continued mumbling her prayer. Then Amira started to cry. Freely and smoothly. It was like something else was pouring out from her mouth with her breath. As she cried, Nana Fatima kept her hand on Amira's forehead, caressing, blowing over her face. Amira shut her eyes but the tears still ran out from under her lids. Nana Fatima was still moaning as she opened her heart to all the grief. When all was done Amira would be able to float away without an ounce of sorrow. With the slightest gesture, she brought Amira to an upright position. Wiping away her tears she mopped the sweat on Amira's brow with the palm of her hand. She fixed her hair and said:

"My pretty, you can't forgive him. If you did you wouldn't be able to forgive yourself…"

With a gentle motion she lifted Amira off the divan and sat her on the ground. Amira knew who she was talking about and like a puppet whose strings had been cut she collapsed.

With her hands in the air Nana Fatima was looking for someone else, a big smile on her face, and she found me. She pulled me to the divan. I could feel the strange coolness of her hand holding onto my shirt. It was like she wasn't made of flesh and bones but of cloud. The slight movement of her fingers set me down on the divan. I understood why Amira could cry. There was something about this woman that pulled you in. A kind of void. A void of mercy. She touched the back of my neck. Took hold. Palmed away the sweat. "You're so very afraid. But you have done it despite your fear. Wait and let's see," she said. Placing the end of the broom stick on my belly, like the needle of a compass in the middle of my body. "Hmm," she said before starting her prayer.

"So that's the way it is... That's the way..."

I kept quiet but it was like she'd taken me aside and was speaking directly to my heart.

"My pretty, you can only really see yourself when others cannot see you. Don't be afraid. You are brave like a lion. Don't be afraid to be a lion."

I didn't cry. But I felt like I might never speak again.

Then with her hands in the air again she searched for Maryam. And that's when Maryam snatched the broomstick out of her hand and raced out of the pavilion, screaming.

"I don't want to be healed."

Maryam was not going to give in.

*

Madam Lilla was still laughing when Maryam's outburst was finally over. The three women of the household were watching, too. And of course, Amira and I had become a part of the episode as a form of revolt against Madam Lilla. After she had called out to Samira, who quickly came back with that dark red velvet pouch, Madam Lilla turned to Maryam and said, "You don't want to be cheated on, is that it? You want something real. A real story with a real end. Fine then, you'll get what you want. A story that's both real and that has a real end. Give it here, Samira!"

Samira held out the velvet pouch. Saying *bismilla*, Madam Lilla opened the pouch and said, "This will change the course of our lives. We won't stop until we have broken all the heartless in this world."

Then she reached into the pouch and pulled out a silver gun with a mother of pearl handle. She unlocked the safety catch, raised the weapon in the air and boom! She fired off a round. It was so sudden that we hardly even realized that she had met our revolt with an even greater one, raising the bar higher, showing us that there were no limits. The gun still in her hand, she went on.

"Ladies, you will break the ones who broke you. You will wound the ones that wounded you. With me you will come to kill a man. Because..."

From a distance Melika came running over to us shouting joyfully.

"I found the swordfish! I found it!"

"Because once the scar forms it will always be with you. After that there is only revenge."

She addressed Maryam.

"Fine then, mademoiselle, seeing that you are too much of a hero to be drawn into my game. But are you brave enough? Do you have the courage to change the course of your life? Or will you run away from this as well?"

There was a terrifying glimmer in her eyes. In a sudden rush of movement totally unlike her, Amira stood up in front of Madam Lilla and cried, "With that Madam Lilla? You're going to change the course of our lives with a gun?"

That's when Maryam did something entirely unexpected. She walked straight over to Madam Lilla. Looked her in the eyes. They were like two cowboys. She put her hands on her hips. With her eyes fixed on Madam Lilla's she spoke to Amira.

"I'm all in, Madam Lilla. I'll go as far as we need to go!" Instead of allowing her secret to come out through a broomstick she must have decided it was better to try Madam Lilla's madness. "But on one condition," she said. Madam Lilla lowered her gun and standing opposite one another like that they both looked like two knights with heads held high, ready to take an oath of honour. Her eyes still fastened on her opponent. "You will tell us the true story. Not all the nonsense you have been telling us up till now, but the truth... And if you do that.... I'm in!"

And that was when Madam Lilla sat down in the pavilion and asked for a cigarette. Somehow Nana Fatima was still smiling, and stroking Melika's head. This woman was watching us as if she were watching the happy ending of a goodhearted film. Then breaking off the branch of a Judas tree, she placed it in Melika's hair. She plucked another branch and put it in her own hair. I didn't know which was more interesting. Madam Lilla's gun, Maryam's sudden fit of madness or the secret of the Judas trees that had no business being there and would tie all our stories together...

Madam Lilla lit a cigarette. She didn't say a word until she'd finished and invited us to her room. She was like someone getting ready to take the plunge, but on the brink of suicide.

Melika was still shouting, "I found my swordfish. I found it!"

18

Now perhaps it was the dizzying pace of the journey or the fleeting desires that flared up in our hearts that made us look different on the surface, but deep down the three of us respected, admired and of course felt pity for a Judas tree that bloomed in the middle of a desert. Maryam, Amira and I knew the value of things. We couldn't mock fate nor underestimate profound love. And we didn't have it in our hearts to bring down Madam Lilla in a place whose climate was as inhospitable for her as it was for the Judas Trees. Madam Lilla was a rare blend of magic that we found infuriating and which tried our patience but which we could never wholeheartedly despise.

The world that Madam Lilla had built was vast enough to contain and indeed surpass the world they say existed. But her magic didn't come from glory but from weakness. Once you recognized the burnt matchsticks upon which her world was standing (and we saw them when Madam Lilla began to tell us the real story) you wanted to give a helping hand. Madam Lilla aroused in us the desire to protect, and the feeling was the same as the care that a fragile and purely joyful little girl would arouse in your heart. Madam Lilla was the oldest woman-child I knew. A purple butterfly one would not deign to take into the palm of your hand and look at too closely in case her wings fell off – and with a purple butterfly like this one it's better to keep your distance.

All three of us were scrupulous women. And yes we were the kind of women prepared to cross a desert to kill a man who had devastated a woman's heart. In the end what more was there to life? What is it about? And we were women who knew without a shadow of a doubt that Madam Lilla was a daredevil. We could give a piece of our lives to Judas trees for nothing in return, considering to whom and what pieces of our lives we had already given. Which is why that night we went up onto the roof of Dido's home. We wouldn't have gone if we didn't value love and matters of the heart and we certainly weren't women to make petty calculations. As Amira, Maryam and I climbed the stairs to the rooftop we didn't talk about of any of this – there was no need. We simply slipped into our white nightgowns again and went up to see Madam Lilla.

She was sitting in one of those white plastic chairs. Shrunken, she looked like a bird. Wisps of hair that had fallen from her bun and her gauzy silks were fluttering and in the swirling motion her body seemed to ebb and flow in a wave of powder. Her eyes were fixed on a distant point so far away. She was like a cicada that had chirped away its flesh until there was nothing left but a shell. She was doubled over. After Maryam had said, 'tell us the truth and no more tales of adventure,' she revealed to us her true face and now she was stuck with it. And our sadness was like the sadness of a slave with a love for astronomy watching the plundering of the library of Alexandria. We had asked for the truth and that truth had ruined our stories. So now we would labour to attach wings to that plane that had suddenly crashed into a white plastic chair. Just like that first night when we were on a dark square shielded from the outside world. Now we knew what could happen on those dark squares. We had to crack our own puzzle in this black square that was ours alone.

Maryam walked over to her and we followed noiselessly behind her. We sat down on the low wall before her. There *was no way she would forgive us. We had done nothing wrong; we had simply done the worst we could have done to her. Now she was nothing but the poor old woman she didn't want to be; from the inside we had succeeded in bringing down all her years of glorious revolt; she had no more interest in the world and she wouldn't forgive us. Her heart was withering before our very eyes, and there was nothing left of Madam Lilla in her face. And what's more... Ah! I suppose this was what hurt the most: her purple nightgown buttons were out of order. No longer billowing, her silk gown stuttered in the wind like an angel's wing in barbed wire.*

Amira took her cell phone out of her pocket. There was no other way for us to show remorse: She started to play Warda's 'So Many Years Without Love'. The same song she had played for us on that first night. As much as our pride permitted we were imploring her to come back to the fairytale she had invited us to join in the beginning. Without even blinking she only let out a pained sigh, a hook of a smile on the corner of her lips far worse than tears.

I poured four glasses of date liquor. Maryam was the bravest among us because she was the most fearful. Slowly she leaned over to Madam Lilla, her hands trembling. Gracefully, she tended to the buttons on her gown: slowly she undid each one then began carefully buttoning them again. Maryam was just barely grazing Madam Lilla's skin, the kiss of a fish. When Maryam and Amira sat back down on the low wall, Warda's voice was echoing over the desert.

I swear to time ... all these years there has been no love!

As I handed out glasses, I hesitated when I came to Madam Lilla. She still wasn't looking at us. Slowly she put her hand in her pocket, took something in the palm of her hand then passed it to the other hand. She waited a little. Then without showing us she placed the ring on her finger. This was the

250

red-stoned ring we saw from above on our first night. She reached out her hand with the ring and took the glass. She still wasn't looking at us but she must have felt us, and from the way her mouth crinkled, her brow softened and her nose lifted, it was clear – she was coming back. When Warda reached the most beautiful moment in the song Madam Lilla began to tap her ring on the glass to the rhythm of the song, just like that first night and, toc ... toc ... toc ... time started running again. In silence we were extremely happy. We waited motionless like children who didn't want their mother to stop fussing over them. Warda was singing to this desert that had given these Judas trees the rare chance to grow.

I swear to time...

Then warplanes roared overhead, jets.... We looked up. But the only thing we heard was the sound of Lilla's ring tapping against her glass.

Tic tic tic... we had finally come to ourselves on the square of a dark crossword puzzle. Life and war was still was barrelling forward on the white squares.

And that was how our most difficult day came to an end. We were exhausted. Once you fire a gun the bullets never come back.

"We want the truth," Maryam had announced that morning, "and no more tales of adventure."

And that was then Madam Lilla had asked for a cigarette and took a drag as she scrunched up her brow without saying a word.

*

After Madam Lilla had told us her "true" story, we found ourselves in the kitchen of the house of Dido, like three empty

251

sacks. Similar to links on a chain and bound to one another like them, we were three women and a young girl. When all the women of a family (providing their hearts are pure) come together they smell something like butter, like bread toasting in a kitchen. It seeps into every corner and you could sit there for a lifetime, speak, fall silent, tells stories and listen; such a cornucopia of life. A supple space composed of their touching, holding, turning, cutting and cleaning. Passing things to one another, turning round to pass again and then placing it on a stovetop, stirring, taking it away, and always something boiling. If there were a divan in the kitchen and you drifted off to sleep all your troubles would disappear and you would wake with a shining "spotless mind".

We sit down, being careful not to disturb all the turning wheels. Our chins are cupped in our hands, elbows pinned on a wooden table to carry the weight of our heads. They were acting as if Madam Lilla hadn't only a short while ago fired off a round and then called us to our room for a long meeting, pretending that our expressions weren't drained of life. Or maybe they had long since known what we had just come to learn.

"Shall I pour you some coffee?" says Samira, thin drops of water on the tips of her fingers. Sweat on her brow. As if she is full of gusto and ready to take on all the work in the world. We nod our heads. She pours the coffee as her mother dices tomatoes. Red mother-of-pearl stains her fingers. She speaks to us over her shoulder.

"Years ago Thirina sent us a machine that allows you to grow Judas trees here, keeps them alive. This device that breathes out little drops of water. We were able to run it on petrol. When she gave this house to my mother there was only one condition: Keep the Judas Trees alive."

Laughing either at the beans she was shucking or how funny her life must have seemed, the old woman went on as if reciting something out of the holy book:

"No man can blight this beautiful flower that Dido brought us. Because we can always give it the season it desires."

"Why did you believe her?" asked Maryam. She didn't mean to say that she was silly to believe in such a thing but rather she was pleading to be converted. With every new bean that slid out of its shell the old woman looked down in wonder and spoke to those strips of green.

"Three books were not enough to bring the evil ones to reason. Those prophets were sent to wish patience upon the good."

Samira caressed Nana Fatima's hair and sat down at the head of the table, a tired hand on her hip.

"Because we believe in our garden. Not so that we can show it to anyone, but for ourselves. Only the Judas Trees..."

The old woman finished her thought.

"We protect them so that we can raise our girls to be strong and graceful. Like our Melika."

The three of them looked at Melika as if she were an ever-unfolding miracle. Melika opened her eyes and pulled her hair up in the air. Then she made a few silly gestures that children make when they are ashamed of being watched. We looked at her and laughed. She was our hope. Melika snatched a wooden sword off the ground and raised it up into the air with two hands and babbled as if she were shouting alone.

"For the fighters of al-Kahina! Advaaance!"

Samira laughed over her shoulder; she kept on mixing something in a bowl while she said, 'That's just the way we are. In the middle of a war ... with the Judas Trees..."

Samira could make light of the situation because she did not doubt her belief. She expected neither understanding nor respect from us. She must have truly believed.

"There are these two women in Lebanon," I said. "In southern Lebanon. On the border with Israel they work to protect the sea turtles. They also have a garden. Right between Hezbollah and the Israeli army. Like you, they're..."

Turning round for the salt on the table, Samira's mother said, "Someone should look after their gardens, too."

Samira laughed to herself.

"Judas Trees and beans."

Still reverently shucking beans the old woman spoke as if listing holy commands.

"Do not let the undeserving into your garden... Do not betray your daughter... Do not show the Judas Trees to those who cannot see them... Learn how to hold a sword... Do not covet, only admire... Never surrender to anyone... Keep walking... Trust your sister..."

She paused and repeated two of the laws:

"Don't betray your daughter. Trust your sister."

Melika suddenly darted out from under the table, brandishing her sword, shouting as she scurried outside.

"Do not betray Dido!"

Nana Fatima laughed again and we didn't know if it was the beans again or the hundred years of life behind her.

Maryam was keeping her cool, unlike me and Amira, and said, "Alright then what about the war? What are you going to do here?"

Samira turned to us, water running from the tap: "Nana Fatima missed the most important part. Never leave the garden!"

Nana Fatima repeated again, "Never leave the garden!"

And the women of the household returned to their work.

I asked Maryam and Amira, "What's going to happen now?"

Rubbing her face, Amira said:

"There's something I have to tell you. About Muhammed."

After rubbing a little more she went on, "And about this matter of the Judas Tree."

Maryam said (and clearly this was something she didn't want to say), "Me too. There is something I have to show you. And yes, it has to do with the Judas Tree." She cursed and felt ashamed for saying something like that when Melika was around. She apologized to three generations of women and they flashed forgiving smiles. She went on, "Oh come on, friends, if I'm really going to believe in all these symbols and signs, I'd say…"

Surprised, Amira said, "You, too?"

"Don't ask," said Maryam.

The two of them looked at me. Maryam cocked her head to show that we should go. We went to our room with half-filled cups of cold coffee. Maryam opened her notebook and read.

*

Dido's Third Tablet

I brought the Judas Trees to this country, sun-kissed sailor. Every spring they will bloom. For a short while. Who knows if years later these Phoenician flowers will remain. Now that you have set out on your journey, stranger, you know how people are: they overlook beauty that does not benefit them and they destroy it. The ignorant are that way because they are under the impression they are making intelligent choices between the practical and the beautiful. But you should be like me, stranger: even in war I can see the earth's sweet alyssum hidden among the weeds.

I don't want you to fear me, brave warrior. Do not look at me the way they do. Do not leave me for one of the gods. Tell me amusing tales. And laugh with me. Let me see my country through your eyes. Let me bring you to the meadows where the young goats graze. Let's laugh at the little noses of the little gods. Later we can warmly laugh at our own noses reddened by wine. Oh! Tell me stories I have never heard, of people I have never known and let us laugh at them. We will laugh so heartily that blooming sweet alyssum will blanket the earth. Let us not be forced to spin beauty out of the earth. Let our footsteps not fall upon the anthills.

I am raising daughters, stranger. Like Judas Trees. I warn them to stay away from men who do not see the sweet alyssum and who do not know the value of the Judas Trees. I teach them how to sing, write poetry, make food from flowers and how to be as graceful as the gods as they brandish their swords. Stranger, I am teaching them how to be strong. The pleasure that comes with vanquishing someone, how to run like deer, swim like dolphins and how to dance like Phoenician women. I teach them magic. I teach them to trust the magic they make with their sisters. They do not fear men, stranger, they fear only themselves. I drive the dark gods from their hearts. Oh brave warrior, the gods speak to me in my dreams. One of these girls will rule these lands a long time after I bid farewell to this side of the world. But in my nightmares I see that beautiful girl of mine (the one the gods say will rule the lands after Dido passes) being devastated. I see that she is destroying her own country, setting fires and leaving behind a wasteland. I see a female eagle thrashing herself against the stones to avoid capture. I am crying as if I have died.

I know the kings of the deserts and the mountains of Africa and Arabia will not take to my brave female eagle. I could endure but she will not. The gods will grow angry and send drought and desert storms. Can my girls overcome the trickery and the traps and the darkness? One of my girls will give birth to that woman ruler and when her heart falters will she set herself alight with her own country? What should I tell them, brave soldier? Come to me and tell me how to conquer this world! Give me that dark secret of the men's world.

Already dear Penelope has begun to worry about me. I wake up in the middle of the night and light all the candles and send out my sailors. They go out far enough to see you but not close enough to be seen by you. Only when they tell me your ship is still there do I fall back asleep. Penelope weeps. As I console her I say that you are there and that for some time you have been mine. Stranger, I tell her that you will not disappoint me. Do not shame me in the eyes of this country: come. I don't want them to invent foul songs and tell sour stories so that they might destroy Dido. I do not have the strength to lose again. I have built you in my mind, stranger. Do not fall short of my dreams, do not shame me. Come.

I am the mother of all the girls to come after me, stranger. Just like those unassailable women of my native lands, I am patient and fruitful. I have bested kings and warriors with my silence, o brave soldier! But I have decided to tell you what I have kept from them. With you I swore to try my love and not my power. Come to me with a heart that knows what is most precious.

No doubt you have been with other women. You have made love to beautiful women. You drank from them and they from you. You mingled with girls and boys, undoubtedly. Come to my country when you have tired of that, stranger. Come to me along the roads of my past to arrive where I have arrived. In the same way that a god might falter at the building of rivers and mountains, come to me with the same noble distress. Because I am here. Because time will pass like this and I will die. Time will pass and storms will not shake, waves will not overwhelm and thunderbolts will not burn, so much I have understood. Come and give meaning to this.

Now I want to look more closely at the Judas Trees. I will continue to rule over these lands and this sea, o brave lover! Just give to me myself. Give hope to my daughters. Make my strong and graceful daughters believe that there can be men who are wise enough to love and show it. Come, stranger, and we will rule together. Come and we will find life in the Judas Tree. Come and we will take strength from sweet alyssum.

Come now brave warrior. Show us the lands and the seas through your eyes. Come. Do not lessen me in their eyes anymore.

*

Amira wasn't surprised but I was.

With only a sigh she started to read one more of Muhammed's letters.

Muhammed's Third Letter

Fine then, so people are dumber than we think but they can still make a real mess of the world. We can hardly work out what's going on. And despite the sheer idiocy they still manage to devise incredibly complex traps for each other, concocted out of their own chaos, it's beyond my comprehension. But you have nothing to worry about. You are humming along. You and others like you have come to this world to enrich us. And we are powerless no matter how hard we fight back!

Not everyone is blessed with a character and not everyone is blessed with a heart. But you have one and praise God it's magnificent. I often think about the day I first discovered your heart like I am replaying the video of Maradonna's famous goal. It had to be the hand of God! A beautiful song was playing, had to be something from Asmahan, and there were tears in your eyes. Then I remember how moved you were to watch a seagull fly differently from the others, alone, perhaps in the distance, not among a flock, all alone. Fine then... So you like to shed a tear or two but in this you can't prove me wrong. Here's a point someone like you needs to keep in mind: Hopelessness is the greatest sin. Sweetie, you need to accept the fact that every now and then you commit this sin. Yes I know I must sound a bit ridiculous so try to forgive me. What I want to say is this: it really wouldn't be such a bad thing if you were to organize day trips for your heart now and then. I have no doubt that birdwatchers from all around the world would rush to Tunisia for such a trip. Kiss those hoopoe birds in your heart for me and please pass on my greetings to Süleyman. And please don't be angry with me for all my idle chitchat, I'm shutting up now.

People who, like me, believe that if you slip into those baggy pants and wear socks and sandals – go for that style and fashion —you find the road to the Prophet. I suppose if we just look strange enough we'll find some kind of heartfelt belief. But for those who fail to grieve with children, with their lovers, with street cats, even with the squawking wild geese, how will they ever hear the word of God? If the Prophet himself came upon them... A fool like me cannot know how the Prophet will temper them. But I suppose through patience and compassion he would call them to silence. Without breaking their hearts he would show them the drought inside. He would tell them their hearts had to be watered with the dew of poetry and love, and maybe he would urge them to go to pastures in the morning to carefully gather dew in their pockets to later drop them in their hearts. But still, as these hearts have lain fallow for hundreds of years I have no doubt the first harvest will be outstanding.

You, my love, are travelling on the same road as the Prophet. If I could redirect the energy you spend punishing yourself out of desperation and fear, I imagine the world would quickly come alive.

Fine then, please do not think I have crossed a line here. I know you don't like this but you must do it: Please say a prayer to God, a besmele. Begin with the name of God. The besmele will call the universe to your aid. God is the universe. When we say, Inshallah or God willing, we understand we are a part of this universe. I'm not talking about all that silly 'send a positive message to the universe' stuff, don't be daft. When we invoke the names of God we announce our belonging to the universe. Now and then you need to win the hearts of angels so you can work together. What do you think?

Fine then, take another look around you now for my sake. Remember the leper's wager. The sweetest part of believing in God is believing in a flawless heart. Till now you have believed in people. You shouldn't be surprised that you've always found yourself in trouble. If you believe people are made in His eyes you could more easily share your compassion. What do you say, sweetie? Can you do it?

Now consider this… This colonialism business really is terrible. It has a little to do with what I've been talking about. Colonialism can even lead people to stop naming children and flowers in their mother tongues. But only our language and its words ring in our hearts. The heart is made up of words. Every word creates a space on the surface of the heart. So then, in this sense the people you see around you are crippled in the same way too. Ask them if they can name flowers in their own language. Ask the Judas Tree. You will see that they don't know it. Ask old compassionate women about the Judas Tree, sweetie. They keep the names of flowers, old prayers and lullabies in their minds. So they frighten everyone, and who knows maybe everyone just wants to forget it all. Only an old woman can stop the erosion.

As a woman, granted, as the princess of them all, I believe that you will challenge all this stuff. No film does well at the box office if it doesn't challenge the status quo. What's more we have no doubt that you can't knock out all the evil in the world with a single punch. Well then why should you do it? There's no end to all these questions!

OK then, I'll give you this. The West will watch you dance with the respect and envy you deserve. But you won't resonate in their hearts. To me it doesn't seem like a risk worth taking. What do you think? So I feel pretty sure that you'll come back. I feel like you'd rather take care of yourself as a human being in Tunisia than show yourself to millions like you're a carpet or an antique ceramic tile. If all this sounds ridiculous you can blame it on my fuzzy head.

I suppose you need to describe your dancing to them in their own words. Sadly this is something you really should do. Because idiots like me end up believing lust is a sin. But every emotion is its own planet. Of course God's planets. And instead of observing them like crafty astronomers it wouldn't hurt to visit them once and a while and walk in the countryside, indeed it would broaden our minds. Belief comes with experiencing all these planets and meeting each other there in solidarity. OK then, but you can't expect everyone to be as brave as you and do this with every inch of their bodies.

Dissatisfaction is a miserable emotion. I want to see you again but if I spent the rest of my life with you I know it still wouldn't be enough. Such caprice. You're right, I need to pull my act together.

Your lowly chevalier,
Muhammed.

Maryam wasn't surprised but I was.

And we stood there humming and hawing like people stranded on a treasure island without a clue as to what to do. Because here's how things unravelled that morning after the gunshots had echoed through the air...

*

Angrily gathering up her skirt, Madam Lilla stormed out of the garden and into the house. In her room she sat down at her mahogany desk. She placed the gun on the dressing table. She was furious. Narrowing her eyes, she looked at us. Would we be able to understand her? She stared at Maryam. Who would still be standing at the end of the story?

"Give me another cigarette," she said and snatched one out of Maryam's hand. She lit up like women of another time and without inhaling she explained, "Ladies, first of all... I wasn't a victim. And I wasn't heartless. I say that because the majority of women assume that women who don't let themselves fall victim have no heart."

"The real story ... the real story is simple." She closed her eyes and rocked back and forth like she was reciting a poetic prayer. "One day I saw a mirage in the desert of a man's heart. In time the mirage turned into a prayer for rain and the prayer became a sea. And with that I stuffed the sand full of fish. When I tired of the mirage and the prayer the sea once again changed into a cemetery. Without so much as trembling the fish died in an instant. And I saw that again I could reinvent the water and the mirage and the sea and fill a man's desert with fish. All passionate love is this. Love finishes when a woman grows weary. Women don't leave men – they leave a graveyard. But I'm not like other women. Ever since I was little I have stood on my own two feet.

Maybe I was seven or so when I started going to weddings with my father's tambour. First it was neighborhoods in Cairo then surrounding villages and other cities. My voice was so full of sorrow that when people heard me they stared at me like I was some kind of animal they were seeing for the first time. Even my mother was afraid and she couldn't love me. Mother was always the woman crying behind my dad and I was the little girl at his side. I grew up with men. So before I could become a woman I had learned how not to be one. My dad used to wrap sacks around me so that I wouldn't look like a girl. The men there loved to cry for the grief of the poor, frail, troubled children. None of them ever thought to ask why those children were so sad – it just seemed easier to cry for them. When I was still a child I learned how men played this dirty game. Before I learned to laugh on my own I first learned how to make others cry. I saw their heartlessness when they threw three pennies at my dad's face and then the way they pitied themselves while they cried at the sound of my voice. I was disgusted. I neither cried nor was heart-broken, most of all I was disgusted by them as I grew older. I was disgusted by my mother, by her weakness. I loathed how she would jump to her feet when I brought home money, a light flickering in her eyes as she slipped into the role of a suffering woman. I loathed how father would wrap me in sacks. How he used to read the expressions on the faces of men listening to me sing, and greedily calculate the money he was going to make. I saw hundreds of brides; they all looked like captured foxes. All done up and finely dressed for a man and when they sat down they looked like water buffaloes. When I was eleven I could recite the Koran by heart. I did it so they could use me at funerals and births. When I was thirteen and my breasts were just developing I had already been to every ceremony there is between cradle and grave. All those faces ... I saw a thousand faces. In my mind they have all merged into one. It is a face that suddenly cries, suddenly laughs, shifting to suit whatever mood. I was disgusted. Absolutely disgusted. Ladies, I grew up in the backstage of humankind.

Then when the money really starting rolling in they decided for one last big win... As you probably have already guessed they decided to marry me off. At one of those ceremonies I had watched from the backstage with disgust... So I was supposed to hop out of the gunny cloth and into the lace. When we're children we make decisions based on what's going on right here (and she put her hand on her stomach). The best decisions are made here I guess. So one night I rounded up all the money there was in the house and I hit the road. In my gunnysack I made my way to Alexandria. That was where I met Mother Wasma. Women of an older time are something else. She was once the head concubine of the Ottoman Palace and she knew that it was a woman's mind and not her flesh that made the money. And so I was taken to her home. She raised me. She must have seen the anger and the power in me because she took me seriously. She took me as her daughter... We sat down and discussed how much we could get for my virginity. That was how I would repay Wasma for the education I would get from her. It was a fair agreement. I was selling something men wanted, I was trading, buying my own life. I would be Wasma's most powerful weapon. Everyone in the Cairo elite – sometimes even women – (she smiled) secretly came to her house. And not only them, there were rich Brits, Americans, Frenchmen and Arabs. We were ladies. Courtesans, escorts as the French say. By the time I was twenty I could speak every Arabic dialect, French and English. Mother Wasma taught me how to work with my anger. May she rest in peace. When she died she left me a gold-plated coffee pot inscribed with the Felak verse, and three-hundred pounds and precious stones. On her deathbed her face was pale as ash. Taking my hand, she said, "Esma Hanım, I beg you to go to the West and start over." So I hopped on a train to Alexandria and from there to the pier and then I sailed to Paris. I took a room at the Ritz, presenting myself as the daughter of an Arab prince. Europeans love that sort of thing. From that day on I danced and sang in the most luxurious venues of Paris and London. I was invited to private parties and met extraordinary people. Princes, kings, ship owners... I hired private tutors to study politics, philosophy, mathematics, astronomy, religion, history and poetry... You name it. The world was my oyster, ladies. And I was gobbling it up. Money flowed. Which was always the easiest part. Because I didn't have a heart. Then I went back to Egypt. From there I travelled to all the Arab countries and lived in many. I took lovers and left them, flowers, diamonds, flowers, more diamonds... But I wanted more. More power. I knew that I deserved more than being a desired woman in a man's world. So I started relaying information, from the English to the Arabs, from the Arabs to the French, from the French to the Americans. I worked for them all. It was a giant puzzle and I was running the show. Just like I wanted. I only did it for the men and their eager eyes – those crazy eyes always watching to see what I'd say next. It was that moment when they would hold their breath and wait on every word. But it wasn't enough to have them as my adoring slaves – I wanted to rule the game. I had grown up in the backstage of life, disgusted by humanity, and now and again I was in the wings, having my fun. I didn't take money but there was one thing I did want from them. I wanted them to be indebted to me. And through those debts of the heart I wove a network over the world. Now if we manage to make this journey it's because of this. I had a few close brushes with death. But danger only raises the stakes in the game. When you live on your wits, life can be the most entertaining game. You take the crème de la crème – men, money, cities and time – and run with it. Ah! I lived the most wonderful life a woman could live. Years went by. And I wasn't getting any older. Because, like I said, I didn't have a heart. I was standing on my own two feet.

Then one spring day I find myself in Beirut and I'm forty-nine years old. I'm sitting at the bar in the Saint George hotel, the setting sun falling on my face, the waves lapping against the hotel jetty. First I saw his shoes. Black patent leather. Then his chic, dark-green, silk gabardine suit. He came in and sat down at the table opposite. With no shame or discomfort, he spent a long time casually looking me over with a teasing smile. I was expecting him to come and over and say hello or send me a drink, expecting and expecting... For some time he made me wait, looking straight into my eyes. Maybe for an hour, he looked at me like he was gazing out over the sea. Then he got up, walked past me and left. That was it. The next day at the same time the same thing happened again. But for even longer. Without blinking and with a sweet air of indifference. The next day the same thing all over again... I should have known he was a deer hunter and that he could have waited as long as it took to kill me with that one shot to the heart. He was waiting for me to turn and bare my heart.

Ladies, love comes to you in a moment of hesitation. Just a slight stumble and you're done. Years of experience, a lifetime of victory, never getting double-crossed or two-timed... Love waits for a slight hesitation and our fortress comes crashing down. Who knows, maybe that's what I was secretly hoping for. My own game wasn't hard enough to really try me. I wanted to put my heart to the test in a wild, unknown forest. That's what we make of life, there are no coincidences. We breathe into life all these signs, magic and serendipity. Who knows, maybe the strongest among us welcome defeat only to feel more alive. What can I say to that? In the same way a soldier might feel phantom tremors in his amputated limb perhaps I wanted to feel something in the empty chambers of my heart. People pray for sadness only if they have never really tasted it. Though we rarely would admit so much we all crave self-destruction at least once in our lives. Forget about getting to heaven, we all burn to whine in our own hell. I was forty-nine years old and maybe just for a moment, I hesitated, wondering if I was living the wrong life. The greatest hunters have the ability to detect that moment of hesitation in their prey. He walked past me and deep down in my stomach and down my spine, I felt his soul. I only heard him breathing when he came over and smelled the back of my neck. I was caught by surprise when he deftly placed his golden lighter on the table. His name inscribed on it. Jezim Anwar. And without saying a word he walked away. A game I had played hundreds of times on others was finally played on me. I gave him permission to play. Love, ladies, is a game played with absence. And the more trust that your absence will be felt deeply the better you play. But the moment you hesitate you're out of the game. I hesitated. Like I said, love comes down to that.

Months passed and I caught myself on countless occasions: when I went to back to the bar in the Saint George and sat down in the same place, holding the lighter and sitting just a half an hour more, and, now here is the worst of it ladies … the worst my dears is when I caught myself staring at the door. Like a miserable woman waiting for life to happen. Like my mother. What I mean is that love is the agony of catching yourself falling to pieces. Finally one day, and it was the wrong day, he showed up. It was the wrong day because I was ready, I'd made all the preparations, or so I thought. He was wearing black shoes and a dark blue suit. And holding a whip. I knew he wasn't looking for me, and that made me angry. He didn't see me and I went mad. I got up and I walked to the bathroom and when he still didn't acknowledge me I nearly lost it. There was no need for him to do anything – I was already thrashing in my own web. I was just about to leave, cursing myself and ready to close the matter altogether, with only the anger I felt towards myself left in my heart when he came out with his cigarillo. He grasped my little bag like he was holding my inner thigh. Oh so slowly. He opened the bag like he was opening my legs. His eyes fixed on mine. Then he plunged his fingers into my bag like he was running them through my hair. Oh so gently. And when he found the lighter he smiled. That's when I knew there was no turning back. All bets were made.

My devastated heart suddenly came to life. But how I loathed that rush of joy. I loathed myself because I could not loathe him. From then on I was at war with myself. He enjoyed watching a panther willingly come to his feet as a kitten.

'My job is catching wild animals, mademoiselle,' he said, 'only the most dangerous ones. And you?'

If it had been another time, another place, another man, I would have laughed coyly and gracefully and asked questions – men love that sort of thing. But like I said, there was that moment of hesitation. Maybe I wanted to do what I had never done and break from a routine. I wanted to tell him my story. Men don't like that at all. They want to carry on about themselves and never listen. And I told him so many things, starting with how I danced. Smiling, he touched my hair and looking at me with a deep admiration that made me wonder if it was real, he said, 'Who knows how terrifying you really are. Men must be quite terrified by you. Who knows how many times you had to withhold stories so as not to frighten men away... You, mademoiselle, look like a Judas Tree that has bloomed in the desert.'

He laughed. I remember my knees going weak. He had this eerie power and you had to shake yourself to keep from falling for the charm. He listened to me all through the night. For the first time a man listened to my own stories as if I was giving away a country's secrets. I couldn't stop. Comical tales, tragedies, tales of woe, I probably told them all. He didn't say a thing. Only this, 'I go to war, mademoiselle, I go to zoos in countries ravaged by war. From there I collect the abandoned animals and sell them in other countries. I seize animals from the heart of Africa, put them in cages and send them to zoos in civilized countries. That's my line of work. People who want to find me need only follow the wars.'

Maybe he said more but I don't remember. That night I listened to my own words. I listened to a part of me I'd never heard before. There was nothing for him to say or ask. We went to bed together. He loved me like a wild animal that night. He tamed me. For a week we didn't set foot outside the Saint George. Oh, I was madly in love! And then one morning he was gone. For a year I looked for him. He left without a trace and I really did wonder if I'd dreamed it all. I thought maybe I'd lost my mind. To forget him I travelled far and wide and I gave myself to all kinds of men. I travelled to many countries and finally one day he greeted me with open arms as I was walking into the Paris Ritz. As if we had agreed to meet there, as if he'd never disappeared, as if he was still love with me, as if he had been searching for me over the past year, too, and was mad with desire. But this time I was bent on defeating the bastard. I would get my revenge. But love overwhelms and revenge looks like a snotty child. I'd already forgiven him before the night was out. Desire for belief is stronger than belief itself. We stayed together at the Ritz for a week and we went to all the music halls in Paris and drank in all the bistros. And later, of course, one morning Jezim Anwar vanished again. This time

I was set on accepting the situation and forgetting him. But the second defeat was nothing like the first. The second defeat leaves the deepest scar. Because there you understand how you longed for defeat and you cannot forgive yourself for that. Loathing, love, grief and passion ... when these are all wrapped together it's tough, and those are the feelings that were surging through my veins. Maybe if it had all happened earlier it wouldn't have seemed so important, I would've got over it. But if a woman falls victim to both love and time, there is no hope. All the men and the wonderful tales have amounted to nothing more than a tiny pebble to fill the chasm he left in my heart. The rest of my life has slipped into the void he left behind.

You asked me if it was true – the story about the baby bear and the pelican that I told you the first night. I worked all the connections I had in those days. During the Gulf War I went to Baghdad. As you'd expect the zoos were abandoned. The animals had either died or had been set free by hooligans. I learned that no transport trucks had arrived which meant that Jezim Anwar wasn't there. There was only a baby bear left in a cage. The poor thing was hungry, thirsty and nearly out of his mind from loneliness. His mother lay dead beside him. The little bear was bashing his head up against the bars. A bloody head. And a pelican, wandering among the cages, his wings caked in mud, one broken, which he dragged behind him. He seemed to be standing there at the cage watching the cub go crazy. Completely still that pelican watched for hours. Then he wandered through the garden, dragging his broken wing, as if he was looking for help, and then he came back to the cage to watch again. Two animals, one caged, the other free, both on the brink of madness. It was a mad idea. I must have been mad with love and anger. I knew that Jezim would come. I was sure he was

in Baghdad. If I could just take the animals somewhere else…
It was crazy, I told you, but then I would have something he
would want from me. Seeing that he never wanted anything
from me I had no other choice but to take what he wanted.
Now don't go and get the wrong idea… I don't know how to
love. And I know absolutely nothing about losing in love. So
I did what I knew how to do: I fought. One night I opened
the cage and lured out the bear with meat and kibble. After
I finally got the two animals to follow me I would take them
to a nearby park where I had a cage ready. But I didn't notice
the soldiers were on to me. And when I did it was too late.
The bear and the pelican were scared and we all took off
running. I lost my shoes and banged up my toes. I was
scared. Then finally we were up against a wall… That's
where they caught me and the pelican and the bear. I must
have been even more crazed than they were. I don't even
remember the stories I told them to get myself out of there.
But things are always easier when you're a middle-aged
woman who's a little bonkers. They took the bear, shot the
pelican and left me there. I sat down on the ground… and
cried so much I could barely see. When the sun came up I
was shoeless and half blind. Without even the strength to
take my own life when I got back to the hotel and saw Jezim's
black patent leather shoes… And ladies, the very same
lighter…"

She paused. The ruins in her face had just suffered
another bombing. She shuddered like a dead animal given a
jolt of electricity. With a bluish shade her secret's curtain
rose and fell before her eyes. Her narrative was cut short.
In that moment she seemed to have changed a detail in the
story before she went on.

"He lit a very young woman's cigarette with the very same
lighter. He gave me a look. I was a mud-splattered, broken-

winged pelican, a crazed bear cub. Jezim looked at me like he was looking at a wall. He walked over. He stuffed his hands in my pocket: the lighter was there. His lips twisted into something like a smile... And he left. That's all... And I didn't say a word. Nothing...

"Ladies, for the last twenty years I've thought about that moment. That moment I didn't speak. For the last twenty years I play the role of Madam Lilla in the daytime. And in the evening, I sit and wait for him in a chair opposite the door, turning jasmine over in the palm of my hand until they are brown. How did this happen, how could this happen? That's what I keep thinking. Whenever there's knock on the door I race over so quickly the jasmine falls beside the door. 'Those flowers grew all by themselves,' I once said. But they didn't, ladies. They came into leaf through sadness. And so after it all, ladies, I am going to kill that man. The tyrant must pay. There should be a price for destroying a garden created by a woman on her own, who built herself a palace out of garbage and in the face of so many hardships; there should be a price for destroying a desert Judas tree. For once, ladies, they should pay the price. Tell me that, have you never thought of killing someone? Or have you never loved someone that badly? Or did you not build yourself – like I did – stone by stone? Tell me that, don't the men who have devastated you, and who have devastated so many other women in the same way, don't they deserve to die? Ladies, these Judas Trees don't grow easily in a desert. Only the blood of our oppressors will cool our hearts? For heaven's sakes come out with it – have you never wanted to put a gun to his head and ask 'why?'"

Now this was not about her story or the fires of love or loathing. For the first time Madam Lilla was really asking us for something. She was begging for our help. Which is why it was the first time she had let herself go. We had seen the ruins, indeed the whole truth. And even her buttons on her gown which were out of order. And so, for us, yes, that man, Jezim Anwar, had to die. To protect the beautiful – sometimes it was the branch of a Judas Tree, sometimes Madam Lilla as a palace made of brushwood – yes, you had to learn how to kill. Amira and I were convinced. Yet Maryam, even after redoing Madam Lilla's buttons, said as she was drifting off to sleep, "There's something else. There's something she's not telling us." Amira said, "You're just being cruel. You know nothing about betrayal." Most likely she meant Muhammed. And she buried her head in her pillow. Maryam was silent. If she could dare to be cruel we would ask Madam Lilla more questions. And maybe then we never would have taken someone's life.

19

Madam Lilla and Nana Fatima were in the garden pavilion. Dawn was just breaking. I watched them from a distance. Madam Lilla was lying on a divan while Nana Fatima pressed her broomstick against her belly. Lilla's head was tilted to one side so I couldn't see her face. When Nana Fatima finished she pulled the stick away and ran her fingers through Madam Lilla's hair:

"Go back to him and lay down your arms, Thirina. He learned to wait for you patiently not from the wrath of a camel but from the stubbornness of the butterfly. Your light comes from him, and now it is time you surrendered to him."

I was dumbstruck, struggling to make sense of what Nana Fatima had just said when Madam Lilla suddenly turned and looked straight at me. I was caught. She sat up on the divan and shouted, "Put on your necklaces. They are coming to pick us up any minute now."

Like a child I raced inside.

"And a very gracious morning to you, madam!"

Standing opposite me was a woman dressed in khaki cargo pants, a safari shirt, hiking boots the size of tankers and a pair of Ray bans – a WOMAN JOURNALIST! Picture this: I was in my nightgown, Amira's sweater draped over my shoulders, my hair down over my face and my heels sticking out of Maryam's boots. As for the WOMAN JOURNALIST, she was right out of a war movie with all the buddy-I-was-there-on-my-own-when-the-shit-went-down-bluster but the way she talked oh… it was like she was issuing fatwas from Cairo's Al-Azhar University, that sort of lingo.

"Good morning," I said in a normal tone of voice.

She was olive-skinned; clearly the seed (her father) or the field (her mother) came from the lower hemisphere. But she only spoke classical Arabic, which people read and never speak, and on top of that she spoke it with a dreadful American accent. Imagine Christiane Amanpour reciting an Islamic ceremonial prayer, it sounded that ridiculous. Yes, this was Arabic, but her insistence and her enthusiasm were the perfect embodiment of an associated American journalist. Breathlessly she went on.

"Gracious to meet you. I am Allison Abou Chaar of CNN International."

The way she dragged out her name 'eeleeseen' and then emphasized every syllable of the word 'een-teer-nash-ee-nul' made you want to say, 'sit down, zero points.' Playing dumb a la Turca, I said, 'Ah...' and I didn't give her my name. Based on the name and surname, I took the mademoiselle for an American with Arab roots. But she was such the model woman journalist she could have been the cover girl for *Vogue* if the magazine did a feature on them. Squinting my eyes I must have looked like a real moron. She went on.

"The reason for my presence in these regions is known: the war in Libya."

If this were happening in Iran or Iraq she would have certainly pronounced the names 'Ay-raq' and 'Ay-ran.' That was the kind of voice she had. I wanted to laugh but I couldn't. I was going to say, "just switch to English, love, no need to bend over backwards," but she was giving it such a fighting try, and classical Arabic with an American accent was just so funny that I couldn't. There really had to be a way to punish these ubiquitous American journalists who hopped around in the morning like jackrabbits nibbling away at people and their lives.

With a sweet look on my face, I listened.

"I and my travel partner Jack (pronounced Jeek) are out here reporting on the war. And your excellency? What matters are you in engaged in, perchance?"

While I am waiting for Maryam and Amira to come out and save me, Madam Lilla comes up behind me. I don't know what just happened in the pavilion but she storms out with her skirt billowing. Seizing the opportunity I dash off to my room, leaving Eeleeseen with her. Maryam and Amira are just up on their feet and I say, "Listen." We press our ears up against the door. As if just speaking in that American-accented classical Arabic wasn't enough the journalist was now hammering out every syllable because she was talking to an old woman...

"Was it Thirina Hanım? Oh, a Hanımefendı?"

The Madam was silent. Imagining her face made the situation even more sweet.

"From what I have gleaned from the women innkeepers you are indeed an esteemed personality. But the matter I fail to grasp is this: what would be your considerations of the Free Libya Resistance? Do you pen your name as the Illustrious Thirina or is it Tirina?"

Madam Lilla was still drawing out her silence.

I say, "I'm telling you, Lilla is going to be in the headline tomorrow in the *New York Times*: 'A traitorous attack on the American press by an old Gaddafi fanatic!' Laughing, Amira throws herself on her bed. Maryam gestures with her hand to say, 'who is that?' In the same drawling accent, I say, "Allison Abou Chaar! CNN een-teer-nash-inal!"

Madam Lilla must have known we were listening because she also started speaking in classical Arabic:

"Ah! My gracious mademoiselle! I am so very delighted to make your esteemed acquaintance! We were expecting someone like you, an exceptional personality, who might remedy all our woes. If you knew just how desperate we are for freedom. Starved for democracy!"

After a pause we realize she's going to change her tactic: the silence doesn't bode well for the American – an idiot who may know journalism but nothing about real people. And pumped full of enthusiasm, she sticks to her trade.

"As you must be aware, this is why we have the honour to be here. Has your excellency made the acquaintance with the Gaddafi family? Are you a resident of Libya? Or are you one of those poor souls subjected to his oppression? In short what is the reason for your presence in these environs? Or have you been in flight for all these years?"

We could tell from Madam Lilla's rising breath that a story was on the way.

"Ah! Don't ask, Mademoiselle. We are in the midst of endless misfortune. If you only knew for what reasons we have come to these dwellings... For the story behind our visitation to this miserable place is filled with sadness. I can only expect that you have marshalled the facts pertaining to the war. Is this true?"

The girl jumped.

"But of course, of course!"

Madam Lilla was writing the play and playing the star role at the same time.

"Then you know that Gaddafi's son, the accursed Saif al-Islam is on the run."

"Yes, yes?"

She was as excited as a medical student taking blood for the first time and finding the vein.

Madam Lilla was now laying it on thick.

"Ah! The scoundrel! The ingrate! The miserable wretch!"

The girl was speechless. She was probably thinking that in

just fifteen minutes she'd be doing an interview with Saif al-Islam, the most wanted man in the world.

Nearly out of breath, she said, "Yes?"

"Well, you see, the vile cretin..."

She stopped and we held our breath behind the door. Suddenly she said, "Have you met my daughters?"

She had us pinned there behind the door, and in a piercing voice she called out to us as if she were calling her kids to come have lunch in the garden.

"Şerfifeeee, Hanifeee, Mebrukeeee!"

Maryam and I had to swallow our laughter. Momentarily holding back her giggles, Amira called out, "Coming mother!"

Jaw-dropped and wide-eyed, Maryam and I whispered, "What?" Amira whispered, "Get into your chadors!"

"But I'm a terrible actor," said Maryam, making a run for it. Amira grabbed her and pushed her towards the door. So we all slipped into our chadors and walked onto the stage.

When Madam Lilla was just about to reveal the tastiest bit of news, her show cut to a commercial break and Allison the Journalist nearly lost it – she thought she had the big fish by the tail. Now she is willing to spend time with these three covered women but only if they can be of some use to her; she must be already counting how many minutes, even seconds, of them she'll have to bear. When all she really wanted to do was throw Madam Lilla to the ground and wrench the information out of her like she was pulling teeth. Madam Lilla turned to me and said, "So Mebruke hanım, I was just telling this writer here that words will not suffice to describe what Saif al-Islam did to our family."

I nodded my head under the chador. That was all from me. Glancing at the front door to the house I could see Samira giggling. Clearly she was the one who got us into this mess in the first place. Seeing I had no flair for this sort of thing,

Madam Lilla quickly turned to Amira, "You tell us about the rascal, Saif."

Heaving a terribly troubled sigh and in a mysterious tone of voice that alluded to the horrors we had supposedly suffered at the hand of the scoundrel Saif al-Islam, she said, "But mother is it right for us to share something so secret with a journalist?"

Madam Lilla was pleased to see the game had moved up a level. And as we all turned to her, Allison said with the sheer incompetence of an impatient glutton, "Of course, sweetie, if you can't convey such information to me then who else can you convey it to?"

Now Maryam had the ball. She wanted to raise the stakes, "Alright then, mother, but are we really going to disclose his current location?"

Any minute now the young reporter would keel over from overexcitement. Madam Lilla knew how to stoke the fire. Thinking for a moment she mumbles and grumbles. And finally to keep the girl alive to suffer even more torture she says, "yes".

Amira takes the ball and runs, "Ah, my dear lady, our family has been in league with the British for years."

Clasping her hands together Madam Lilla stirs her on.

"But of course. We adore the English."

"Yes," says Amira, positioning herself to dish out more baloney. Who knew where she might take this. Mustering all her talents she adopts a new voice for the role.

"We are a family of informants. Yes... Our father served as a commander for the Free Libya Resistance in the north. After all this is about our country beyond all else and so we had to step away for a while. This is the way of our clan, sacrificing our lives for the country. Yes..."

Amira pauses for a moment and Madam Lilla picks up on

the reference to the father and to buy time she says, "Yes, my husband was a brave commander. Yes, Şerife, do tell this young writer all about him."

With a confidence that only comes with a well-prepared lie, Amira barrels forward.

"Gaddafi slaughtered our brothers and sisters. Our esteemed father sent us here to be safe. We were going to travel to England but it is time for freedom! It is time for revenge!"

Sensing this outburst was going to last the girl's eyes bounced between the four of us like ping-pong balls. For the love of God, she only wanted someone to tell her where Saif al-Islam was hiding. Amira didn't draw it out for too long.

"Esteemed Lady, we have been told that Saif al-Islam will be here in just five or six days. But now it's no longer safe for us to stay. We have no choice but to leave."

The girl's eyes opened so wide there was hardly any room left for her nose and her mouth. Straightaway she fished her phone out of a pocket in her cargo pants. Maryam finished with a double-check.

"Esteemed writer, only Fatima Hanım, the oldest of the innkeepers here, knows this. We implore you not to let anyone else know. But Saif will indeed be meeting with traitors in this place to arrange for his escape."

"Of course, of course," said Allison who was dying to give the good news to her editor. Now she only needed to get rid of us as soon as possible.

And with that our theatre-in-the-round came to an end, a comedy in which a journalist's greed is more than her knowledge could buy. Before the curtain had even touched the stage Miss Een-ter-nash-inal was gone with both hands glued to her phone. Madam Lilla went inside first and she started to laugh. Clutching our sides we threw ourselves down on our beds, our throats aching from holding back the laughter. Madam Lilla announced, "Good morning, ladies! It's going to be a wonderful day!"

"It already is," said Maryam.

Any sadness from the night before seemed washed away in the waters of the Nile. Now and then Madam Lilla flashed me a look, wondering if I was going to ask her about what I'd seen in the pavilion. I avoided her gaze, trying not to make her feel uneasy. When she settled down she clapped her hands. "OK then. Put on your necklaces. They're coming to pick us up."

*

It seemed like the sun was beating down on just that point in the world, its light shimmering off the sliver necklace that hung between Amira's breasts. Given to her by the old, blue-faced man as if it were some kind of key, it seemed made for Amira's olive-colored skin, sparkling like a mirror as it slid over the smooth, moist, mother-of-pearl surface of her chest that rose and fell with her breathing.

The silver chain that ran between Maryam's strong collarbone would get twisted when she craned her neck to one side. Part of it would stick to her skin. When the sweat dries the weight of the charm pulls the chain from her skin and the charm falls back down between her collarbone – I am watching how it happens.

Madam Lilla never lets go of her necklace. When she touches the silver charm her forefinger is tucked under her other fingers. She places the charm directly over her sternum, searching for the centre with her fingers. There the slightest, graceful, trembling worry in her hands...

We were behind Dido's house. After we had said goodbye

282

to everyone and told Samira that she should keep Allison busy in the house until we had left, we went out to wait. Madam Lilla said, "How lucky you all are…"

Still holding her necklace, she went on when she was sure that Maryam and Amira were listening, "You're the heroes of a story. No one can take you prisoner. No one can tell you to stay. You're not obliged to make a decision. How lucky… "

The words went straight to Amira's heart. Her voice was like a half-open tin of preserves, the sharp, jagged metal peeling back.

"Yes."

That was all she said, nothing more. Madam Lilla smiled, looking away, and with sadness in her voice she said, "And in the middle of a desert of a country whose every nook and cranny is observed from space but not really seen."

Deadpan, Maryam said, "We even made it past CNN eenteernashunal…"

There is a flurry of dust in the distance. It's the same car that came with our necklaces. It comes closer then stops beside us. Heat shimmering off the hood, our faces crinkling in the bright light and the heat. Out steps the same dashing young man from the Lavazza commercial. Amira leans forward and her necklace unpeels from her breast; Maryam's chain quivers as she cranes her neck; Madam Lilla's necklace sits calmly in her sternum. Without saying a word we get into the car. Madam Lilla rides shotgun and the three of us, following the usual stage directions, sit in the back. Silently the young man steps on the gas – he might have said good morning but I wasn't even paying attention. After driving for a few minutes we come to a fork in the road. The young man stops and looks at a hill across from us. There is a horse on the peak. Its tasselled harness creates an undulating shadow. On top of the horse sits a man. Madam Lilla sees him. She takes off her necklace, holds it in the sunlight, levelling the glimmer on the man. He raises his hand. From the way he moves it's clear he's the blue-faced man. He's wearing a Prussian blue scarf, fluttering in the wind. Self-possessed, Madam Lilla puts her necklace back on. "Man, oh man," says Amira, astonished.

Her eyes fixed on the road and one arm draped out of the open window, Madam Lilla slowly nods her head. The old man, who has fallen to unrequited love, sends us off into the desert. And that's how we left.

The young man's cologne fills the car. It smells something like adventure. Like a dove in heat, Amira is moving, eager. Maryam looks frustrated with Amira's fixation on the man. Madam Lilla is steeped in a grave silence. Looking at the man, Amira says to Madam Lilla, "We could have at least stopped and said hello. The poor guy has come all the way out here for us."

As if angry with Amira for imposing her concerns Madam Lilla suddenly explodes:

"For a man, mademoiselle, I have taken off my faerie shirt. But if all the men in the world went up on all the mountaintops in the world and waited for me on horseback, if they all kissed my feet, not one of them would give back a single button from that shirt."

What had just happened? Why was she so angry? Maryam was looking out of the window with seemingly no interest in the exchange. Amira was still obsessed with the young man. I couldn't be sure if she was paying any attention to Madam Lilla either. I wondered if Nana Fatima had been referring to the blue-faced man when she held the broomstick over Lilla's stomach and said, 'Go back to him, Thirina, give yourself back to him?' Maybe women who chose to disregard the praise of princes and degrade themselves were like this: a display of love only reminded them of a broken device in their hearts. Amira's eyes are fixed on the young man as her cheeks flush bright red. She goes on, "But the poor man has been so gracious to us."

Spinning angrily around, Madam Lilla looks Amira in the eye. But she doesn't even notice – she's that focused on the young man. Maryam and I are watching them. The man is checking Amira out in the rear-view mirror. This is really happening in the middle of the desert, and so early in the morning. With a glance Madam Lilla's understands what's happening and for a moment she seems to delight in the hormones fluttering through the car. Flirtatiously she asks the man, "No music? Amy Winehouse or something like that?"

We smile.

Stirring up the love that was rising in the car and spilling out of the windows, Madam Lilla starts up a new little game.

"That's just what I was saying, dear Amira, you can never trust them. You must never give in. What's a man anyway? The dirt on our hands. A creature that knows nothing of humility. If you are not an elusive deer they will turn you into one of those doleful looking cows."

Turning her head back to the window, Maryam quietly smiled and I did too. Teasing through dramatic pauses, Lilla carries on with her speech.

"Take this young man for example … please give us your name Apollo."

The young man throws back his head, his white teeth glimmering in the sunlight, dramatically shifts into a higher gear and opens his mouth as if he might actually give us his name.

"We have immense respect for you, Tin Abutut. As for my father's love for you … well you already know. Everyone does."

That was it. He didn't give us his name and he didn't say any more than that. She flashed a sugary smile that suggested she was wondering whether she should dance with this young fox, mulling it over for a split second, and then Madam Lilla went on, "And we have great respect for your father. So you have been warned about speaking to us. Wonderful! Well then, tell me what he said about me?"

Raising his chin, the young man only smiles to show he's not going to fall for it and he is silent.

After a brief pause Madam Lilla shared with us her theories about men, which lasted the whole four-and-a-half hour journey, her sarcasm making everybody laugh except Amira. Each story was more outrageous than the next. And each one started the same way: 'my dear Amira'. The young man was like stone, and, to give him credit, he didn't once open his mouth to protest. Was it his Tuareg upbringing or something else, Madam Lilla couldn't get a word out of him. But for her the pleasure comes from the difficulty in the challenge. Meanwhile Amira kept waiting for the young man to say something but not so much as a peep.

Finally Madam Lilla reached a new height.

"Of course the most important thing, my dear Amira, is this: if a man says nothing don't be fooled into thinking anything is actually going on up there and that he has simply chosen not to speak. If he doesn't speak it's because he's got nothing to say. Especially with smart women because that's their strongest weapon against them. They know that silence can bring women to their knees. The young man here is playing just that card. He also needs his roots to be ripped out altogether. Do you see what I am saying, my dear Amira?"

In the back seat we all laugh and shrink in shame. Madam Lilla, however, will not stop before she twists the knife in his stomach and smiling all the while. With love she has devastated this young man's father but now she's not going to let his son live.

Finally we stop in the middle of a sea of sand. In all directions nothing but an endless shimmering yellow sea. Standing there are seven camels and three men. The young man steps out of the car first and we follow. From Lilla's movements we understand that we should collect our things and head for the camels. Amira lingers behind. Turning around I look. The young man is sitting on the sand. Amira is standing over him. Their shadows are shimmering in the rising heat. The man says nothing, he only looks up. He reaches out and holds her ankle. She seems about to lose balance and I hear: "Don't hold anything else. Hold me."

Slowly he leans over and kisses her ankle. In that moment she seems prepared to give to this stranger (or the fantasy she has built around him) not only herself, but every remaining second of her life. I know this is exactly how she feels. Amira looks at me intently, as if her brow is begging for mercy and understanding. She wants to stay. Leave us and stay behind... Which is why in that moment I think Madam Lilla is bringing us to a war we declared by default. Another war that is lost for all the women who are the victims of men as well as their fantasies about women. And with that we set out into the desert. Maybe there we will find the strength we're looking for. As Nana Fatima said, 'if nobody sees you maybe you will see yourself.' Walking ahead Madam Lilla calls out to us over her shoulder, "Oh, you're so lucky..."

20

Muhammed's Fourth Letter

Now that you are reading these letters, well then... you have come back to Tunisia! Hurray! Do you know what this is like? Dawn is breaking in the forest and all is well!

I couldn't imagine you in another city. It was strange. And now you have come to Tunis, and I can see you there with my own eyes. You're wandering through the street market and I'm watching you, because I'm following you. You can't escape me even when I'm gone. You walk and walk and walk and suddenly spin around and... Hey! A piece of baklava for all the kids out on the street. It's on me!

You are looking right at me...

And add a soda to go with the baklava!

Now I wish I could be there with you in Tunis. I could have been the light that now falls from eyelashes that flutter over these letters, the cool ceramic tiles under your bare feet. You know that I'm not all that bad with those kinds of things. I would give you an armful of those little orange flowers on the noses of those peppers on the branch. Without thinking twice I would promise that when your hair fell over your face I would tuck the fallen strands in place with admiration. So I would always win with the first good morning and every good night lost in the honey slumber that would be mine. And no one could ask more from you. We would sleep and wake up together. What more is there than that? Our branches bending under the weight of our roses, we would break. We would pray with pure and peaceful minds. The pebbles we would gather from the sea would never dry and fade and all the cheerful fisherman and rosy-faced green grocers would take care of all the orphans in the world. So you see my love, if we could do that then we could have faith in one another. The God I know would forgive us for that. Day and night I would bask in the breath he gave to you. I would give thanks to God. What more could there be...

Fine then, yes, all this can never really happen. All because of me and my flaws. More than anything else I wanted to be a more capable person for you. But this defeat does not mean that we have broken our backs in the long jump of love. We are among the ones who leap up and vanish into thin air. You and I share a love in a league all its own. We are unrivalled – we are both going to win in the end. Indeed we are the only referees. And that means we are at such a high level it's impossible to describe. And so I have no doubt in my mind that we will hold up that cup together.

My love, please, you should always keep these things in mind. Let's work for it and if we have no other choice let's hope for it. And if there is no other way let's have faith in goodness. Otherwise it will all just weigh us down, sweetie. Compared to what we have, what is this earth? Nothing but a ball of cotton. Even space cannot carry fallen loves. In short the fact that we are finished without falling is the lesser of two evils. Sweetie, this is the after life of our love, we are already in heaven.

Now that we already have one foot in heaven we can push aside some other awkward issues. I suppose I should say a few words about my decision to disappear. What can I say? Ever since you left I just couldn't stand being around any more, my little sweetheart. Always with the same losers, and always the same old, boring routines. Your absence should take the seat of honour in the corner of grief. But I understand this: what we call a 'country' is a fantasy. And when the fantasy falls apart we are nothing but refugees even when we stand in the centre of our capital city. What's more, when I look around I don't see the possibility of balanced justice and joyous piety walking hand in hand.

But that's not important. For time is the concern of unbelievers. Do you know that I was left alone, which hurt me a little. I feel like there's always this enormous ball of paper in my mouth and when I chew it grows. I said to myself that I should head out to sea to save myself from drowning and if nothing else there is the chance that I will wash up on another shore and be saved.

This is nothing new. This country has always oppressed us. We love it the way we would love an orphan defeated by base injustices. In other words this country is worse off than you think, as savage as an unloved orphan. We try to tousle his hair and embrace him but he only tears us apart for fear that we might abandon him again. That's why he threatens our lives. But my life wouldn't satisfy even a fraction of its needs. More importantly there's nothing like blood to make people thirsty. They might devour me whole but this would only stoke other appetites.

I suppose I've thought about this enough and I've made my decision – best not to be anybody. It just seemed like a good idea to board a boat with all those nobodies. Nothing is as crystal clear as fading away and losing yourself. An existence more peaceful than fading away into a flow has not yet been invented. Is there a more essential way of 'being' than curling up one night like the Arabic letter vav and becoming whole?

In any event God sees you. And then to become the letter mim that shrinks to a dot on the page and disappears. Think about it, is there any better way to be 'one'? Little one, you know I'd get by if there were just a single ray of hope shining through the leaves of a walnut tree. Hey! Don't look at me like that. It's not really that melodramatic. I'm fine. Don't worry. Like all the others who can't swim I'm completely comfortable in the sea. Honey, if I am lucky I am about to disappear altogether. I'm simply not here and neither am I there.

I won't draw this out any more. You are my only unbroken dream. You're really tough, aren't you? Even in the hand of a miserable klutz like me you are as nimble as a drop of water. Now I'm thinking about how glorious it would be to disappear with you. We wouldn't even be nobodies, we would be absence itself. We would complete each other like two curled up vav letters, our tails in each other's bellies, like that, existing and then dying. Life on this planet isn't right for anything else. People can only get lost on their own, at least for now. Thank God for that. I mean in the forest everything's running smoothly. The weather's balmy. It's the best way to think about it, don't mind the rest.

If you're still upset when you get back to this country, honey, then just take off. All things considered the best is to live large. When you fail to live small this is your best revenge. As for all the different sizes of life... Life should be rich and open to the point where you could feel almost absent, that small. Besides when you dance you add space to space, the air around you expands. All I know is how to get by, and I've already told you that. Anyway...

Your absence isn't darkness. Your absence is a flood of light, leaving people no other choice but to shut their eyes.

Come on then, sweetie. Let's walk. Beautifully. If you walk beautifully your destination comes to you.

Grace me with the crumb of a prayer. My heart is always locked in a prayer for you.

Your puppet on limp strings,
Muhammed

*

"So that means that you actually ... I mean since the beginning... Breaking the bride's neck in the hamam and all that ... I mean you actually did all that, and those things didn't happen to you... In other words you wanted to get lost... Seeing that Muhammed Efendi was already talking about it ... I mean because this Muslim Romeo said those things you... Amira! Are you trying to destroy yourself? Amira! I'm talking to you."

It was the first time Maryam was speaking with real surprise in her voice. She wanted to hold Amira responsible for finding herself in the middle of the desert, as she had so many times before. Most likely the best thing to do was keep quiet, maintain a solemn silence, and understand without knowing; in short, we had to be like a mirage. And so a dreamy, oriental and entirely mystical stage would perfectly suit the course of that day and the evening to come. But the "desert tea" we had been steeping throughout the day under the sheltering sky wasn't all that fresh.

*

The three men started walking towards us and Madam Lilla checked to see if our necklaces were visible. They were all wearing headscarves – one blue, one black and one with a black and white pattern. She pulled my necklace out from under my shirt. The fuss she was making over the necklaces seemed awkward and old-fashioned in comparison to the brusque style of the men. They immediately hurried us up onto the camels while Madam Lilla slowly mounted as if she were delighting in a documentary film about herself that was finally being shot. Each camel had a canopy made of fine white cloth. And Madam Lilla's camel...

"Ah ... he hasn't forgotten how much I love dark-blue silk..."

Her canopy was made of the sweetest, loveliest night-blue silk; and as a love letter sent by the blue-faced man with no hope of an answer, it fluttered in the wind like a flag. Fleetingly stroking her necklace, she pulled herself up onto her camel with the men helping. We got on, too. Maryam went first, I was in the middle and Amira brought up the rear. Of course Madam Lilla rode ahead. Once the men had placed our bags up on the camels, which they did in the twinkling of an eye, we were ready to go. Two of the men chose to walk alongside us, thinking one of us might topple off. The man in black was next to me and the man wearing black and white was between Maryam and Amira. The little man in blue rode on the camel in the rear. With her hair blowing in the wind, Madam Lilla set off on course. Not a word was said. The desert began.

It seemed as if we had come to believe deeply not only in Madam Lilla but in her lovers, too. The only official documents we had were the necklaces around our necks, and our only escorts were the men of Lilla's former lover. And we couldn't even see their faces as they led us across the desert. We were travelling with these men but we only could make out their feet. And we went on.

Here time covers everything like a great physical mass. You can see it. It comes right at you. It is long, deep and wide. And when you see this yellow headless mass of time from a distance, you understand that you will talk to yourself about things you never talked about before, or so you think. But the time and the space can be so overwhelming that you feel drowsy and you postpone the conversation with yourself. A voice inside you says, 'In any event those words will come when the time comes.' But time is not something that comes and goes, time is now, a bright, yellow mass that pulls you within. You are in the heart of time. So for a long time in the desert you are quiet. You aren't really thinking. So as not to be swept away in this sandy presence, you must press your mind to keep a hold on the names of things. But your effort is like a child in the face of the ancient desert. When the desert dashes its mind upon you, unleashing that great swathe of time and mass, you understand that it is futile to persist in the same old way of thinking.

For the first time we were travelling without looking at each other's faces. Under the sun we were all shimmering waves of heat rising into the sky; the outlines of our bodies splintering into eternal vibration; our shapes and the world around us separating as we moved higher and higher. We were roasting in the heat.

Madam Lilla kept sniffing the air. Though there wasn't much to smell in the heat she seemed hungry, as if a faint scent kept eluding her. From under her dark blue canopy, she gazed out over that blank, infinite desert as if it was an infinite circus. There must have been layers and layers of memories in what she saw. Beneath everything we could see she must have seen so much more. Every passing moment she must have seen versions of herself from past stages in her life: there to one side is a thirty-three year old Lilla riding camelback into the distance and Madam Lilla of today looks at her and smiles at all the foxes bounding through the mind of her former self; then over there is the forty-two year old Lilla on horseback, galloping beside the blue-faced man. Lilla now sees the worry carved into her younger face and she feels a pang of sorrow; and perhaps an entirely different Lilla in her fifties is passing over this very spot in a plane above, dabbing at her mascara with a handkerchief. She looks up to see that even then she was already on the way to killing Jezim Anwar. Probably cursing so much life spent on such a mission. Maybe she could have turned out to be a different woman, sitting in a garden and fanning herself with a newspaper after finishing the crossword puzzle, and forgetting the name of her grandson. But instead she's gazing out over the desert like she's looking through her album with moving photos. She is a woman with tremendous stories, a woman who sees so much when she looks at nothing, and who must live without sharing these stories. She must keep her mind busy. She must laugh at her life and the desert because she's learned on countless occasions that no mirage has a direct equivalent in the real world. Here was a Madam Lilla we would never know, steeped in all her years. Now swaying from side to side on her camel, which Maryam had aptly nicknamed Rosinante, Madam Lilla was stewing like strong tea. Yes, Maryam was right, this woman is living in another world altogether, because she sees the images of a magnificent life covered by layers of time.

Whenever I turned around I saw Amira looking down at her foot. She'd also taken off her shoes when she got up on the camel. But her feet were now different – something else altogether. She was looking down at the place that had been kissed. Now she adores her ankles in a way she never did before. Madam Lilla was right. It was a sheer lie, this thing about loving yourself, whoever made that up. You only learn to love yourself after you have been loved. I look down at my feet. Just feet. I look at Maryam's feet and her ankles, body parts that are still unaware. Then I look at Lilla's feet thrown up on her camel's back. I look and look and look. The song Lilla played for us on our first night runs through my head:

How long it's been without love
I look and the song is spinning.

Only Amira's feet have been refreshed with love.

With that kiss the body becomes one. But when those lips go away the body is divided: there is a foot, a hand, a belly. Maryam and I are like this. Pieces and parts.

Maryam has many parts. Beside Amira she is her male counterpart. When Amira isn't around there is a genderless aspect that comes back to her. And there is a part that struggles to knead dough despite a head without hair. There's an angry part but also a part that does up Madam Lilla's buttons. She struggles to love something. If she can, her locks will open. And then she would fall apart. There is something she isn't saying. There is something Maryam never says. I look at all the feet again. In fact there is something they are all hiding. All but a mirage. A figment of the imagination.

When the sky starts to turn red you can catch the tail end of time. When the sun reaches its appointed place in the sky it dies. In their chadors the men pitch tents against the wind. Pat-pat-pat went the wind and their scarves and the tents were intertwined. After twisting and hammering and covering they are done and the bodies of the men separate from the cloth. Frugal like three pigeons: piling one piece of garbage on top of another and calling it sweet home and faithfully settling down. They make a fire and we all sit round the flames. I expect them to roll bread in the palms of their hands or go hunting and roast an animal on a spit, just like in the movies. But it doesn't happen. Instead they crack open tins of tuna and pull slices of bread out of plastic bags. They eat from under their veils and we take little bites. Nobody says a word. We aren't there – only our feet. We stretch out to each other. And the men's feet are there – more prominent than their eyes.

When we finish eating they lean close to the fire with their hands on their chests and say their names from under their veils.

"Furkan." With the black-and-white patterned veil. He has young, eager feet. Toes that were allowed to grow freely and so there is laughter between them. Each one sits like a shameless little boy never accused of a thing. Feeling neither beautiful nor ugly. Forever walking and smiling without an ounce more sadness than the world has ever given them, they have raced and jumped and have always been calmly scratched. These feet are so light you get the impression their soles have always hovered just above the sand; and their toenails have never touched stone. Light and shadowy like the fine line between night and day.

"Tariq." The giant of a man in the black veil. Whose wrists were incredibly thin despite the vast open space of the desert... whose feet were still walking though covered in deep scratches and so many scars... he must have had faith in the road... with every step he took there was the slightest hesitation and his foot didn't strike the ground directly but rolled a little to either side. Sinking into the sand, his heel slid from side to side. With every step the desert sand filed down his feet a little more. No doubt this ever-so-slight hesitation before every footfall wore down his skin much more than other walkers.

The third man never lifted his little head out from under his blue veil. And he never said a word. He slowly pushed his feet out from under his robe... And the moment we saw them...

"I am Tin Abutut," she said. Revealing her face. "His daughter..."

Her expression is blank. She looks at Madam Lilla with something close to admiration. Her eyes lined with kohl are as empty as the desert. She pulled out her necklace, a token of her words. It was the same as ours – a silver necklace. Once she was sure Madam Lilla had seen it she put it away and covered her face. Furkan and Tariq bowed their heads. Amira and I were shocked. Maryam crossed her arms as if she suddenly felt a chill. And Madam Lilla... She was startled for only a moment and then – as if nothing out of the ordinary had just happened, as if there was nothing strange about this young woman, indeed the daughter of the blue-faced man who was travelling with us in man's clothing – she leaned closer to the fire and changed our names:

Houeida, Rasha, Rana.

As if in a dream Madam Lilla rose to her feet and started walking. There must have been an expression on her face she didn't want anyone to see. Her feet sinking into the sand, she left us. Shaking her skirt and the sand around it, the girl went into her tent. She was a chess player who had just made her opening move. And she had stepped back to wait.

Plucking embers out of the fire, Furkan and Tariq moved a little further on. Sitting opposite one another they lit a smaller fire and took out little pipes. Slowly they began to crumble the hashish in the palms of their hands. They were doing it so slowly it seemed as if they were already smoking through the tips of their fingers. They filled their pipes. Gravely they lit them, only their eyes gleaming. Two or three puffs later and they were still silent. But then they began as if picking up a conversation from the night before.

"The holy book says that 'humankind must consider why they were created.' Why do you think we were created Tariq?" asked Furkan.

Without hesitation, Tariq answered.

"The book says, 'Your Creator has given you the power to see his love and compassion for you.' If we are of His breath then that is our binding duty, Faruk. It is not about thinking but about showing compassion and conscience. Surely that is why we were created!"

They paused. Then Tariq calmly read from the Alaq verse.

"He made us out of love, fascination and care."

Furkan was restless again.

"But the Book says, 'Pay attention to those who glorify their fancies.' But in that case what makes love possible without ambition?"

They thought about it together. Tariq spoke.

"Draw away the blankets that cover ambition, Furkan. And look closely at what is underneath. But first get lost. Now you are on the thin line between light and darkness. You are on the razor's edge of life. Lose yourself, young brother. Lose yourself until you reach the core."

And they lay down and slept. It was such a strange conversation that I couldn't be quite sure if the three of us lying there awake beside the fire were nothing but a dream.

The scene was strange enough to make us forget the possible story of this girl who had been named Tin Abutut. Dusting the sand off her hands, Maryam brought her legs to her chest and smiled.

"Yes, azizi. We're in the middle of another strange scene in this adventure. Let's make the best of it."

"What is going on here, girls!? This adventure is nothing but one strange day after another," I said. Resting her chin on her knees, Amira said, "This is really weird..."

"Where do you start?" asked Maryam, "that girl there ... there's something strange about her. If you ask me..."

Looking pensively down at her feet and wiggling her toes, she said, "This thing about getting lost...."

"What are you talking about," Maryam asked Amira. She looked up at us absentmindedly.

"What are you saying, girl. Out with it," I said impatiently and Amira reached for her bag and pulled out her letters. She began to read. When she finished Muhammed's fourth letter it was the first time Maryam spoke with such surprise.

"So that means that you actually ... I mean since the beginning ... breaking the bride's neck in the hamam and all that... I mean you actually did all that, and those things didn't happen to you...?

Amira's eyes were glazed over and still. Muhammed had told her to 'get lost'. And that's just what she did. Now there is hardly any room to move. We're in the middle of the desert.

"Amira," I said. "Sometimes people set traps for themselves without even knowing. Is that what you did?"

Maryam asked: "Amira are we here right now because of this Muhammed?"

300

Amira's voice was strained. "I didn't forgive Muhammed and I'm alone, Maryam. But you have a wound far worse than cancer. Something you can't forgive yourself for. I have no idea what it is. But you're out here to lose yourself. You don't even want to see yourself. Isn't that it?"

Maryam was calm and, like Amira, she rested her chin on her legs.

"You can breathe on her but a breath that can blow you right into hell, and you just can't say when and where."

Both looked at me at the same time.

"That's enough," I said, slapping the sand out of my hands, "Tell me why in the world I need to get lost in your breathing? Explain that riddle for me?"

They were both staring at the fire. Even calmer now, they looked as if they had already answered me and I hadn't heard. Maryam stopped for a spell and then said, "Eh!" or something like that and she was leaning back as if protesting against her own hesitation. She pulled her notebook out of her bag. Looking over at me, her eyebrows raised, she said, "Azizi, allow me to repeat to you what Madam Lilla said to me when we were crossing the border, 'don't take yourself so seriously. Otherwise you'll end up taking your own life.'"

And with that she started to read...

*

Dido's Fourth Tablet

Hey, lofty soldier! So you won't come. Then the sorceresses with marked cheeks were right: there will be no miracle. The gods will all love me as if I am one of their own. They will never show compassion and make me happy. This morning I turned my face to the swamps of Carthage. I turned my

301

back on the sea. No longer am I searching the horizon for ships. I am only hoping for a storm. Today I will consecrate animals to the gods so that they will tear your ships from the sea and your image from my mind. Seven days have passed and you have not arrived.

And so I will confess, stranger! My enemies never received the punishment that was due. What they have done to me is already forgotten and no justice was done. They are now no different than all the other frogs in the swamps of Carthage. I have swallowed such rage, stranger, only to stay on my feet, and my stomach is full of bile. They are under the impression that a ruler can maintain the throne by simply wiping out all her enemies. They are under the impression that a queen lives by killing. Yet a ruler only maintains rule if she can remain quiet in the face of fools. And preserving pride in the face of fools is like being cut with a dull knife.

I am a weary queen, stranger. And you are not coming. And if you do you will bring me no miracle. By expecting such a miracle from you I am throwing myself into a terrible pit of fire. Sadly life has left me no other choice. Having seen my misery the most dangerous thing for me now is to believe in you. Don't come! Go away! Sail away from my shores. There is not enough room in these swamps for another frog!

I have fallen out of the gods' favor because I convinced myself to believe in you. But I do not care at all about the gods and so I have forsaken them. Even Penelope now looks at me with pity. I have grown so small that I took shelter in her who once took shelter in me. Your love cannot heal me. So go, stranger!

Last night I told them to shut the lighthouse. So even if you did come you would never find the pier. Carthage is now in darkness and you will be lost. And, like me, you will drown. Like me you will wrestle with the gods under the earth. I have warned all of Carthage not to light their candles tonight. The entire country is feigning death so that you will have no sign from us. The palace lies on its back like a cockroach so that you will pass by without ever seeing. And so you see the extent to which we fear you stranger.

I pray for the sun not to rise in the morning. I pray that Carthage will be hidden from you even in daylight. Let the gods bring you a dream. Let them call you to other seas, to other women, to other lands. On the shores of this swamp, yes, with tears in my eyes, I am praying to the gods for this.
You have shown me my own misery, stranger. Silk is no longer silk, glass is no longer glass. I will shed the blood of seven oxen at dawn. Let the gods return me to my former self. Let them not allow the reflection of my defeated self to appear in the mirror again. Today I am sacrificing all the wheat of my country to the sun. Let Carthage go without bread, as long as you pass by and leave us. Let your ship take away the nightmare you have brought with you. Bring this shrunken, fearful, wretched Dido back to the shores whence you came. Give me back my old life, stranger. Give me back the birds, and my voice will fade in their song. Judas Trees and lilac-coloured glass. Go and return to me my country, stranger. Have mercy on me. Let not the glory of Carthage fall.

You are the sin of a queen who only for once has chosen to believe in gods and miracles instead of herself. Go back to the hell you came from.

Hey, cruel arrogance! Go and let me lose myself. Let me lose myself so that no eye can see me. Ah! If only it were possible to wipe out the history of this place with black magic. So that no one would remember, not even the gods.

I appeal to the gods, indeed I curse you from the shores of Carthage. I appeal to the gods to try your heart. Let the gods give you fantasies that will never end. So you can never relinquish them, even when you know them to be false. So that you will sail into oblivion. So that you will not sail to victory but to your doom. And your beloved servants should cry out like Penelope when you sink into the abyss. Let neither the hands of the gods nor the doctors touch that dark core of your heart.

Hey, shameless traitor! If I had the courage and the strength to once again sail upon the Mediterranean I would set out at dawn. If it were not too late to become another, I would set sail. But now it is too late to sever life in the middle and become another. So I will fade away and vanish like a defeated wretch. Hey stranger, of course I would one day fall to a fantasy. I would fall to my knees only before my nightmare like all the other rulers who have bested the truth. A ruler cannot disappear, simply go away. Rather she is defeated, falls and dies by the sword. Now looking at my miserable state in the dark of night, I am not such a ruler. I am but a daughter of a shepherdess who has done everything through wits and ambition and now I am losing it all with my heart and my dreams. However I cannot lock myself in a cave nor can I allow myself to be swept away with the sand in the desert like a shepherdess. There is no place left for me on this earth.

And then you too shall be cursed with all my might. Become even more visible when you want to disappear. When you wish to leave your feet shall be locked to the earth. Go stranger! Go so that my eyes will no longer see me.

*

The fire had gone out. The embers were breathing crimson. In the dark night we could only see the tips of our toes. "What if we get lost altogether?" I said. We were now consumed in darkness. Maryam reached out and took my foot. "We'll be found, azizi," she said. "Just have faith." We were just about to laugh when we saw the girl come out of her tent holding a large satellite phone. She disappeared in the darkness. As we were setting out on this journey towards the womb of the desert that strips everything of its name here was this young girl, with darkness in her eyes. We didn't know that she was hiding a story that told the essence of the desert.

21

"Because women show no mercy! Because time stands still in the desert! That is what makes a desert a desert!" said Madam Lilla. The words came out of her like a knife that she twirled before us. Then she was quiet as if waiting to see *which one of us would step up to edge of the blade. We were silent, as if on the brink of a terrible disaster in the middle of the desert, in the darkness of our second night in the tent. Amira and I were waiting for Madam Lilla to tell us how we were going to get out of this mess when Maryam turned to Madam Lilla, looked her in the eye, and said, "I believe we have the right to a question. And you are going to be completely honest with us."*

Madam Lilla seemed to have lost her resolve and her eloquence. And considering Maryam's state there seemed to be something far more pressing than finding a way out of our predicament. Madam Lilla was trapped in the middle of the desert and she needed our help. Maryam asked, "There is something else you didn't tell us, Madam."

Madam Lilla looked at me and Amira. No one was going to help her out of this one. She had no choice but to respond to Maryam. After everything that had happened that morning there was simply no other choice.

*

The sun was high in the sky and we had been on camelback for hours. In front was Tariq then came Madam Lilla, Maryam, me, Furkan, and finally Amira and Tin Abutut.

The order didn't fall into place naturally. An hour after we had set out in the morning Tin Abutut tentatively made her way over to Amira while Furkan kept riding between me and Maryam. Tin Abutut and Amira fell into conversation. It was impossible to hear. I could see Maryam now and then looking over her shoulder, trying to make out what they were saying or catch Amira's eye. And it went on like that throughout the day and on until nightfall. When we stopped for a break Amira kept away from us. Something like fear was swimming in her eyes. Maryam was growing more and more tense. Only after the fire was lit and we had eaten and Tin Abutut and Lilla retired to their tents did Amira get up and come over to us. Her head bowed, she whispered,

"We're in deep trouble. The girl ... seems she's up to something. Her dad, the blue-faced man, doesn't know she's here. I couldn't figure out if she has Tariq and Furkan involved in this. But this certainly has to do with Madam Lilla. I suppose she... I don't know. She's either going to kill her or hand her over to the English."

Turning she looked at us out of the corner of her eye. She lowered her head and playing with the sand she whispered, "She wants to take revenge on Madam Lilla for her mother. This love for Madam Lilla turned out to be a nightmare for all of them. Her father even gave his own daughter the name Tin Abutut. The name Madam Lilla goes by around here. As far as I can understand, when Madam showed up they gave this girl here the job of finishing her off. So when our good old Lilla ends up in the desert ... the girl is determined ... just so you know."

"And?" said Maryam, hanging her head and staring into the fire. Amira looked at me and tried not to be angry with Maryam, "And she said to me, 'I have no business with

307

you. If you leave me Lilla I'll send you back to Tunisia by helicopter.'"

"And if we don't?" I asked.

Amira buried her head in her chest, "I'm telling you the girl is determined. Is that clear enough for you?"

Taking a handful of sand, Maryam let out a deep sigh and said, "No one is going to kill that woman because I am going to do it myself." And she went over to the tent. We went in after her. Madam Lilla was sitting on the ground, cross-legged, looking at numbered pieces of paper under the light of a torch. As soon as we stepped inside she looked up and said calmly, as if she had been expecting us, "we need to make a plan." Maryam sat down on the ground and swiping at the papers said in a hushed voice, "Do you have any idea what is going on around here?"

Raising her eyebrows, Madam Lilla was silent to show how inappropriate it was to behave so rashly. Then running her eyes over the pages on the floor again she said, "so just as I expected," and she went on without pause: "We need to make a few minor adjustments in the plan. This means that I will have to call upon the help of someone I would rather not see at all. Which is problematic."

"Madam, this girl is going to kill you. And if we don't leave you she's going to kill us too. It seems you don't know what's really going on here."

Madam Lilla sharply cut her off:

"Everything is perfectly clear … a girl stigmatized by my love has come to avenge her mother. She thinks she'll gain her mother's love if she murders me…"

Maryam opened her eyes wide and leaned so close to Madam Lilla. I thought she might bite her:

"Why do you think she would do that?"

She looked up without an eyelash trembling and said those words.

"Because women never show mercy. Because time stands still in the desert. That's what makes a desert real."

Then she looked up at me and Amira, her head held high.

"Don't be afraid. Nothing is going to happen. If you help me we'll get out of here."

Before she could turn back to her numbers on the slips of paper, Maryam said, "just a minute, just one minute, Madam!"

She took the torch out of her hand and held it under her face.

"We are here because of you. And you can't get out without our help. I am going to ask you a question and you are going to give me an answer."

Madam Lilla turned up her nose and waited for the attack.

"Just one question," said Maryam, "but this time you're going to tell us the whole truth. I am asking you about a detail you have overlooked."

They looked like two gods that had risen up above the clouds, lightning crackling in their eyes. Maryam sat back down cross-legged and asked, "Madam, who was that young woman? At the hotel, in Baghdad, beside Jezim Anwar, the one who was carrying the same lighter he gave you."

She looked up at Maryam for only a second before turning off the torch. In the dark tent she began:

"After I tell you this, there will be nothing left to hide. I'm not telling you this to get you to accept my plan and not because you have forced my hand. I am telling you this so you'll know. You need to know that if you strive for a great life you must risk the penance of your sins..."

She paused. When she began again her voice seemed to come from another world:

309

"The one with Jezim Anwar ... she was my daughter."

I heard Maryam swallow a massive lump in her throat. Madam Lilla began her story.

"I saw her three times in my life. But she only saw me once, that day in Baghdad, in the hotel lobby. I first saw her when she was born. A black birthmark ran down her neck all the way to her collarbone, it looked like a vine... I took it as a sign that I should leave the baby and forget about her. When people decide to do shameful things they look for signs. I was so young and I couldn't stop. I had just begun to take my revenge on life. A baby would soften me... I wouldn't dare give birth to another me. So I left her in Alexandria. One day I would return. Always one day. When I was strong enough, when I had enough money, enough ... when I was no longer afraid. But she came to me before that day came. When I had thrown myself into the middle of a war in a fit of madness, tracking down a man who made off with zoo animals, she was there, an abandoned daughter searching for her mother. Who was crazier? We were two women risking our lives for people who didn't love us. Who was Jezim Anwar? The scoundrel whom we took to be a film star was nothing but a two-bit extra in our story."

She stopped again. For a few seconds it seemed like she was asleep. Waking, she went on, "I am telling you all this so that you will understand – the greatest crime is to betray one of your own. The price is too high to pay. If you betray your daughter or your sister your soul will never recover."

All of a sudden I remembered Nana Fatima in Yafran. She had said something like this when she was shucking beans: "Never betray a daughter or a sister."

Then I thought of another scene that had almost slipped my mind. That morning, right before we set off, in the pavilion Nana Fatima placed her broomstick on Madam

Lilla's stomach and said, "Go back to him, Thirina." How did it go? "Go back and surrender to him, Thirina. He learned his patience from the persistent butterfly not the angry camel." The details rushing back into my mind were so overwhelming that I suddenly interrupted Madam Lilla in the middle of her story.

"Who was Nana Fatima talking about, Madam? That morning in the tent she said, 'Go back to him and surrender.' Who was she talking about?"

Even in her lowest moments Madam Lilla could pull herself together like an army rising for battle when there was talk of surrender. "That is not the matter at hand," she snapped, cutting me off. And with that she went back to the lobby in Baghdad. With every turn in her story her voice sunk deeper into the mire:

"It wasn't hard to recognize her. There was the birthmark on her neck. And her face... She looked so much like me... Maybe I would look like her if I were the one who raised her. But when I suddenly saw her like that... I was terrified. Lighting her cigarette with Jezim Anwar's lighter ... she knew the whole story. Why I was there and what Jezim Anwar meant to me. I don't know how she did it. Let's just say she was her mother's daughter. She was very young, so young. And while I was covered in mud and with no shoes, and Jezim so coldly passed me by... I was already a stone. My daughter ... then I didn't even know her name ... Leila ... Leila ... she walked over to me and ... looked at me. She said..."

She couldn't go on. She turned away from us. And for a little while we listened to the muffled sobs of an old woman. It wasn't hard to understand that she was telling this story for the first time.

"I am telling you all this because... The day we met..."

Maryam asked, "What did Leila say?"

As if using a part of her voice she had never used before, Madam Lilla said, "'You stole my heart, mother. And so I stole yours.' That's what she said."

I was the only one who noticed Maryam crying in the darkness. A tear had fallen on my hand resting on the ground.

I assumed that was the hardest part for Madam Lilla to tell. I assumed that was the end of her dark story. But it wasn't. She went on. We didn't want to listen but she wanted to share. She took her gun out of the velvet pouch and placed it on the ground.

"When something horrible happens – it's been like this ever since I was a child – I tell myself, 'now you have two choices. You either fall or you get up and keep walking.' I don't know any other way. I turned around and walked."

Caressing her gun she was an eerie image, silently crying: "It was this gun. Leila took her own life with this gun."

We were frozen. Without looking at any of us and with her hand still on the gun she let out something like a scream from her soul but as low as a cat: "But I paid for it." She stopped again and this time spoke to convince herself: "I paid for it."

For some time we sat in silence. The effort it took her to tell her story surpassed the terrible weight of the story itself.

"Once I was afraid ... so afraid ... I thought I couldn't raise her. They scared me. I was afraid and now... there's nothing left but the empty pride of Madam Lilla. Don't be afraid. You mustn't be afraid."

When she found the strength to raise her head she looked at Maryam. She had something to say. She was exhausted. Silent. Only when she caught her breath was she able to speak: "This is the real reason I have set out on this journey

312

with you. I am trying to atone for a sin. I shall take revenge for her ... with her. A revenge for both of our hearts... I saw her three times. The third time... I thought I'd lost my mind, I thought everything was over. They gave me the gun. I told the men who were burying her that I was her older sister. I suppose you can go insane if you choose to. But it didn't happen like that."

Looking at Amira, she went on: "I heard you talking about losing yourself. Losing yourself is something else. After I left Leila in Baghdad I went out into the desert. I wandered far and wide. If I could have dared to die before Jezim Anwar, I would have killed myself with this gun. But I had to kill him first. I left this gun in Yafran so I wouldn't take my own life with it. I said that when I find a girl who is worthy enough to set out on this journey with me ... I can't do this alone. I need to have my daughter's heart with mine. So that is the real reason we have set out on this trip together."

Amira asked, "Why are you telling us this, Madam? Don't you think you've already punished yourself enough?"

There was a strange cruelty in her voice and I didn't expect this from Amira.

"Because, my dear Amira, only my equals can judge me. Was I supposed to explain myself to the vengeful who are thirsting for blood?"

A second tear fell from Maryam's cheek and struck my hand. But her voice was strong: "We will inform you of our decision, Madam Lilla."

Taking her notebook, she left the tent. I followed her out. We sat down at the fire. A little later Amira came and joined us. Maryam didn't say a word. She only opened her book and started to read.

*

313

Dido's Fifth Tablet

I am praying for the dead, stranger... For now they must die. The dead do not hear me and the gods lash me with their whips. When they are to forgive me they are asleep and when I remember my crime they are more alive than the living. Hey warrior! Do the sleepless dead come to you in your dreams?

O honourable sailor, I know that everything will sour. The gods will not bring down a miracle from the sky. For I am guilty. And you will not come. Because Dido is cursed by her crime. Dido should have died with her dead. My victory is proof of my sin. My soul is a tangle of corpses.

My husband the king of Phoenicia and my guards and sweet ladies of the kingdom ... none of them died so that I might live, stranger. But now the gods are asking me to account for the dead because I am still alive. The sea had made for you a gilded passage and the sun has lit a pathway on the water for your ship. A golden road that I can tread upon. When I stand on the hilltop where my palace stands and look out we come eye to eye. And like the locals here can you see the cursed fate in my eyes? O brave commander! Do you also carry in your body the bodies of those you betrayed? When Phoenicia was burning I carried them all to the Mediterranean. Even the sea has not yet cleansed me. Every night my sin pulls me deeper down, the hooks in my flesh.

How many people have been killed by the oversight of a spoiled princess? Killed by a favour... How many slaughtered souls because she never cared to look? How many hearts have burned because she withheld love? How many women have been sent to the dark underworld with a laugh? How many

*men belittled by disregarding the value of their treasures?
How many children were killed because she pretended not to
know? I was but a girl who betrayed her gifts from the gods,
drunk with power and abundance. I held my mirror so close
to my face there remained no room for another. The life of that
princess laid to waste by her indulgences will now remain the
suppurating sin of a queen who founded her own country
tooth and nail.*

*Hey, stranger! I am not going to account for this hungry and
savage rabble. A moment off guard and they will raze this
county to the ground. Not for my sins – they would kill me
out of a thirst for blood. Their decrees would be so ignorant
they will amount to nothing in the face of my miserable sins.
I wanted you to come, noble sailor! I wanted to surrender to
you my sins not my heart. So that an equal is tried in the
traps of power and nobility would judge me. I shall shed tears
and tear myself apart before you and you shall see how I
punish myself and thus I, Elissa, not Queen Dido, shall be
forgiven. Oh glorious warrior, I do believe that I am entitled
to a fair trial and to you. You! The last right given to me by
the gods. As my blood has not been shed and dried it still
pollutes my body. Clearly my penance will remain so long as
I live. Even if all the gods were to forgive me and all the locals
worship me and if every night I were to poke out these eyes,
my misery would not abate. Those who do not receive a
merciless but fair trial are always punished more than they
deserve. I needed you.*

*And now you will not come. I know that with the birth of a
new day tomorrow, I know, that you will leave this shore.
The birds are no longer singing. And the flowers no longer
come back to life in the rain. There is no longer a trace of*

reproach on my lips. The wind no longer blows through my soul. My heart has withered. This morning I even forgot to look out to sea. Tomorrow with the rising sun, I know, you will leave as if you never came. I will wait until I forget the nightmare you dragged me through. Carthage will wait. And the days will roll away as if they had never been. To remind herself of her strength, Dido will declare new wars. Because she has not forgotten the young and sinful princess Elissa, Queen Dido will run to the swords that will kill her.

*

"What are you guilty of, Maryam?" asked Amira, her voice hoarse. Now she no longer trusted Madam Lilla, who just told us how she had betrayed her daughter, or Maryam, whose secret seemed to be greater than we had thought. She must have felt so alone in the middle of the desert. Maryam looked at the fire. Without taking her eyes off the flame she said, "Alright then, Amira, why didn't you forgive the man you love most? How could you have been so fragile and merciless at the same time?"

Silence again. Then Amira read another one of Muhammed's letters...

*

Muhammed's Fifth Letter

"I don't know my own worth, so will you know it for me?" Or so you said one day, and now look how I am counting that same worth like I'm counting prayer beads. Day and night. But I know, don't say it, I'm counting them after I've pulled them all off and they have scattered on the ground. Now I am

counting your worth as if I am holding all the elusive little drops of mercury that have spilled out of a broken thermostat. Sweetie, maybe I'm losing my mind.

You are the only living thing that moves faster than my own imagination. So my wretched sin only grows. If this heart I have broken wasn't yours I might have wished to spend the rest of my life on my knees praying for forgiveness. But now having ruined the heart of an angel there is nothing left to do but stay quiet and wait for this life to end. Who am I to undertake such a task as fixing the broken heart of an angel? Now I am nothing but a 'who', my angel.

I know that you didn't tell me about your anger. Your grace and your compassion jammed a shotgun of words. But all you need to do is aim, sweetie: My heart is already sealed.

Maybe men are just like that, sweetie, we are out to conquer a country we cannot even understand. All this ambition over land they cannot even decide what to do with. A woman's skin is not enough, nor her heart – we aren't satisfied until they have surrendered their soul. Even after we have raced over the lands of your neck, towards the valley of your ribs and arrived at the source of the Nile, your heart, we are not convinced that we have truly conquered. When it comes to women, we are all angry and restless, like Alexander the Great. In essence we know we don't deserve this and we cannot rest clear with the idea of a conquered heart. We want to see what adorns the most intimate cabins of a woman's heart. But we don't know that once you walk in you'll have to stay. You once said, "If I don't know my worth, will you know it for me?" I promised you. Sweetie, when we take those vows we don't know how much you will take them to heart.

So it isn't fair, eh? Well not at all. A heart can be broken, betrayed, but I know we don't have the right to shake each other's faith in life. Such a crime only works on promises, you taught me so much. And I understand that even my not knowing the value of your conquered flesh wouldn't hurt you that deeply. But once you surrendered your faith in life to me I understood that I was the sum of a tremendous lie... Committing such a sin and asking God's forgiveness, I could only live with that if you weren't in my life. From now on every sin you commit is mine. Every heart you have broken and every will you have thwarted will be the cross I have to bear. If you were to take a person's life the blood would be on my hands. If only I could be justly punished in this world or the world beyond.

You remember when I said, "Leave everything and hold onto me," right? I wish you didn't. Then you would have forgotten how you humoured me. If only I had made you angry, without touching your heart, then there might have been grounds for due justice. But twisting the wings of an angel like you and just leaving you there... Such punishment doesn't happen even in fairytales, what do you say to that, sweetie? But you see no one is cleverer than a fairytale. I'm not even a robber, only a mountain man trickster. Not even Hira mountain can keep me covered.

For I'm as guilty as if I slaughtered all those pure souls. It is written in the Maide verse, "If you kill one, you have killed all of humanity." I am trying to pay for stabbing your soul by wrapping my arms around rabid dogs scratching away at their bleeding sores. It's so miserable Satan himself might die laughing, don't you think?

Yesterday I separated that rifle into seven pieces, sweetie. Then I took it and buried everything at my mother's grave. I don't even know what in the world I was thinking. But my stupidity went further than that. I sat down and I swallowed the last two bullets in the casing. One for me and one for you. After you left my idiocy expanded geometrically, sweetie, if you haven't gathered this much already. And all this was no end result, you might have guessed that, too, seeing that I'm still writing this letter.

Sometimes I say to myself that I should go kill those fools, mow them down one by one, the same men who levelled their guns on you. But even if you beat back all the demons, can you bring back an angel?

I have come to understand that birds fly to desolate islands to die. I learned so much after you left: so as not to stain the hopes of this world with their blood the shirtless fairies go to close their eyes in different worlds.

But justice should be possible, sweetie. For a miserable wretch like me it's far too comfortable to keep wrestling with my conscience. Who am I to decide on my own punishment! With every moment I suffer a crisis of conscience, I am ashamed of my pride. And because I still see myself as a Muslim I cannot put a bullet in my head. I will have to burn in ice because I have fallen for an angel that did not have the heart to bow to me. Sweetie, my lips burn even with the names of God.

Vav
Mim
Muhammed

*

"Madam Lilla…" I said, "she betrayed everyone. Maybe she has betrayed us…"

It was like they couldn't hear me. They had both switched onto a channel I couldn't access. Maryam asked again.

"What is this crime of his that you cannot forgive, Amira? Supposedly you're so strong but then why are you so weak around me? If you loved Muhammed that much why did you let that guy kiss your foot?"

Without pausing Amira pivoted back to her question.

"I let that man kiss my foot because my heart is like a stone. Now answer me. What did you do? If you're supposedly so ruthless then why are you so gentle with me?"

Maryam replied: "Because you are just a young girl."

And then they only looked at the flames. A little later we all went back into the tent. Madam Lilla was waiting for us there. She was holding one of the cards with a number on it.

22

"I'm fed up with your lies, your stories, your treason, fed up with it all, Madam. You have betrayed us all. The whole world knows just who you are, Madam! The whole world! You betrayed us too. With your lies, false promises and your stories you've dragged us out into the desert."

Amira left the tent. In the middle of all the other tents she stopped in the darkness. Maryam and I were still in our tent. We could hear Amira crying outside and the swish of footsteps in the sand, moving quickly towards her. But we couldn't go out. We only waited, keeping still. Considering everything that had happened that day we had no other choice.

*

With long faces we came out of our tent. None of us were speaking to Madam Lilla. Furkan and Tariq were already getting the camels ready and we still hadn't said a word to each other. Maryam only made a weary attempt to joke with Furkan. They laughed at something I couldn't understand. Soon Furkan was riding next to her. I was behind them. Then Taraq and Madam Lilla, side by side. They weren't speaking at all. At the back, Amira and Tin Abutut were keeping a good distance from the group.

"Then the man sewed himself into his own quilt. Ha ha ha!"

Now Furkan was telling Maryam a story and so loudly I could hear everything. It seemed interesting. A noble Tuareg goes to Istanbul in Ottoman times. Wandering the city streets he comes across a quilter and he is dazzled by the shimmering satin, the dancing sunlight on the cotton fluffer, the embroidered shapes on the cotton and satin, and the quilter's dusty but clean little shop. Now this man is weary of all his wives. And because his heart is empty – or as Furqan put it, he no longer has desires – he becomes enamoured with quilting. When he returns to Timbuktu he decides that he can no longer live in a country where there are no quilting materials let alone a climate that requires quilts. But he's in no position to leave behind his wife and children. Night and day he keeps dreaming of quilts, crying and drinking himself to sleep. And in the end he comes up with an idea: he makes a deal with a tradesman, who brings him the satin and cotton and everything else he needs from Istanbul. Now the next part is tragic. The man is a butterfingers with the needle and he can hardly even separate the satins. His wives go crazy but he doesn't let them touch a thing. In the end they take a stand and say, 'It's the quilt or us.' That night he drinks and he drinks...

"Then he sews himself into the quilt. Ha ha ha!"

The moment Furkan finishes Madam Lilla is suddenly shouting.

"Furkan, desire and love never kills just one person. Leila will also die ... she will also die..."

She stopped and started telling her story at the top of her lungs. She wanted Tin Abutut to hear.

"Once upon a time there was an old man who lived in a city. He chained himself to a tree and the key to the lock was nowhere to be found. And he lived like that. But he never stopped writing, filling one notebook after another. When people asked him about his plight he would say, 'Ah, for the sake of love'. Years passed and no one could understand the connection between love and his chain. And the man died of old age still chained to the tree. He was quickly buried and everyone began to wonder about the notebooks. 'But what if,' they asked, 'what if the old man wrote down the reason in those notebooks?' And with that they raced over to them and began rifling through. But they were empty. The pages had got wet and then dried and were all wrinkled. Then an old woman they had never seen before appeared and announced to the crowd, 'He would write with his saliva. You can't read any of it.'

The astonished crowd was brimming with curiosity.

'Did you know the deceased?' they asked.

'He knew me,' said the old woman.

"And she told her tale. Many years ago the old man and the woman fell in love when they were young. The girl started a cruel game. She said to the man, 'If you come for me I won't be yours. All I can do is tie you to a tree. And every day you will write me a letter. I will come to read them and if I like them I will be yours.'

"But the man was illiterate. So some evenings the girl would look at the blank pages wet with saliva and give herself to the man if she felt like it, or if she didn't she wouldn't even pass by the tree. After the old woman finished her story she said, 'it was the beginning of the end when he decided to use my own cruelty against me. The games of youth are the torture devices of maturity. I didn't know that then. But when I finally wanted to untie him and let him go he was already a madman in his own world. Even when I opened my legs and wiggled before him he didn't look: he was still writing things in his notebook he never showed me. Like that he killed me. Now don't get the wrong idea and think he's the only one lying in the ground. Bring me those chains so I can chain myself to his gravestone.'"

Furkan laughed at the story. Tariq glanced at Madam Lilla

for just a moment: he had understood what she was trying to say. Then Tin Abutut's voice rang out from behind us:

"I have a story, too … Tin Abutut!"

It wasn't clear if she was addressing Madam Lilla (for the old, blue-faced man called her that) or if the name of her story was Tin Abutut. In a voice loud enough for Madam Lilla to hear Tin Abutut began her story:

"In a time before time and in a fairytale before the real and in a place so very far from here there once was a charming young man who lived in the desert. He was the most noble of all the noblemen, the keenest of all the warriors. All the women were so deeply in love with him, but it was an unrequited love; they knew they couldn't have him and so they only wished for him to be happy. And then one day an enormous wooden bird landed in the middle of the desert. From under its wing appeared a young woman. She was dressed in many layers of silk, and fluttered in the wind like a good omen. The young man assumed that woman was sent to him from the clouds. They raced through the desert on horseback, bonded in a cloud of hashish. But one day when the man felt they were the only two people left in the world and after he had overcome the initial pangs of love and became accustomed to her scent the giant wooden bird came down to the desert again. And the woman hopped on its wing and they were gone. Desperately the young man rode his horses about the desert, kicking up sand in their wake. But it was all in vain for the woman would never return. And as he was wondering if he would be able to live through the pain an iron bird lands on the desert floor. From inside the bird bandits leap out and throw nets over the man and take him prisoner. They wanted something from him, something the woman left behind. As if the pain of heartbreak were not enough the young man now sees that he'd been deceived. They were not going to let him die of sorrow, and right there they slashed his stomach. His heart ached so terribly that his flesh felt no pain. Later he married and had children but he never loved anyone again. In his sleep he would mutter the name of the woman who came to him on the wooden bird. He was disgusted by his wife and his children. His heart had withered and he raised his children as if they were a curse. They vowed that they would one day take that woman's life. They would lift the spell that had taken hold of their father's heart. It would be the only way for them to avenge their mother who had gone crazy with the love she had for their father."

And with that Tin Abutut had issued her verdict on Madam Lilla. The sun had nearly set. This was another love story from Madam Lilla, one we had never heard, one filled with secrets; we were listening to a story that could lead to our being killed in the middle of the desert.

So when night fell and Amira cried out, "We are fed up with your lies!" she had every right. Maryam and I stared at Madam Lilla for some time and then we went outside. We couldn't stay with her any longer. We sat down at the fire. There was no sign of Amira. We waited for her till morning. Still no sign of her anywhere. And not once did Madam Lilla even so much as stick her head out of her tent.

Once the sun was up over the horizon Furkan and Tariq came out of their tents. Arm in arm Amira and Tin Abutut came out of another tent. Amira's eyes were swollen from crying. She was leaning on Tin Abutut. She looked devastated. She looked as helpless and lifeless as a gutted fish: another mother had betrayed her. Maryam and I walked over to them. Madam Lilla was still in her tent. Furkan and Tariq didn't seem to be in any hurry. They weren't preparing for us to set out. Tin Abutut left Amira with us and then she went over to Madam Lilla's tent and cried out:

"Get up! You old witch! Wake up. Get out here. Get ready for your final journey!"

"Don't kill her here," shouted Amira, "I don't want to see it."

In that moment Tin Abutut looked forty years older, and I suppose she had the face of her mother when she said, "No. Why would I kill her! The Brits will do that. Just like you told that American journalist in Yafran. You're an English agent who knows where Saif al-Islam is hiding out, ha! The British found that bit of information quite interesting. Get your things together. The helicopter's coming to get you."

"And what about us?" shouted Maryam, still holding Amira by the arm. Tin Abutut spun round like the wife of a feudal lord.

"Amira saved you. The three of you are going back to Tunisia. But first we're going to take care of this old witch. The English have promised me they will return your body to me once they are done with you. Then my sisters and I will decide what to do next. Tin Abutut. I will then be free of that accursed name."

Madam Lilla pulled open the flap of her tent. Slowly she stepped outside. She stood there tall like a queen, fearless of being executed. Her large silver necklace rested prominently on her chest. She ran her eyes over everyone. She flashed us a disgusted look. "You miserable fools!" she said. "You common women. I thought maybe you were different…"

"Enough!" shouted Amira. "We don't want to hear any more out of you."

Madam Lilla slowly drew her hand out from behind her back. She was holding Muhammed's letters.

"But I suppose you want to take these with you. These precious letters."

We heard the whirring of a helicopter. Amira grew restless. Tin Abutut shouted at Madam, "Give the girl her letters!" And Lilla started to laugh.

"Let her come and take them. Otherwise these precious documents are coming with me to the Brits."

The three of us walked over to Lilla. Still looking at us in disgust, she hissed through her teeth.

"You fools! You'll never achieve anything in your lives. You'll never be anyone. Because you're weak and insignificant."

We could no longer hear her voice over the circling blades of the helicopter. Tin Abutut was shouting at all of us, "Quick! Quick! They're here!"

As sand swirled up in the air Maryam suddenly leapt behind Tin Abutut, drew a gun and pointed it at her head. Lilla was shouting, "Hurry up! Furkan and Tariq are also armed!"

By the time the chopper landed the two already had their guns drawn. Maryam's entire body was shaking. Madam was shouting at her, "Shoot! Shoot!"

Tin Abutut had nearly struggled free of Maryam. Amira and I couldn't get close to them, fearing the gun might go off. Madam Lilla shouted through the clamour:

"Maryaaaam! Shoot!"

Maryam waited a little more. And then Madam Lilla snatched the gun out of her hand and put a bullet in Furkan's leg and one in Tariq's foot. And she shouted, "Run! To the chopper! Run!"

Tin Abutut was still shouting at Furkan and Tariq. "Get them! They aren't the Brits!"

When the camels began to flee from the confusion one of

them knocked Tin Abutut to the ground. And we made a break for it. We scrambled towards the chopper. Two figures clothed entirely in black lifted Madam Lilla and pushed her inside. From inside the helicopter she recited the Felak verse at the top of her lungs. Ripping off her necklace, she threw it to the ground. She shouted one more time, "From the evil of the blowers of knots!"

Taking a deep breath Lilla sat down next to Amira and put her arm around her. She kissed her on the forehead.

"God bless. I knew you'd be able to do it!" Amira was as cold as ice, like stone, staring wide eyed at Lilla. She was glowing with life again.

Earlier that night Amira had found Tin Abutut's satellite phone and sent a mayday message to the number Madam had given her. Now we expected Maryam to ask Lilla who had come to rescue us and where we were going. But suddenly she broke down and started to sob. Cool and collected, Madam Lilla looked at her, and as if we had all just sat down in a waiting room and nothing particularly out of the ordinary had just happened, she said through the chuff-chuff-chuff of the helicopter blades:

"You're pregnant, Maryam. You are trying to have a miscarriage. The way you threw yourself off the camel, nauseous all the time, cutting all your hair... you didn't have an abortion because you think it's a sin and so you have come on this trip to lose your child, right? Is that your secret? Tell me."

Maryam's lips fluttered as she tried to say something but only horrifying sounds came out. When they finally became words she only managed to sputter through her teeth:

"Madam. I left her. I ... I was afraid... And now you see, Madam! I can't protect her. And I can't protect Amira either... I couldn't shoot. And what about my daughter? Do

328

you understand? Do you? I'm not a real woman. Nothing like that. I can't. She has no father. Her father is one of the kids in Tahrir. And I'm all alone... protecting myself. I turned myself into a man... and what if she turns out like me? I have no idea ... I only have these swords. A bald head. I just want to forget it all, Madam. Forget that I'm afraid... but I love her so much. How could I forget her? I can't do it. I can't!"

Our feet were entangled. How could we reach out and hold her? Madam stopped us. "Leave her!" she shouted. "Let her cry." Like ice, Madam was back to her former self and with a face like stone she asked, "Where is she?"

These sounds came out of Maryam, something like braying. And the two armed men dressed in black who had come for us uncovered their faces... they were women. They weren't looking at us. Maryam was shouting, "I couldn't save Amira, Madam. I can't do it!"

Lilla screamed even louder, "Where is she?"

Maryam started hitting herself in the face. Amira tried to get a hold on her but she couldn't. In a daze I couldn't reach her either.

"I ... my daughter ... I'm going ... going to see heeeeeeer...."

It was like she was losing her mind.

"I'm afraid, Madam. I'm so very afraid, Madam. Please help me!"

And that's how Maryam came to sort herself out. Tears welled up in Madam Lilla's eyes as Maryam put her hands in Lilla's lap.

"We'll take care of it," she said. "Just don't be afraid. We are all in this together."

Maryam had become a tiny little woman. Maybe all the screaming and the shouting were for her child but in a way it seemed like she was giving birth to a heavily swaddled woman right then and there. She was breaking all her swords; she was surrendering to Lilla.

"Where is she, my dear? Tell me that," said Madam Lilla in her softest voice. Indeed she was still shouting over the clamour but her voice fell lightly into the human ear in drops of compassion that brought confidence.

"Far away, Madam! I can't go there alone, Madam!"

As she cried, 'mummy, mummy!' Maryam's voice in the human ear was like the saliva of a lion licking her own wounds. It wasn't hard to see this was the first time she'd asked someone for help.

Taking Maryam by the hand, Madam Lilla looked out over the desert. Amira and I looked at each other. Maryam was doubled over between us, clutching Lilla's hands. I put my hand on Maryam's back and Amira put her hand on mine. And we stayed like that. The bright yellow desert racing beneath us. Some time later when Maryam had stopped crying, Madam Lilla spoke as if she were heading out for a walk in the countryside:

"Maryam don't sit like that. You'll get sick to you stomach. Put your head up."

Madam Lilla could suddenly turn the extraordinary into the ordinary and quickly lighten any misfortune. Everything seemed entirely normal. Everything seemed like it would all work out.

A light touch on my back. One of the young women with dark kohl around her eyes and a smiling face said, "They are expecting you in Alexandria." She patted me lightly on the back. She was consoling us without knowing what had happened. We assumed they were only waiting for us in Alexandria. In the back of her jeans Maryam had stuffed not only her notebook but Muhammed's letters, too, and they rustled as she rocked back and forth. Maybe she wasn't able to save Amira but she had managed to hold onto her letters.

I took them out, put them in my lap and started to read. Every time it seemed like a page might fly away I held them more tightly in my hands or tucked them under my arms and legs. As I read through them I came to know the essence of Maryam's secret in her story of Dido, but more importantly there was Amira's secret about Muhammed. The desert had united the three of us and with these stories in my lap they were the closest they could be to my womb. As we sped through the sky the stories of two women spiralled in the desert wind and took root in my lap.

*

Dido's Fourth Tablet

I am Queen Dido's servant, master of the slave girls. I am Elissa's companion, her confidante. I am Penelope. And these are my words.

Dido lived. I watched her. I was the one who boarded that Phoenician boat with her. I could have stayed behind to live out my own life. But I, Penelope, I gave myself to the fate of Dido. She called me Penelope and I did not seek another name. I was born into the palace a slave. I learned by heart how to be happy when she was happy. But I was not kept a slave, I chose to remain one. What I have to say now are the words of a free woman. I decided to put these words to parchment when the mysterious traveller's ship came to Carthage. Let these words be said and known until the Mediterranean runs dry. So that generations to come will have mercy on Dido. I had this tablet prepared without the order of the Queen. These tablets will be buried seven layers under ground along with the secrets of Dido. Those inscribing these words onto stone are three women slaves who have sworn to be buried with their work. Their names are Zin, Dira and Sura. They have told the gods they will sacrifice their own lives to warn our future daughters.

Thus Dido's tale shall unfold the way I tell it.

*

For seven days and seven nights the stranger's ship was anchored in the open waters. Seven times Queen Dido died and was born again. Then on the eighth day the warriors set foot in Carthage. When the stranger arrived the Queen was exhausted. She had succumbed to a battle with her own self. The women of Carthage offered sacrifices to the gods. They made a pact with the gods: they would shed the blood of white oxen so that the stranger would fall in love with Dido.

Elissa took my hand as the ship approached the shore. In the same way the Queen took my hand when we boarded the ship in Phoenicia. And the same way she took my hand when she decided to rule over the savages of this land. The Queen took my hand. I was gripped with fear. Elissa can no longer see me. The Queen now no longer sees herself. If it is not Phoenicia she is leaving behind then what is she leaving behind this time? The Queen fell before the war started. I was gripped with fear. All of Carthage saw this impending defeat. Dido was not heeding us. I pleaded to the gods: "Do no let this happen: For Dido wants to fall."

Dido said, "An eagle came to Carthage." But I have seen it

with my own eyes, this stranger was no wild eagle. Dido said, "What a beautiful-faced brave warrior." We saw him and his obscure smile. Dido said, "His face is full of scars. He has come to me with stories." The prophetesses read the scars on his face which said, "Here lies the wrath of a soldier who could not vanquish anyone." Dido said, "A noble man is coming." But I saw with my own eyes a bandit dressed in a nobleman's furs. Dido said, "Either my love or death comes on that ship. This time the gods must show me mercy." I saw that something worse than death was nigh. Taking me by the hand, Dido looked at me and said, "Will the stranger love me?" That was the day that Carthage fell.

*

The stranger came. His name was Aeneas. He looked deep into Dido's eyes. He had dark eyes and on his right cheek was a deep scar left by a sword. He had dark curly hair. And like a wild animal he had hair on his body. He was neither ashamed of his hair nor would he bow his head. Cunning was the stranger for he knew how to make a queen fall in love and bend a knee: the stranger was making bold to her.

He began by speaking of Dido's beauty and all his legendary victories along the coast of the Mediterranean. Yet the brazen airs of this young warrior suggested he sought neither protection from Queen Dido nor a part of her country. The stranger reached into Dido's chest, took her heart and turned it in the palm of his hand. The stranger wanted the light that gave life to Dido. He went down on his knee and all of Carthage beheld the stranger. Looking at Dido they saw how the Queen desired to hang her head lower than his. The stranger did not conquer Dido. Dido wanted to be the stranger, to be the conqueror. She had crossed the borders of her own country and was now in foreign lands.

Clapping her hands together she rained orders down on her servants. Dido had never before clapped her hands like this, nor given orders in that way. Like ravenous hyenas the warriors glared at our women. Dido's dress billowed in the wind, showing her feet. Dido never showed her feet. Linen and beds were unfurled on the terraces and purple silk nettings were drawn. The fires were lit and lambs were soon turning on the spit. Swaying left and right, Dido lavished the sky with every turn. Dido never walked like that. Dido ordered the girls to be merry. And they began to dance. And having met with more generosity than they had expected the warriors could see that their commander had devastated Dido and they laughed. Dido laughed with them. By then she was blind. I, Penelope, had to remain silent. Dido had the right to be happy. They sat down to a banquet. Dido listened to Aeneas. Like a young and simple-minded girl, she marvelled at what he had to say. Aeneas spoke to her of Troy. He told her of the horror and his defeat and his flight as Troy fell. As Aeneas told his tale his defeat seemed more like some glorious victory. Like a wounded snake he slithered underneath her pity. Aeneas spoke until Dido believed he was a miracle. Giving herself up, she said, "I knew that you would come. I knew you were like me." The stranger drove Dido's horses without a whip.

Glancing at Dido the girls were giggling. "How quickly the queen surrendered to this charlatan?" They didn't know how weary queens were capable of giving away their minds, their thrones and their gods only to be hopelessly deceived. But I told myself it would be Dido herself who would undo this spell of her own making.

I am Penelope. The gods will not forgive me. Because I remained silent. The stranger had come to Carthage. Dido gazed upon Aeneas in the same way Penelope gazed at Dido. I became a prisoner of this traitorous pleasure.

*

I am Penelope and I have never been in love. Because Dido taught us never to surrender. Dido taught us to know that we will always remain alone. Dido taught us that mystery lives in our own breath. Blowing we fill the sails of our hearts, this is what Dido taught the girls of Carthage. Now she was breathing with all her might. Pushing out all the air in her lungs to blow away from the hills of Carthage this eagle called Aeneas. When Dido finished breathing Aeneas' eyes would go dim, his arms weak. If Aeneas had left before Elissa's breath had finished, her vessel would have struck rocks. The sea of Carthage would go dry.

On the first night Elissa did not take the stranger to bed. Aeneas lay silently in ambush. When Elissa retired to her room she called for me. There she was looking at her naked reflection in the glass. Dido said, "Aeneas is younger than me." I replied, "Let us not be deceived by appearances my Queen. Men are more skillful than women in the hunt and more primitive in their lack of mercy and heartbreaking in their blindness." To which Dido responded, "With magic I will make him lose his head." And I said, "My Queen first be sure that such magic will not swallow up Carthage." Dido, "I am old now. Aeneas wants a country and I want to love." I said, "But this time my Queen you want to be loved, too." And for the first time I told her what she must do. "Give the order," I said. "Tell the soldiers to burn his ship and Aeneas will be yours. Take him prisoner." Dido cried, "No! He will

335

not be taken prisoner. He will stay in Africa because he is a slave to my love." I said, "Men despise the lands that they have not conquered with the sword of ambition and the blood of wrath. They should be given no offers."

I had presented Dido with my servility. Now Dido hoped for the servility of a stranger wrapped in animal furs. Dido is no longer Dido. She has to be protected from Elissa. Penelope must become Dido. What she learned from Dido will lead her to be the guardian of Carthage and Elissa's heart. That is how I decided for wickedness to be brought upon Dido to make her put an end to this dream that would bring a curse to Carthage. If I told her she would not listen. With her own eyes she had to see her wrongdoing. She had to come to the light and put on her armour again.

With the rising sun Dido made ready fruit and bread. She would take Aeneas into the pastures. Spring lambs were turning on the spit. Flasks were filled with wine. Dido was blossoming like a wild flower. Throughout the day Aeneas worked his charms setting the groundwork for lies that would stoke her desires. I, Penelope, saw it in his eyes: how delighted he was, a hunter with spear in hand, in anticipation of feasting upon his prey. He was the most dangerous kind of hunter. But Aeneas thinks nothing of his prey, and only of himself. She believes she will make him a slave to her love. While Aeneas planned to beguile her and then break her wings. Dido asked me to join them. She wanted me to fall in love with him, too. So I might be her partner in crime. I should fall in love with her so that yet another could watch her tumble into hell. Aeneas was the most dangerous of warriors. He had no concern for the country he was to conquer. Aeneas was only pursuing himself. He would not stay; he would leave Carthage; that was all too clear.

We walk into the pastures. Dido looks at Aeneas and he gazes into the distance, over the sea and up at the hills. He tells Dido how loneliness and grief weigh heavily on his heart. Dido has embarked on his tale, swaying from side to side. The expression on his face causes her to leap from grief to joy and from joy to fantasy and from fantasy to truth. He would finish a story before he started and start before he finished. He had the shimmering eyes of a wild dog. "I am nothing," he said. "Are you nothing as well, Dido?" He groped for her heart and found it.

By the time Dido made the decision to save him from herself a net is cast over us. There is no escape for the queen any more. "How beautiful you are, Dido, like the sun," says Aeneas, "But no, I cannot fall for such beauty." Dido then looks at him so closely she is blinded. She believes him so fully that she no longer needs to listen. She feeds him fine meats and pours wine through his lips. "I want to love you, Dido," he says and then gazes into the distance. The demons in him are stirring. "But I can't love you, leave me. I am an evil man, Dido. Do not love me," says Aeneas. She has forgotten all that she has taught us.

Dido speaks of Phoenicia. Of the orange-tree orchards, the rosebuds and how we boarded the ship. It seems Aeneas is listening, as if listening to the words of the gods. Then he stops. Dido hesitates. Her voice quivering, she does not know if she should carry on. Before she gives up, he says, "Tell me a little more, Dido, light comes trippingly off your tongue." Her voice finds strength again only to see once that the eyes of Aeneas drift away. She is lightheaded. Just before her heart breaks, Aeneas takes her hands. "Tell me Dido, your voice is the sun breaking through cloud." Dido is weary. She grows old in the face of his madness. To soothe her doubt she asks questions to take his truth by the throat. Aeneas is silent. And in the silence she begins to tremble with fear. She wants him to break the silence, even with lies. Dido is now afraid of defeating Aeneas.

When we return to the palace the feast awaits. Dido wants Aeneas to get drunk and she will drink, too. She wants all of Carthage to be drunk, for no one to see the truth. The ladies and foreign soldiers sup wine from each other's mouths. Aeneas calls the women musicians and he raises his arms up in the air. He moves to the fire and dances there. Dido gazes at his arms and his chest. She is burning with desire. He never stops. Dido catches him and tries to make him look at her. He doesn't stop. Dido rises and takes Aeneas by the arm. She is standing there helpless. All of Carthage watches this prey throw herself into the hunter's arms.

That night in hope that the manhood of Aeneas would not satisfy Dido I sacrifice animals to the gods. Till dawn I brew magic spells in the cauldrons. I listen at Dido's door. Now the fate of Carthage lies between the legs of a rogue. I curse the gods of the seas who brought that ship here.

In the morning Dido steps out onto her balcony. Her white silks flutter in the breeze. She looks at her arms. From my balcony I can see the bruises on her arms. Aeneas has left his mark on Elissa. Smiling, Dido looks down at her arms. Then she calls for me and gives me an order.

"Quick, Penelope, bring me the ointments and let us use cream to cover my arms. Have the girls find golden bracelets to cover these bruises. I want to be ready for Aeneas this evening."

Dido's arms are in pain but she is joyful. I don't know what becomes of a queen who loves her wounds.

I am Penelope and this is how I decided to play a game with Aeneas to devastate Elissa's soul before he had broken Dido's heart. Let the knife of Penelope slit her throat before she became the hunter's wasted prey, tossed aside after the kill. The queen can heal a wound inflicted by her own dagger. Just let not Carthage kneel down before Aeneas.

*

I am Penelope and I have learned that I can bear the sight of Dido fading. But my heart cannot agree to the queen's defeat. When Aeneas leaves, Dido's feather will fall out; let it fall. The birds of Dido will fall silent when she sees the monster that lives in Aeneas; let them go silent. When she comes to realize that Aeneas does not love her, her heart will rot, and so let it. Only make it so that Carthage does not crumble upon the queen. Let not my sister, my queen, my soul be ashamed of herself. I am Penelope and I have asked so much from the gods. And so that is how I began to set the trap that would bleed my own sister's heart.

First I chose those girls with the liveliest breasts, the tautest bellies, the shapeliest legs and the sweetest inner thighs! And the most playful! I made them ready with my own hands. I molded them until each one was a mermaid and I rubbed them with scents, poured drops of syrup onto their lips, rubbed their feet with almond oil, their breasts with jasmine oil and their thighs with orange blossom essence. When each was her own flower garden, her own den of sin, I spoke with them. I told them to go to Aeneas in the morning. Before he was fully awake. They would meet him when his sword was already hard. That hairy beast would be shocked and think he was making love to fairies in a dream. He would surrender his wild soul and his feverish body to those fingers. I laid a trap for him made up of heavenly flowers. Two days and two nights had passed when Aeneas fell asleep alone and that morning he was caught in our web. That morning the most beautiful girls in Carthage opened their legs to save the queen. When Aeneas embraced them they screamed and moaned and wailed. Our girls cried out with all their might so that the betrayal would ring in the deaf ears of Dido. Let her hear that Aeneas is undiscerning; may it be Dido's flesh or the flesh of another; his heart cannot know the difference.

Dido laughed and she cried. Her mouth watered and then her lips went dry. Dido's chest split open and her belly grew. Dido died and came back to life. Swallows flew from her hair, rosebuds shot out of her neck and the gold on her wrists went pale. She had revealed her garden to Aeneas, which she had never done before, and now it was full of snakes. And they were strangling her. And Dido did not say one word. She gave herself up like an adolescent slave and she bore her pain like an ancient queen. And like that, one by one, she locked all her doors. The walls turned to copper and the locks were as strong as diamonds. And that is how we won our war that we waged against the heartless Aeneas. Carthage was saved. In gratitude I offered up my sacrifices to the gods.

I am Penelope and I say this to all of our girls of future generations. I am Penelope, a slave who has seen the devastation of a queen. Oh listen to what I have to say, beautiful young girls! It is with great sadness that I say to you that we cannot defeat those glossy-haired hunters so captivating and so cruel, who, like Aeneas, feed their souls on flesh. Pray to the gods to keep Aeneas at bay. Give sacrifices so that such people do not fall to you. Because, I,

Penelope, am a poor slave who falsely believed that we had succeeded. I assumed that Dido would have his head. But that accursed evening he was allowed to see the queen; the base animal that did not esteem his conquest at all wanted the unconditional surrender of that country. As if he truly loved her, Aeneas fell to his knees before the throne. And he said not a word. This ill-starred sailor knew that his words would no longer deceive her. Taking out his blade he held it in the moonlight. "Forgive me, Dido," he said. "I am your slave!" And slowly he began to cut his manhood. Oh! Dido Oh! I saw the queen and she could not bear to see it happen. I saw how she killed herself instead of killing a scoundrel. She raced over to him and kneeled. And there they made love. Blood dripped from his manhood. He was willing to shed his own blood to capture his prey. Carthage would fall because that is what the gods had decreed.

*

Years before Dido had said to us, to all the girls, with all the stars in the sky reflected in her eyes, "Put yourselves first." On the steps of the palace that she founded, on the first day in Carthage, she had said, "If you can bear your own strength you can bear anything." She had said, "Do not be afraid my daughters. Do not be afraid of yourselves. And do not…" She raised her hand in the air, her thumb and forefinger touching:

"Do not underestimate yourselves. That is when the hunter will find you. The eye of a hunter knows your limit and he will find you. You become prey."

And now as we chisel these words on the stone with our scribes we shed tears. Last of all Dido taught us how a queen can long for defeat. Oh Dido! You were once our queen. Even when you chose to become the slave, the prey, the spoils of a rogue, you were beautiful. Oh, Dido! We are your daughters. Your hands between our breasts. Elissa, Oh! Your flesh on our flesh and your heart upon our hearts. We know that you fell willingly.

I am Penelope, and to the young girls to come after us I will whisper in their ears the fate of Dido's secret.

One morning with tears in his eyes, Aeneas said, "I must leave." He spoke of wars, his soul, waves, honour and kings. He spoke as if he could deceive a queen with magnificence and not with a compassionate heart. Dido looked at him like a goat might look at a stone, an eagle at a lamb, an elephant at an ant. Then she gave up. The girls of Carthage watched and Dido relented. "Go," she said and twirling in her silks she went into the palace. Aeneas was still speaking when Dido shut the doors of the palace. Festivals were held there until his sails were unfurled; Aeneas was not invited. When he left with the rising sun the candles in the palace were put out and Dido fell silent. The Prophetesses said that she was 'beyond repair,' and they quickly made ready charms of opium as a cure. And the women of Carthage hid the daggers and swords to keep Dido from cutting her jugular vein. For seven days and seven nights the city waited for the queen to fall. I am Penelope and I watched how the queen stared at the ceiling for seven days and seven nights. And one morning Dido sat up in bed. She got out of bed like the day she rose to found Carthage. She said, "Make ready the camels. I am leaving this place." Dido wiped the tears from her glassy eyes. Taking my cheeks in her hands, she said, "To you, Penelope, I entrust Carthage to you. You will look after the palace and the harbour with our girls. I am going Penelope because I am

342

with child. I must give birth to a daughter so that I may leave this ruin, from my hips I must give forth a heart that will bring me back from the dead. To heal I must start life anew. I need a wise woman who knows these lands and her healing herbs, which can keep me on the right path, and as companions I need the two strongest women here. I will set out on a journey. I will go to Ithaca where I will start a life with a new name. The palace has crumbled and I cannot remain beneath the rubble. A lifetime has come to an end on these shores and I cannot watch my own demise. If there is new life in my loins then I must follow where this leads because here I can only wait. I will set out Penelope. Everything left behind you will put down in the annals.

Concoct a story for them Penelope. Such a story that only the girls that come after me will know the truth. Let no others ever know the true story of Dido. Say that she took her own life. Say that she was beaten. Tell the story in such a way that only the girls who live by their breath and the wind will know the truth.

I am a queen, Penelope, and though I might have fallen into a heartless trap I will not allow myself to be defeated by my own hand. I might lose at war but I will never bow to pain. I will not kneel before the shadow of a mortal that I have made with my own breath. If I fall out of favour before my own eyes I will never rise to my feet again. Now I must walk, Penelope, and if I stop I will lose this breath. The soldiers will not follow. Only you! No one else will know that I have left. You are my sister, Penelope. For my sake write the wrong history for the mortals and the gods. Fool them, Penelope, so that no one will come after me. Now go and choose those who will travel with me. And do not shed tears. This road is the harbinger of *victory. Do not cry, Penelope, for the legend of Dido begins again. And if no one knows that now then all the better."*

And with that Dido left. And I, Penelope, did as I was told and told no other person her true story apart from the two who left with her. I did not cry. Because if there is something I know it is that the queens who founded Carthage by breathing can rebuild palaces of glass even when no eyes will ever gaze upon them. With Dido's departure I understood that a queen must follow her breath more than anything else. Once upon a time Dido said the ones who are brave enough to write their own stories should not wait for mercy.

Once upon a time, as Dido said, we should not wait for the mercy of those brave enough to write our own stories. A queen must not forget that the essence of a dream is always in her possession. Our girls must know that in their hearts lies the essence of a queen.

I am Penelope and Carthage was entrusted to me. I am Penelope, sister of Dido. Now I must come up with a story that will satisfy the curious eyes. I will tell them that Dido took her own life. Luckily the stories of queens who have killed themselves for love would surely satisfy the hungry souls. But the story shall be written in a way that only our wise daughters will be brave enough to uncover the secret. I am Penelope, sister of Dido. I will most certainly find a way. Now I shall bury these tablets seven layers deep in the earth. To find them and the truth those seeking them will have to breathe to lift those seven layers. The truth shall be known only to our girls who deserve so much.

*

Muhammed's Sixth Letter

Sweetie, it wasn't the gun I levelled on you but the lie I told you. I know that's what struck you. You can pull a bullet out of flesh but the scar left behind by such a lie will never go away. I know. I am leaving because I know this. There's only one thing that you don't know about me, and my crime, and I wanted to talk to you about it before I left. What I am trying to say is that there was something I didn't know.

Years ago when I came to the club where you danced I was an ignorant and savage man. And like all the other ignorant and savage men around me I had been made to believe by men like me that I wasn't really like that. Amira, we were going to burn down all the dens of iniquity. We were a bunch of fools that took belief to be a bloody calculus. I am not asking your forgiveness, I am asking you to understand: we were kids who thought to smash was to touch, to break was to love and to be angry was to believe. All the love in the world couldn't fix us.

When we put on those ski masks and burst into that club to gun down sinful women like you that we called abhorrent witches, we thought we were heroic bouncers for God and we were ready to wash our souls in blood. We weren't in the state of mind to know that those who are silly adolescents in the eyes of women can take no refuge in God. And when you called out to our ragged bunch, "Brothers! For the love of God stop!" I tried to convince myself that you were the most beautiful devil spinning lies. Later, still dressed in your dancing clothes, you shouted out those verses from the Ğaşiye sura:

"Let them look up at the sky to marvel at how it was raised/ Let them look up at the mountains to marvel at how

345

they stand/Let them look to the earth to see how it unfolds/Then remind them, you are but the messenger/For you are not an imposing tyrant."

I felt like I couldn't breathe under my mask. I was ashamed. Not of you. I was ashamed how our ragged band had strove to something that the Holy Prophet Muhammed, may God grant him peace and prosperity, would not even deign to consider. Like I said, to have faith is to primp in the face of the Prophet's belief that men can be virtuous. That night my heart went out. And I have never recovered.

That dictator Ben Ali threw me in the dungeon. And I felt better. I deserved so much pain for breaking the neck of a beautiful black swan like you. When I got out I was a new man. In that cell I sometimes prayed for you and I prayed to God to forgive you if you ever sinned. And I prayed for the grace of God and I prayed to remain human...

When I got out of jail I was the one who found you, Amira. It wasn't a coincidence. I cherished every detail. And later you believed me and then that night you gave yourself to me... It was the first time I touched a woman... Oh how we laughed, sweetie, didn't we? To make you laugh I played up my ignorance. After it was all over and we lay in bed... Oh God I'm so ashamed to think of it ... how I got up and pretended to be an astronaut, saying, "A small step for humankind but one large step for a man." And the way you laughed and laughed, peals of laughter... That's when I assumed I had been forgiven. That was the day you told me how the night we stormed the club your dad had beaten you and your mom watched as you lay there broken... When I held you in my arms and I read to you, read to you, read to you... You thought that I was trying to heal you. But sweetie, I was licking my own wounds.

346

Honey, how abominable one can be – I learned so much from myself. I could see myself in the space you opened up for me. In you I was challenged. I saw the evil in my heart. That night I wanted to tell you I was the one that broke you. I wanted to tell you that I was the one who pointed my gun at you, revealing where you secretly danced and provoking your father to beat you... But I couldn't. I couldn't exchange your love for suicide. People are so weak... People can house so many satanic verses. You cannot protect that sweet soul from yourself if there is a chance it can be yours.

One day you said to me, "If a man is treated well enough he turns out to be a scoundrel. Why not you?" You were afraid. It was like you felt there was a secret in the source of such goodness, love and grace. That day I wanted to tell you. I wanted to go down on my knees and ask for your forgiveness. It didn't happen. You heard nothing from me. I don't know how you learned my secret and I don't want to know. Like I said, I don't wish for forgiveness, I only wish to be an ordinary person in your life you can't even remember where you first met. And how you met.

The last time I saw you, you said, "My heart no longer beats. It's cold." I curse myself for having done such a thing to someone with such a rain forest of a heart. But I know that someone as pitiful as me could never really break you. Life will spring out of you again. You will breathe magic again into the world. Stop breathing for me and breathe into life. Life will give you back everything I know you deserve, all the angels. Amira, we need a book that tells us how to love women. Otherwise we'll forever remain dried-up fools. We need a book that will teach us to expand the breath of women and to unfurl our sails in its strong winds. Otherwise all the love in the world won't fix us.

I dream of you in a freshly watered garden in the setting sun. You are wearing a white dress fluttering in the breeze. The birds are swirling about your hair, circling butterflies. Your soul like sweet water rising to the surface, cool and clean. You are walking barefoot. Blue beads dangle from the branches. I don't know why but I hear a child's voice coming from somewhere, so cheerful. There is a house in the garden. It is a beautiful mid-afternoon. You see a purple bug of extraordinary beauty and, bending over, you push your hair behind your ear. You smile at the bug. Your heart flutters. Amira, you are always so happy in my dreams. You seem to have a heart that was never hurt. Like a little girl who's never been disappointed, you twirl in your skirt. You don't even remember me. This is what I wish for you. I am praying for that day, Amira.

Always with love,
Muhammed

Egypt

A giant yacht is moored in the marina. We never could have expected leaving Alexandria like this. A little later we would be on the Mediterranean. We are holding all these suitcases.

Taking my first step up on the boat, I shout, "I got the seventh rule! I got the goddesses' seventh rule!"

Amira bumps into my back and Maryam, who is fiddling with a slingshot, bumps into Amira. Madam Lilla is wearing a hat with a brim that's almost a metre long. This was our departure from Egypt.

23

The famous Firdevs Hanım's hands were clasped below her waist, her fingernails painted red. When she saw us she flung open her arms and said: "Hmm ... three young women who have run down their angels!" Mouths open and our eyes like saucers, we were speechless as we stared at the crowd of women in the magnificent hall. Only Madam Lilla understood.

"You are going to indulge their angels, Firdevs!" cried Madam Lilla and in that moment we could not have fathomed the old, strange stories Madam Lilla and Firdevs must have shared. Everything that had happened earlier in the Union Hotel ceremonial hall was like nothing we'd ever seen.

*

When our helicopter landed in the airport in Alexandria our sadness had already been purged by the desert sand. We felt as crystal clear and alive as the soul of a child who has woken up after a lengthy illness. One way or another we'd made it out of the desert alive. Our minds were still too preoccupied to boast but we nevertheless received an invisible medal of honour from Madam Lilla, which she presented to us with a pat on the back. And when she asked us for the necklaces we had put on before we set out into the desert and ceremonially threw them out of the helicopter with a prayer, we had been freed from all those misadventures. Like someone who had just saved her skin we felt reborn. We had blossomed. Like joyful soldiers who bonded with each other for having survived the war we forgot to even ask who won.

And when we saw that purple limousine waiting for us at the airport in Alexandria there was no need for us to think any more. Now we were wrapped up in a new story that had nothing to do with the one that came before.

After reading the note the chauffer (maybe a man, maybe a woman) gave Madam Lilla, she let out a 'hmm' and said to us, "You are going to meet Firdevs Hanım. And you're lucky because we got here just on time for Hypatia's birthday. All the girls will be with her in the Union hotel."

Naturally I turned to look at Maryam our Egyptian sister. She didn't seem to have understood anything. Her elbow against the window she asked Lilla because she knew that I was curious.

"When you say Hypatia? Do you mean *the* Hypatia ?"

I said, "Well there aren't any Hypatias I can say that I know in Turkey." And like an academic rushing through a list of boring footnotes, Maryam said, "She was a mathematician and astronomer in Ancient Egypt. When Christianity first emerged, the library of Alexandria was looted and she was lynched by angry young Christians who took her for a sorceress. She's an important sister."

"Oh my God," I said, "has she got her own national holiday?" I asked, cheekily.

Flashing me an angry look, she only said, "No."

Madam Lilla picked up from where she left off.

"Only Firdevs's girls celebrate her. And when I say Firdevs's girls... Anyway you'll see them soon enough. You might be a little surprised."

"I don't think there's anything left to surprise us," said Amira with sly grin. Madam Lilla fired back right away, "Mademoiselle I hope that wonder never leaves you for the alternative is death. When the wonder is gone your heart truly stops beating."

I let my eyes wander over the city of Alexandria that was rolling by and the driver's face in the rear-view mirror. She doesn't really look like a woman and she doesn't really look like a man either. And Alexandria doesn't really look like Alexandria. Like any other city whose name is the stuff of films, fairytales and fables, the dreamy pictures in your mind never seem to match the real thing. I think the driver must be a woman. Even a man doesn't look that manly. She seemed covered by extremely thin glass. You could never ask her why she was like this, about the story behind her look. Deep down you sensed this story to do with her resignation from womanhood was full of sadness and you never could muster enough courage to ask.

Alexandria is loud and chaotic: a city best seen from a distance. Like a famous painting it's best to look and not touch. All of Alexandria now seems to be leaning on car horns as if hopeful and determined to make music all together. This is a city that shouts at the top of her lungs but fails to say anything at all. As if once upon a time the city was a woman who lost her mind and became a man when she was attacked by a band of savages.

The tail-end traces of womanhood flutter over the driver's face like cirrus clouds. Her furrowed brow casts shadows over the soft curve of her mouth. In her expression in the rear-view window occasionally the sun breaks through the clouds and then it's overcast again. In those moments when she looks at us with curiosity she's a woman but when her arm is hanging out of the window and she's waving at passing cars like a minibus driver, gesturing for them to hurry up and pass, the cottony clouds of womanhood have drifted away from her face.

Considering the odd colonial houses that line the roads the city clearly has a past but Alexandria must have grown weary of it because she has chosen to cover up and hide. Like any other city unsure of how to express its history, its story looks besieged by vibrantly colourful shops, storefront windows and billboards that dot the landscape. This is a city besieged by its own history, cloaked in all this noise, covered in sandy brown earth that keep the ghosts of the past from rising.

"This is nothing like Cairo," said Maryam. "I mean Tahrir."

"All the cameras were in Tahrir. That's why," I said.

Looking out the window, Maryam cocked an eyebrow and laughed.

"I never quite worked out how you could have a revolution with people who don't believe it's happening unless they see it on TV."

Looking out of the other window, Amira said calmly, "It's just the opposite. The youth are looking for something that never appeared on TV and so was never tainted. But once something ends up on TV it disappears in real life."

Maryam: "That's also true. The rotten side of Tahrir came out when they created all those popular faces for the revolution. That's when real people left the streets. And when people went and spoke on TV on the people's behalf, it was the end of Tahrir. It was like the hierarchy was put in place."

Madam Lilla unexpectedly entered the conversation.

"This is the problem of your generation, ladies. You want the world but you don't want to manage it. You don't want a leader. Out of the question. You want a revolution without getting in the mud. It isn't practical!"

Maryam looked at her and said, "It's a generation, Madam Lilla, that learned that earlier generations and their revolutionaries have all wasted away. Apart from Che who died early enough, there is no one they can open up their hearts to. We need to come up with a new language ... to rediscover our emotions."

"Yes," said Amira, "and especially when we are talking about the Arab world. Just give us a little time!"

Maryam and Amira spoke in hushed tones because they were talking about revolutions, their countries, indeed they were talking about themselves. But Lilla was full of life as she plunged deeper into the topic, our episode in the desert already a thing of the past.

"You can't make it happen without a leader, ladies. I am telling you that you have got to have a leader. Humankind is not as advanced as you might think. If people are going to make a real sacrifice they still need someone to fall in love with. And with no sacrifice there's no revolution."

After a awkward pause, she went on, "And you need to look after yourselves. Ladies, the crucial point here is the women. One way or another men will set up a new system and be the soldiers that support it. Only women take prophets and revolutions seriously. You need to look after yourselves and not get duped this time around. The world has lost its faith. And the world hasn't got any plans. But we can do it better. Women can always do it better."

Distressed, Maryam whispered, "It's hard, Madam. Very hard."

Then Lilla said, "But there's still more left to do."

Her eyes fixed on the road, she took a deep breath and breathing out she said, "You'll see."

Conquering that thousand-headed beast called traffic, we made it to the Union Hotel by nightfall. The two girls from the helicopter (I recognized their eyes) were waiting for us in the doorway, dressed in jeans, one wearing a headscarf, the other with thick, curly hair. Without saying a word they took us upstairs and down a corridor. Tired, rundown and dragging our feet, we stumbled after them single-file and finally stopped at a large door. Both girls signalled for us to remain quiet and they opened the door...

A large room with high ceilings and an enormous chandelier that wasn't lit. The corners of the rooms are cloaked in darkness. On the walls are paintings that have faded to match the browning walls. From inside comes a smell: sandalwood oil and an old theatre house curtain. Apart from five thick, tall columns nothing else divides the room. The wooden floor is covered in black smudges. This is one of those halls that makes you think of waltzing because it's so big or so old. In the centre of the room is a spiral of candles. And all types of women of all ages are inside, enough to fill the entire room. They are standing at a certain distance from one another. And in the middle of the spiral stands a heavy-set woman with platinum blonde hair pulled up in a Farah Diba bun, waving her hands in the air as she speaks. We don't have to ask: she must be Firdevs Hanım. We've arrived in the middle of something and so we wait on the sidelines, listening. This much I can catch from her speech:

"... we will be here. Like grains of wheat, like water underground. With the elegance of jasmine and with the perseverance of worms. We are the keepers of good and evil. The keepers of dignity and indulgence, vengeance and forgiveness. We are precious, so very precious. We have given birth to life and death. Raised them all. We will be here. Because we have always been here and we have always known this. We will remember what we have forgotten. We will remember that we have given birth to gods. We will never forget that we were the first to know the science of earth and sky. And we will raise our daughters to be stronger than us, more joyous and more free. We will lend helping hands. And in doing so we will encourage more. We will keep our faith in each other. We will keep our faith in a god that loves us. Girls, a happy birthday to Hypatia!"

I leaned closer to Madam Lilla who was behind me.

"What is this? Some kind of cult?"

On her face was the elation and pride of a woman in an airport waiting to see a friend she hasn't seen in years.

"The girls of Firdevs!"

Maryam leaned into Lilla's ear.

"Are there eighty women here?"

Madam Lilla proudly nodded her head and under her breath Maryam whispered, "That's what I figured."

Into my ear, she said, "They say that Dido had eighty girls. The story goes that when she was crossing the Mediterranean she stopped at Cyprus and gathered up eighty young girls before she carried on to Carthage. She entrusted the city to them."

Our arms crossed, Amira and I raised our eyebrows in surprise.

"Then what happened to them?" I asked and Maryam took me by the arm to shush me. But I couldn't help myself and I asked, "Why aren't you here?"

Looking deeply into my eyes, she didn't reply.

Then the ceremony seems to end. The women slowly start to leave the inner circle, waiting for women in the outside rings to step away. And suddenly the strange and mystic mood is gone and there is only laughing and hushed gossip. Groups of four or five form and then naturally disperse only to come together again in a new number. Now and then I catch the following words that I can't really understand:

"Chinese … Bangladesh … Tahrir … T-shirts… The young women who have left the Muslim brotherhood…"

Centremost in the circle Firdevs Hanım is the last to leave. Like a captain on a sinking ship, her hands are clasped below her waist. When one of the girls who brought us inside goes to her and points us out, whispering into her ear, Firdevs Hanım is already looking at us, or rather she's looking at Madam Lilla. Then she addressed us directly, *"And so here are three women who have run down their angels!"*

I looked at Madam Lilla, who was holding back a joy taking shape on her face, trying to keep a serious expression. In a flat voice she responded to Firdevs Hanım:

"Firdevs you shall be the one to indulge their angels!"

Amira abruptly asked Madam Lilla, "Was it Firdevs Hanım who sent us the helicopter?"

Nodding, Lilla whispered, "You could say that."

There wasn't even enough time to ask, 'well then who did?' Firdevs Hanım was now beside us, her enormous stature hardly leaving us any room, squeezing out even Madam Lilla's ample soul. This woman took up all the space around her. Now leading us out of the hall with her arms open wide we could do nothing but let ourselves go as she was speaking.

"I'll have the girls prepare a room for you. They will find something for you to wear. And I'll have them send you something to eat."

Firdevs was the kind of woman who made you feel small and insignificant in her presence. She had more breadth than depth. We were surprised to see that she hadn't even greeted Madam Lilla. And then we found ourselves in a room, dumbfounded by everything we had just seen – the ceremony, the ritual or whatever it was. It was a strange room with embroidered bed covers, oil paintings of scenes of Alexandria's colonial period on the walls, machine woven rugs on the floor and the sharp scent of dust in the air. Outside the door Firdevs and Madam Lilla were speaking. Our ears pressed against the door, we listened in on the conversation.

Madam: "I'm grateful Firdevs. I can't thank you enough..."

Firdevs: "What are you after, Esma?"

(Silence ... Lilla was trying to cope with the belittling tone in this unsavoury first salvo.)

Madam: "You're still angry with me..."

Firdevs: "I'm not angry, Esma, but hurt."

(Silence. Lilla changed tack.)

Madam: "You know why I'm going."

Firdevs: "I ... What reason could you have for leaving us? As for your daughter..."

Madam: "I entrusted her to you, Firdevs. You shouldn't have told her who I was. You shouldn't have allowed her to come after me. You betrayed me..."

Firdevs: "I couldn't allow you to betray your own daughter, Esma. And I never would have imagined she'd take her own life."

(Silence. Was Lilla on the brink of tears?)

Madam: "It's all over now Firdevs. Now..."

(Lilla took a deep breath.)

Madam: "Think of those three young women in there as my own. They're all special in their own way and... And I can't leave them in the middle of this trip. They need to learn to believe in themselves. To believe in life... You know. The same old story. They're tired."

(Silence. It seemed Firdevs was ready to forget everything and make a fresh start)

Firdevs: "And you Esma? Do you still believe?"

(Silence. If this was the Lilla we knew she wasn't going to answer and she didn't. Firdevs went on.)

Firdevs: "Is he still waiting for you?"

Silence.

Firdevs: "He believes in you, Esma. You should go back to him. At this point you should give yourself to him."

Unable to stop myself I whispered with my head still pressed against the door:

"Who the hell is she talking about? This guy waiting for Madam Lilla…"

Their fingers on their lips, Maryam and Amira shushed me and the rest of my sentence melted in my mouth:

"Nana Fatima told Lilla something about going back to somebody."

Lilla went on in a softer, halting voice, "I have one more thing to do, Firdevs. When I take care of that… I don't know… Maybe you're right… It's been a lifetime… But that doesn't mean that people change…"

Silence again. It lasted some time. When the conversation finished we heard the rustling of cloth; this was the kind of conversation between people who have so much to say but do it with eyes and hands instead of words. And then more rustling: they must have embraced. Breezing over the issue, Madam Lilla then said, "In the morning I'll send you these young ladies. Speak to them, Firdevs. They need to get to know you. They're all smart girls. This is why more than anything…"

Firdevs seemed more at ease and in almost a cheerful tone of voice, "No need to worry, Esma. I understand. Like you said… The same old story."

They laughed together. It was a poignant, sorrowful laugh. In that gentle laugh you felt the depth that comes with a long friendship, one that has brewed over years. Then the laughter turned to sighs and Lilla asked, "How is Walid Bey? God willing they are all thriving. Please send them my deepest thanks. If the two of you didn't help us out in the middle of the desert we'd be…"

"There's no need to thank me. Walid Bey is doing just fine, mademoiselle … he's a husband. And standing where he needs to stand." answered Firdevs, most likely twirling her hands in the air. And they laughed again. Firdevs said, "Come on. Let's go have a glass of liquor and you can tell me how boring Tunisia has been. And I'll tell you about our new girls and what we're doing."

Speaking in low voices they carefully walked down the stairs – they must have been holding onto one another.

"Ok tell me then," Maryam said turning to me.

Picking up from where I left off I said, "So like I was saying … that morning we left Yafran Nana Fatima said something to Lilla like, 'Go back to him, give yourself up to him,' obviously referring to somebody and now look, Firdevs is saying the same thing, 'Go back to him.' So who it is?"

With both hands on her hips and her eyes wide as saucers like a child at a circus for the first time, Amira says, "Who knows which lover she's talking about. Forget about it … but wasn't that strange? Maryam do you know anything about all this stuff? So these kinds of things are going on in Egypt? A cult of women. That's amazing!"

Maryam laughed. As usual it wasn't what Amira had said but the way she had said it. Maryam said, "Who do you think am I, *sweetie*? An Egyptian ambassador? You think I'd keep tabs on some group of strange women? These women have their own mission. What do I know about them? People in the revolution and the academy don't go for this sort of thing."

Her eyes spinning like pinwheels, Amira said, "But in the morning we're definitely going to see Firdevs, mademoiselle!"

She stopped for a second then went on like a comic book superhero:

"And they'll probably sacrifice us to the gods on some altar!"

Was this the same woman in the desert just a day ago? This little girl? Indeed she wore the expression of a little girl who has just hopped off a swing but the night before she was a sorrowful woman who lamented having rashly given herself to a man only to feel her heart flutter. Biting down on her lower lip, Maryam must have been thinking the same thing because she went over to Amira as if she were her child. Taking her little face in her hands, she squeezed,

"*Sweetie* we were actually thinking of handing you over to them and making a quick getaway!"

Looking at these two made you think long and hard about how two women could mean so much to each other. In turns they become each other's mother, sister, husband, brother, daughter … her face in Maryam's hands, Amira crinkled her brow:

"Oh!"

"What's wrong my little sweetie pie?" said Maryam still squeezing as if practising how she might love the daughter she left behind. And without admitting so much to herself Amira was practising how to be a young girl loved by her mother.

Placing her hand on her stomach, Amira said, "I'm on my period."

A strange expression fell over Maryam's face and she said, "How strange," and went quiet. "Me too. Just now."

I thought about how men can never change each other's

physical chemistry, no matter how close they might be. But when women start to really talk, even their eggs get in on the conversation.

We spent half the night looking for sanitary pads. In the end they wrapped gauze they had found in the medicine cabinet around the little hotel towels and stuffed them between their legs and we all went to bed. I looked over at them. Playing the part of young girls I could see how they relished the well-needed break from the burdens of being grown women. They were incredibly beautiful. I thought of Muhammed's letters and Dido's tablets ... Maryam and Amira were the kind of women who could write the ends to the stories that others had started for them. And like all truly strong women they didn't show it. With softened hearts they fell asleep. Dreaming, their hands and their feet were twitching but what was to come the next morning had to be far more interesting than their dreams.

24

"If someone has a scar on her face and you don't ask her about it she won't think you're being kind, she'll just think you didn't see her face."

That was the line Firdevs Hanım dropped like a bomb when she overheard our conversation as we were getting out of her limo that morning. Maryam was having a go at me: "If you're that curious you should've just asked. I can't ask those sorts of questions."

I snapped back in response, "We're in your country now, azizi, aren't we? Why can't you just ask? Or will you lose face if you come out and say, 'hey driver, how did you end up like this?' You just mention the scar and take it from there."

Amira butted in, "She's going to know you're talking about her."

I was curious to know why this woman driver looked so much like a man. I was sure it had something to do with the slits in her ear lobes. It looked like her earrings had been ripped right out, leaving ear lobes dangling in two pieces. But Maryam was worried about her street cred and Amira didn't want to ask such an intimate question in Tunisian Arabic and look like the typical overly curious tourist. But they had hit that time of the month at the same time and so we tumbled out of the limo like a crackling ball of nervous energy. Firdevs Hanım's sudden intervention caught us off guard, which is why we were even less prepared for the sudden intimacy she'd forced on us.

"If someone has a scar on her face and you don't ask her

about it she won't think you're being kind, she'll just think you didn't see her face." People like to become partners through their scars. Maybe Maryam Hanım doesn't want someone else to tell her story because she might end up having to tell her own. Take her hair for example, maybe she doesn't want to have to explain why she keeps it so short."

This was certainly a touchy topic for Maryam. And Firdevs had just stuffed her hands and her legs into the metaphorical bell jar that Amira and I had been so careful to avoid, keeping away for days, always waiting for the right moment. Maryam immediately parried the bold attack.

"My personal issues have nothing to do with you, Firdevs Hanım. We're only making a courtesy call here. You helped us and so we're here to thank you."

Flashing a wry smile Firdevs Hanım said, 'Hah!' Then she stared at Maryam long enough for things to get uncomfortable. The expression on her face belonged either to an executioner choosing the right sword for the job or an old woman looking at a young version of herself in a family album. Then she simply said, "Don't be angry, dear". So softly and suddenly that Maryam was left alone with her bad vibes. And without waiting for an answer she turned and started up the broad white steps leading into the house. Turning around she looked at us with a smile, one thin eyebrow raised.

"Please come in. Let's go inside where we can politely meet one another before we get too tangled up in our personal issues."

Firdevs Hanım moved like an enormous stately galleon gliding over the surface of the sea. There was something about this platinum blonde that put you on edge. It was like a powerful electric cloud hovered over her and if you stayed there for too long you might never leave. Your instinct was to run but when you tried to go for it you got this creepy feeling that something terrible might happen. This was a presence so oppressing you could hardly articulate your own anxiety to yourself.

In a broad entrance hall with high ceilings sat a little ornamental pool. In the middle stood the statue of a goddess. At the opposite end of the hall two staircases curved out from each other and up to the second floor, like the ones you see in those old Hollywood pictures. In fact this was so Hollywood you wouldn't be surprised if Ginger Rogers and Gene Kelly came tap dancing down those steps... As I was mulling the scene over in my head, Firdevs Hanım stopped with a hand on the bannister and said, "I was thinking of champagne. We need to have something to celebrate women who have come back from the dead, don't you think?"

Her suffocating aura must have had the same brain-numbing effect on Amira because she asked a really ridiculous question: "What a stylish statue! Is that you?" The expression on her face making it clear no cannonball we shot would ever breach her city walls, Firdevs Hanım calmly said, "I am glad you asked. That's Athena. Every woman has a goddess within. Mine is Athena. Shall we find yours?"

Maryam pouted. Her nervous energy was still getting the better of any wonder or curiosity. But Amira was quickly taken in and quickened her steps. Mayram and I fell behind.

"Which one was Athena?" I asked.

"Azizi, can't you guess? She's the goddess of strength and logic. Born out of Zeus's head. She just popped out whole."

"Wow! So a real tough cookie?"

"More like a man-woman, azizi."

At the top of the stairs we stopped at two open rooms facing each other. Both were filled with young and middle-aged women. On the right were young goths all dressed in black, sitting at computers, and on the left were colourfully dressed middle-aged women. I vaguely recognized the faces of some of them from last night's ceremony. But some were new. The curly-haired girl from the helicopter sat at a computer in the goth room. I couldn't find the other one. As I was taking a closer look inside the computer room I didn't realize that Firdevs Hanım was right behind of me.

"You met my daughter the other day. Now she's at her computer performing the fine art of hacking, but she's also an extraordinary Fu Jitsu master!"

"Sorry?" I said.

"I gather you aren't familiar with the martial arts?"

"No," I said. "I'm rubbish at that sort of thing."

Narrowing her eyes, Firdevs Hanım peered into mine as if she was trying to read my mind. I squinted back at her but also kept an eye on the young crowd in the computer room. We stayed like that for a few seconds with our eyes narrowed. Then the absurd moment ended as if nothing had happened and Firdevs Hanım turned to the room filled with young women and computers and began to explain.

"Maryam Hanım must already know this but there have been some very important developments regarding the women in Tahrir."

Hopping up and down, Amira jumped in. "I swear the most important development we've heard has to do with sexual harassment." Filled with the same national pride, Maryam and Firdevs Hanım glowered at Amira from Tunisia. Firdevs Hanım went on, "The centre of such activity isn't Tahrir, dear Amira. And if such an unpleasant encounter really must happen the one thing a woman could ask for is for it to happen in Tahrir Square. If nothing else all your brothers and sisters will be there to help."

Maryam looked at Amira as if to say, 'Well take that for an answer!' I saw that she had cooled off and she suddenly moved closer to Firdevs Hanım, who went on, "Maybe you missed this while you were on the road. The police dragged off one of our girls. Almost all her clothes came off in the process. And then there was all this talk about the colour of her bra: it was blue. Now we as women..."

Maryam made a sound but it wasn't like she was trying to say something. More like she'd choked on saliva and the sound of the pain in her throat had slipped out. Firdevs Hanım caught on immediately:

"Now don't you dare let yourself feel guilty about being here, Maryam. Considering what Esma told me last night, you have done everything you could for the revolution. And everyone deserves a rest, you have earned the right to catch your breath. We as Egypt are happy to take to care of you. Just relax!"

I had no idea that Maryam felt that way. Listening to Firdevs Hanım we could see Maryam's face softening and, yes, she was feeling guilty. Firdevs went on with her delivery.

"We have also organized an event. Women from all walks of life went to Tahrir on behalf of our sisters. It wasn't easy reconciling political differences but it was a beginning. It was a watershed moment for the women of Egypt. Leftists and religious believers came together in support of our sisters, raising their voices in their honour. Now we are in the process of expanding the network. Of course for this..."

Her eyes wide open, Maryam interrupted Firdevs Hanım whose voice was beginning to wane, "Did they come? I mean did everyone come?"

She touched Maryam's arm and smiled.

"Yes."

Tears welled up in Maryam's eyes. And when she smiled a single tear was pushed into the corner of her eye before it streamed down over her cheek. Now squeezing Maryam's arm, Firdevs Hanım went on, "You saved the girls of Egypt, Maryam. People like you who were the first ones in Tahrir."

Maryam struggled to wave her hand in the air to downplay her role and as she buried her smiling face in her neck it was as if everything – her daughter whom she she had failed to protect and Amira whom she also failed to safeguard and the flight from her own country – the pain of it all was pressed into a single drop of rose oil that ran down her cheek.

Firdevs Hanım let out a high, heartwarming laugh and said, "Don't worry Maryam. Even the girls who left the Muslim brotherhood were there."

"And in that room," said Firdevs Hanım quickly moving on. Suddenly she let go of Maryam's arm that hung there in the air for a second. And again there was the fraction of a second of tension. Firdevs Hanım was incapable of staying any longer in the warm glow she had created and if you stayed there too long she would eventually leave you. But in her tense mode it seemed like she could fix her eyes on someone for an eternity. And then, as if nothing out of the ordinary had happened, she would suddenly flip all the feelings in her soul. Strange. And you couldn't quite be sure if the moment ever really happened. Were you together or did you make up the moment? She was a woman who knew how to pull the strings of her own tension. She was just starting to speak again, gliding to the other door, when five women came out of the room and showed her their T-shirts.

"What do you think?"

On each T-shirt was the face of a woman. Chinese, Asian, Indian faces...

Firdevs Hanım turned to us.

"What do you think? Do you like them?"

"What's the issue?" asked Amira and Firdevs Hanım eagerly explained.

"We are thinking of different ways to protest alienation. Everything we wear is made by these women and yet we never see their faces. Especially in the West. They have no idea who made the products they get from Bangladesh and Pakistan and China. So we came up with this idea. We all wrote about it on Facebook. We said we wanted the photographs of women working under slave labour conditions in the textile industry. In the end they sent us their photos and we printed the T-shirts."

"Wow!" I said. Picking up on my enthusiasm, Firdevs turned to me:

"And now we're thinking about doing this: we are going to make it possible for those workers to sew secret notes into labels: Information about their working conditions. Let's see if it works. We're still in the planning stages. There are a few crucial points we always must keep in mind. One is reaching women in the West. Right now our girls are working to bring down popular women's sites. In their place we plan to post letters about everything we are going through here. And of course the political situation in Egypt ... that's what we are working for."

"Where does the money come from?" said Maryam all of a sudden.

"That part is easy, Maryam. My husband and I are both very rich."

Like a single woman might talk down to a married women,

Maryam added, "So your husband gives you permission to do all this?"

"A husband doesn't need to know everything, Maryam. Besides they don't really want to know in the first place. So no use pushing it. In the end I have my own money. Now come along. Let's see if the champagne has chilled. Over a glass on the terrace I can tell you all about the matter of the watermill which I am sure you are all dying to know about. And you can tell me about the goddess in you."

"I can tell you right now that we don't have anything like that in us," I said, laughing. Firdevs Hanım laughed, too.

"That's what you think."

We began another trip up a flight of stairs, following Firdevs Hanım's broad hips. The walls were suddenly covered with all kinds of posters and photographs and we began to understand where Firdevs Hanım got her money. These were enormous, faded black-and-white photographs of a young Firdevs. Her face was now much larger and worn but the colour of her hair and her hairstyle hadn't changed. Looking at these hyper-polished close-ups of her in her fake eyelashes, full make-up and feather boa and then all the different coloured movie posters, I could see that she was a genuine moviestar. "Ah," said Maryam, whispering in my ear. "Now I remember, azizi! She was the classic femme fatale in all the old movies! Of course!"

A few steps ahead of us Firdevs Hanım quietly laughed without turning around. But then she did and made the face of a true femme fatale and said in a tough, stony voice, "The femme fatale, eh? Oh please, my dear Maryam! Coming from you? You should know that any city woman in this culture who knows what she wants is labelled a femme fatale. A pure and chaste village girl is good, but when you have desires, and a cigarette always dangling from your lips, well, then you're pure evil. Please! How could you say such a thing?"

And gripping the bannister she threw back her head and let out a long theatrical laugh. She looked at Maryam who started to laugh. Clearly Firdevs was imitating her own laugh of years ago when she would play the evil blonde. When she finished her scene, she said, "Ah! Ah!" and she hauled her hips up over the last few steps.

When she had caught her breath, she said, "Esma and I grew up in the same house. She must have told you about Mother Wasma. She raised us. Esma went to Europe and I stayed here. The only thing left for me to do was take the role of femme fatale. And so I did. Sometimes I still play it. I couldn't care less. My own god loves me."

When Maryam asked us to describe our own god, Amira was pouring champagne into broad glasses with such joy she looked as if she had been weaned on the drink and denied the taste for all these years.

"Just a minute," Firdevs Hanım said and she placed three glasses in the shape of a triangle and a single glass on top. "If we are going to do this we should do it right." Champagne overflowed from the top glass and cascaded into the glasses below. Firdevs Hanım let out another laugh. We joined in as we raised our glasses. As soon as we'd taken that first sip she said, "My dear friends, my god is one that loves me. This is what you need too."

Holding her glass up to the light, she went on, "Seeing that you're women who have taken to the road you must have already severed all your bonds. First you cut the deal you made out of love for your father and later you made deals with the people for whom you felt love and compassion. So this means you are one of them. But which god are you?"

Amira was feeling the champagne and twisting and teasing.

"In what sense?"

"I'm asking what goddess lives in you?"

Firdevs seemed ready to answer her own question. Her mood was brightening and the tension in the air was gone.

"Wait, wait. Let me say it. Amira... Of course! Aphrodite. And you Maryam... Yes, you are Hecate, but you still have time."

I waited, thinking it was my turn now but Firdevs Hanım started to talk about Hecate and Aphrodite.

"Aphrodite turns the wheels of her life on seduction and inspiration. While Hecate is a woman of wisdom. She has experienced everything, pain and joy. She is always waiting at the door, ready to help her daughters. Now considering everything Esma has told me, Maryam, you're at the last bend in the road, and once you make it around you will become Hecate. Esma has the same goddess. She was Artemis in her youth but now she is Hecate."

"Which one was Artemis?" I asked, hoping she might pick a goddess for me. She didn't let me down.

"And considering what Esma has said to me about you..."

"What did she say?"

Firdevs Hanım laughed.

"No more than what you have already showed her. But mulling over what I was told, you must be an Artemis. A virgin!"

"What?"

Firdevs let out another laugh and then calmed me down. "I'm not speaking about physical virginity. This is a spiritual matter. For you this is a matter of producing, writing and taking inspiration from the world."

A glass of champagne in her hand, Amira was now

steeped in the *Breakfast at Tiffany's* mood, poking fun at me.

"Darling, are you sad because I nabbed Aphrodite!"

We laughed at the way she batted her eyelids and wiggled her bottom in her imitation of Aphrodite. Coming into her element, Firdevs Hanım threw herself onto one of the white wicker chairs on the terrace and swinging her glass of champagne in the air she began to explain.

"Esma sent you to me so that I could help. So you should leave this place feeling better than when you arrived. And Esma ... girls, you need to keep a close eye on her. Because she ... ah ... I mean she ... she's always chasing after life. I mean, she couldn't stay like me ... anyway my dears ... right now the matter is you. This matter of the goddesses ... you're all smart women so I'm not going to waste too much of your time with them and other mysteries. But this age of ours is very deceiving for women like us."

Maryam now wore her professorial expression, one hand on her temple and the other holding a glass of champagne. She asked, "When you say women like us...?"

Hardly bothered by the interruption, Firdevs answered, "My dear Maryam, I know your story. Which makes it easier for me to understand why you cut your hair. You must have wanted to forget. You must have felt compelled, like our woman driver, to resign from womanhood. This only shows that you have more than one woman in you. As for Amira ... oh! Amira. Esma and I know all too well what you've been through. As a woman with a word and a woman who dances ... this crowd isn't easy to confront. That's why..."

Maryam cut her off again.

"What did Madam Lilla tell you about us?"

Putting her glass on the glass coffee table, Firdevs leaned over and clasped her hands, thinking. Then she smiled and said, "Ladies, have you still not understood? For people like us your stories are already written on your faces. There's no need for us to speak of them. We only need to help each other. Women like us recognize women who have worn out their angels. We can see it in their eyes."

She stopped for a moment and looked over our faces and went on.

"I am a woman who has come to certain compromises only later in life. To be Firdevs and to stay that way. To have this house, and these chairs and this champagne. I didn't race after life like Esma and that's why I had to come to an agreement. With Walid, with the city, with men and women. To live that way I had to sacrifice a few of my inner women. My Artemis and maybe even my Aphrodite. But you're not in the same boat. You have refused to make these deals. You did not give up on any of your inner women. Which is why your souls need support."

Again she paused to give us time to digest what she'd just said or to see if we would challenge her. Looking up she saw that we were listening and she continued.

"Here we have developed a method that fits our needs. It was a method that originally came from a woman like us: Madam Katherine Fowler. Esma made a point of asking me to tell to you about it. In the beginning this might seem a little funny or strange but you'll see how useful it can be. It's a speaking method. We do it like this..."

She got up and pulled the two empty chairs towards her. She sat down in one and started:

"You take empty chairs. You can also draw pictures of them. What you do is line up your inner women, sit them down in the chairs. For Amira it's the dancer, the writer, the woman-child... For Maryam it is the man-woman, the woman-woman, and so on... Then you encourage them to speak to each other and come to an agreement. All the women in you must feel nourished and fulfilled. Otherwise you won't find happiness. But they must work things out before you decide which one will be most present. You must get them to come to a decision as to how much life they will get out of you. Do you understand?"

I asked, "Well then what good comes of doing that? And what happens if they can't agree?"

"Of course you're a writer and so..."

"Well, you can't really say that."

Firdevs Hanım took a sip of champagne, raised an eyebrow and smiled as if to say, 'Now would you check out the little devil.' Then she added, "What you're doing right now, mademoiselle, isn't important. You are already doing enough providing you are still concerned with the wounds of others. You don't always need a pen in hand, ready to get everything down on paper."

I looked at my champagne. Firdevs Hanım now turned to Amira and Maryam.

"It isn't necessary for your inner women to come to an agreement. If you have this conversation frequently enough then over time, perhaps years later, you'll find that your inner voice has coalesced around one voice. That's when wisdom begins. By the time you get to be as old as me and Esma you'll be speaking through one voice. Then your inner goddess comes to life."

Maryam leaned back in her chair, her stomach shaking to the tune of a sarcastic chuckle.

"Why don't you just come out with it and say we've got a long way to go."

Firdevs stopped, closed and opened her eyes. Then she said this: "That's all there is to life! It's that short."

She added: "But until then..."

376

"Until then you should keep the basic principles of a goddess in mind. One: Never apologize for something you didn't do. Two: Don't try to over explain yourself. Three: Never underestimate your achievements. Four: Never begin a sentence, 'Now I might be wrong but....' Five: Never answer questions you don't want to answer. Six: Don't be afraid to say no. As for the seventh rule..."

Maryam butted in with thorns in her voice: "Now are you going to tell us that all we need to do is find ourselves a ruling king, Firdevs Hanım?"

"You decide if you want to find a king or a jester. But you must come up with your own seventh rule. Every goddess has this right. But it might be a good idea to get on with it. Like I said..."

Again she blinked in slow motion, "Life is that short."

Silence. Though I doubt we would have admitted this I suppose we were all trying to bring up an inventory of inner women and wondering how faithful we could be to those rules. Then a man shouting below broke the silence. He bellowed:

"The Singaporean stock market! Yes! Yes! No! What does the Japanese market have to do with it, brother! The key thing is..."

Firdevs Hanım's expression suddenly changed. Frozen in that blonde femme fatale look she had when we first met her. Her eyes went glassy. The man continued shouting as he huffed up the stairs.

"The kids weren't following Nasdaq! That's unbelievable."

Firdevs Hanım looked at us with compassion in her eyes, asking for us to understand. She was no longer the strong, untouchable woman who had just been lecturing us – now she looked ashamed. Years flittered across her face and in waves it seemed like you could hear the words, 'well what else can you do?' And when that fat, old man with a sour expression on his face, Walid Bey, husband to Firdevs Hanım, noisily burst onto the terrace, his bad energy gusted all over the place, the same kind of energy you always feel when a man busts unexpectedly into the middle of a scene without giving a damn. Trying to appear charming, he said, "Champagne? What a pleasant idea?" And with that our interior monologues abruptly came to end and the champagne went flat. Amira took Firdevs Hanım's hand. For a second. Without even noticing it, Firdevs shook her hand. The curtain had already fallen. Amira dropped her glass and shards exploded over the stone floor. Firdevs Hanım cried out, "Walid! Don't come out here! Don't! There's glass everywhere!"

Walid's hand hung in the air and his hunger for champagne growled in his gut. But the place really was covered in glass and Firdevs wanted to protect our shards from Walid. As she hurried us out of the house we said nothing about what had happened that day. Except for one thing of course.

25

"So what exactly are you saying, mademoiselle Aphrodite?" asked Maryam, "Are you telling me that God doesn't love women?"

With her finger Amira was scraping the last bits of coffee out of the bottom of her cup. "Not exactly," she said, "but let's say we're not his favourites. If someone like Muhammed even says so..."

"He was just being ignorant," said Maryam leaning back in her white plastic chair. We were sitting in a coffeehouse. "The believers who succeeded in making him out to be genderless know that He or She loves them."

"When so many believers have made him a man is that still possible?" asked Amira. "In my opinion Firdevs is right. We need to create a God that loves us."

"Don't be ridiculous," interrupted Maryam. We were silent. I was willing to bet that right then we were all thinking about our inner goddess and more importantly about how we were going to get all the different women in our heads to sit down and talk. I could picture Amira talking politics in her dance outfit and Maryam chanting slogans in Tahrir Square with a baby on her back... Like any woman who looks good in photographs, in my mind I watched them wake up alone. Later they went to bed alone. In the middle of the night when they were startled by a sound and woke they would speak aloud. So what Muhammed and Firdevs said was important. We were so alone that maybe we needed a compassionate goddess to speak with.

When we sat down at one of those coffeehouses at the harbour, Amira said, "This is the second time I've heard this thing about a god who loves women ... my Muhammed said something about it as well." And she started to tell the story:

One day Amira and Muhammed were travelling from a city on the Tunisian coast to Tabarka. Over lunch in a hotel Muhammed points out something in the garden. A tennis umpire's chair covered with all different colours of paint. For years they must have used it as a painting ladder. Muhammed then says:

"Leftovers like that from the fifties were abandoned in the southern hemisphere. They say so much, don't they? What do you think, my love?"

That tennis umpire's chair that no one actually used for tennis prompted a conversation on the subject. Muhammed went on to explain how Western civilization still spoke of an airy happiness it promised through these leftovers.

"When you look at the state of that umpire's chair you understand more clearly the revenge they got from that dream of civilization. I can imagine the pent-up anger they must have felt when they had to climb up that thing. This is a far more humiliating form of oppression than suffering at the hand of a Western soldier. Especially when you imagine a typical short, potbellied Arab, don't you think? Think of all the battles waged in his head so that he could come to grips with that umpire's chair!"

Muhammed was laughing heartily as he said all of this. Then they talked about the old film projectors that were left behind years ago, abandoned when the open-air cinemas were shut down. As far as Amira could remember Muhammed said something like, "This part of the world rejected its dream of absolute civilization with the anger of a lover scratching out the eyes of her lost love." And he added, "Of course the holes only remind you that the lover's gone. Those blank spots overwhelm everything else in the picture."

Amira looked around her. I suppose she was thinking how empty the world was without seeing things through Muhammed's eyes. Her face scrunched up with sadness; she was silent. Maryam said, "And? So what are you saying then? The umpire's chair and everything..."

It was when her finger began to scrape at the coffee that lined her cup. "How should I know?" she said. "Muhammed was strange that day. When we went for a walk along the coast he saw women in chadors and veils over their faces. Beside them were these young tough guys and little kids, naked, running in and out of the sea, laughing. But the women only put their feet in the water, one step forward and one step back. Muhammed was in a bad mood – I'd never seen him like that before – and he said, 'maybe we made a mistake, sweetie. We were forced to climb that tennis chair back then and to get our revenge we took it out on women. Now it seems to me, that we wanted a God who loved men more. We were so humiliated that we needed a God on our side. A God that would really stick it to the women who laughed at us. But our...' and he looked at me. For the first time he touched my hair in public and he said, 'now I need God to love you more. Now I believe that God loves a woman like you as she is.' That's what he said..."

"Azizi," said Maryam, looking at me. "Muhammed loved

you so much he lost his faith and love of the world. That's what happened."

"But," interrupted Amira, "just imagine a father-god figure that could really love us the way we are ... wouldn't we walk this earth differently? I mean we'd be that much better off. We could have believed. And not just in God. If he loved us ... like Firdevs was saying, you know, we'd love ourselves so much more. And that's what Muhammed was saying..."

"Say it," said Maryam, "what else did the heathen let slip?"

"'Do you think God loves women, Amira?' That's what he asked me."

"Most likely just his guilty conscience," I said. "I mean because he couldn't really talk about what they did to you, what he did to you. The raid for example."

"It's possible," said Amira, leaning closer to her cup and nibbling dried coffee off her finger.

And that's when Maryam said it: *"And so what are you saying, Mademoiselle Aphrodite? Are you saying that God doesn't love women?"*

"That's nonsense," she said and we were quiet.

We said nothing else on the topic. Maryam picked up a paper from the table next to us and started to read, her brow crinkled, her lower lip hanging and a distracted look on her face. She put the paper down and I saw the photograph of the girl in the blue bra. It was the news about the protests that was getting to her. But the devil got the better of me.

"This isn't about God, if only our homelands could love us for who we are. That would be enough, don't you think, azizi?"

An eyebrow bent she looked up at me and said nothing. I went on.

"So what are you going to do? Are you going to see your daughter when we get to Lebanon?

She cut me off.

"Azizi, pride brings nothing but trouble."

"Excuse me?"

"That's just the way it is," she said, gravely nodding her head a couple times. "Pride is nothing but trouble. Whether it's talk of God loving me or not. Or whether my homeland is going to love me back. Blah blah blah... All this comes to nothing. You have to love. You have to let go. That's the deal. The rest is just pride."

"Oh Lord," I said, broken. I wasn't angry. Because I knew that Maryam was speaking to her broken heart. She was kicking her own heart because it was broken for the same reason, because she thought it was full of pride. With astonishing speed Amira changed the topic.

"Now this Walid Bey... Firdevs Hanım really found a guy to fall in love with. I don't know how women like her do it. Don't they ever get bored?"

"Of course they do," I said, " but some of them don't feel secure unless they're with someone who's going to love them til death. To me it seems like some women set up their lives like it's this massive company they are going to manage. And they do it mainly out of fear. It's strange. They get stronger from the fear. But I wonder how Madam Lilla holds out? All the time alone, I mean, the idea that she's going to die alone."

I looked to see Maryam with her phone. It was the first time she'd taken it out. She was checking her Twitter. Most likely she was trying to see what her friends were saying about the protests for the girl in the blue bra. Unwittingly

383

she was biting her lips and her fingernails. I had never seen her do that before.

"Hey! Who am I talking to here?" I said, but she didn't look up. She hadn't even heard me. "Azizi, do you think that Dido made a new life for herself with her baby in new lands? Was she a loner like Madam Lilla or did she find herself a Walid who made it possible for her to set up a new firm?"

Maryam didn't look up – she really hadn't heard anything I'd just said. Before I could open my mouth and shout, 'Hey,' Amira grabbed me by the arm and shushed me. So the two of us just sat and watched. Our elbows propped on the table we stared at Maryam. And her Twitter séance went on and on. Once or twice her hand moved to write something and then she stopped. She didn't even know we were there. And so we just leaned deeper into the table and looked at each other. "What do you think?" I said. "What sort of life did Muhammed make for himself abroad?" Amira shrugged and frowned and stared blankly at the table.

"I mean alone or in terms of adopting a new lifestyle…" I said, but she cut me off.

"I don't think so!" She made a face that made her look much older; I took her hand and smiled:

"For what it's worth there's something you can be sure about," I said, "God loves you."

She buried her head in her arms. When the waiter came over we prised ourselves away from the table. Suddenly we all had the same tough Middle Eastern woman look. Suddenly we had all buttoned up our souls. "Three more cups!" says Maryam all of a sudden, guiltily emerging from the whirl of the Twittersphere. "Azizi," I say, "hey, over here." I had to be sure she would hear me this time.

"Look at me! Our countries are always expecting us to give some reaction. Reaction, reaction, reaction! They don't even give you time to think! There's no time to hoover up all the information. You have the right to take a break. This femme fatale of so many years can't be wrong about that!"

Like a fool I smiled to myself. Biting her lower lip, Maryam looked at me.

"Well what do you know," she says, "someone has sprung back to life. Asking all these questions, giving advice and everything. What's happened to you?"

Truth is I hadn't even noticed.

"Firdevs has had a good effect on you," says Amira, smiling, "the goddess thing and all that. You liked that stuff. Right?"

"Could be. What do I know? This thing about Artemis. The idea that I could be a 'virgin' for the rest of my life. In other words, alone. You see I write and so I am alone, and I'll keep writing, and to know what I am gives me a sense of comfort. It's my destiny or something like that. No other responsibilities. Fantastic!"

Maryam flashes me a reluctant smile.

"So far so good, azizi. It gives someone a sense of comfort. We are puppets in the hand of fate and there's nothing better than that. If nothing else, I could believe in God for just that reason, but that's just between you and me."

"You might be right about that!" said Amira as she leaned back in her chair.

"In my opinion life is way too hard for people. Somewhere someone scribbles something down and we do the best we can. And you know, the rest is up to God."

"This doing-the-best-we-can bit, that's the issue," says Maryam, thoughtfully.

"If Firdevs is right," I begin, "whatever is it that you, well, it gets better with the presence of a god that loves you. Because you grow stronger…"

"I swear everything Firdevs said was really good for me too," started Amira, but Maryam cut her off.

"It was good to hear what Muhammed was telling you from someone else. You still love him, *sweetie,* and so you're looking for approval from someone else…"

"OK," said Amira bluntly and as she raised her hand she knocked over her coffee cup which loudly crashed on the floor. All the coffee, however, had gone straight into Maryam's lap and over her phone and the newspaper. But before we could even cry out, someone else had beat us to it.

"Maryam! Ah! What are you doing here?"

With two hands up in the air and a broad coffee stain over her shirt Maryam sputtered and groaned. Startled like a lizard that was suddenly exposed from under a pillow.

"Weren't you in Tunisia?" interrogated the plump woman who was about our age. On her right shoulder was a computer bag and on her left was a bag packed full of papers and to keep them from sliding off she had to keep hiking one shoulder higher than the other. In jeans, stubby shoes and glasses at the end of her nose she was the perfect academic. With astonishing speed Maryam came up with a lie.

"I was in Tunisia when I caught the trail of a woman's cult with links to Dido in Alexandria and so I came here. In any case I'm going back. I won't be staying long. In fact we were just leaving. We'd love for you to sit down with us but…"

She had already picked up her phone and cigarettes from the table. Clearly she'd been caught by someone she didn't want to see and so we got up too.

"When are you coming back to Cairo? People in Tahrir

are waiting for you. We need you..."

"I..." began Maryam and she stumbled into the rest of the sentence clearly not knowing what she was going to say.

"In any case now... I mean, I ... You know that I need to be working..."

Amira took Maryam by the arm and made a face at the woman (no doubt Amira thought she looked tough when she actually looked really funny) and she said.

"Maryam will come back when she wants to. That's just the way it is!"

"You've lost a lot of weight," said the woman, looking Maryam over suspiciously.

Her faced contorted, Maryam tried to make light of the comment.

"Ah! I did get rid of a couple pounds. You know, the food in Tunisia!"

"And she's madly in love! It could be all the sex!" says Amira all of a sudden, taking Maryam by the arm and walking away.

"Please excuse us," Maryam says over her shoulder, "but we need to run, we're terribly late!"

And we raced around the corner.

"At this rate you'll never get to be a goddess my, friend" says Amira to Maryam, laughing.

"What was it Firdevs Hanim said, 'No need to over-explain!?'"

Out of breath, I asked Maryam, "How many months have you really been out of the country, azizi?" As we crossed the street, Maryam had no choice but to shout through the jungle of cars, "For the past three months. I went to Beirut, gave birth and from there I went to London, and then to Tunisia."

"How many months old, Maryam?" asked Amira

suddenly stopping in the middle of the street. Taking her by the arm and leading us both to the other side, Maryam said, "Two months and twenty-four days."

"How could you leave a baby like that?" Amira said quickly under her breath. Suddenly in that moment and with such conviction ... she looked at Maryam as if she had been left behind. When we got to the sidewalk Maryam inspected her clothes; the coffee stain on her shirt looked like dried blood.

"Woman you got it all over my shirt! We need to get back to the hotel."

With the eyes of a child fixed on her mother, almost hypnotized, Amira asked the question she should have asked days ago but for whatever reason had to ask now. She wasn't going to move before she got an answer.

"What's going to happen to the baby, Maryam?"

"When I make a decision, I'll let you know Amira Hanım," she said gruffly.

This time I asked, "You're actually going to see her, aren't you, Maryam? This 'far away' place is Lebanon after all, isn't it?"

She put her arms in ours. She didn't say a word.

Now Amira spoke to Maryam as a mother.

"If you go ... I mean if you want to go and see her..."

"And?" said Maryam peering into Amira's face and smiling as if she were caressing a child. Stopping on the pavement, Amira threw her arm around Maryam's shoulder like an old army friend. "If God isn't going to love you, you always have us. That's all I have to say!"

Maryam smiled, sad and sweet. Wending our way through a crowd of men who occasionally threw glances at our hips and our breasts and rarely at our faces, we walked back to the hotel. I thought about how some trips you can't do on your own, and how some babies you can't make on your own.

When we got back to the hotel Madam Lilla was talking to a man in the lobby, a bunch of papers in her hand. Dressed in her purple silks and sitting up straight, she seemed engaged in fierce negotiations. I could only hear her say, "No, no. Not Beirut. We absolutely must go to Tripoli." Meanwhile Maryam and Amira were talking about how they needed to check up on the status of the hamam affair back in Tunisia. Amira was forced to remember that she still had to confront this matter of the bride she had tried to forget about despite all the distress; and that she still had to ask Madam Lilla to what extent Eyüp Bey had taken care of things. Suddenly Madam Lilla pulled out a roll of cash and placed it in front of the man and the strained negotiations between Amira and Maryam seemed a thing of the past.

"Good sir, you are going to be carrying some very weighty women. We need the best boat there is!"

"You're not as heavy as you used to be, Esma Hanım," said the man, flashing a sardonic grin and Lilla said, "Fine then" as she took back half of the money.

Amira and Maryam were watching her and the man, two cats locked in a showdown, poised to scratch each other's eyes out. Speaking to myself, I said, "So just like Dido we set sail on the Mediterranean, the last leg of the journey, eh? But if Dido was right... What was it she said? 'There are mortals who write their own stories. The gods love them as their equals. With a harsh and merciless love.' I mean if a single god were to love us, with only a dash of affection..."

Laughing, Amira came out with (and I really didn't expect a joke like this from her), "So you say he would just bottle it up?"

We laughed. Madam Lilla and the captain were suddenly reminded of their feline face-off and they turned to us with even greater offence in their eyes.

"What?" shouted Lilla, and with the frustration of a woman being teased she said, "Aren't we weighty women?"

I must have been thinking that sometimes even Lilla's goddess didn't love her enough when Amira let out a peal of laughter and cried, "They couldn't even get us up on the scales, Madam!"

Like a child who had won all the marbles in a game, lights flashing in her eyes, Amira looked at me and Maryam.

"Friends, I've got the seventh rule: 'A goddess is never weighed on someone else's scale!' How's that?"

From a distance Madam Lilla flashed Amira a look of pride.

"Eh? And so what do you say, Captain?"

"As you can see the ladies are right here. Can you carry them?"

26

"On the contrary – life is long. No twinkling of an eye. And there's only one condition. You must embrace fate with a fresh heart. Only apathetic lives are short. There is always the time to do everything you want to do. There is no wrong story. Whatever your fate or your trials, just be sure that you are truly in the moment. Life is short if you are not."

With a Stella in hand, Madam Lilla said all this in the Spit Fire bar, the TV showing Tahir Square in yellow lights. The mass was moving in the night, like the interconnected organs of a body pressing into each other. Now and then the roar of the body drowned out the voice of the worried broadcaster. That night there was a new clash in Tahir and there were even rumours that one of the young protestors had been abducted. Now protestors with startled and worried expressions on their faces were giving statements about the betrayal they had suffered at the hands of the army and how plainclothed soldiers had fired on their friends, wounding and even killing some. Then Muslim Brotherhood politicians appeared on the screen with the air of 'responsible' statesmen who had long since figured everything out, speaking as if the revolution was over. Maryam was watching her other life unfold on a TV screen while Amira and I were looking at Madam Lilla.

"Only when you're afraid," said Madam Lilla, tapping her beer into Maryam's, "Only then are you pushed out of your own life. We will keep walking, ladies. Whatever happens. Come on then, to our health."

We clinked glasses. Distracted, Maryam spilled half her

beer over the table. Finally ungluing her eyes from the screen, she looked at us, "Wake up, mademoiselle!" laughed Madam Lilla. "There's nothing you're going to miss. No need to worry, life does not come to an end without being fulfilled."

"Or until you surrender?" I asked.

Unsure of what I was implying, she raised an eyebrow and looked at me. I went on, "Who is this person you're supposed to surrender to, Madam Lilla? Fatima Nina in Yafran mentioned him and so did Firdevs Hanım. Who is it?" The speaker on TV was announcing, "Soldiers in Tahrir have begun their largest push against the protestors." And the mass in the square shook like a creature straining to readjust its body parts. Everyone in the bar stood up. History had let in another goal. It was one of those moments when there was no referee to call an offside and on the faces of the Egyptians in the bar fell the dark shadow of wounded pride. People suddenly stood up, knocking over beers, which dripped off tables and onto the floor – but no one cared. Tahrir was at war and the Spit Fire was watching its defeat. These people in the bar watching the protesters being beaten in Tahrir seemed the most afraid and as spectators they seemed the first to accept defeat. Maryam and Amira were up on their feet, their eyes locked on the screen.

Madam Lilla stared at me like she was looking at a snake. People always look like that when I ask the hard, unwanted questions that need to be asked. I considered how long it had been since I'd experienced such a moment. So long since I had asked a question that touched the core of a person's life … for the first time in a while I felt like I was really breathing. Madam Lilla asked, "So you really want to know? Or are you just curious to see if you can get me to talk?"

I suppose this time I looked at her like I was looking at a snake. People were now talking across tables, occasionally

392

looking down at their phones, checking Twitter feeds, sharing new information. People twisting their moustaches; hands on hips, hands in the air, hands over their faces as they communally cowered. Tahrir was not about to surrender and with blood, sweat and tears on its cheeks the communal crowd, men and women, surged at the violent plainclothes police force. Tahrir would rather fall than be taken and the bar was grieving as they watched on.

"I don't know," I said, "today Firdevs said something like, 'if you ignore a woman's scar she might think you don't care about the story behind it.' I guess I believe that."

Sipping from her beer, Lilla looked up with a smile and nodded, "Well when it comes to scars it isn't quite like that, Mademoiselle. You must have understood that when we were in the limo… when I was speaking to the driver. But you still insist on asking. If you're so fixated on knowing who Madam Lilla needs to surrender to … well then give me a cigarette!"

She dramatically lit up. Blowing out the smoke without really inhaling she started to explain.

"My little lady, it's easier to love other people's scars. The problem is learning to love our own. That's when we really start to think about what we're doing with our lives. Do you know what real darkness is? Let me explain…"

As the images on the TV grew more savage the clamour in the Spit Fire crested into a painful howl. Edgy as a racehorse about to be released from the starting stall, Maryam looked up at the screen with tears in her eyes. Amira was on her feet, looking at Tahrir Square as if she was watching the fate of her own country unfold. Maryam went over to her and they held hands without looking at each other. Two women witnessing the end of a revolution they both believed in, and it seemed to me they had nothing left but themselves. But for Madam Lilla life was longer than the revolution and her story

*was greater than her country's story. I suppose that night
was the first time I decided to chronicle this trip, while the
world was going up in flames around us and in a hushed
voice Madam Lilla told me her story.*

*

"Why don't we drink tonight?" said Amira full of energy.
Right after she'd said those words: *"They can't get us up on
those scales, Madam!"* There was a joy in her voice that
called out for celebration. Or maybe it was calling out for
us to soothe Maryam in her melancholy. Or maybe both at
the same time.

Reluctantly Maryam said, "There is this place the
protestors in Alexandria would talk about but Madam Lilla
... I don't know if she'd go to a place like that. A place called
Spit Fire."

"Aren't you afraid of running into someone, azizi?" I
asked Maryam. Laughing, she answered, "Amira would
rough up anyone who asked too many questions."

Then Lilla turned to the captain and said, "We came to
Alexandria earlier than planned. So the boat we've booked
isn't ready yet. We could still wait for that boat but then
you would be deprived of the joy and honour of meeting
women like us. Think about it." And she got up and held
out her hand as if gracing the man with the opportunity and
they shook. She came over to us "Ladies, I say we get drunk
in some beautiful setting tonight. What do you think?"

Steeped in woman-to-woman camaraderie, Amira said
"We're going to the Spit Fire tonight ... just to let you
know!"

We all packed into the limo. Lilla was in a cheerful mood,
full of life. Leaning over to our driver she quickly said,

"That hat looks great on you, my good lady." And our male driver suddenly shifted into womanhood. She almost giggled. Like a man flirting with a young woman, Lilla went on "But if you ask me, little lady, you might want to try lighter colours. Yellow for example. Yellow and hmm … bright green."

As Lilla spoke the man-woman in the driver's seat became more of a woman. And there was no longer any trace of a scar or any awkwardness. I thought about what Firdevs had to say about openly talking about a person's scar. Madam carried on with her jokes. Without creating any tension, she alluded to the question of gender and downplayed the issue at the same time. Lilla took off the flower she had pinned to her lapel. "Oh! Just a minute! Now don't move," she muttered as she deftly stuck the needle through the driver's cap. With a shy smile on her face she inspected the flower in the rearview mirror. She was pleased. She mumbled a short thank you.

Sweeping away the awkward moment, Madam Lilla said, "Ladies, I was thinking that seeing as we nearly burned to a crisp during our trip through the desert we should at least give our souls a cool cleaning as we cross the Mediterranean."

Maryam smiled. "If we're going to drown then we should do it in a big sea?"

Opening her eyes, Amira took Maryam by the arm. "Now that should be your seventh rule! If a goddess is to drown she does it in a big sea!"

I told Lilla about Firdevs' spiel about our goddeses. She smiled. And she said to Maryam, "Now there's no need for us to drown. Just like your Dido, we are off to found our own Carthage. You can be my girls and you can raise your own. That way…"

"I still haven't made that decision, Madam," said Maryam sharply. Looking at Amira she continued, "I have neither the patience nor the strategic thinking to find myself a Walid goon like Firdevs."

Looking out the window Madam Lilla flashed a wry smile.

"What is it then, Madam?" I said. "What do you think about Firdevs? After all she did say, 'Like Madam I didn't go running after life.'"

The limo slammed on the brakes. Suddenly through the darkness we saw the eyes of many children peering into the limo. They could only see the shadows of their own reflections, blank gazes. They held limes which they were trying to sell to the people in the passing cars. The little green fruit stood out brightly against their dark palms and the darkness of the night.

Maryam sat upright. Like a grounded child watching her friends play outside, she looked out the window. She was trying to show herself through the tinted glass. Closely she followed the gazes as they came closer to the glass. From both sides they were searching for each other, like lost travellers in the night, blind in a crowded port. The traffic started moving again. As the car lurched forward Maryam reluctantly leaned back and looked one more time at the kids. She looked at those lime sellers and they stood still in the middle of the road as if one of their own was in the car and they had just lost her without ever catching a glimpse of her. Turning into thin shadows in the headlights they scrambled off and were gone.

When Madam Lilla saw Maryam so moved she ignored my question and caressed her short hair.

"Your homeland is everywhere. It's wherever you are. Your homeland isn't Tahrir. As long as you keep looking at those children like that ... it's right here."

Lilla placed her hand on her heart. Then she touched Maryam's head, "Egypt is here, always in you. The time for you to return will come. And not broken and guilty like this, but full of joy."

"That's if we make it alive to other side," said Maryam with a bitter smile.

"Or if the natives don't eat us alive when we get there!" said Amira, chewing on a fingernail. Turning to Madam Lilla, she said "Madam Lilla, were you able to reach Eyüp Bey? Any news? I mean about the bride?"

Madam Lilla skipped over the questions with a haste I'd only understand later. She used my earlier question to change the subject. "Firdevs is trying to teach the women in this country who have always felt worthless to feel precious. From the birthday of Hypatia to this whole thing with the goddesses. She is trying to create a spell that women without adventure in their lives can believe in. She is doing everything she can. She has embraced her fate. And of course you…"

Lilla left her sentence hanging. We were in the front of the bar. Men were smoking cigarettes cupped in the palms of their hands, heads bowed, throwing us sideway glances. As the girls blew out smoke they looked at us condescendingly. It wasn't such a great thing to pull up in a limo and we felt duly ashamed. On behalf of the group, Maryam slightly hid her face, as if she were apologizing.

With a single finger Amira touched Maryam's spine at the curve to make her sit upright, and, imitating Firdevs, she said, "Goddesses never offer needless apologies!"

"You've really taken a shine to these rules," said Maryam.

Madam Lilla was greeting people at the door with her regal style, which always annoyed people who were meeting her for the first time. "Good evening ladies and gentlemen! I hope that you are enjoying yourselves!"

"You call this enjoyment?" hissed one of the girls through her teeth. She took a hard drag on her fag then flung its butt to the ground and made a move for the door. Madam Lilla was in fine form. "Ah! There's no point if there's no fun, sweet bird! If you can't kick back then you don't get the taste of life. Ha ha ha!"

Maryam sidled up to Lilla and flung open the door to get inside before the revolutionary could smack her. Amira seemed about to laugh.

In a long, narrow corridor packed with round tables men and women, young and old, sat together waving their hands to the rhythm of discussions on the plight of their country. Two big TVs were showing live coverage of Tahrir Square where people were beginning to gather. Occasionally conversations around the tables stopped for a breath when someone pointed to a screen and then they plunged back into a heated discussion. It all surged forward with bursts of laughter, moustaches thoughtfully twisted, beards absentmindedly stroked and sentences chopped short with, 'Just a minute. Wait up, but actually...' Every table seemed to be trying urgently to reach a conclusion, as if a moment later they'd be questioned on the fate of the country, asked for a personal decision, and when they failed to come up with a consensus all eyes turned back to the screen.

At least one person per table was busy predicting how many people were in the square comparing it with the night before; the fate of Egypt seemed to rest on a rough head count. The bar was shrouded in a cloud of cigarette smoke that made it all look like a dream. Occasionally people with burning eyes went outside to watch the crowds of Alexandria that weren't watching the crowds in Tahrir. The people outside were caught between the difference of life on TV and the life flowing by on the street. They were never out with the real life for very long. Once back inside they slumped down in front of the TV. They returned seamlessly to the world of Tahrir.

On the one hand it seemed they were welcoming the images on the screen but they also looked like hungry opium addicts who were taking a hit from a pipe they had left only a couple minutes ago. There was a nervous energy in the air. When their voices faded you could almost hear their heartbeats.

So when Maryam and Amira stepped inside they merged with this communal heartbeat, locked to the image of the surging crowd. Madam Lilla and I were the only people alone with each other. We alone had noticed the old man at the bar who was eyeing Lilla from his seat under the light reflecting off the bottles. She pulled me with her away from the mass. We sat down at a table opposite the bar with our backs to the TV.

Seeing that Maryam and Amira were more interested in Tahrir, Madam Lilla turned to me, "We are all in this life together, sweetie. Me and Firdevs, too. Even Tahrir..."

As she spoke her eyes drifted to the man at the bar. Clearly he was the boss of the place. Now and then he gave her an under-the-brow look. Lilla still didn't realize that I was close to her secret.

"It's just that Firdevs chose a safer path. I could have chosen the same and lived a life with someone in a home. Instead of wandering the deserts and rushing to war zones. If I found such a life comfortable I could have found myself a Walid ... but if you ask me, those Walids are fare more frightening than the idea of being abducted in the desert. Ha ha ha!"

All of a sudden Lilla was in full flirt mode. Not with me

of course, she was working the man at the bar. She still hadn't realized that I knew what she was doing. She continued, "Indeed we are all living the life we can live best. The one we fear less. The life that gives us what we need."

"What do you fear most, Madam Lilla?" I asked.

"Surrendering, mademoiselle. Surrendering! Because then…"

"You'll be defeated?"

"I'll become mortal. If I set out along one road, if you choose one path you're already choosing an end…"

The waiter came over to our table with a plate full of fruit.

"Mademoiselle, this is for you. From Necib Bey, with his regards."

Madam Lilla flirtatiously pouted her lips and with a slight nod she conveyed her thanks. Ogling, she looked over at the bar. Only for a second. No more. Then turning back to me, "As for me … I still can't risk losing this life I lead. The surprises and the excitement."

She must have taken the look in my eye to be an allusion to her age because she tilted her head to one side and smiled, "Yes, and I'm still going."

I smiled back at her. I looked up at the screen, at Tahrir. Maryam and Amira were lost in the unfolding drama. With the hope of bringing them over to our table, I said, "Today Firdevs Hanım was saying that life only lasted so long." And I blinked. "That short."

Then Lilla raised her voice, addressing Maryam and Amira.

"On the contrary, life is very long…"

That's how Madam Lilla started her story. She had asked me for a cigarette … she began to tell the true story that Maryam and Amira would learn much later. Tahrir was full of noise. It was clear I was the only one who was going to hear the story of her life which was longer than the revolution and bigger than the country. By the time she finished Necib Bey was gone. She hadn't even noticed. It was clear from the story that men were never important – the important thing was the story she had made. The secrets of all secrets she had just revealed was hardly mysterious – like all the other stories – and it had always been around us.

After she had finished we were silent.

Maryam could see how far we'd drifted from the tense atmosphere in the Spit Fire. She snapped, "Aren't you a journalist, azizi! What's with the indifference? Madam Lilla … you … aren't you Egyptian? Don't you have any interest in what's going on in Tahrir?"

Lilla looked at me and then speaking to Maryam but really addressing me, "We are already talking about a revolution."

There was no way for Maryam to know what she meant by that.

Suddenly a group from the right side made a clear cut through the roaring crowd in Tahrir. Placing four beers down on our table, the middle-aged waiter said full of excitement, "The Ultras are finally on the scene. Things are going to change now."

It was like he was watching a football match and commenting on the arrival of a strong centre forward.

Maryam opened her mouth wide and gasped for air. Still on her feet and glued to the screen, Amira cried out joyously, "The Ultras have arrived! Maryam, come and look!"

Maryam took another gulp of air and sat down. I didn't know what was happening. But I guess Lilla did. Calmly rising from her chair she undid the top button of Maryam's blouse. Then she did something strange, she mumbled a prayer and then blew three times over Maryam's face.

It is impossible to heal your own wounds but when you move to help another you end up healing yourself. But for me to explain that I need to weave the story behind Maryam's strange moment in the bar and the mystery that lay behind the secrets Lilla had just told me. A crude and funny moment in the most unexpected of circumstances would take me there.

27

"Poverty puts people on the same playing field. Crushed under the same rock people are all the same. You wouldn't know it. You're not poor," said Madam Lilla. This was the lecture she gave me before we set out on the Mediterranean. Here's what happened the morning after we left the bar and came back to the hotel without saying a word.

*

I drew the curtains. The sky and the sea were the same grey. That night Alexandria had been washed with rain but she still didn't want to get out of bed. Maryam was twisted in white sheets and Amira was wandering around the room as if she had lost something, scratching her head.

"I'm going to find a coffee," she repeats three times before she starts to dress. I looked out the window.

"Mornings make my head spin," I announce. With one eye closed and her face crinkled, Amira replies, "Huh?"

My hot breath clouds the windowpane as I write my name, "I was saying that mornings... I think every novelist starts a book with the desire to be the hero. But we actually write because we can't be the hero."

Amira made a sound to show she wasn't listening. On the street below a bus was moving through the city. Kids were hanging off the back of the bus like a bunch of dark grapes. As it slowed they jumped off together, then huddled arm in arm until the next bus arrived. Watching them laugh as they dangled from each other's shoulders you might have thought it was a sunny morning. "Like dark grapes…" I thought to myself and I wanted to write those words on the glass. Not for any real reason, I suppose I just had the urge to put pen to paper. It was that longing you get when you wake up with the remnants of a dream and you try to get back to sleep to recover it. Feeling the weight of the lager from the night before, Maryam looked up at Amira and, with her eyes still shut demanded, "Amiraaaa! Coffeeee!" like a spoiled child. Then she buried her head back in her pillow.

Amira pulled on her jeans, wriggled into her shirt and left. I sat down on the broad window ledge and thought about the story Madam Lilla had told me last night. It hurt me to think that if no one wrote it down it would be like water flowing through mountains that no person has ever seen. Just like those words, "dark grapes". I shivered as I remembered a sentence in Madam Lilla's story that stood out.

"I loved you, Esma. I loved you like my blind eye."

*

Why hadn't I ever thought of it? I suppose it was because we'd never considered that in Madam Lilla's magnificent life such a key issue could be so small, simple, and right there before our eyes. We had never thought that Madam Lilla's half-blind butler could have been the real reason she had set out on this fantastical journey and all the other journeys in her magnificent life. Only his patent leather shoes and his blind eye alluded to a deeper past. I suppose we were all too young to know that a man enslaved to a woman through love could actually take her prisoner. Looking out of the window I considered why we had come on this trip. We were learning how to be each other. And when we did the journey would end.

Amira would learn to become as manly as Maryam, and Maryam would learn to become as womanly as Amira; Madam Lilla would learn to become as young as us; and I, instead of writing their story, would become a character in their novel ... and maybe a little bit about surrendering, too.

That's just what Lilla said the other day when she was telling me her story, "Is that what you're curious to know, mademoiselle? What will happen to you when you surrender. And what it means for a woman like me to surrender."

"Yes," I had said. Just when the military launched its largest assault on the crowd in Tahrir. Among all the noise Lilla was telling me the greatest secret of her heart.

"When you love someone ... when you let someone love you ... fine then, when you surrender ... when you surrender, right at your core ... yes, right near the belly button ... you notice a scar you didn't know you already had. And the ache never really goes away until you are with the one you have surrendered to. Now there is something else that you think about more than just staying alive. And so you get smaller, softer, weaker. Do you see what I mean?"

The clamour in Tahrir had consumed the Spit Fire. Embracing their fate and each other, people in the square threw stones at guns. They shouted in the face of the muzzles and the clubs. They charged at their own fears as if they had nothing left to lose. They had surrendered to the moment, willing to accept whatever might happen. They were no longer flesh but steel.

"It is safer to lead a meaningless life racing from one place to the next. It was always like that..." She looked me in the eye to judge if I would to be able to understand what she was about to say. And then she went on, "Do you remember Eyüp Bey? He loved me very much. How many times did I tell him, that it wasn't him..."

She stopped. The sound from the TV was cutting out, a bad connection, but the footage ran on for a few seconds in silence. Men at the neighbouring table leaned right over to get a closer look at the screen as they shouted. "Did you see it? Did you? You see that's how they get hit in the eyes."

"God damn it! Those kids pop up out of the crowd to see what's going on and the soldiers aim right for their eyes!"

"Mother… they've taken out so many eyes like that! Mother f—kers!"

They cursed a couple times more before glumly sinking back into silence, staring at the screen.

"What do you mean, 'that it wasn't him', Madam?" I asked. She took a sip from her beer, trembling.

"That my daughter wasn't his. Leila … but … he doesn't believe it. He didn't for years. He's had this conviction that he is the father. And he said so much in the end, when we parted, *'I loved you. Esma. I loved you like my blind eye.'* That's what he always said to me, for years. Watching other men come and go, he never gave up. And he's still waiting, always will be. It kills me to see him wait like that. That's how he surrendered to me. But I… "

The men next to us started shouting again. If they screamed any louder their voices would carry all the way to the streets of Cairo and into the ears of the soldiers in Tahrir.

"Look, look. Did you see it? Those two kids there. Right there! Look! They both have patches over their eyes! Lions! They're already out of the hospital and back in Tahrir!"

The other man said under his breath (I think tears were welling up in his eyes), "lions." The expressions on their faces tugged between laughing and crying, their cheeks trembling.

"But me," continued Madam Lilla, "The moment I surrender is the moment I begin to get old and die. One embrace and I am swept off my feet. Because ... then my heart would be under siege. It would be easier to surrender to the enemy. At the most your honour takes a blow but if I were to surrender to someone I loved ... I would be a slave."

"But I don't understand at all, Madam," I said, directly and with unusual honesty, "I don't understand how people can let themselves fall back into a bank of snow. They must be crazy."

She touched my cheek. Touched me as if I was a picture of her forty years ago. For a moment it felt as if there was nothing we could learn from each other. And that's when Maryam was affronted by our indifference and Lilla said, *"We were already talking about a revolution."*

The men at the neighbouring table were taut like bows, stretched out toward the screen. A space was opening in the middle of Tahrir. The Ultras had showed up. And in less than five minutes everything in the Spit Fire changed. And then we drank. Even after Maryam had her outburst we kept on drinking.

*

Looking up from her pillow, Maryam asked, "Where's Amira? Why isn't she back with my coffee?"

We heard her laughing in the corridor. It didn't sound like she was coming inside any time soon so I went out to find her. Maryam stumbled after me. Amira was sitting on the floor with a middle-aged maid in a headscarf. She was looking down at her phone and explaining, "No, sister, it's

407

not like that. Now look, not everyone on Twitter can see your daughter. Her friends can see her and her friend's friends and their friends, you get it?"

"What's going on here?" I said.

Laughing, Amira said,

"I'm teaching Warda here about Twitter. Come over."

Maryam and I sat down next to the woman. She didn't seem very interested to see us. Trying not to laugh we pieced together a story from everything Amira was saying. It seems the maid had a daughter studying computer engineering who'd told her about Twitter, and when her mother was trying to figure out just what Twitter was all about she stumbled on the profile picture of her daughter without a headscarf. The picture made her very uncomfortable. Warda's daughter was due back at the hotel in Alexandria any time now. She poured us each a coffee from her thermos. Maryam and I lit up a cigarette and joined the conversation in the corridor. Warda was a very anxious mother. "Sister, I can't look after this girl on my own. I tell her not to go, and she races off anyway. I'm terrified something is going to happen to her."

With every sip of coffee I could see Maryam's face soften and soon enough she was back on earth and consoling Warda. "Sister, there's no need to be afraid. Nothing's going to happen. She has friends there. And you can see how Twitter helps. You write and the words come up right away on the screen. And your friends know where you are and how you're doing."

It wasn't long before Warda was edging closer to Maryam – she was after all an Egyptian.

"Why did she put a picture up without her headscarf? Isn't that shameless? Did she go to Tahrir to find a husband?"

"Sister, if she's going to find a husband it's better she find him in Tahrir Square. Forget about it, don't let it bother you."

Taking her phone, Maryam looked at the picture of Warda's daughter.

"Looks like she has a head on her shoulders. Nothing's going to happen to this one."

I had a look, too. The picture was heavily photoshopped, real chic, hair blowing in the wind, a big smile. She was a beautiful young woman – it was that kind of picture.

"She's smart," said Warda, her chest suddenly expanding with pride. "She's always first in her class."

"She wouldn't be in Tahrir if she didn't have brains."

A little embarrassed to reveal that she'd been keeping an eye on us, Warda said, "Your older friend, she left early with Firdevs Hanım. They went to the cemetery. Firdevs told me. It seems the older madam's daughter has died. God bless her soul. She died young of course."

We looked at each other in shock. Lilla hadn't even told us her daughter was buried in Alexandria and she certainly hadn't told us that she was going to her grave that morning.

"They should be back soon," said Warda. "It's been a while now."

Amira asked, "And when will your daughter be coming?"

"She's already on the way. How I've missed her. But I'm going to be real angry when she gets here. This is simply unacceptable. No such photos like that without a headscarf."

"They're starting a revolution, sister! I'm also Muslim but forget about headscarves and all that for now. Does she normally wear one?"

Warda was defensive "I thought she did ... but now with Tahrir and everything I have no idea what she's up to."

No sooner had she finished speaking than we heard hurried footsteps at the end of corridor. Straightening her back, Warda said, "There she is. That's how she runs up the stairs." Here eyes flickered and her entire face was lit up with joy. But the moment her daughter appeared at the top of the stairs Warda stamped out her joyous expression, clasped her hands and slipped into angry mother mode. Emotionless, she said, "Welcome. What took you so long?"

The girl stopped in her tracks as if she had just hit a wall. She was a tiny little thing, her head wrapped tightly in a scarf. Her eyebrows were thick, unplucked. Above her lips was the shadow of a moustache, unwaxed. Her arms looked like little bundles and so did her legs. Her backpack only made her little round body look more like a ball. There wasn't a trace of that super-chic Twitter profile photo. She looked like a fun, free-spirited girl who was holding it back in the face of her mother's authoritarianism. Without saying a word she kissed her mother who promptly poured a cup of coffee and handed it to her daughter like it was a form of punishment.

Then, in a flat tone of voice, "Meet these sisters. They were just asking me what you were doing in Tahrir. Sister Maryam is from there."

We looked at each other in disbelief and I even clucked my tongue in disapproval. We all said hello. Sincere and full of warmth, Maryam immediately relieved us of the role of controlling older sisters.

"Sister, how are you?" she asked. "How's Tahrir?"

The name itself was an icebreaker. Hardly breathing the girl was off and running, "Did you see what happened last night? It was a major attack. But the kids fought back ... of course I didn't go. It was late."

She looked at her mother. Did she know she was in

Tahrir? Turning back to us, she went on, "Later ... did you see it? The Ultras came!"

When Maryam heard the name her coffee trembled in her hand.

After describing just what happened, she asked Maryam, "Do you know them, sister? They're the real thing. I have a friend, Housam. In fact last night..."

She bit her tongue. She'd remembered she couldn't explain such things in front of her mother. Maryam was breathless again.

"Are you OK?" I asked and she nodded silently. She was trying to keep focused on what the girl was saying.

"The Ultras burst in on the scene. And of course Tahrir went crazy. Everyone up on their feet. I have no idea what we'd do without them."

"Just who are these Ultras?" I asked. "Ever since last night..."

Quickly Amira filled in the gaps.

"They're actually fans from a football club. But also a political group. They're the ones who really got things going in Tahrir and in El Kasbah Square in Tunisia. They do some really crazy stuff. Both really funny and really radical."

"Like Beşiktaş Çarşı!" I said. They looked at me but the girl was keen to say more about Tahrir and I had to leave it there.

"Sister, Maryam, these Ultras..."

With a knot in her throat, Maryam asked, "Who do you know from the Ultras?"

"Houssam!" cried the girl in excitement and then remembering her mother she added, "He's a friend from school."

In a strangely dark mood, Maryam asked, "Was Kamal there?"

"Sister, do you know Kamal abi? He's a very brave man. He was there last night. In fact he was out in the front."

Her mother couldn't help but interrupt:

"How do you know who was there or not?"

Treating her more like an enemy than a mother, she responded, "I keep telling you, it's all on Twitter. That's how I know."

"I know about your photo. You have been far too disrespectful. What is this with you not wearing your headscarf!"

"That's how it is. You wouldn't understand."

She quickly stood up and something fell out of her bag. Before her mother could see it Maryam picked it up and was just handing the object back to the girl when her mother snatched it out of Maryam's hand.

"What's this? Have you gone and turned into a thug?"

Warda dangled the slingshot in front of her daughter who only stood taller, "Give me that!"

"What are you doing with this? Are you out there shooting stones at soldiers?"

"Why shouldn't I? I'm doing it for you! For women like you!"

"I don't want a hero. I want my daughter!"

"Here I am. You don't like it?"

I was a little embarrassed and Maryam and Amira looked tense. We tried thanking Warda for the coffee but neither mother nor daughter even knew we were there any more. Tugging the slingshot back and forth between them, they were pushing the boundaries of good manners. My head bowed and my face flushed, I walked into our room. Maryam and Amira hurried in behind me. Before we could even close the door Madam Lilla appeared in the doorway. On her head sat a hat with an enormous brim. It could have been from a Sixties film.

412

"What's going on?" she said, angrily.

"They are having an argument," I said, "about the square."

"Hmmm," said Lilla, turning to me and smiling at my naiveté.

"Poverty puts people on the same playing field. Crushed under the same rock people are all the same. You wouldn't know it. You're not poor..."

"Madam," said Maryam. "This morning you..."

Lilla cut her off. "I did a little shopping. For all of us. We can't go to Beirut looking like a bunch of bums. I hope you like everything. The bags are ready downstairs. Get your things together. We don't have much time left. The captain is waiting for us in the marina."

Turning to me, Maryam whispered, "I wonder which one of her old flames we'll get stuck with this time."

"Pardon me?" asked Lilla.

Maryam didn't repeat herself. Looking at that crazy hat on Lilla's head we could see that she was already having problems coping with her visit to her daughter's grave. By now we knew her well enough. In weakness she seemed even more magnificent.

Once she left Amira was as curious as a child again, "I wonder what she got for us?"

"Of course, dear! You mademoiselle are thinking about your new little trinkets and not how we are going to be cheated in the middle of the sea," said Maryam angrily.

Amira was combing her hair in front of the mirror. "That woman is strange. Did you see the hat she wore to the cemetery? I swear she's like Sophia Loren."

"Come on," I said. "It's not like that. She can't surrender."

"Surrender to what?" said Maryam condescendingly.

"To herself," I said and I stopped. But I suppose the

413

traitor got the better of me and I went on, "Just like you, azizi. Just like you."

Maryam narrowed her eyes, trying to understand what I was saying. I rushed on. "So who's this Kamal, azizi?"

Amira's brush stopped mid-stroke, "Yeeeeees! Of course. Come on. What's the deal with this Kamal?"

Maryam was short of breath. Amira wanted some answers. "Now forget all this oh-I'm-having-a-heart-attack drama. You are going to tell us. Was it you and Kamal in Tahrir…"

Exasperated Maryam reached for her trousers and her shirt but Amira wouldn't let the subject go.

"Just a minute! Is he the one? Tell me right now." She sat down and took Maryam by the collar. "Yeeees! You got knocked up by one of the Ultras?"

Maryam suddenly caught her breath. Framed in those words her secret seemed lighter, not cracked and faded.

On the other side of the door Warda was shouting at her daughter more loudly than before.

Maryam stood up, flung open the door and shouted, "Enough already! Sister, give me that slingshot. You're blowing this way out of proportion. And young lady you need to treat your mother with respect. No more misbehaving. You don't need to get on a high horse because you're out there fighting for the revolution. I am taking this slingshot. A souvenir from Alexandria."

She came back inside, slamming the door behind her. She stuck the slingshot in her back pocket. "Come on," she said, "let's get out of here."

"You go, girl," I said and nothing more. As Maryam walked out of the room I looked at the slingshot sticking out of her back pocket. She looked like a kid from Palestine. I looked at her back. I looked at a woman who only learned how to surrender very late in life.

28

"I've come up with a rule, too!" I said as we waited to board the yacht. Ahead of me the captain was helping Madam Lilla climb the gangplank. She held his hand tightly, prolonging the human touch, drawing out his desire. She looked over her shoulder, one eyebrow raised. I had interrupted their moment. Maryam bumped into Amira who was right behind me. "The goddess rule … I found my seventh rule. My own rule."

Amira and Maryam slumped their shoulders; they were fed up with the subject. But I continued, "A goddess will do whatever she was made to do when she came into this world. A goddess never surrenders to her fate, she chooses it."

Madam Lilla says to the captain, "Please, show us the way," and with the air of an esteemed passenger aboard a cruise ship she made a faint gesture with her hand to show that we should be left alone. Ever so gently and sweetly, Amira pushed me onto the boat. Behind us Maryam flung open her arms wide and hurried us along. Neither asked me about my rule and the epiphany that brought it on. But now I felt like I was setting out on the Mediterranean with the clarity of a goddess who had chosen her fate; but surely from the outside I looked like a nutcase who thought she was Queen Elizabeth. I was in a good mood. And here's how I got there.

*

"You never know what a woman might need in Lebanon," answered Lilla, her eyes twinkling, her lips fluttering flirtatiously. Amira, Maryam and I were standing next to

415

five fully packed, stylish suitcases in the middle of the hotel lobby, looking like three question marks. As Lilla handed out generous tips to the hotel staff in true regal style, Amira whispered to me, "I really want to know. Did Lilla go to the cemetery with that hat or did she buy it afterwards?"

"She must have bought it after," I said. "You know, she doesn't surrender ... That's how she fights back her sadness."

"Azizi, look, I'll say this one more time. If this captain is one of her old flames ... we didn't really ask who he was or who he's connected to..." mumbled Maryam.

"It's not the right time," I said.

Madam Lilla let out a dramatic laugh as she joked with the staff. She was making a serious effort to shake off the dust from the cemetery. Even if we'd had the courage to break up Lilla's little act in which she played 'the marvellous woman', none of us would have wanted to pick up the pieces afterward. In the end we were her travel companions and we would rather have perished in the Mediterranean than plunder the magnificent palace she had built. Then Firdevs Hanım turned up. Ignoring Madam Lilla, who was still carrying on with the staff at the reception, gossiping with the bellboys and fussing over our luggage, she came over to us.

"So it's time to hit the road."

"Sadly so," said Maryam, stuffing her slingshot deeper into her back pocket.

Firdevs nodded. I might have misread those shadows falling over her face if Walid hadn't showed up rambling on about Singapore and Hong Kong right after her. In her eyes I could see the last ember of ambition going out.

"Don't say that," she said. "You could stay."

Firdevs' two daughters came to say goodbye, along with

416

some other women. The crowd behind Firdevs grew as she watched us get ready to go. We stood there awkwardly with no baggage, and the crowd of well-wishers continued to grow. It was a strange moment. A thought ran through my head, "she has collected so much along the way that she can no longer move." I saw the same thought on her face. As the crowd grew, Lilla kept looking back at us and Firdevs but she didn't come over to us. She didn't want to speak with Firdevs, who would only remind her of their trip to the cemetery. She didn't want to accept what they had been through.

Or it seemed that way to me.

Maryam had something to say to Firdevs. Something like, "If I had the courage I would stay." She took the slingshot out of her pocket. It was a keepsake from the Ultras, from a life she could not embrace. Amira was looking at Lilla. She was learning. It looked like she was memorizing the mise-en-scène of the play *A Wonderful Woman*, which from the outside seemed so flimsy and sometimes so artificial it was embarrassing to watch. Amira felt that one day she might need it.

In the strange silence all of this might have happened, but then again maybe it didn't.

"When you get back..." Firdevs started to speak to Maryam then hesitated and her words trailed off. Maryam picked them up.

"If I come back, yes, I will let you know. To Cairo ... if I come back, I will invite you there."

"We're here," said Firdevs. It seemed strange to think of the idea that there was no other place she could be. But at that point there wasn't a soul who knew how to reach any one of us. Letters and messages must have been piling up somewhere. Like a wire a thought crackled in Amira's mind, Muhammed might have come back but she hadn't received the news.

I had wanted to write so badly when I was sitting on the window ledge in the morning. If I could have just sat down to write I might have been able to tell the difference between what was real and what I was making up.

Madam Lilla called out to us, "Did you forget anything?"

Amira and Maryam went over to her – there was really nothing we could have forgotten. But then I found myself walking to the reception desk where I plucked a cheap ballpoint pen out of a container and grabbed a little pad of Union Hotel stationery and stuffed them into my back pocket.

Firdevs didn't make an effort to say goodbye to Madam Lilla. Turning around, she walked into the inner lobby, and her entourage moved with her. Meanwhile Walid Bey was still pacing back and forth, barking into his phone. And with that we stepped into a cab leaving behind a life that would go on without us. Madam Lilla hurried out of the door so quickly that she must have felt that sticky, cloying feeling that comes with a settled life. When we all settled into the taxi she changed into the brave commander we last saw while we were setting out into the desert. She enunciated three words for the driver.

"To the marina!"

Lilla always looked younger when she was leaving a place behind. I could understand it now. But Maryam never seemed to understand. She looked lost like a child with no love for school. And this time she was really annoyed we were leaving. She'd been reluctant to leave Tunisia and Yafran but leaving Alexandria was the hardest. She was running from an unfinished story. I knew this because I knew the story behind the slingshot in her back pocket. And I knew about Kamal. In the taxi I started making notes so that I wouldn't forget.

*

It was the second day that people began to gather spontaneously in Tahrir. Maryam had convinced herself that she needed to get married. She had decided that the best candidate would be a fellow academic from her university. The unpleasant feeling she'd had while reaching the decision only grew as days passed and she secretly began to wish for a problem that might help her escape this feeling. The man's name was Necib. It had to be Necib... once they both had their bios written up on the same page. He and Maryam loved the same books, watched the same movies, seemed to want the same things out of life and they both spoke with the same conviction. They had never kissed but they were both sure they wanted children. Always stressing how perfect they were for each other they struggled not feel bored. They both pretended to be the kind of people they were supposed to be. The pretence was so perfect that neither dared to interrupt the game. They were just about to get married to please friends and family when the second morning in Tahrir broke. Maryam didn't have to go. Tahrir still hadn't taken its vital place in the history of Eygpt.

On that second day so many men and women like Maryam, who needed a deluge to show them the truth of their own feelings, had gone to Tahrir to unleash storms that were already brewing in their heads. Of course the goal was to bring down Mubarek, but who wouldn't want history to turn your life upside down if you were already life's plaything. People like Maraym went to Tahrir to write a part of history that was greater than their own lives. There was no turning back. And like so many others Maryam didn't want to go back to her other life, she didn't want to leave the square. She didn't leave for the struggle that was Tahrir, a struggle against the military after the fall of Mubarek and all the related politics.

But like so many others caught in that tumultuous time she was possessed. Like every Mecnun she had a Leila. And like every Leila, that man, (for Maryam it was Kamal) was not the sum of himself. He symbolized Tahrir and escape, never returning, leaping boundaries, vanquishing fear, freedom, justice, *the other side of the turnstile* and, lastly, revolution.

But more than this, like every Leila this man was so beguiling because he showed Maryam that she could be a Mecnun. She had fallen in love with her capacity to fall in love. Kamal was charming because he didn't really fit the part of an academic or a revolutionary or a leader. He was young, a high-school drop out, the leader of a football fan club that stormed Tahrir as if they were out of their minds. But there was something about him. He could laugh until he was beyond himself. The way his jawbone dropped and his cheeks caved when he shouted, and his beard shimmered in the lights of Tahrir and his brotherly compassion when he helped the other women who had faltered and finally when he took Maryam by the arm as she fled the police and he put his arm around her waist and helped her up over the iron gate that surrounded the square and did it all without causing her the slightest pain and without looking at her face and the genuine concern he showed when he asked, worried and out of breath, "Are you OK?"

"Come with me," he said. She thought at last someone was finally speaking clearly, as she raced with him through streets she didn't know. If she ran any faster she would leave behind her life altogether. It seemed a new door was opening and if she hurried she could step inside. They ran and they ran. Now and then Kamal looked over his shoulder, smiling, slowing down for her, picking up speed, then losing themselves along the dark streets. Only God could see them and He was in Maryam that night. Finally they stopped at the entrance of an apartment building. Out of breath, Kamal pulled out his key, opened the door, stepped inside and looked at Maryam. There is no need to draw this out. There was half a loaf of bread and a radio on the table covered in newspaper. On the wall an Ultra emblem and a messy portrait of Che Guevara in oil paint. The last two letters of the word 'Basta' were scrunched and falling, like it always is with unplanned writing on the wall. In the sink were three dirty plates and a beer glass covered in grease. On a single bed were pamphlets and the crumpled sheets that hung over the edge. This was a place Maryam should not have been to and where she could do things she shouldn't do. Egypt would be a totally different place the day after so Maryam would be an entirely different person.

Kamal approached her slowly and gracefully. When their breathing had died down they could only hear the drip from the tap. After making love it was still the same sound but the world had changed. They sat down together naked and smoked, "That was some getaway, don't you think?" said Kamal. Maryam was silent, feeling the very sound of her voice would give her away, and she nodded and smiled. She could feel her cheeks flushing. She felt beautiful. It was the first time she felt that way. In the days to come they went to Tahrir together and they came home together; they ran and they ate and they made love; they cried and threw stones, taking cover and taking punches; they stumbled and got up and ran and in the end they always made love. She was already pregnant. From the moment she knew she ran even faster, she fell more, she threw more stones and they made love more. That strange thing that happens to women who are pregnant but who shouldn't be and who want the baby but shouldn't, happened to Maryam, too. She wasn't thinking. Her body was governed by something more powerful than thought. The clamour around her was so great it had silenced her inner conversations and in her heart swelled an unqualified but unquestionable feeling of goodness.

She didn't know what she believed as now something even more reasonable than belief itself surrounded her heart like sweet butter. She felt like she would be protected, she felt that things that cannot happen could.

She could have had an abortion but she couldn't even bring herself to think of rooting out this intoxicating and completely new feeling of peace, joy, contentedness and wild happiness. So she went to work, gave lectures, collected a few of her things from home and went back to Kamal, and they made love and went to Tahrir and screamed and later they laughed and fell asleep right away and when she woke up she had no time to think about what had happened.

When she was almost too big she found herself at the airport. She bought a ticket and flew to Beirut and from there she went to Tripoli where she gave birth and left the baby.

Maryam still has a secret that I can't write... but I must continue.

She wandered aimlessly as if out of her mind. She went to London where she met with academic friends. She pretended to laugh and carry on. Her soul curled up in the pit of her stomach and she was as still as someone sleeping after torture, somewhere between life and death. Somehow she tried to get back to her old life but she knew that wasn't possible. As if she didn't know that she was chasing a dream she found herself in Tunisia. She didn't know that she was going to Dido's Carthage until she ran into us and told me about Dido. She was startled by the fact that she didn't know that she was following a fairytale in the back of her mind. And it was only later that she came to realize she was writing this tale herself, concocting a new ending to Dido's myth to make a good ending for her own story. In Yafran. That night we were all together. That night Lilla fell apart. That night Maryam redid the buttons on Madam Lilla's shirt. That night she understood we could make it together and that it wasn't the baby or life she feared but loneliness. In the desert she realized deep down that her baby was a part of her destiny and that she was already going back to her. Even without admitting the journey to herself, she was already doing it. Something in her snapped.

She had set herself up for a sad, accursed life locked shut and she would wither alone, lonely and pale. Returning to hope frightened her more than a life of grief. That was why she had bellowed and cried in the helicopter. She reached down into her guts and pulled out the bullet. From that deep sleep her soul came back to life and she felt the pain.

That's how it had to be. That is how it happened. I had put it down on paper...

Did Kamal look for her? He must have. Did she miss him? Maybe. But the revolution was over. She was thrown out of the maelstrom that she had hoped would send her to

423

another life but when it finally stopped, Egypt, Tahrir and people were the same. She was the only one who had changed. She cut off all her hair.

Maryam was now looking in on her life from the outside. She no longer looked at her own face the same way and she no longer believed God loved her. When she met Amira and I and then later Madam Lilla she'd already lost all hope of another life. We were the only story she could fit in. That was why she had agreed to come on our trip. The solution to her solitude was our strange quartet. We were forced to take her to the place she most feared which was also the place she most wanted to go. That was why she was angry with Madam Lilla. Like a child angrily embracing her mother because she is both afraid of the sea and desperately wants to go in. It was only Madam Lilla who knew from the beginning that once Maryam got used to the sea she would love swimming.

*

I scribbled this down on Union Hotel stationery when we were in the taxi. I held my breath as I wrote and when I placed the last full stop I let out a heavy sigh and I was back inside the car. I added a note in the cramped space at the bottom of the page. Characters in novels most likely enjoy being watched, but as for me...

"No way!" said Amira, shocked. The car stopped. There before us in the marina was a shiny black yacht the size of a ship that looked like it belonged to a Russian oligarch. The captain was smoking a cigarette beside it, waiting for us. Lilla said to us, "You can trust the Captain. The owners don't know we're using it. You can always trust criminals." And she laughed.

We got out of the taxi and the captain signalled to a thin, dark-skinned cabin boy beside him who rushed over to our bags and whisked them up onto the ship. "Let's get a move on," the captain said. "We need to set out before the sun sets."

Like an actor in a film, Madam Lilla stepped onto the boat, her hand in the captain's hand. As I followed them ... well that's when I said, *"I found my own rule..."*

With the tolerance you show a lunatic, Amira pushed me towards the boat and Maryam with her slingshot in hand was waving her arms with that let's-get-going routine. I wanted to tell them that I would write the end to both their stories. But I didn't. I was going to write Muhammed's seventh letter and Dido's seventh tablet. In the end I had found the seventh rule. I would write it down and it was definitely going to turn out just the way I wrote it. And that's how we set out on the Mediterranean.

29

"It's so much busier on land. But the horizon is never moving. It's beautiful here because you can't see what's ahead," said Amira as she looked down at the rich foam the boat churned up in its wake. Those white caps in the dark blue water seemed as strange as what Amira had just said. Night was falling. Our first day on the boat had come to a close with those words, but here's how we got there.

*

"We don't do this boat any favours," said Maryam as she took aim at the cabin boy. He was making it clear that serving a rough group like us was beneath him. She stretched out the rubber band of her slingshot and let go. We certainly weren't doing the boat any favours but we were enjoying ourselves more than any picture-perfect Russian model ever could.

With our feet curled under our big bums, parked on the stern of the boat we were talking loudly over the sound of the churning waters. The cabin boy reluctantly served a set of ridiculous fruit cocktails. He had the long face and upturned nose of a salesman at a luxury boutique. We sank deeper into the dark-green cushions. We made ourselves comfortable. Amira stretched out, Maryam took aim with her slingshot. She was going shoot the world right in the eyes.

Madam Lilla was settling into her cabin as if we were permanently moving onto the boat. In the movie she had running in her head we were on the Titanic and her closet was packed with all her things from Alexandria – silks and satin, flared skirts and brocades – all that she would need before we arrived in New York. She must have missed the feel of fabric. The trip would only last a couple of days but of course Madam Lilla had a different measure for time.

"Seems Lilla is going on a journey around the world in eighty days on this boat," said Maryam.

"No doubt we'll be invited to the captain's quarters for dinner tonight!" commented Amira.

"Lilla and the captain will dance the first dance together."

Still on her back, Amira flung open her arms and twirled her wrists as she made the announcement for the evening, "Captain Stubing and the Love Boat's amazing guests. The episode, The Return of Madam Lilla!"

We all laughed. The three of us had grown up in the 1980s and we'd all seen *The Love Boat* on the television. I added, "Of course at the end of the episode we shouldn't end up like the Three Black Fish on the grill."

I was laughing on my own now. Neither Amira nor Maryam had understood. "Don't you get it?" I asked. They looked at me blankly. "No way! So you don't know the *Little Black Fish*? From Behrengi." They didn't. "How's that? Aren't you guys supposed to be Arabic? He's actually an Iranian writer. You know the one who was killed under the Shah…" They had no idea who I was talking about.

Maryam tired of the joke. She wanted an explanation. "Alright already. If you have something to say then spill it."

"There's this little black fish who leaves his home with a knife around his waist. He's looking for adventure. He ends up in a pelican's gullet. But teaming up with the other fish he manages to cut a way out and they escape. And it's then that…"

I stopped, feeling a little foolish but Amira was curious to know how the story ended. "And?"

"The end is a little … I mean it's like … my mother's version of the story ended with the fish going back home to tell his story but … in the real story he doesn't go back home. They never hear from him again."

I was silent. In that moment the fate of the Little Black Fish seemed overloaded with meaning for someone who was on a boat crossing the Mediterranean and who was confused about writing a book and being an actual character in that book.

"In the end does he come home or not?" asked Maryam, indifferently.

"How should I know," I said.

We were silent for a few moments. And it seemed the subject was closed.

Maryam kept sniffing the strange smell the rubber band left in the palm of her hand. Rubber, plastic, latex, a hero … she was thinking and began to tell us her thoughts.

"Something's happened to superheroes, azizi. They all seem depressed recently. Have you noticed?"

I was still musing about the Little Black Fish while Amira had her arms on the back of the boat, her chin on her hands, lost in all the foam bubbling up from the propeller. Maryam continued her theory.

"Even Superman was depressed. Batman started the trend. Then Spiderman got the blues. The world's only going from bad to worse, azizi. Even superheroes are on the therapy couch. Their heads all turned around."

"Maybe it's because women superheroes have come along," said Amira. I thought of all the films I'd recently seen with heavily armed women in tights. Perfect beauty, incredible strength, extraordinarily smart, exceptionally

428

wise, and always flying off somewhere... A crew of super-ladies that didn't look anything like our ragtag trio of Little Black Fish.

I noticed an orange butterfly with black and white spots, the last thing I expected to see in such a place. Freeing itself from the wind, it had managed to land on the deck of the boat.

"Maybe telling a story, or writing it down, is just the hopeless search for a home."

"The library in Alexandria!" said Maryam, and she thoughtfully covered her mouth but suddenly catching a whiff of rubber from the sling again she scrunched up her face. She hesitated then continued, "Alexander the Great wanted to establish a place where he could gather every story ever told because he could never go home. So it was a home where all the stories were collected. But the place he chose was opposite his old homeland of Macedonia. Only the sea was in between ... the reason for the lighthouse in Alexandria..."

"Brava, my love!" I said to Mayram, and excitedly I went on, "the story is hopelessly trying to find a home. Or like miserable Alexander, you put up a lighthouse and wait for the house to find you."

"And?" said Amira, "In this story does anyone end up going home?"

I saw a different question in her eyes. A question about Muhammed. When he came back – if he did – would she be there, too? If we made it out of this trip alive would Amira return to Tunisia and lead a normal life? Or like a butterfly would she pass away before the story ended...

"Is that a butterfly?" asked Amira, distracted.

Maryam looked at our new voyager on the boat, "It happens sometimes. In Alexandria there can be these sudden gusts of them. The wind must have blown this one all the way out here."

For some time we gazed at the butterfly. We watched it opening and closing its wings, as if on the brink of coming to a decision. It mustn't die before three pairs of eyes could marvel at its wings. Then we saw them and its story was told. Maybe Madam Lilla was right, "No life ended unachieved." Even lives that lasted just one day.

"I can write it," I said.

"Yes, you can, just steady yourself, Rocky," teased Maryam.

"I mean the end of your story ... I can write the end of our story," I added.

Joyful as a butterfly, Amira asked, "What will it be like?" And almost at the same time Maryam said "So you don't need us then?"

She took out her slingshot. Stretched it. Inspected it. She was really asking me, it wasn't a joke. I tried to loosen up the mood with the beginning of a smile, and with no luck because Maryam kept pulling back the rubber and snapping.

The silence went on for a few seconds then in a crystal clear voice Almira asked, "Will the ending be the same for all of us? Are we really not needed anymore?"

Cocking an eyebrow slighter higher and making a sly face, Maryam drew the slingshot at me and asked again, "What do you say?"

We were like three sisters who had all hopped in the same bed to sleep through a winter's night. Their imploring eyes were fixed on mine. They had pulled the blanket from me and the monster under the bed was about to nibble on my toes. I knew what I had to say to get back under the covers. But I couldn't.

Amira rescued me, "What could you write without us? There'd be no flavour in it."

Lowering my head, I laughed. Maryam was still looking at me. Her voice wasn't as soft as Amira's. "What will happen if you do write it? Isn't it destiny you are writing?

"Not yours..." I said, and I fell silent before I went on. "I guess it's a little bit of my own."

"And?" said Amira, "what happens in the end?"

The butterfly lifted up off the deck and landed on the table in front of us, as if repeating Amira's question. Slowly and curiously, it unfurled its wings. It didn't want to end its brief life before the end of the film. This was a brave, adventuresome butterfly; it deserved so much.

"I suppose in the end," I said, "I mean I suppose that ... hmmm..."

Maryam suddenly stood up, threw back her arm and hurled the slingshot out into the farthest wave. Then she let herself fall back like a sack and laughed.

"And so it's entirely clear, no? In our story the mademoiselle here will be the character who writes the story."

"Yes," I said with such a foolish joy the two of them laughed. Then we heard Madam Lilla say, "No, sir! No, sir!"

Amira stood up and stretched.

"I was just going to the bathroom. Let's see which cruel tyrant Lilla is waging war against now."

Amira left me and Maryam alone. Maryam took her chance with a question. "What are you going to write then? I mean really?"

"How should I know? I suppose I'll go for a happy ending."

"Maybe you'll write our destiny?"

"I wish."

431

"If you could, how would you do it?" She looked at me, searching for an answer.

"Yours?"

"You know exactly what I mean. What do you think I should do?"

"Well, I think ... considering that I'm not going to write something that can't happen..."

"Are you going to tell me or not, azizi? Get to the point."

"Alright then..." I smiled. "Then I would write it like this."

And I told Maryam her story...

*

"What's up?" Maryam asked Amira who had come back up onto the deck. Maryam didn't know that her voice was crisp and her eyes were shining because of the story I had just told her, the fate that I had woven for her.

"It's nothing," said Amira. "Lilla's schooling the cabin boy. She's teaching him how to make a hot toddy."

"What in the world's that?" I said.

"I just found out," said Amira, "you see he was putting a little lemon in hot water and according to him there's no cognac but Lilla insists on the cognac. Of course it's his first time dealing with Lilla. He'll get used to her."

"How's the bathroom?" asked Maryam.

"Like the Kremlin Palace. You have got to go," said Amira.

Maryam stood up and went below.

I was in the mood for stories now. I wanted to write everyone's story. I turned to Amira. "How do you think I should finish your story if I was going to write it?"

"Mine?"

"Yes."

"Just make something up but just make sure that in the final scene I'm dancing."

"Are you sure?"

She placed her arm on the back of the boat, her chin in her hands, watching the foam again. "Is Muhammed there with me?"

"Should he be?"

"In your opinion?"

"It depends how we depict him."

"Are we the ones writing it then?"

"In a way."

She was thinking about how she would write her own destiny.

"Don't look that far down, you'll get seasick."

"No, I get that way when I look at the horizon."

"Allah, Allah."

"Hmmmm.... That's the way it is."

"Are you alright?"

It was as she was looking at the churning foam in the wake of the boat, a thick white line in the Mediterranean sea that she said, *"It's so much busier on land. But the horizon is never moving. It's beautiful here because you can't see what's ahead."*

Her pure childlike air didn't match those words. But I didn't write them – she said them. But if I wrote them I wouldn't have written them like that. I would write it like this.

I told Amira the end of her story...

30

With our wrists on the table covered in croissant crumbs, twirling our oily fingers in the air, coffees swaying to the rhythm of the waves, Madam Lilla said, "The world will fix it. But only sometimes."

"Of course, of course," interrupted Amira, trying to get a foothold in the conversation, "a morning like this couldn't be a better time to solve the world's problems."

I forced a smile. "There are these journalists I know in Beirut. We need to tell them what we have come up with as soon as possible so the world can benefit from our brilliant ideas!"

Struggling to smile Maryam got up from the breakfast table and made for the Kremlin Palace. She whispered to Amira, "We need to talk about this." Madam Lilla didn't hear. She was too busy trying to get her lighter to work, clicking again and again. Through pursed lips she said, "If they only had something close to a Turkish coffee…"

"Oh, that would be so nice right now," I said.

She looked deeply at me "Maybe you could read my fortune, mademoiselle? It seems you're going to be writing story endings for our friends."

Though there was no reason for me to feel guilty, the way she blew smoke in my face implied I should. "I told you," she said, "people who write end up alone. Be careful. You might end up all alone in the middle of the sea."

"How would you know anything about writing Madam…" I asked.

She only smiled. "If only they had Turkish coffee," she said again. Madam Lilla didn't know how she was going to bring her

story to an end. Did she want me to write it? Maybe I just had
seasickness. I had been writing all morning without looking up.

*

"That's enough! Azizi, what are you doing!?"

When Maryam woke up and came out onto the deck I'd had two coffees, five cigarettes and I had filled three toilet covers with text. On the fourth one I was drawing a plan for the narrative technique. Before I could say, "Notes on our journey", Maryam leaned over the scheme to have a closer look. She didn't ask for an explanation but I gave her one all the same.

"I'm coming up with narrative techniques in light of the material at hand."

"Hmm..." she replied.

I wasn't sure if she was asking for an explanation. So I went on, "Seeing as these toilet covers are round I thought this kind of narrative would work. A circular narrative. A ring whose ends never touch. When I pulled one out it ripped into pieces and I couldn't patch it together. This is how women tell stories. They begin somewhere in the middle then go back to the start and from there they carry on till the end. Don't you agree?"

"Are you writing everything down?" asked Maryam. She sounded neither cold nor encouraging. It was if she was asking someone she had never met.

"Well, like I said yesterday, I might," I said. I forced a smile. She wasn't convinced.

"How would I know ... when I see you like that ... oh God, whatever. Just write whatever it is you are going to write. In any case..."

"In any case what?"

435

"In the end you're just going to make it all up."

"Of course," I said, "I'll just make it all up."

"But don't go overboard," she said, teasingly.

"I won't go overboard," I said, laughing. Coming back up on deck, Amira joyously announced, "The cabin boy has made croissants. And they're divine." I gathered up my papers so quickly she didn't even see them. Her hair was a mess and she looked like a shimmering but groggy seabird that had just woken up in the sea. On top of her white night gown she wore a long woollen sweater. She called out to the sea, "Good morning!"

To the right and left, she curtsied to the Mediterranean.

"Breakfast must have something to do with happiness," I said. "Cemal Süreya had a poem that went like that. A Turkish poet."

"The guy wrote an ode to breakfast?" laughed Amira.

"You wouldn't know, sweetheart. You don't have a real breakfast where you're from. You could write poems about the breakfasts in our country."

Madam Lilla came out with her face made up, and her hair all done up in glimmering hair clips. She was going to have her breakfast in the ballroom of the Titanic.

"Ah! Breakfast in Istanbul," she said, "you are right, mademoiselle. They have an Ottoman breakfast there. Long and leisurely. A gentleman's breakfast."

"Good morning, Madam," we all said. As she settled into her corner, smoothing out her skirt, I lingered a bit longer on the topic. "If you could crack the problem of breakfast in northern Africa you could solve all sorts of other problems. You definitely need some kind of cultural exchange. I mean for the happiness of Arabs!"

The cabin boy came out with the croissants still steaming on the plate.

"I mean how much longer are you going to have to put up with dried-up croissants? In the spirit of a Mediterranean union..."

My speech about breakfast naturally fell flat in the face of the crispy appeal of the croissants. Only after taking her second hurried bite was Maryam able to talk, "Don't worry, azizi! When the revolution pulls through in Tahrir we'll see to the matter right away. We're considering a breakfast reform, it's in the programme."

"That sounds perfect. In fact you might even be better off creating an emergency action plan. We need to end this torture as soon as possible."

"Of course, azizi. In fact we could even add 'breakfast as betrayal to the nation' to the list of Mubarek's crimes."

"Exactly."

Madam Lilla and Amira laughed as they watched Maryam and I conduct our 'revolutionary diplomacy'.

Maryam went on, "What we have been dealing with until now has to do with finding a way to collect the political method experiences accumulated in the squares and gathering them in a single pot at the centre of breakfast."

"Where do you think that should be done, azizi? I might have a suggestion," I said.

"Go ahead."

"I'm thinking Cordoba. When you think about it you see that throughout history Andalusia is a key crossroad of civilizations, a geography of so many different breakfasts."

"Sounds good. I'll inform the Egyptian delegation right away. We should call for an emergency meeting. So...."

Gravely taking a big bite out of her croissant and munching, Maryam went on, "I wonder if we could use Andalusia as an umbrella concept. 'Andalusia Reinvented' for example? Would that work for you?"

437

"With my respects. Of course you know best. To my mind, 'Andalusia Again', is just the right name."

"In that case let's get on with it, azizi"

"Right away."

"In fact," said Amira, she wasn't just joking around like we were. "This isn't such a bad idea. I wish there was some kind of solidarity group. If the revolutionaries of Egypt, Tunisia, Spain and Greece could all come together, I mean to talk about more serious things than breakfast, just a thought."

Nodding our heads gravely we continued to munch the croissants. Madam Lilla, however, was taking little bites. She was that much more refined. Her words rang out clearly "I agree." It was an unexpected ovation. And she went on, "Who knows, maybe they would even solve the question of Palestine."

"That question will never be solved," said Maryam. "I agree," said Amira. The croissants no longer tasted so good. No one at that table was willing to joke about Palestine. The mood turned awkward and we fell silent.

"To my mind," said the cabin boy and we looked up to see that he was listening to us from a corner. He paused, uncertain if he should continue. The glances we shot him suggested that we found him rather suspect. With the severity of a board chairman, Madam Lilla said, "Please, good sir." No doubt surprised that someone had just addressed him as 'good sir' he was so startled that he went on despite our discouraging looks.

"I have an idea. An idea."

"In terms of solving the problem of Palestine?" asked Lilla, her gravitas still very much intact.

With some effort the cabin boy went on, "To my mind … a nuclear bomb and boom! There'd be nothing left of Israel.

Then all the surviving Palestinians and Israelis move to Cyprus where they all get Cypriot citizenship. And they carry on from there."

Narrowing her eyes and nodding, Lilla listened as if she were up against a diplomatic genius. The three of us concentrated on our croissants. If we looked at each other we might have cracked up laughing but the cabin boy went on.

"Just finish the matter once and for all. There's no other way!"

Then he waved his hand in the air as if saying, damn it all. It was the revolt of someone who cursed the same problem every night. He spoke like a man who was trying to accept the fact that his girlfriend, whose picture he still carried around in his wallet, was never coming back, that sort of pain.

"Don't you think it's like that?"

We were silent while Lilla kept nodding, lost in thought. She must have thought that his far-fetched theory needed some grounding so she raised the bar.

"And considering it won't be very long before Cyprus is completely under water they will all have to find another place. Or live on boats."

Trying to develop his theory with this added Atlantis element, the cabin boy realized he was sinking and he started collecting plates. After sweeping up croissant crumbs and the remnants of our astonishment, he was about to go inside when Lilla said, "but perhaps you're right, sir. We have all suffered enough. Arabs don't like the Palestinians but they are in love with Palestine. Perhaps it's time to do away with this lie."

Maryam and Amira were now meaningfully munching again as they nodded their heads in agreement. Maryam said, "They are despised and driven out of every other Arab

439

country but Palestine is always the 'apple of the eye'. All the Arab countries have exploited the situation there and they're still not done."

Satisfied that he had started a new element of the conversation based on his strange solution, the cabin boy picked up the last few plates and went inside.

"Palestine is their land of milk and honey," I said when the captain, whom we'd hardly seen since we left, lurched onto the deck with the weight of a galleon.

"Good morning, madam! May I have a word?"

"Of course, captain!" said Madam, like a sailboat unfurling its sails.

"Perhaps a tête-à-tête…"

"Oh no, please go ahead. I have no problem with the ladies hearing."

"Fine then, Madam … I'm afraid we won't be able to take you as far as Tripoli. We have no choice but to leave you in Beirut."

"I don't understand, captain. That was not our agreement," said Lilla with the certainty of winning the discussion.

"The arrangement has changed, Madam. Our boss is on to us."

In her softest voice and with all her good intentions, Amira said, "What difference does it make, captain? It will hardly take more time to go as far as Tripoli."

Angrily, Maryam turned to me and said, "I told you so." Looking at me, her lips trembled, she said bitterly, "OK. We'll get off in Beirut. There's no need to draw this out. We're in no mood for yet another adventure, Madam."

The captain jumped on the opening, "I'll refund a portion of your payment. There's nothing else I can do, Madam. Please forgive me. I don't want a bullet in the back of my head. You know how Russians can be."

440

Not entirely grasping why leaving us in Beirut instead of Tripoli was such a perilous matter, Amira asked Madam, "We could get off in Beirut and go…"

Lilla cut her off, "Out of the question! That was not the plan."

"Just what was the plan then, Madam?" asked Maryam, fed up. Lilla leaned back and looked at the captain with pouted lips.

"My apologies again," the captain said and hurried back inside.

After he had left, Lilla looked at us. Maryam didn't repeat the question and in a softer tone of voice, Amira said, "Just what was the plan, Madam?"

"First Tripoli … to take care of … business. Then travel to Beirut where we would celebrate!"

"So you were thinking of putting a bullet in a man's head and then celebrating? How pleasant," grumbled Maryam.

"Madam, are you still … I mean … are you still planning…" said Amira.

"What did you think? That I would abort the mission?"

"No, not that," said Amira, "it's just that we're here now."

"And?" Lilla asked, imperiously. It was as if in a moment she had brought everything back to the start. Something snapped in Amira's expression. Lilla wasn't even looking at her any more. The end of her story wasn't going to pan out the way she'd expected and she was angry. Maybe we had got too swept away in everything that had happened to us along the way but Lilla was still locked on her target.

Maryam said, "Oh come on, dear. We've already solved Palestine so surely we can we work this out too? Right, Madam?"

Lilla seemed to soften a little. Under the table I saw Maryam nudge Amira's leg. And that's when Lilla said,

"The world will fix it. But only sometimes." Amira and Maryam went to the loo. Clearly they were up to something – and it had to do with Lilla.

Meanwhile Lilla commented, "Now I'm going to have to send word to my friends in Beirut, to let them know I'm coming early. I suppose the captain can manage that."

Then Lilla and I talked about Turkish coffee. But I couldn't be sure. Was she now asking me for an end to her story? I said what I had to say, "It's easy to write the end for the girls but writing your finale ... yours will be too grand, Madam. I don't think I'd be able to manage it."

She was taking such quick drags off her cigarette the tip was dangerously bright, "No, mademoiselle," she said, "mine is only a little longer. In fact all of our stories are the same."

"Then would you like a happy ending?" I asked. "I can write it along those lines."

She looked beyond me "Do you know how many bodies lie at the body of this sea?" Looking out over the waters, she went on, "Strange that it's still so blue. All the people who have drowned just trying to get from one shore to the other, no one knows their stories. Mademoiselle, if you ask me, any old ending will do. In any case mine has gone on far longer than is necessary."

"In that case I'd write something like this Madam ... would you like to hear?"

The ash from her cigarette fell into her lap, burning a black-rimmed hole in her long silk dress.

"No," she said.

442

31

"Beirut is a city where the endings of stories are nothing like the ones you write," said Madam Lilla, "isn't that true?"

In the Café Orient, which was built directly over the sea, high society customers sat in big armchairs behind ice buckets holding bottles of white and rosé wine, puffing on water pipes and watching our arrival. Like a small and unsavoury royal family we stood on the deck as we approached the dock in the mild afternoon sun. It was a magnificent arrival into Beirut that quickly turned into a comedy because an old man was waiting for us on the shore, his arms spread wide and his belly shaking with laughter. We might have looked like showroom girls who had just stepped out of a giant oyster if the fatso on the shore hadn't been jumping up and down and shouting, "Stop Solidere! Stop Solidere!"

Lilla didn't expect me to answer her. With her back to me she was facing Beirut. So I addressed her back and Beirut, "Yes, it always looks more ridiculous than I imagined."

As the man on the shore called out to Lilla his belly bounced so vigorously it seemed like laughter was alive and wriggling out of him.

"Welcome, Samira! Welcome and glory be upon us! Stop Solidere!"

Waiting for the gangplank to be lowered, Madam Lilla smiled indulgently at the man and said to me, "And always more enchanting than you imagined!"

Considering everything I had scribbled down on toilet seat covers while locked away in my cabin, she had a point.

*

I went to the toilet and collected all the covers. I went into the cabin and sat down at a little desk made of rosewood. I thought about whose finale I should write first. Amira's. Of course. The whole trip started because of her. She was the one who got us up and moving and who started the escape. So all our endings should be connected to hers. And her ending certainly had to have something to do with Muhammed. So...

The door swung open. Outside stood the cabin boy, but he wasn't quite at the door. I gave him a dull, 'hello?' A question. He nodded. Blankly we looked at each other. I stood up and shut the door.

So should Muhammed come back or not? He shouldn't. He should take Amira with him. Somewhere in Europe. Yes, that's the best option. But then what would they do there? Of course, of course...

The door swung open again. Now I was staring straight at the cabin boy's ass. He was bent over fiddling with something. He looked at me through his legs.

"What's happening?" I said. He shook his head to say, I didn't open the door. I stood up and shut the door again.

In that case Muhammed has to write another letter. Considering all the ones I've already read it could go something like this...

"Hey, sweetie, I felt I should tell you that we have crossed the Mediterranean and made it to Italy. We made it. The moment we got up on Italy's southern shore I gave a speech that began, 'Hey, Romans!' But the old flavour of this place is gone and no one paid any attention. But it was still good fun. This place is like something right out of those Sicilian scenes

from The Godfather. *The only difference is that the foreign language makes my own film seem more about my relationship within the Arab mafia. Now I am working with this Lebanese hot shot. Let's just say I have my place in the mafia's social responsibility wing. We are trying to bring new standards to the business of human trafficking. I am focused on widening the narrow channel that runs from black Africa to Europe. The Undocumented People of Europe, Leave it to Us. That's our slogan. Do you like it, sweetheart? We provide work and transportation for the undocumented, bodies but no head count. The undocumented! Let's just say I am keeping the documents for the undocumented. In Europe there are libraries that keep track of everything and I keep the tabs on the people who aren't officially on the list. Sweetheart, my life is terrible here. So I can't say come and join me. But I've put together a little money. Maybe I could meet you somewhere on the Spanish coast? Or in Cordoba. Only a place like Andalusia could handle a woman like you. What do you say? Maybe you would let me serve you my heart with a platter of fresh seafood? Maybe it still has some flavour, what do you think, sweetie?*

Bang! The door swung open. This time it wasn't just the cabin boy's ass, but the captain's, too. They were either inspecting something on the floor or searching for something. They both looked at me through their legs.

"Is there a problem?" I asked, annoyed.

With expressions on their faces that said there definitely was, they both said: "No..."

"I gather the door's broken?"

"No..." they chimed.

Doing my best to make it clear that I wouldn't tolerate the door swinging open like that again, I slammed it shut. Then I started writing again.

This wasn't happening. Muhammed's letter couldn't be like that. So I gave up on it. So I boldly had a go at writing the end of Maryam's story.

… Suad Massi is playing in her house in Cairo. The windows are open to the early morning air. At her desk she is writing the ending to Dido's story. Her baby is sleeping in another room. The house smells of her. Is there a man there? No. As she writes the final section she smiles, she is content. Her hair is longer, curly. When the call to prayer echoes through the air she thinks of us: me and Amira. She sits down at her computer to write an email. She turns on her laptop. Her hands hovering in the blue light of the screen … she rolls a joint. Smiling as she twists. "Ladies," she begins. "You are about to embark on the most important journey of your lives." The same words Lilla had told us at the start of our trip. She is sad that we aren't there. That there is no longer a journey. For a moment it seems silly to write to us and she gets up and goes to the window. She listens to the birds filling in the gaps in the muezzin's morning prayer. Her baby wakes and Maryam lets the joint to go out in the ashtray. She lets out a deep sigh. There is a knock on the door…

This time the door has quietly swung open and I only notice when it begins to bang to the rhythm of the rocking boat. Now I am really fed up and I rise to my feet. The captain and the cabin boy are still there.

"For the love of God what in the world are you doing there?" I bellow, not realizing that I am shouting now.

The captain makes a face, "It doesn't concern you!"

"But then why is this door always opening?"

The captain gives me a ridiculous answer, "Doors are made to be opened!"

"No sir," I say, "they are made to be closed."

446

And bang, I slam it shut. I am sure they are cursing me on the other side.

There is a knock on the door but who can it be? With the door always opening and closing Maryam's story goes stale. So I give up on it and turn to Madam Lilla.

…First of all Jezim Anwar has got to die, that's for sure. But how should Madam Lilla kill him? Strange how it seems perfectly normal to think about murdering someone. A day or two from now she is probably going to kill a man and this isn't just a part of a film script, it is really going to happen. But now the most important thing is how I am going to bring this to life in my story. It was impossible. Did someone once liken novelists to serial killers? If so, she was absolutely right…

Madam Lilla is climbing the steps of a vast mansion nestled in a garden. She has taken her gun out of her burgundy velvet pouch. It's mid-afternoon, when the heat grinds everything to a standstill. This is Jezim Anwar's house. Not a soul is around. (Why? Like one of those scenes from The Godfather shot in Sicily.) Jezim Anwar is having his afternoon nap alone on the balcony, and because he wants peace and quiet all the staff have left. Her hands trembling, Lilla takes out her gun, puts her finger on the trigger…

Bang! The door opened again and I turned and fired as Maryam hurried in and quickly shut the door behind her. She didn't realize she had just taken a bullet.

"Azizi, we're in hot water."

Closing the safety on my gun, I stuffed it under my belt. "Really?" I said wretchedly.

"There's cocaine on this boat."

"What do you mean cocaine?"

"The Columbian kind! The real stuff! Cocaine, cocaine!"

"Aha!" I said and stopped. I must have looked lost in a daze. But Maryam had already decided to take the matter into her own hands – you could see it in her face.

"Amira knows. But I haven't told Lilla. Now this is what we are going to do…"

She stopped, her gaze fixed.

"What are we going to do?" I said.

"We're going to jump off this boat and swim. How should I know? Pray or something. I mean we should all pray. What's more the captain and cabin boy couldn't find the stash. They've been looking for some time. I overheard them talking about it."

"So they're looking for cocaine outside my door…"

"The moment this boat docks in Beirut we need to disappear. Do you know a safe place in Beirut, a place you can trust?"

I thought for a moment. A safe place in Beirut? I felt like laughing. Maryam wasn't in the mood. "I know," I said. I couldn't quite believe what was running through my head but I didn't have a choice. Off to Beirut and the rest is up to a gracious God. It was always like that.

Maryam continued, "Now, in this situation … hmmm … you go and pack up Lilla's things. She's too slow, she'd never jump to it. Amira should stay with her until we get to the shore. I'll pack what I can of our things into one bag. Once the boat comes to a stop… Let's just pray that no one's waiting for us in Beirut."

She stopped and shook her head in despair, "May God help us."

"Amen!" I said and silently I prayed that the only person who could help us in Beirut was actually in town. It was the sort of city where if God didn't come to the rescue, friends did. Of course it would have helped if I really did have a gun with me. But what was I going to do with it? This was the difference between writing a story and being a hero in one. You know what to do with a gun.

There was no sign of the captain or the cabin boy. I hurried into Lilla's cabin. I opened the cupboard and started choosing what I thought were the most precious items in her silk collection. Who knows what sort of celebration she had in mind but she certainly had a real hoard of dresses. Among the piles of cloth, I found her burgundy velvet pouch. But there was something else inside. A bottle. "No way!" I said. The word cyanide was printed on the side of the bottle. Was Madam Lilla planning to kill herself at the end of her mission, while we were busy celebrating? A grand drama for the grand finale? This was cheap melodrama no novelist would stoop to. But considering Madam Lilla.... yes, an exit that would look chic only in real life. If it were me I wouldn't write it that way, no way. I stood there with the bottle in my hand. What was I going to do with this now? What would I make of this scene if I were to write it? If I were the hero in a book? The door opened. Quickly I stuffed the bottle in my pocket. I looked at the door; no one was there. It had opened on its own. I kept the bottle in my pocket. I figured it might come in handy at the end of the story.

I shut the door and I gathered up two sets of clothing for Lilla and a few other powdery scented items and put them in a bag. I noticed that she didn't have any medicine. But then again why would a woman carrying poison also keep vitamins and osteoporosis pills? I saw her brush covered with hair. It looked like years of hair. She must have spent so much time combing her hair alone. I left it in the room. The memory of her hair could stay there. I was deciding

449

what part of her from her previous life would be taken or left behind. I remembered the cocaine, and I was convinced that for now the story needed a crude action sequence. I ran my hand through the closet one more time. And yes. A lighter. That lighter. The name Jezim Anwar written in Arabic. I tried clicking open the flame like you would with any other lighter. Like someone unsure of the future, I made a wish. If the flame came out on the first go everything would turn out alright. It didn't light. I put the thing in my pocket. I was pillaging Lilla's memories to write a story. Like any other writer I was under the impression that this was acceptable. For people like me every holy relic that belongs to someone else is a talisman that can help you write. What horrible people we are. When we aren't chosen to play in the games other people make up we go and steal their toys and make up stories. In fact people like me...

"Are you ready?" said Amira, coming inside. I started. Caught red handed. I stuffed both hands in my pockets. Poison in the right and the lighter in the left.

"Are you done? Did you pack up her things? Beirut's on the horizon."

I don't know why but I pulled out the lighter and I handed it to her. By writing the ends of their stories I felt that I was betraying them all and so I suppose I was seeking some kind of forgiveness. Something like that. Amira took the lighter and turned it over in her hand, "The famous Jezim Anwar lighter." Whispering to herself. "May God help us!"

I picked up the bag and went up onto the deck. Beirut lay before us with her dark yellow buildings and steeped in her strange sweet smell. I had missed this place. We were approaching in a boat that was packed with cocaine and I had a bottle of cyanide in my pocket and a gun destined to kill a man. I didn't even know if my friend who was supposed to help us was even there... it was still a beautiful sight to behold. We were all up on deck as the boat sped towards the city. We were heading for the dock at the luxury Café Orient on the point of the esplanade. There was no sign of the captain or the cabin boy. There was no unusual activity on the shore. Slowly we came together on the deck. Like a statue of a woman, Lilla stood at the very end. She was so accustomed to other people handling her affairs, she wasn't even thinking about who might have packed her bags or who was carrying them. Amira stood beside her. Maryam beside me. With a sigh I said to Maryam, "Oh, how I love this city, azizi!"

That's when Lilla said, without turning around, *"Beirut is a city where the endings of stories are nothing like the ones you write."*

The man on the shore was flailing his arms and shouting, *"Stop Solidere! Stop Solidere!"*

Maryam whispered in my ear, "Well there you have it. A new man. In any event it doesn't look like anyone else is waiting for us... azizi, if we can just dodge this bullet I promise we will end the story just the way you want to."

I checked the bottle in my pocket. Smiling, I only nodded. In Beirut Arabic I said, "I'm right on it."

The man shaking his belly on the dock of the Café Orient cried, "Welcome, Samira! Samira! Welcome!"

Out of the Café stepped four enormous blond men. They walked straight to the dock. Behind them came a man shaped like a Turkish wrestler dressed in a suit – you didn't need be a gangster film buff to know this was the guy in charge. They stopped behind the bouncing fat man who had raced over to greet us. The captain's face turned as blue as the Mediterranean.

451

Lebanon

"Beirut is a city where endings of stories are not like the ones you ever write."

Madam Lilla was right when she said those words. This story wasn't going to end the way I wrote it. More to the point, I wasn't going to write it the way it would unfold. You'll see what I mean when you get there...

32

One: An Israeli attack on Lebanon is possible. Indeed Iran's nuclear program is pushing Israel to the limits. On her southern border, Hezbollah, diehard supporters of Iran, maintain control; a single rocket suddenly launched over the border and war would break out.

Two: With a strong political presence in Lebanon and support for the Assad Regime, along with Iran, Hezbollah is ready to pull the trigger. A regime collapse in Syria would mean a brutal civil war in Lebanon. Every day in Beirut supporters of the Assad regime are protesting in front of the Syrian Embassy on Makdisi Avenue in Hamra.

Three: As in previous states of emergency, the city is packed with secret service agents. Now this might not apply to tourists but for those who know the city the tension on the streets of Beirut is palpable – you can feel it on the back of your neck.

Four: When old and middle-aged men in the coffeehouses shout at the top of their lungs about the coming of war there's no real problem but when people are talking of war in hushed tones … it's a serious matter. These days in Beirut the situation is serious.

Five: This is Lebanon. Anything can happen at any moment. And nothing could happen at all.

Against this background we were sitting around a wooden table in a little house in the mountains looking at a pink tomato resting on the middle of a little white plate. The tomato had such character it seemed like it was staring up at the handsome, middle-aged man who sat among us and who was leaning over the table with a fruit knife in hand. He says, "Now let's see what happens next." In that moment he wasn't referring to the fate of Lebanon or the plight of the Assad regime. But as he slowly sliced the tomato the seeds of the Middle East emerged, and they were blood red. Light from the setting sun streamed through tree branches and played on Amira's hair and then Maryam's and then Lilla's, painting the strands red. And then the unexpected happened. Nothing we had been through that morning could have prepared us for it.

*

When the four blond bodyguards and the stocky man built like a wrestler came out of the Café Orient and walked over to the dock we thought the game was up. The expression on the captain's face spelled out the words, 'the end'. As the boat glided up to a stop a second group of men emerged from the café. They had dark skin and were well-dressed. They walked up to the fat man. He fell silent. They were his men. They positioned themselves on the shore at the point where the boat would dock. As the boat touched the marina there was a brief exchange between our man and the Russians. It lasted no more than a few seconds. Turning back to the boat, our man was smiling again as if nothing was wrong.

"Welcome, Samira!"

Before we had stepped foot on solid ground, the four

Russians were already up on the boat. There was no sign of the captain and his cabin boy. The expression on the face of our friend said, 'you should smile, too, just make like everything's normal and hurry up.' Lilla seemed to get the drift. With a startling quickness she hopped off the boat.

The moment she hit the ground our man, went crazy with joy and threw his arms around her, hugging her so tightly you'd think he might break her bones, "Samira! Dear sister!"

We were hardly startled to hear Madam Lilla's Beirut name. I couldn't take my hand out of my pocket. I was clasping the cyanide for fear that revealing the little bottle would turn out to be more significant than our getting caught with cocaine. Along the esplanade the trendy young Beirut ladies full of botox and with silicone breasts draped to either side, sprawled out on armchairs lined up on the wave breakers, were now and then puffing on a nargile or sipping from a glass of wine. The fully tanned gents beside them had gel in their hair and sported enormous watches on their wrists. The ladies had their hair blown out and wore full make-up, tight pants, low tops and condescending gazes that were directed at us. A wave of disappointment ran through them after seeing a scruffy bunch like us come out of such an enormous yacht.

Like water we slipped through the Café Orient and onto the street. In Kornis three black jeeps were lined up along the pavement. Our man directed us to the Hummer in the middle, waving his arms. He'd either had a lot to drink, or a lot of something else, his eyes were bloodshot. But then again he had such a pudgy face you could hardly see his eyes. Leading us over to the Hummer, he must have grabbed Lilla's arm too tightly because she cried out, "Enough already. Pierre! You're going to break my arm!"

Pierre Efendi kept his grip on her arm but Lilla swiftly captured his hand and brought the display of affection down to the level of holding hands. Then Maryam grabbed his other hand and said, "Hello Pierre! I'm Maryam. Are we safe?" And she nodded in the direction of the Russian Mafia.

Though Pierre Efendi's face was gripped with joy, as with almost every Lebanese

man there was something deeper at play in his eyes. In answer to Maryam's question, it said something like, 'Don't worry, we've handled it.'

Madam Lilla asked, "What's going on?" It was the first time we heard something like that from her. But thanks to Pierre's flood of emotion she didn't expect an answer nor did she ask after her bags. In any case we had already made the jump into another scene. Pierre quickly scrutinized all our faces. I noticed how Maryam thanked him for rescuing us. In Beirut dialect. For the first time. Interesting.

As Pierre hurried us into the Hummer, he seemed cheerful – not because we had just escaped the Russian mob but as if we were setting out on a picnic.

"I let the driver go, Samira. So I will be your chauffeur today. Ha ha ha!"

After we shut the back door and Lilla hopped in the front, she turned and whispered. "Pierre is completely bonkers! It's all because of the hotel."

I was the only one who narrowed my eyes when Lilla added superciliously, "But how could you not know?"

"Saint George my dear! Because they closed Saint George down!"

Amira and Maryam were watching a new world pass by the windows. I pretended to know where we were but I was lost. The only thing I remembered from my previous visit to the city was that the famous Saint George Hotel was shut down and left to ruin when the city centre fell to privatization.

"Meet my young friends, Pierre," said Madam happily. "Young," laughed Pierre, "we are the young ones, Samira. They are still children!"

As we drove along the coast road in the direction of the Christian neighbourhood Jemayzi, Pierre turned to us, "Ladies, I don't believe that any of you are of the ripe old age to remember the bar at Saint George?"

All three of us pretended to laugh even though we were mainly worried about getting away from the cocaine as fast as we could. Looking at us in the rear-view mirror, Pierre was waiting for an answer. He went on, "Anyone who has seen Saint George isn't young!" He squeezed Lilla's arm, "You haven't changed at all, Samira!"

"Don't be ridiculous," said Lilla, trying not to smile; and without turning around, she introduced us to Pierre. "Our friend here was the last manager of the Saint George Hotel. We spent so many days together..." She paused to make it amply clear she didn't want Pierre to know the whole story before she went on, "He knows Jezim Anwar quite well."

"Ah, Jezim! What a wonderful scoundrel! Ladies, till this day Samira was the only one who ever brought that bastard to his knees! You know that, don't you, Samira! Ha ha ha! Since you the Don Juan has never been back up on his feet!"

In the back seat we looked at each other. Lilla's head was so still that we understood we were supposed to stay silent. We were not to ask any questions. She was making it clear that Pierre wasn't going to be privy to her plan. The ensuing conversation made that clear, "Samira, why are you all of a sudden thinking of seeing Jezim? What brought him to mind? Or is the mademoiselle out to visit all the hearts she's broken? Ha ha ha..."

It was all too clear that Pierre didn't know the story we knew. He must have been the sort of man who drowned out everything he knew and everything he wasn't supposed to know in laughter. Now he was laughing vigorously to ignore the danger signals coming from Maryam and Madam Lilla's nervous energy. His clucking laughter sounded like elevator music.

"Jezim is still in the same house in Tripoli, isn't he?" asked Lilla. "Yes," Pierre sputtered through his laughter. "But he's not the same man! Oh he's aged, Samira. He's not like us. He's got a wife and his life is a living hell."

Lilla didn't answer. There was no need because Pierre had just slammed on the brakes, bringing the jeep to a sudden halt in front of the Saint George Hotel.

"Look Samira! Just take a look!"

The abandoned building, once the Saint George Hotel, looked like an enormous frigate that by the stroke of some ill-omen was frozen as it was being lowered into the sea. Outside a "Stop Solidere" sign flapped mournfully in the wind like a flag announcing a cholera epidemic. Out of the corner of her eye Lilla looked at the place. She wasn't indifferent, it was just that she was afraid of turning into stone if she looked for too long. No part of her plan entailed stopping in front of the St George and getting emotional about the past. Clearly this was why she had wanted to go straight to Tripoli before coming to Beirut. Now her face wore the expression of a woman at the funeral of a man she had failed to kill by her own hand.

"What days those were, eh? Samira. We'd still be young if those Solidere bastards hadn't stopped restoration because they couldn't buy our beautiful hotel. Huh, what you think," said Pierre.

Lilla cut him off. "Where are we going to stay, Pierre?"

For the first time he stopped the incessant giggling and looked at her. He gave her such a look...

It was years and years ago. Lilla had come to the Hotel Saint George. Either she was singing or dancing or shuttling secrets from one country to the next. No doubt she wore gloves. Those gloves must have been made of pale lilac silk. No doubt her hair was in the style of Farah Diba. She came with her valises, her make-up bag and her shoulder bag filled with powders and pearls and pressed handkerchiefs. The tips of her stiletto heels echoed off the marble floors in the lobby.

Jezim Anwar was already giving her the eye but she didn't notice. Constantly clicking open the flame of his golden lighter, he went to speak with Pierre at reception. "Who's the wild cat?" he said. Pierre understood the scoundrel's intention but he also knew there was no way to stop two lonely panthers from finding each other. His patent leather shoes squeaked on the marble floor. "So that's Samira then," he said, " she lives up to all the talk!" His eyes shimmered and Pierre could see him constructing the trap for a queen who would never be his lover.

From then on Pierre kept a close eye on them. He watched Anwar's every move, how he scaled her walls before the castle fell and how she lay in wait for him, all the while blind to his presence... Pierre was always invisible to her eyes.

Now he looked at her the way he looked at her back then. He saw that nothing had changed at all, and that no matter how much they had aged they would never change, and that Samira was still a young woman. And so he reluctantly imitated his own laughter and merely answered the question.

"My dear Samira, you said that you had to stay in Hamra so I booked in the Hotel Cavelier. And as for dinner..."

As they began arguing over dinner arrangements – we'll have dinner, no we won't, oh yes we will, oh no we won't – Maryam kept throwing glances over her shoulder and finally said, "we need to find this friend of yours."

I responded, "Why do you keep looking back? Are we being followed?" And she only pouted to say that she had no idea. I looked at Amira, who was trying to piece together Lilla and Pierre's shared past. Maryam took out her phone and handed it to me. I still knew the number of my friend, Fawaz, from my time in Beirut. This was the only city where I'd memorized numbers, just to be on the safe side. I sent a message.

After squeezing through heavy traffic and arriving at the Hotel Cavelier in Hamra, Fawaz was already waiting for us. Pierre left us at reception and as soon as he stepped out of the hotel Maryam called for a taxi – again in Beirut dialect! Fifteen minutes later we were making our way into the mountains north of Beirut. The moment Lilla heard talk of mountains she didn't even ask exactly where it was that we were going. For the first time she had surrendered to us on the road. She was wearing the same broad-brimmed hat she had on when she had come back from the cemetery in Alexandria. There was clearly something she wanted to forget.

Nobody wanted to know where we were going but I felt the need to explain, "Fawaz is my best friend here. He's an academic but he's also an old warhorse. Out of the left wing movement. But now…"

More interested in the logistics, Maryam said, "Madam, are we going to Tripoli tomorrow?"

Why the rush? Weren't we going to try and discourage Lilla from going? Weren't we going to stop her from killing a man? Amira must have felt the same way because she furrowed her brow and shot Maryam a quizzical look. Maryam didn't look at us.

Lilla said, "Yes. We need to be there by evening. So when night falls..." and then clearly altering the original ending of her sentence she said, "We can go back to Beirut. And then..."

I was the only one who knew the way she really wanted to end that sentence because I had the cyanide. But now wasn't the time to tell Maryam or Amira.

Maryam said, "Good, then our driver friend here can pick us up in the morning and take us to Tripoli."

I took Maryam's hand. I whispered, "What's going on?" Placing my hand back in my lap, she closed her eyes at me as if to say, 'It's OK. There's no need to worry.' She negotiated the ride with the driver in flawless Beirut Arabic, telling him to come pick us up at noon, and that was that.

"It's here," I said. Fawaz was waiting for us among the fruit trees with open arms. How was I going to introduce Lilla? Amira and Maryam were easy. I decided to go with Samira, which seemed to be her known name in Beirut.

Fawaz had the large body of a middle-aged man but when he walked over it seemed his footsteps hardly hit the ground and time began flowing. His eyes were smiling. A witty remark was playing on his lips but before he came out with it you were already ready to laugh. His hands were open as if ready to gesture warmly. He had prepared a dinner which he began joyously describing in detail and told us how he had fired up the barbeque with a hair dryer.

As he led us into the garden, Lilla clasped her hands and whispered to me, "What a handsome man!"

I let out a laugh. Fawaz turned and said, "What's up?"

I quickly cobbled together an answer, "It's just that it's been some time since we sat down to eat with a gentleman and we are all in a good mood."

And so we sat down at the garden table. Before the table

was even set and before anyone even had a sip of water and before all the social niceties were made, we were deep in politics and hardly breathing at all. I have no idea how we got started. Apart from Lilla we were all waving our arms about in the air – that's all I can remember. Fire and coal crackled in the grill and maybe the fire was going out but we weren't even watching it. We were talking about the Middle East. I asked about Beirut, or one of us surely did. We got drunk on all the talk. Maybe for half an hour, an hour. This was something like drinking the Beirut water, breathing Beirut air. Even up in the mountains it felt like we really couldn't start breathing until we had got all this out. We spoke without stopping until Fawaz slammed his hands down on the table and said, "Let's go."

And we took a deep breath. He brought out marinated meat and arak. I brought out plates from the kitchen. Amira brought out thin pita bread. Maryam gathered up spices from the kitchen table. Fawaz put out fresh zahter and romaine lettuce, slowly sliced mild cream cheese and drizzled olive oil on top. He added green olives and soon the entire table was shimmering with food soaked in olive oil. It was a rundown, old table covered with a perfectly delicious display. We set that table like it was a beautiful, free verse poem.

Madam silently watched, as silent as she has never been. She must have still felt frustrated with having ended up in Beirut. She seemed to be holding her breath. We were still riding the choppy waves of the conversation with fitful starts. "But in Syria…" "and then there's Iran… " "But the gulf Arabs…" "But in Turkey, America, Israel…" In every sentence we calculated death tolls. Roughly, till water mingled with arak. Water poured into that carafe and magical white clouds swirled like cigarette smoke and everyone fell silent. In that moment it seemed we were witnessing the process for the first time – I suppose it's like that every time – and silently we watched. It is a chemistry that silences the Middle East.

"But the most important thing," said Fawaz. We assumed he had something to add to the political discussion but he went inside and came back with a pink tomato on a large white porcelain plate.

"The most important thing is this beauty which is your destiny. I have been keeping it since yesterday and now that you're here let's cut it in your honour."

"What's this, Fawaz?" I said, as we all leaned over the tomato.

"Tomato with arak. A pink, mountain tomato. When you make a little hole here at the top and let it steep for a day in arak it becomes the world's greatest arak aperitif. Let's slice it and see…"

Slowly leaning over the tomato as if it might be startled and try to escape, he went on, "…or so they say. The Middle East is a place where human life isn't valued, or so they think. It's not true. The Middle East is a place where some are overvalued and some are not valued at all. And the thing that keeps this system in place is…"

The pink juice of the tomato spread over the plate.

"Air… that's what keeps it moving. There's nothing you have to do in Beirut. Because something's always happening. Life is in full swing even when you're doing nothing. You get dragged right into it and…"

As tomato slices fell a cloud of arak swilled onto the plate.

"And this presents you with an enchanted life. There is always something holy you can sacrifice yourself for. What a comfort! There's no longer any need to search for meaning because there's already so much of it on open display. There is already so much blood. And when there is blood there is always meaning. To believe this…"

The slices fell heavily onto the plate.

"It's easier to believe in this than to believe in God. A whole generation will be swept away like this. Then another. In any event they won't forget and they will find a cause for blood. When they find it there's no need to find any other. There is no need for you to know anything in the Middle East."

Slices lay on the plate and the smell of arak was in the air.

"And so it's done," said Fawaz, "let's see how it turned out."

He didn't speak of the Middle East and nothing about the war that was closing in on his country. He only spoke of a tomato that lay in the centre of the centre of all this. *Now let's see how it turned out?*

There was nothing left of the cocaine or the boat or anything about what was to come. For a moment that tomato was the centre of the world. For a moment. And the moment would have grown but Fawaz asked, "And why are you ladies here? And in the middle of a war!"

Our forks hung in the air. There was nothing to say. If Lilla really had come to a war to find a man she once loved the situation was really no different for us. We had gone to the centre of war for one another and without anyone else.

While I was thinking that no one would say a thing and that one of us would certainly come up with a lie and that Madam would certainly create a story, Maryam replied "There's a commune in Dar el-Amar set up by old Philippine maids. Do you know it? We're going there."

Maryam's face was lit with the clarity of having made a very important decision. As if she hadn't even heard

Maryam, Lilla responded to something Fawaz had said earlier, "In the Middle East … the most important thing … is to know which lives are precious. This you must decide before you take one."

Fawaz flashed me a look that said, who's this crazy?

"This tomato," I said, "is superb! Do you think you could do this with normal tomatoes?"

33

Amira placed Anwar's golden lighter on the brown Formica table in the Abou Hassan Meyhane. She put it there as a question. There was no need to say more. Ignoring Amira and Maryam, Madam Lilla turned to me.

"But the most important of all..."

She blew smoke into my face.

"Yes ... the most important is to keep your Madam Lilla alive. Instead of the soul of a scoundrel... Yes, mademoiselle, that's what I'm asking you..."

She blew another puff of smoke in my face.

"A hero in a novel must deserve to be a hero, don't you think? This is more important than the life of some wretch like Jezim Anwar. What will become of me if I don't kill him? An old woman. Who doesn't even deserve to be written about in her own book? Isn't that so madam author? Only if I kill him..."

"Madam Lilla!" cried Maryam, interrupting. And just like the women in old black and white movies, Lilla snuffed out her half-finished cigarette.

"That's what I'm saying, I need to stay Madam Lilla!"

When she reached out for the lighter her hands were trembling and Maryam leapt up and grabbed the golden curse.

"Listen to me!" she said. She paused and repeated herself as if she wasn't convinced by her voice. "Everyone is going to listen."

Maryam held Jezim Anwar's lighter in the same way she held the slingshot in Alexandria. It looked like she could bring down a regime with a lighter. We had been drinking since afternoon and into the night and our eyes were bloodshot. Inspired by the drink when we left Fawaz's house, we decided to keep going and so we went to Abou Hassan's tavern. Oum Kalthoum had been playing at the tavern for years on repeat. We had only been there two hours and we'd already heard the musical Inta Omri twice. Amira, Maryam and Madam Lilla looked as beautiful as the song.

*

As we left Fawaz's mountain home and got into the taxi before heading down to the centre of Beirut, he took me by the arm and whispered, "What business do you have with these people? It's like you don't really know where you're going."

This was like saying to someone in the middle of a dream, indeed just when she is being swept away in the spirit of the dream, 'you're having a dream.' And I answered him the way you would answer someone in a dream, laughing, "Well, no one is waiting for me. And seeing as no one is telling me to stay I'm going with the ones who are telling me to come."

"Where are you going? Alright, to Dar el-Amar. But after that?"

That's when I realized I didn't know about after that. I would go wherever the actors go after all the filming is done. The hollow silence made Fawaz really worried. "You should go back to Istanbul. Back home. When you called and told me you were coming I called Nuray in Istanbul. They're all worried about you."

I smiled, "Me, too." I said. "Sometimes I really do worry about myself. Fawaz, I suppose I..."

Lilla and the girls were all in the car looking at us in the darkening sky. I finished quickly. "I am going where the story ends. Wherever that is. You understand? I don't have any hope for that country any more. I guess I don't have the struggle in me."

Fawaz was someone who had seen many friends off to war, to death, to the unknown. He knew the only thing a real friend could do in such a situation was to give them a warm hug and say 'call me'. And that's what he did.

The moment I got into the car I turned to Maryam cheerfully, playing up my good mood to stall any questions about me and Fawaz, and I said, "You speak such good Beirut Arabic, azizi. How so?"

But before she could answer Amira butted in with the more direct question, "So what's the deal with this commune in Tripoli set up by Philippine women, Mademoiselle Maryam?"

The taxi drove on.

Since we had arrived in Beirut Lilla had gone almost completely silent and seemed hardly interested in anything we said. She must have set out on the journey before any of us. Her gun wasn't actually in hand but perhaps she had Jezim Anwar in her sights, her finger on the trigger. And just like our first dinner together we were merely extras mumbling through our lines.

The car wound its way down through the mountains to Beirut, with no one stopping us at checkpoints. Like a dream the road unravelled perfectly. Making funny faces, Maryam held my hand and Amira's. Then she placed our hands on her knees. Clearly something bright and cheerful was running through her mind.

Her light-hearted sisterly gestures made me feel more and more like a traitor. One hand still in my pocket, I was clutching the bottle of cyanide. I felt awful not because I had stolen something but because I had plundered Lilla's stuff so I could write a story. To write fiction I'd become a life thief... . The bottle of cyanide was like a talisman. I had the power to write the end of the story as long as it stayed with me. But I was outside this story as it unfolded in real life.

I pulled out the bottle and I showed it to them. Madam's spirit was somewhere so very far away that she didn't even notice. Maryam and Amira looked at me as if to say, 'so what?' I nodded at Lilla. They got it. Maryam looked angrily out the window and Amira nervously bit her lower lip. Nothing was said but now we all knew that Lilla wasn't just out to kill someone: she had set out on this trip with the intention of taking her own life. We were her pall bearers.

"Let's go somewhere and drink!"

Maryam looked at me and Amira as if to say, 'now get on board with me right this instant.' Then it came to me. Leaning over to the driver, I said, "Good sir! Do you know Abou Hassan? It's on the left as you go down to Karakas from Hamra."

As if he had just heard a password the driver chuckled and merrily shifted gears and Maryam's mood brightened. "Ole!"

Lilla was right: the yellow lights of Beirut were shimmering in a way that foretold that this story wasn't going to end the way I'd wanted to write it. At least now I felt good in my heart. With the peace of mind that comes with choosing life over the written word, I put the bottle of cyanide back in my pocket.

From the outside Abou Hassan looked like a miserable little fast food kiosk. With the dark blue and white awning and white fluorescent lights it looked about as appealing as a roadside rest stop. But when you went inside ... the same tape was playing from so many years ago. 'İnta Omri' by Oum Kalthoum... You are my life! It was an extraordinary improvisational intro. We climbed up a narrow stairwell to the top floor. My favourite brown Formica table right next to the window was free. Cheerfully the waiter asked his well-worn lines.

"Halk Rakı?

"Of course!"

We were surrounded by familiarity, banter and music. We sat down across from each other at the table... it created that warm feeling from way back in the 1970s when you are asleep on a night journey in a minibus warmed by the shared breath of the passengers huddled together and listening to Orhan Gencebay. Though that was my memory, they all had others of their own, of familiarity and time passing. For a moment we were just at ease.

The appetizers were already on the table: fresh meatballs, liver sliced paper-thin, leaves of mint, mild cheese drizzled with olive oil, hummus with ground beef, fattoush salad, fried lamb, boiled artichoke hearts with garlic, Lebanese sausages and tabouli... and just when I was about to ask, the waiter beat me to it.

"Shall I bring some chicken wings?"

Keeping up with the tradition I answered, "A little later..."

But we never managed to get to the wings...

Maryam began the conversation. "So, Madam Lilla, do tell us. What's the plan? How are we going to do it?"

Lilla was still in that far away place. Dreamy and slightly drunk, she looked at Maryam.

Maryam continued, "I mean this man... What was his name again? Jezim Anwar ... just how are we supposed to bump him off? Do you have a plan?"

Madam must have sensed that slight softness in Maryam's voice, which signalled to her that Amira and I were now on board, and with an eyebrow raised she asked, "Why do you ask? Are we doing it together?"

"Come again?" said Maryam, opening her arms. And then, full of confidence, she added, "can you do it on your own?"

Lilla looked at us with something close to contempt.

"So you have doubts!"

"We want to know how this ends?"

Leaning over the table, Amira repeated the question with her eyes. Maryam came right out and underlined the point because she was all too familiar with Lilla's talent for wiggling out from under these kinds of questions.

"What happens after that, Madam Lilla? Have you made a plan for what comes next?"

Lilla ran her eyes over the three of us, as if sensing we had made a secret pact. The eyes stopped on me. Immediately she went for divide and conquer. Speaking in Beirut Arabic, she looked at Maryam and said slyly, "But of course, sweetheart!" She paused then continued "Now tell me mademoiselle. Why do you speak such good Beirut Arabic? And Amira's right. What's all this about a Philippine women's commune in Dar el-Amar? The ladies here want to know. Isn't that right?"

Lilla looked at me and Amira, expecting support for the move she had made against Maryam. But Maryam was already pushing forward.

"We know about the cyanide..."

Lilla looked at me one more time. She understood that I was the one down below getting the bags ready before we left the boat so I must have been the one who found the cyanide. But she didn't even blink. She raised an eyebrow slowly and she casually adjusted her hair.

"You don't have to do anything. I have thought it all through."

"You've arranged your own funeral in other words!" said Amira, angrily.

Lilla put her hand on Amira's and lightly tapped it and said as if consoling her, "As I've already said, my dear Amira, you don't have to do a thing. And you in particular shouldn't worry. As I promised, when you go back to Tunisia your dance school will be ready. Eyüp Bey is setting it up. And it seems the matter with the hamam has been settled, too."

Amira angrily pulled her hand away and pushed aside the matter of the hamam and her dance school.

"Is that what I'm asking you! Is that what I'm asking? For the love of God, Madam? Without you..."

"Yes? Without me?"

Amira pulled out Anwar's golden lighter. And started clicking. Her eyes fixed on Lilla. She was staring right back at her. It was a silent face-off. Amira was a young girl already betrayed once by her mother. So was Lilla another mother who would not be there when life beat her down again? Or was she not going to let this mother leave her? Would she say, "You aren't going anywhere because you have to protect me?"

Maryam was looking at the two of them. She knew there was nothing else she could do now. It was one of those moments when Amira's eyes turned to stone. In those moments she was stronger than all of us, stronger than the three of us combined. Lilla did not want to have to bear too much of the increasingly oppressive silence. And so she batted away the tragic moment. Pulling a cigarette out of Maryam's pack and popping it into her mouth, she looked at Amira. She looked at her. She looked at her as if to say,

'Light my cigarette and trust me. Just give me a light and I'll tell you something. Something you are going to want to hear.'

"It doesn't work," said Amira and she put Anwar's lighter down on the table; there was no need to say any more. Lilla took Maryam's lighter and lit her cigarette. Turning to me, she said, *"More important than anything else..."*

Then blowing smoke at me, *"Yes ... the most important is to keep your Madam Lilla alive. Instead of a scoundrel... Yes, mademoiselle, I am telling you..."*

Maryam cut her off in the middle of her pronouncement, *"Listen to me!"* she said.

We heard someone coming up the stairs and then a voice, "Aaaaa!" that cut right through the gloom that had settled over our table. We all looked up to see who it was, this young woman who was looking right at me. I cried out as if I was reaching for a lifesaver: "Çağıl!"

The woman came running over to me. Her voice rang out like crystal as she took hold of me. Hugging we swayed from side to side. Locked together we were like two women rocking a baby. We asked each other the same question at the same time, "What are you doing here?"

And we both laughed. But the heavy mood still hung over the table. Nevertheless I introduced Çağıl to our group as if we were just having a casual night out and chatting.

"This is my daughter!"

Çağıl shook everybody's hand and nodded, her cheeks turning rosy when she smiled. "Come sit down," I said and she squeezed in next to Maryam. Çağıl was a little tipsy and a little nervous and there was a fresh scar on her face. Before I could ask her about it she was already explaining why I had called her my daughter.

"You see, I was deported from England because I didn't

475

have all my papers in order. So I came to Beirut with nothing." She turned to me with tears in her eyes. "She told me 'Hey! Pull yourself together!' and taught me all about journalism. Now I'm at the BBC in London."

Everyone nodded. Apart from me no one was completely free of the suspense that had come from the showdown with Anwar's lighter.

Çağıl turned to me, "I trained up to be a war correspondent. Now I'm going to Syria. Are you coming? Are you writing?"

Touching her hair, I said, "No. I'm doing something else now."

She waited for me to go on. So I had to come up with something, "It's not clear yet. So tell me then, young lady, what are you up to? What happened to your face?"

She touched the scar and with something close to joy she said, "Oh, this? Nothing serious. On the way through Istanbul I said why not check out a protest march, and I got hit with a gas canister. The bastards fired at short range. So the scar. It'll be gone in a week or two."

She ran her hand over the scar like it was a medal of honour, and she almost looked proud. Then turning to the others at the table, she said, "She even gave me her lucky pen. When I was doing my first scoop in Beirut! 'Everything will be fine,' she said, and it was."

Now everyone was smiling. Not at what Çağıl was saying. They were smiling at this young woman because she was some kind of meteor from the planet of optimism that had just crashed into our table.

"So you're going into Syria?" I asked.

And like a primary school child breathlessly reciting a poem she had learned by heart for her teacher, she explained, "I guess I'll join up with one of these human aid groups. Though I might not tell them I'm a journalist. I tried crossing the border in Antakya but no chance. But there's a guy I know here from some time back who's in one of the villages on the border. I'm going to meet with him. I mean we were going to meet here but..."

She looked around to see if there was anyone else in the tavern.

"Aren't you scared?" Amira asked Çağıl.

"Oh you bet," she replied, as my hand involuntarily went to her hair, like I was her older sister. She went on, "But it really is very exciting!"

Everyone at the table laughed.

"Now, there's my daughter," I said, pride welling up inside me.

Then turning to the table, I said, "This woman is not just a war correspondent, she's also a fine flamenco dancer!"

As praise rose up from the table Çağıl blushed a deeper shade of pink. She was beaming. Then her phone rang. In a flash she was no longer a shy little girl but a tough war correspondent rattling off fluent Beirut Arabic, "And so where are you? I'm here... Where? Next to Barbar? OK, OK, I'm coming ... OK that's it then!"

Turning to me, she said, "The idiot! The guy doesn't want to come here because it's a Shiite tavern ... well, fine then ... hmmm ... I need to go. How long are staying?"

Turning back to the table, I looked at Lilla. They were all silent. I said to Çağıl, "We don't know. When you get back try the Hotel Cavalier. If I'm still around that's where I'll be."

"OK," she said and with another flush to the cheeks she nodded respectfully at everyone and hurried out. As if letting out a deep sigh I sunk back down in my seat. I could feel the extent of my smile from the tension in my cheeks but I couldn't close my mouth.

Rubbing my back, Maryam said, "'My daughter!' Huh!"

"That's just how it is..." I said, embarrassed.

"She's really sweet," said Amira. Apart from Madam Lilla everyone let out a sigh. The silence reminded us where we were. But we continued in more relaxed tones. Çağıl had left behind the subtle taste of good tidings, intimating good things to come. A sea breeze that reminded me I had a life somewhere and that I was more than just a thief in other people's lives. That warm feeling you get hours after eating when a fig seed slips out from between your teeth and then crunch ... the good cheer of a younger woman had pulled us together. With a feeling of responsibility we couldn't articulate, we had rallied our spirits. Everyone was a little stronger, we were all a little more ... grown-up. Mature.

Maryam gravely topped up all our glasses. She seemed to be preparing for a major negotiation. "Now, I have a few things to say."

Lilla was staring out of the window blankly and Maryam warned her in a soft voice, "Madam, I am serious. Please listen."

Lilla reluctantly turned to face us.

"You were wondering why I speak such good Beirut Arabic..." said Maryam. Turning to Amira, she continued "And about this commune in Tripoli and the Philippine women..."

Taking a gulp of arak, she looked like either a young man mustering his courage to declare his love or a tough young girl fearing rejection.

"I had a nanny. Called Nunu. Or at least that's what I call her. Her real name is Nadine. She's from the Philippines. When she was young she came to work in Egypt after working in Beirut. She's a good person. So gentle. Hardly even there. You know the kind of woman

478

you only really feel when they are gone. Anyway, the only Arabic she knew was Beirut Arabic. So I learned it from her. She never liked Egypt. Always wanted to go back to Lebanon. She finally she came back here after I grew up. Now you wouldn't really call it a commune but she rented a house with a few other Philippine women. And they started running a nursery. When I was close to giving birth … people yearn for that gentleness when they're close to giving birth. It has nothing to do with the mind or ideas, just that unconditional warmth. Madam … I left the child with her. She's there."

Lilla gripped her glass of arak. She clicked her ring three times on the glass. She was still angry with us. We had rummaged through her secrets. We had taken away all the secret weapons of a woman who was never going to surrender. At last she spoke. Like ice, "And so?"

"And so," said Maryam, "I'm going there to get my baby, Madam."

Instantly I pulled out a celebratory cigarette and lit up.

Amira slapped her legs, "You don't say?"

Tears welled up in our eyes. Maryam curled her lips to hold back a smile. On her face was that mixture of worry and joy you see on the faces of people riding an enormous emotional rollercoaster. There wasn't the slightest movement on Lilla's face; she was still striking her ring against her glass to the same rhythm. In the same icy tone of voice she said, "Well, and then what?"

"The rest I can't handle without you. Madam…"

"Sorry?" said Lilla without a sign of letting up.

But Maryam had come to a decision and she felt a surge of relief, she was patient and undeterred by any obstacle. Smiling from deep down, she said, "Please don't be like this. Without you she will never have a grandmother!"

Lilla let out a bitter laugh, "Ah! Now that really makes me laugh. A granny? Me?"

She looked long and hard at each of us, waiting to see who might join her in laughter, almost imploring. This woman had never surrendered to a man, to life, to love, to poverty or danger or to anyone. And now? For us?

I took out the bottle of cyanide and placed it on the table. Beside the lighter. Pushed it between the hummus and the cheese to a point where only we could see it.

Amira put her hands on the table. "Madam," she said. In her silence it seemed as if she wanted to gently take Lilla's hand and not say any more. But she went on, "We have so much more to do than deal with death. With you..."

Lilla still wore a forced smile to encourage us to laugh all this away, but her voice had turned sour and trailed off. Reaching out she swiped the bottle off the table as if trying to cover up a shameful secret. Then she put it back. She was no longer looking at us. It seemed like I should say something, "Yes, things better than death ... like raising girls ... just like you've said."

And Maryam finished the discussion, "We're not coming with you to kill a man, Madam. That's been nonsense from the start. But considering we now have a better plan I think it's time to tell you. You can't kill Jezim Anwar. You shouldn't kill him."

Arching her eyebrows, Lilla gestured the words, 'you don't say?' Amira and I had bashfully lowered our heads to show our agreement with Maryam and Lilla began to spin her glass. Her eyes slightly unfocused, she said, "So you ladies mean business then. In that case..."

She downed half a glass of arak and when she slammed her glass down on the table she was directing the scene again, just the way she liked it. She took a deep breath, let out a long breath, leaned back and looked at us. Nodding her head for some time. She worked up such silence that we couldn't say a word. We were sure that she had agreed with us, and that she hadn't.

I put the cyanide in my pocket. Slowly Maryam placed the lighter on the table. There was nothing else for us to do.

34

After the sun sets in Tunisia and before the sky darkens there is a precise sliver in time. I call it the Lilac Hour. Though it only lasts about ten minutes. Maryam from Egypt, and Amira, Madam Lilla and one-eyed Eyüp from Tunisia also call it that. In the Lilac Hour birds come together and warble. From now on they are called the Birds of the Lilac Hour. They are silent throughout the day but at this time they take to the jasmine trees and sing hurriedly to one another before nightfall. In such chatter they must be telling their stories to the end... I hear it all. The construction work at home that's been going on all day is over.

In Madam Lilla's back garden I am sitting at a little wooden table that Eyüp Bey has put out for me. I am sitting on a two-person swing, which squeaks sweetly as it swings. When it hits the table I fear it might knock over the jasmine rakı Lilla has made, spilling the contents over my ticket to Istanbul. I have put paper on the table and I have a pen but I haven't written a word. I look up at hundreds of blue beads Lilla has strung up in the trees. The Siamese kitten we brought back with us from far away is winding round my feet. Taking herself for a tiger, she lies in ambush, ready to pounce on a bug.

I can hear Amira inside, walking on the second floor. So slowly she must be dreaming. Lilla is on the first floor with Eyüp, planning something together. Maryam is taking a bath. The baby must be sleeping. A sign freshly painted in oils is leaning against a wall, waiting to dry.

They come into the garden. Lilla and Eyüp Bey. Both holding clippers. They are going to trim the jasmine that has overtaken the wall of the house. The moment they touch or clip a branch the birds take flight. The stories they have to tell are left untold. As the stories take flight Lilla and Eyüp Bey keep trimming branches and soon the house seems to breath again. The wall looks like the right-hand page of a primary school pupil's notebook, cool and clean. Peering up at the upper branches, the clippings fall on their heads that now and again touch. Madam Lilla and Eyüp Bey, standing there like that, two matches stuck together when they burn. Calm, warm and soft. "Is that the same woman?" I ask myself. Holding her clipper and narrowing her eyes, she looks up at the birds swirling overhead, jasmine raining down on her head as the branches tremble, pausing when her hair touches the top of Eyüp's head ... where is that woman in that car that raced from Tripoli to Dar al-Amar?

*

The driver doesn't ask questions. He needs to get these four strange women out of the place, and fast. He steps on the accelerator and every piece of the old Mercedes seems to shake and rattle. Amira is holding a Siamese kitten in the palm of her hand and she places it in Lilla's lap. Lilla is laughing and crying. With her handkerchief she wipes away tears of joy and sadness. She looks down at the kitten in her lap as the snot of tears and the spit of laughter meet in a stifled sneeze. Now Maryam is riding shotgun. Lilla is back right, Amira in the middle and I am on the left. In the long silence Lilla cries and the driver looks disturbed. Gently he asks, "Madam, shall I put on Fairuz? Oum Kalthoum?"

Slowly we all start to laugh. Even Lilla. Opening and closing her trembling palms over the kitten, she squeezes love into the little creature, "Oh little, little you! Little lovely! Lovely!"

For a moment we all look at the kitten. With those blank and fearful eyes, she is the one to tell the new ending or beginning.

Maryam says to the driver, "Put on Fairuz ... good sir, do you know the shortcut to Dar al-Amar? The mountain road?"

His mood brightening, he says, "I do," and he throws a good-humoured glance in the rearview mirror, taking on the role of a vagabond, "A smile does you a world of good, sister!"

We all let out another round of laughter. Maryam says, "Wait, we're just warming up. Let's make sure we pick up the little one first." Wiping her face with her handkerchief, Lilla lets out a sigh. She looks out the window and smiles.

"Life is so strange!"

It sounds especially poignant coming from Madam Lilla. After everything that's happened the night before and earlier that day there is nothing else to say.

*

The cyanide was still in my pocket when we left Abou Hassan. Lilla was silent and we were too. We split up in the Hotel Cavelier and somehow drifted off to sleep. In the morning we all packed into the old Mercedes with a nasty group hangover. But the driver was in his element. It must have been Lilla's mood. He was dressed in a suit. Jumping out he opened and closed doors for us... these were formalities you didn't normally see from Beirut taxi drivers.

484

As we head north the car stops in the Christian neighbourhood before turning onto the mountain road. We are completely silent. It still isn't clear where we were going. The driver pulls over, saying, "Ladies, I'm just going to pick up some künefe. You'll have some, won't you?" His words seem entirely out of place. Humbly he crawls out of the car and comes back with künefe in slices of white bread. It's a Beirut breakfast special but it's wasted on us. He looks downcast when his noble gesture is unappreciated. Lilla is in the front and we are in our usual places in the back. When we finally get out of the city the poor man has to ask, "Just where are we going, Madam? I heard talk of Tripoli but this morning Maryam Hanım said that…"

Lilla cut him off without even glancing at us, "To Tripoli! And when our business is done there … we can go wherever Maryam Hanım wants to go…"

There's dissent from the back and Lilla explodes in exaggerated rage, "After travelling so far, ladies, I will not go back without seeing him! What was it Maryam hanım said? I can't do it alone. I can't do anything without you. Isn't that right?"

The three of us knew she was capable of doing it. She did it in the desert. She pulled out a gun and pulled the trigger. She could do it again. And when it came to Anwar she would definitely shoot. I was startled and Amira looked hurt and Maryam was angry but Lilla turned, and in her most Madam-like air she issued the holy decree to the driver who was standing by.

"To Tripoli, good sir! And at the double!"

Two hours later we were at a fork in the road…

"Yes, this is it. His mansion is at the end of this road."

Pressed up against the front window Madam Lilla pointed

to the mountain road. And so we made our way up the road towards the mountains before forking off again onto a thin winding road that climbed even higher and which was lined with trees.

"Wait!" she cried, and the driver stopped the car. "Yes, yes, it's this one!"

She is pointing at an old mansion. It has an old iron door. A majestic door but the lock was broken and the paint was peeling from the metal while the wings were tied up with thick rope.

Lilla took a deep breath as the car ame to a halt. Carefully she pulled her burgundy velvet pouch out of her handbag. Her hands were steady. She took out the gun. She looked long and hard at the driver.

"Good sir," she begins. "Good sir... this is a matter of honour. I am about to take the life of a scoundrel. And you will wait for me here. In return I will pay you one thousand dollars. But that's not the issue. You seem a gentleman of some life experience. So you should understand why a woman of my age would take up arms. Isn't that so?"

The driver nods like an aide-de-camp and without a flicker of fear in his eyes he seems thrilled to have been tasked with a sacred duty.

"Fine then," says Madam.

"Now wait just a minute," says Amira holding her back but she has nothing more to say. She looks at me, and then at Maryam, who has that angry look on her face, and opens her arms to say, 'what else can I do?'

"But this can't happen," stutters Amir. "Madam how could you? On your own? You..."

Wasting no time listening to Amira ramble, Lilla flings opens the door and gets out.

At the same time Amira says, "I'm coming, too."

So I get out too. Maryam gets out of the other side, an empty look on her face. Lilla doesn't even look back. She's hardly concerned whether we come with her or not. Maryam is so angry she's not even grumbling, her face has gone dark. Amira is hurrying after Lilla, looking back at us to make sure we're coming.

Lilla is now in front of the door quickly untying the ropes. She opens the door and steps inside then stops. Looking straight ahead, she says to Amira, "I spoke to Eyüp Bey last night."

She slightly turns her head in my direction but doesn't make eye contact, staring into space. "As for the matter of the bride in the hamam ... no one has testified against you. The prosecutor still wants to open a case but Eyüp knows of the crimes he's committed under the Ben Ali dictatorship ... Eyüp Bey has worked it all out." Turning to Amira, she makes her point, "In other words, there is no need for you to come with me, dear Amira."

Suddenly the reason we hit the road is gone. Everything we have experienced, which is about to culminate in the killing of a man, seems meaningless. We are jumping into a new world in which the air is nothing like we know and we have forgotten how to breath, and this is happening at the most exciting part of the story. I suppose that's why when Lilla stops speaking, takes a breath and walks ahead without looking over her shoulder we follow. She puts her gun in her belt, in the middle of her waist. We hurry along after her. We are going to war, to a killing. We should have been the ones who were angry, but it was Lilla who was angry with us.

"You still haven't understood that I am doing this for all of us!" she hissed between her teeth.

A dilapidated, two-storey villa with a veranda opening onto a garden. Surely it was once white but now it's the colour of mud. The garden is filthy and there aren't any flowers. There are some cabbage, green onion, dried cucumber saplings and rotten tomatoes. It is a garden in ruin. In the middle of the veranda are dirty jars of cheese and in one corner is a pile of mouldy green olives. The ground is littered with everything from plastic coffee cups to bags of pasta. Chickens graze over the rotting rubbish scattered about the garden. And there is an army of thin, stray cats. In the garden on a rusty cast-iron table that must once have been white sits a bowl of lentils. On the veranda is a large gilded armchair, the upholstery torn to pieces. In front of the door lie bottles of arak, most of them broken. Under the foot of one of the chairs is a TV remote – for balance. In all her glory Lilla stands in the middle of all that rubbish. Settling her breath, she opens her mouth to cry out that name. And then...

"The whole lot of you can go to hell! I'm fed up! Let this house of a pig be a grave for you all, and I'll be free of this place!"

Shooing away chickens, stumbling and cursing, a fat woman hurries out from behind the house. Lilla slowly closes her mouth. Like a bundle of bad vibes the woman nearly rolls right into us. Wrapped around her waist and tucked into her belt is a whip. Her sour face is all crinkled from the heat and the sun. Her dress is completely faded. Her hair is bleached blonde. She hardly has any teeth. Seeing us there she stops in her tracks. But she doesn't look at all surprised. Her hands on her hips, her eyes squinted and her jaw dropped in disgust, she croaks, "Cat, pigeon or snake?"

We are rooted to the spot. Our silence probably makes her think we're dense and not startled. Almost spitting, teasing and ironically polite, she asks:

"Pray tell, ladies, which one do you desire?"

As if offering another choice with every word, she twirls her hand from side to side "Cat? Snake? Or shall it be a pigeon?" she shrieks.

Lilla is silent and the woman wearily walks over to us. Coming close she sizes up Lilla's shoes, her clothes and then her face. She goes straight for the personal 'you,' keeping the tone real rude. "Hah ... you must be one from Jezim Efendi's youth. Did you come to have a look at his pigeons? I look after the cats and the snakes but as for the pigeons you'll have to speak to Jezim, lady! And he's not here so get going and come back later."

"And who are you?" asks Lilla in her loftiest Arabic. Madam's courtesy is like a starched handkerchief in the hand of madman walking around in his underpants. The woman must find the grand-dame style amusing because she puckers her lips and apes Lilla's style, "Alia, my sweet! Married to that asshole Jezim! Oh do come in! Perhaps you have something to say?"

And she steps closer and squeals, "What's that? Is that a gun? A gun?"

Unruffled, Lilla maintains the Dartanyan grace that befits a duel. Her head high, her words come out like a white glove snapping across the woman's face, "This has nothing to do with you, madam!"

The woman starts to laugh, "And? So you've come to knock off that idiot, Jezim? Ha ha ha!"

While the woman laughs Lilla looks at us. Lines she has prepared for her dramatic scene are now almost certainly meaningless and she seems to be asking us for a prompt. Maryam was about to say something when the woman suddenly goes berserk.

Through crazed guffaws she says, "Do it girl, shoot him!

Let the flea-infested dog die in the dust! You see cause he's only got one left…"

Lilla's eyes are wide open in surprise and the woman dressed in rags realizes Lilla hasn't understood her meaning. "But don't you know, sweet tea? He's only got one leg. I fed the dirty bastard's other leg to the lions!"

She opens her eyes wide to mock 'ladies' like us for being afraid and she keeps laughing. Then one of the cats sneezes under Lilla's skirt, shooting snot over her shoes … there is definitely nothing left of the scene Lilla had in mind.

The woman continues, "I like you, girl!" she says, slapping Lilla on the shoulder and laughing, "So you really came to kill the old mule! Brava! Of all the women he's talked about you turn out to be the one with some guts."

In a flurry of laughter she walks into the house leaving us in the middle of the garden. But then she turns around at the door and lets out another laugh and says, gesturing as if we are having a hard time understanding, "Sit, sit! I'll be right back! Ha ha ha!"

"Shall we sit?" Amira asks Maryam, who seems on the verge of laughing. She raises an eyebrow to say she has no idea and rubs her lips. I start picking up overturned chairs. It is like we are spectators about to watch a play.

Lilla is still frozen, standing tall on her two feet. She still doesn't want to believe the final scene she had in mind might be cut altogether. God knows what's really running through her mind as she turns and says to us as if in a dream, "So a lion ate his leg."

Maryam pulls over a chair for her. Lilla gives in and sits. She's no longer the lead actor. Her shoulders slump. The woman returns with a motley mix of glasses and little jars and a bottle filled with a hazy liquid. She continues jabbering in the same teasing tone, "And you're quite the looker, eh! Of course you've fallen to pieces, too, clearly, but you must have been a wild cat back in the day."

She picks up the bowl of lentils, hurls it to the ground and puts down the two glasses and three little jars. She waves the bottle at Lilla, "We can throw one back, sweetie pants? It'd do you some good!"

Maryam tries a new direction, "Alia, my sweet, are you selling any of these cats?"

"Oh yeah, sister!" she says, her toothless grin and her beady eyes teasing. Nudging Lilla's arm, "Your Jezim was once a tiger but now he's just a little pussy cat! What do you say to that?"

She fills the glasses with homemade liquor and in one go she downs her glass. We pretend to drink, keeping the glass well away from our lips. Lilla still isn't moving. "Jezim will be here soon. You can draw your gun and pot the wooden-legged bastard."

Adopting the woman's style, Maryam says, "Sister, I don't think you're getting this. This woman here has really come to kill your husband. Are you going to just let her do it?"

She realizes she's finally been asked a question and opening her legs, her skirt drooping between them, she puts one hand on her knee and says, "It makes no difference to me any more, my pretty!"

In a rough street tone, Maryam laughs and says, "Really?" The woman now seems more relaxed. Lilla looks like a statue while Amira covers her mouth to stifle the laughter as the woman begins her story, "Now let me tell you, sister…"

*

"....But what beauty! I swear those circus owners would fight over me. 'She dances like Nana, the legendary belly dancer, and with snakes!' That's what they'd always say. But I'm a real daredevil. So I insisted on having the lion. The Shah gave me one so how could I ever leave him? I told you that already, right? I did, I did. Anyway ... I picked the lion up at Shah Rıza Pahlavi's palace. They would have celebrations on the birthday of the King's horse and they called me to dance. That's when my first husband croaked. One of my pythons bit him on stage. The wretched drunk! He was blasted out of his brains and the bastard was bent on using my snakes in his magic act. Go for it, I said. Of course I knew the snake would get angry and bite him. Good riddance. I'm no walk in the park! Ha ha ha! So my husband's dead and I'm a woman in mourning, right... Ha ha ha! Then the shah gives me this lion cub. I take the little guy with me to Istanbul. I buy a house with a garden. It's me and the lion living together. I was really obsessed with him. Wasn't so interested in the snakes any more. So I start teaching him tricks and training him. We go from one circus to another. Years go by. But the neighbours complain. Of course the guy grows and gets bigger and starts roaring, which means the whole neighbourhood is up in arms and the Beşiktaş newspaper declares war on me. They want to beat me up but there's the lion and the shameless bastards are too scared. Anyway that's when I get an offer to join a tour in Kenya. I get them to make a cage on the back of a Magirus truck and I set out with my lion. Of course we had our adventures on the road. In Egypt they wanted to cut his stomach open, thinking I was hiding drugs in there. Anyway we survived that but then we ran out of money on the road, shovelling out bribes here there at all the borders, and I end up in Sudan with nothing left. But God pulls through for me and I get this real sweet gig. You see the Masai have this crazy thing for lions. They used to be common, all over the place, but they were overhunted, and they never saw them anymore. For a dollar I showed them the lion. Oh, the money I earned back then. What money! With all that money we finally made it to Kenya. Back then it was a different place and we put together some great shows. I stayed there for a while and that's when I fell in love with this Indian who said, 'Let's go to India.' And so we set out. Of course with him the journey lasts for months. We'd stop, do a show, oh, we really loved each other. And then that year a man calls me from Istanbul and tells me that Saddam has a son who has a pet lion and he invites me to come and train it. So I set out for Iraq with the Indian. But he doesn't want to come all the way. Fed up with him anyway I just leave him there. I get to Iraq only to find out that this Saddam's a real maniac and his son is even crazier. And it turns out that war is about to break out. What do I know? I got there just when the war started and I had to find a way to get out with the lion. That's when that disgraceful dog Anwar turns up. 'Come,' he says, 'I'll save you both.' I had to save my skin so I agreed. I wish I hadn't. The lowlife tricked me. Turns out he sold the lion behind my back and the bastards there were going to send him to America or England. I realized too late, the idiot I am. Seems the same men were supposed to get us out of Baghdad. They wouldn't help us unless we gave them the lion. They came for the animal but he would only listen to me. 'You bastard,' I cried, 'bite him and take his leg off!' The lion broke free even though they had plugged him with a tranquilizer but before it worked he tore off Anwar's leg. Well … if you're going to tug on my mane I'm going to mess with your leg, Jezim Efendi! And we came here. What else was there to do?

I had nowhere else to go, my lion was gone, and I had no
other reason to live. I had nothing left but grimy Jezim.
We're together till one of us dies. You see this whip?
Whenever I think of my lion I crack it over Jezim's wooden
leg. Gives him a real fright. The dirty bastard doesn't have
a leg but he still feels the pain. Now if I can just pawn off
these cats, snakes and pigeons, I'll have my teeth done right
away. Look four missing in the front here... and then look
seven missing here in the back. If I can get these done I
won't be half as ugly and I can hit the stage again. I'll do it.
That animal Jezim doesn't believe me but I am going to do
it. I still got more in me."

That was the end of Alia's story. She wiped away the
white spittle that had collected in the corner of her mouth
then looked at Madam, slapped her knee and laughed,
"And? What did the animal do to you? Tell me all about it."

In the face of this woman's tawdry style Lilla's queenly
airs were starting to make her look more like an robot when
all of a sudden, "Aliaaaa! Aliaaaaa! You crazy bitch! Where
are you? Come and take these!

And there was Jezim Anwar. When he saw us he stopped
at the door with birdcages in both hands. This was not the
man Lilla had told us about. This was not even a rough draft
of the man she had told us about. He didn't look like someone
who owned a golden lighter; he looked like a man who'd
never seen one. He was nothing but a bag of skin and bones
with a little head hammered so deeply into his body there
was hardly any neck left. His trousers were too long and held
up by a ragged old belt. The hat on the top of his head didn't
look like a sumptuous relic of times past but some old hand-
me-down he had pinched from a street market. Jezim Anwar
looked like an abandoned old flourmill in ruins.

All three of us stood up. We were ready to take any necessary precautions. Alia was snickering as she stepped back towards the house. She was getting ready to sit back and enjoy watching whatever might happen to Anwar. Leaning over the table, Lilla slowly rose to her feet. "Madam!" was all Maryam said. But Lilla was beyond us. She was moving in slow motion. Her hand went to her waist and drew her gun. Standing like a statue she still hadn't taken aim. Anwar narrowed his eyes and ... he recognized her. "Esma," he said and smiled, which made his face look like a collection of copper-coloured metal sheets and then there was fear and in his fear he recalled his old greasy charms and the metal sheets seem to crush down on his face.

It wasn't easy for her to hear her name through those lips after so many years and she felt a tremor in her neck that coursed down through her body and her silks seemed to tremble. But her gun was entirely still. As she slowly raised the weapon, Anwar, a man who knew his crimes, raised his arms. The cages trembled with fear, trembled and shook and crashed to the ground. The pigeons were set free and the snotty cats pounced. They chased after the birds.

Alia chased after the cats and then there were more and more cats. Cracking her whip, she cried, "Pigeons born of swine! You bitches are riling up the cats are you? Idiot Jezim's pigeons! The bastard's birds!"

Suddenly there was chaos. Cats, pigeons, Alia, chickens and more chickens, Alia, pigeons, cats. They all raced about the garden. Lilla seemed to grow taller and the miserable wretch Anwar seemed to shrink, both in a cloud of dust while Alia cracked her whip, crack ... then, bang, Anwar fell into the dust, the whip wrapped around his wooden leg.

Alia was shouting, "Dog spawn! Why did you let the

pigeons go like that? You cowardly beast! Are you a fucking man!?"

Anwar lay still on the ground. His eyes locked on Lilla. It was a pathetic sight indeed. But this wouldn't stop her. She clicked off the safety. Then in the twinkling of an eye, in a thin sliver of time, so slight ... Jezim Anwar smiled. Trying to appear loveable or maybe charming, he grunted and in his ghastly appearance there wasn't a trace of pride. He was nothing more than a weed that wanted to live. Lilla studied the look in his eye. To see if this was real. It was. There was a man lying there. A ruined windmill. A millstone grinding nothing but itself. The flour was full of worms. A mad woman. A wooden leg. In a filthy garden. Chickens grazing through cat shit, snotty cats, broken glasses, an old couple living like bugs, a finished story, missing teeth, a ragged piece of life, a man's dirty wretched life ... the gun in her hand slowly falls to one side.

Maryam jumped and took Lilla by the arm. Through the whirling of dust and the continuous clamour, she said, "Let's go, Madam! This is no place for us. You'll just get your clothes dirty..." Lilla looked down at her dress. A Siamese kitten was at her feet, a tiny little thing. It seemed she couldn't move because of the kitten. It was like the kitten was keeping her from moving on.

Amira ran over and scooped up the animal that curled up in the palm of her hand. Taking Lilla by the hand, she said, "Let's go Madam. This man is already dead!"

As if in a trance Lilla started walking. In a moment she would pass Jezim Anwar. She took a step and then one more, one more and just as she was about to pass, he said, "What's that, Esma? Still don't have the guts!?" and he laughed.

Bang, bang, bang!

496

We were frozen. But only for an instant. Maryam raced with Lilla towards the door. Alia was still darting about the garden, riling up all the animals as she screamed. Jezim Anwar watched us go. He wanted to die. But after Maryam had grabbed the gun from Lilla, she had aimed for the wooden leg. The leg he didn't have … and I had left the cyanide on the garden table.

*

It was far easier getting a baby on the plane than a Siamese cat. We had to fill out a pile of paperwork for the animal. Lilla took a Xanax – you can find them anywhere in Beirut – and she slept until we got to Tunis. For two days after we had arrived in Tunis, Amira carried the baby in her lap; Maryam couldn't even touch her. Whenever she did the baby started to cry. It took a few days until she finally took her in her arms. So we left them to work it out. On the night of the third day the baby cried and fell silent before Amira had the time to get up and that's when we knew that Maryam had become a mother. She was awkward but she was trying and when she needed the compassion and the patience she would run to Amira right away. Lilla was more like the conductor of an orchestra. The moment she had arrived home that first night she decided the house had to be renovated. If this place was going to become a dance school it had to be done the best way possible and in fine style. And when it came to looking after a baby everything had to be perfectly crisp and clean. If Amira and Maryam were going to be staying for a while they were going to need their own rooms. And if she was going to surrender to Eyüp Bey…

*

"Welcome back," said Eyüp Bey.

His head bowed he seemed to hold all his emotion in his one eye: he knew Lilla didn't like over-the-top sentimentality. He had come to pick us up at the airport. Swiftly he helped Lilla with a bag she was holding and on the way to the car, Lilla said, "Eyüp Bey, could I take your arm?"

I'm convinced he grew ten centimetres in that moment. Without saying a word he looked at Lilla. He was a man who had waited years for this woman and now he wanted her to wait, if only a few seconds. One ... two ... and he couldn't wait to three. He was probably afraid of ruining the moment because he wasn't used to being loved. Calmly and as if they had done the same for years, "Of course, Esma."

And he extended his arm. Not Madam, but Esma! And no other word was said on the matter. It was a pact. Years went by in a glance. When he saw the baby in Amira's arms ... he wouldn't say a thing but with her arm in Eyüp Bey's arm she smiled and said, "Life's so strange, Eyüp Bey..."

Then she looked at the baby in the same way she had looked at her in Dar el-Amar. It was as if in that moment she was a grandmother and she had lived the life she had chosen not to live in an instant.

"How are things here?" she asked Eyüp Bey.

"Radical Islamists tried to burn down Carthage," he answered and she pouted, "Then we have work to do."

She was as calm as a Don Quixote waving his sword at real giants.

*

"Doesn't Dar al-Amar mean Moon House?" I asked and no one answered. Amira quickly nodded to dodge the question. We were standing in front of a farmhouse. A house of women, a house of the moons. There was a warm aura surrounding it, which must have been because it was full of women seeking shelter. Every brick seemed molded out of mud with the care of little girls making meatballs, making a house to befit a fairytale so sweet that it must have been dreamt up in the dreams of other girls. The garden wasn't very big but there were vegetables and strawberries in little plots divided by low wooden boards. The strawberries looked like tiny red jokes made by the earth. The garden was so delicate you felt like you had to tiptoe through it.

Amira, Madam Lilla and I got out of the car and started walking towards the house. Maryam was rooted to the spot. Standing next to the car. Madam Lilla looked over her shoulder. Her head lowered, she slowly went over to Maryam. She walked right up to her and stopped. Silence. She waited. Maryam's heart was beating so violently she felt her chest might collapse. Lilla waited for the pounding to subside. With Maryam. Without making a sound. Then reaching out, Lilla said, "You know I can't do it alone."

The rising tension in Maryam's chest rushed out in sobs and almost sounded like laughter. She put her arm in Lilla's. Maryam looked older than her then. Ahead of us they went to the door and knocked. Maryam rested her hand on the frame. A little old Filipina opened the door. So small and so old you would think she might die of surprise. When she saw Maryam she let out a silent scream. She flung open her arms and Maryam's tall, thin body crumpled and fell into the woman's arms. She looked at us over Maryam's shoulder. Weeping. Three times she said, "Welcome." Each word meant something different. Every word a long sentence.

"I knew you would come and you didn't disappoint me ... you are doing the right thing by coming for her ... don't be afraid, we won't speak of the past."

Freeing herself from the old woman's bosom Maryam looked at us with misty eyes and said, "my nanny". With both her hands the woman shook Lilla's hand. She looked at all of us with gratitude in her eyes for bringing Maryam here. Taking Maryam's arms she looked at her with pride and she said, "She's sleeping…"

Then she put her arm in Maryam's and gestured for us to follow. We came to a closed door. Maryam stopped. Quickly Lilla stepped up behind her and placed her hand on Maryam's back. Only then did Maryam reach for the handle. As the door opened the sight of the sleeping baby fell over us. Maryam smiled like a little girl unaware of disappointment. The palm of Lilla's hand was still resting on her back. She had lived such a very different life but now gazing at Maryam's child it seemed that Madam Lilla was surrendering to a weakness she had always eluded. Mischievously, Amira said, "let's wake her up," and she was the first to take the baby in her arms. Maryam still didn't have it in her. She felt inadequate, she felt afraid. Her palm still on Maryam's back, Lilla said, "Don't worry. Don't worry. We'll work it all out."

It was the first time I saw that expression on Lilla's face. As she relaxed she began to look more her age. She had accepted it. Felt the moment. Loved the moment.

*

When Eyüp Bey came to meet us at the airport, he definitely noticed the difference in Madam Lilla. And from then on he was as happy as he could be with just one eye. Now and then he even tried cracking jokes. They weren't funny but he always laughed. And we indulged him. He worked like crazy. But most importantly he offered to make the sign for the dance school even though he had never done anything like that before. Amira agreed. And so he started painting the letters in oils.

THE WOMEN WHO BLOW ON KNOTS DANCE SCHOOL

So in that lilac hour when the birds were chattering in the jasmine tree his sign was drying. When the Siamese kitten wasn't rubbing against my leg she would go over and sniff at the sign, driven away by the scent every time. As Lilla continued trimming branches a shower of jasmine flowers fell on the sign. Naturally Lilla didn't last very long, bored with such a mundane activity: first she was angry at the scissors, then Eyüp Bey, then the jasmine and finally she put her clippers down on the table. She saw me sitting on the two-seat swing with papers before me and a pen in my hand. Something crossed her mind. She came over.

"Are you writing?" she asked.

"No," I said, "nothing for now."

"You will," she said, "I know."

I just looked at her and said nothing.

Upstairs Maryam was shouting to Amira from another room.

"When did you last change her nappy? And when did we last give her milk?"

Amira laughed as she answered.

For a moment I thought Maryam and Amira were the same woman, half man and half woman. As for Madam Lilla standing above me...

"Don't write about what we did to Jezim Anwar," said Lilla, sitting down next to me on the swing. "What happened happened. Do you understand that I did it all for you?" She put her arm around my shoulder and I put my head on her chest. She patted me on the shoulder in an awkward show of compassion. "You can make up a good ending for the bastard anyway…"

And so I made up such an ending for the bastard. At the end of the day Maryam, Amira and Madam Lilla were more than just a story. They were more precious than characters in a novel. You see that's why I didn't write Maryam's last tablet and Amira's last letter. I left them before they rounded out at number seven. I left them as they were. I left them as they should be.

Maryam and Amira were in the kitchen looking for glasses for jasmine rakı and soon the glasses were clinking. I was in Lilla's arms. Dropping a glass, Maryam cursed and Amira laughed. The baby woke up. In a white dress Amira walked over to us barefoot. She stopped, leaned over, tucked her hair behind an ear and merrily said, "There is this incredible purple bug. Did you see it?"

We were still. Madam Lilla knew her breath was falling over my eyelashes like a prayer. It was the first time a ticket to Istanbul seemed to be the right choice. It was the first time I understood what Madam Lilla had done for us all. We did not need a god to love us if we had a courageous mother…

Maybe this wasn't why we had set out in the first place but we had made it to this garden. In the end you make a decision to leave but you never know where you're going to end up. When you decide to write a road trip story the road surely writes the ending for you. *Thinking of everything we had been through I'd have to say I have trouble believing it all really happened. I hope you won't have such trouble…*